HOSTILE

HOLLYWOOD GUARDIANS **BOOK THREE**

HEATHER ASHLEY

Copyright © 2022 by Heather Ashley

All rights reserved.

No part of this book may be reproduced in any form or by any electronic or mechanical means, including information storage and retrieval systems, without written permission from the author, except for the use of brief quotations in a book review.

ISBN: 9798866065394

Cover Design by Sarah Kil Creative Studio

Contact the Author:
heather@heatherashleywrites.com
www.heatherashleywrites.com

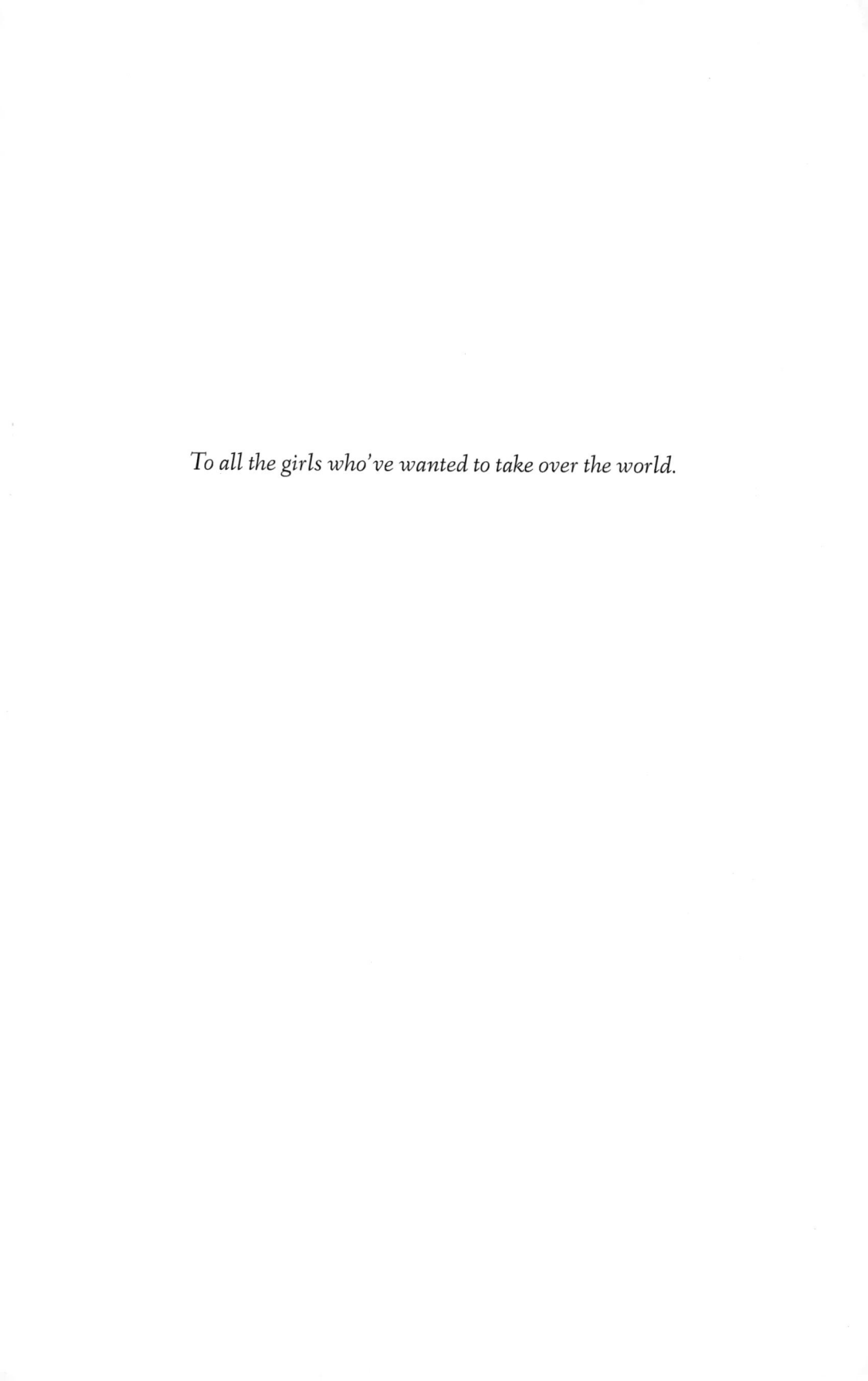

To all the girls who've wanted to take over the world.

TRIGGER WARNING

This book contains graphic situations of both a violent and sexual nature typical of dark romance books. If you have triggers, proceed with caution.

CHAPTER 1
PENELOPE

"I KNEW you weren't fit to be CEO."

With those seven words, one of my worst fears has been realized —I'm failing.

"Someone get Collin on the phone. We need to initiate a vote of no confidence in *Miss* Driscoll," Franklin sneers, glaring down his large nose at me as if I'm shit on the bottom of his thousand-dollar shoe.

I hold up my hand. "If everyone could just—"

"When your father died, we couldn't believe he left the company in your hands. I don't know what he was thinking," Hannah says while shaking her head in disappointment, her perfectly styled hair swaying with the movement. Whether she's more disappointed in my father or me isn't clear, but my shoulders curl inward and I have to force them back out.

These people are sharks scenting weakness in the water like blood. If I give them a hint of vulnerability, they'll attack. I can already sense it about to play out even though technically what happened is *their* fault, not mine.

"You're going to ruin us all and I, for one, am not going to stand here and wait for it to happen," Ira chimes in, moving away from the rest of the board members who congregated in my entryway as soon as the evening news headlines hit. He slinks across the room to the bar my father always kept well-stocked with expensive liquor and helps himself to a glass. "I say we vote."

"If you'd all—"

"Has anyone managed to reach Collin yet?" Valerie asks right over top of me, cutting me off yet again. Heat flames in my face and spreads down my neck, but what can I do about their blatant disrespect?

I was never meant to be CEO of my father's company.

I know it.

The Board knows it.

They've tolerated me this long because they know what I'm working on will be a game changer and the company has continued to see record profits the last four quarters. Tonight it's become clear their patience has run out.

You know what the worst part is?

This hostile takeover attempt they're so up in arms over? It's because *they* got an offer to buy us out and declined. See? The blame lies with the Board.

Not one of them bothered to tell me about it, though.

Assholes.

Naturally, I'm an easy scapegoat. They never wanted to have to listen to a twenty-five-year-old woman with social anxiety and zero business skills in the first place. I still haven't figured out what my father was thinking leaving me in charge of Driscoll Tech. The best I've come up with is he wanted to make sure the AI framework we've been building doesn't end up in the hands of the Board.

If that's the case, he chose right because I will *never* let the Board sell my creation even if it costs me everything.

It's not a great place to be when you're operating at odds with your Board of Directors, but it's where I've spent the last year and I've found my only defense against them is knowledge.

I've learned more about hostile takeovers in the last two hours than I ever thought I'd need. People think code is boring, but business ethics and law are the real stars of that shit show. The dull aching throb in my temples is a testament to how in over my head I am.

"Collin's on his way and then we can get this handled and get on with our nights. I was *supposed* to be at a gala for the underprivileged youth of Beverly Hills," Valerie whines as she tucks her phone back into her clutch. She's in formalwear and I want to laugh my ass off and explain to her that I doubt Beverly Hills has any underprivileged youth, but I keep my mouth shut—something I've gotten exceptionally good at these last twelve months.

The muscles in my shoulders are practically screaming as I force my spine to stay straight and my chin to stay lifted. The last thing I want to do is deal with my uncle right now. Uncle Collin and I used to be close back before my parents died, but when the will was read and he learned he'd remain CFO and the company was left to me with the request I become CEO, everything changed.

This whole night has been a disaster and it looks like it's not going to end anytime soon. My only hope is to somehow convince the Board to hold off on a vote until tomorrow, but any time I try to speak they cut me off. How can I possibly expect them to do anything I ask if I can't even get them to move from the entryway into the formal living room?

Maybe I can convince Uncle Collin to handle them, just for tonight. Then tomorrow, I can slip my CEO skin back on after I've had a chance to come up with some kind of plan.

"Listen," I start but they're all still having their own conversations. I don't know if I have the energy to yell over top of them. A couple of hours ago, I made a call and I'm expecting them to show up at any minute. I don't want the Board to know what I've done, the kinds of things I read about online that can happen when these hostile takeover attempts go wrong. It'll just be more ammunition for them to use against me, so I need to get them out of here before my doorbell rings.

Once a hostile takeover fails, there's a terrifying history of kidnapping, murder, ransom, and torture all because of money. I'd say that's bodyguard worthy, even if I might be overreacting by calling them in. Better safe than dead.

I finally get tired of the board members speaking over me and shove my fingers between my lips, blowing an ear-piercing whistle that immediately silences the room. "That's better. I understand tonight has been a shock, but you knew this was coming. The second you turned down Fields' offer, they had the green light to take it to the shareholders, yet none of you said a thing. If you think I'm going to stand by while you undermine my father's last wishes and force me out, you're dumber than I thought. We'll meet in the morning and discuss this further. Now get the hell out of my house."

Somehow, I manage to keep my voice steady and cool, composed even as I'm falling apart inside from the hatred so clearly being aimed in my direction. I can't falter now. Not when their greedy eyes are trained on me waiting for me to slip up. If I didn't know any better, I'd say this whole thing was a set up so they'd have a reason to push me out, something that warrants further investigation.

No one speaks as the seconds drag on until finally, Nathan Carpenter, the man who's been with my father from the beginning finally opens his mouth. "No."

With that one word, every hope this night could end in a way that would let me regain some of my control evaporates like water on a desert road. The five of them start up their discussion again, turning their backs on me as if I don't exist. To them, I don't. Not anymore.

What should bother me most tonight is Fields AI's attempt to steal the company my parents built. But I'm not convinced that's what's making my stomach feel like it's made of stone—not entirely. A certain curly-haired, wild-eyed playboy comes to mind even as I try to shove thoughts of him away. A rush of energy shoots down my spine, but don't get excited—it's not from attraction.

Nope.

He digs under my skin like a parasite on a consistent basis and I can't help but want to punch him right in his stupidly gorgeous face, and I'm not a violent person.

Indy Foster.

I hope Connor sends somebody else—*anybody* else.

The nail of my thumb finds its way between my teeth as I nibble at it, a habit I've had since I was little and never really shook. I look over the room as the absolute certainty no one wants me here—in my own house and the company my father built—sweeps across my skin.

Reading people is not one of my strengths, but I know this for certain. Right now, I'm at the bottom of a pool looking up, struggling to get a clear picture of what's going on through thousands of gallons of murky water.

Numbers flash behind my eyelids as I close my eyes, trying to make sense of what's happening and find a way out. But people are chaotic.

It's why I've mostly shut them out of my life, perfectly content to spend my time solving puzzles and working to better a humanity I've never really fit into.

The phone I forgot is in my hand vibrates, and without looking, I know it's because they're here. My security team. My *bodyguards*. I scoff because when did my life get so out of control? Everything is deteriorating, and I'm clawing at nothing but air, trying to stop the momentum, but it's not working. No matter how hard I cling to the things I think I have command over, the more the universe proves me wrong.

Clearly the Board isn't going anywhere so the tiny hope I had they wouldn't cross paths with whoever Hollywood Guardians sent me bursts into flames and dissipates in a puff of smoke.

My fingers tremble as I wrap them around the cool metal of the brass handle. I draw a breath deep down into my lungs, filling them until they ache before blowing the air back out. The last thing I ever want to project to people on the outside is that I lack confidence.

I'm faking my way through all of this, and I don't even know why I bother. It's not like everyone can't see right through it. I throw the weight of my body back as I tug on the heavy oak door, swinging it open to reveal who Connor sent me.

The voices behind me disappear and I don't know if it's because they stopped talking to see who's here, or if it's because everything else fails to exist the second I lay my eyes on who's at my door.

My gaze quickly sweeps over the two figures standing on my doorstep—one I'm not familiar with who wears a tie and pushes his glasses up higher on his face while avoiding eye contact with me at all costs, and the other I'm a little *too* acquainted with. My nose wrinkles in distaste when I finish my perusal.

Sure, Indy Foster's attractive. Absurdly, unfairly, insanely hot. His messy curls and dimpled smile have probably won him entrance into any woman's panties he wanted, and that effortless charm he throws around like confetti ensures everyone loves him. But to me? He's just an arrogant jackass who's never taken anything seriously a day in his life.

The worst part? I'm not immune to his sharp jawline dotted with two-day-old stubble or the way his black jeans hug his muscular thighs. As much as I like to pretend he doesn't affect me, I'm a liar. A tiny bolt of excitement fires through my entire body, settling in a place that's been mostly ignored for way too long.

His full lips tilt up into a sinful smirk as if he knows what he does to me. Even though I lock myself down. Even though I always attempt to be a blank canvas and give nothing away. An infuriating dimple pops out and my fingers twitch at my sides with the urge to reach out and touch. Would his jaw be rough against my palm? Would it feel jagged? Would it slice my skin open and make me bleed?

"I hear you need some help, *Duchess*," he drawls while strutting past me inside the house without waiting for an invitation.

My few interactions with Indy always make me want to regress to a time when I was a child, stomping my foot and throwing a tantrum at his behavior. When he calls me Duchess, I want to kick him in the balls with the stiletto end of my shoe.

As he's passing by, I grab his arm, the leather of the jacket he's wearing buttery soft underneath the pads of my fingers. "Wait. The Board of Directors is inside."

Indy raises an eyebrow. "So?"

"They're upset and I don't know how they'll react to you being here. If they think I'm some scared child who can't handle a few threats, it's not going to help my case in staying CEO. I'm already hanging by a thread." I chew on my thumb with my heart thundering chaotically in my chest as Indy studies me. I can't believe I just admitted my weakness to the same guy who lives to torment me.

Sometimes when he looks at me with those dark gray eyes, I feel like he sees right through every façade I put up to the rest of the world and strips me bare right down to the rawest version of me.

Finally, his lips tip up into a dangerous, predatory kind of smile. It's not nice and I shiver, something he doesn't miss if the heat that ignites in his stare is real. "I said I was here to help, Duchess. Your problems are now my problems."

With that potentially ominous statement, he stalks into the room and bellows for everyone to get the fuck out. I rush in after him and the confused and enraged faces of the Board fall on me like a weighted blanket, only this isn't comforting. At all.

"Who is this?" Hannah purrs, the only member of the board who's managed to ignore the tension and hostility in the air in favor of her baser instincts. She saunters closer to Indy and a gross twist of irritation surges up inside of me.

"He's right, you need to leave. Now. We'll discuss the future of Driscoll Tech in the morning after we've had a chance to calm down," I say rather than answer her question.

The other guy that'd been on my doorstep walks inside, shrugs and steps around me, not really looking in any way apologetic about his abysmal manners. Ugh, this is going to be beyond exhausting.

"I'm not going anywhere until—"

Franklin's cut off mid-sentence by Indy grabbing his shirt and dragging him to the front door. He tosses him out on his ass and for the first time all day, I have to bite my cheek to keep from grinning. That might've been the best thing I've seen all year.

Indy prowls back inside. "Anyone else want to stay past their welcome?"

After that, the other four board members bolt pretty quickly. Who knew a little violence would do the trick?

When they're gone and the door's closed behind them, I let out a sigh of relief and type out a quick text letting my uncle know not to come over.

"See, Duchess? That wasn't so hard, was it?" Indy drawls, coming to stand in front of me.

"My name is Penelope," I tell him for the hundredth time, keeping my voice as even as I possibly can. I've already let it slip that the nickname irritates me—it's why he insists on using it. I might be grateful for what he just did, but that doesn't change every other time we've interacted in the past. For some reason, after Bali, Indy treats me like his latest toy.

I know what you're thinking, and it's not like that. I'm not the same kind of plaything as the other women. The ones he screws and tosses aside, forgetting them as quickly as he shone his Sauron-like attention on them. For a fraction of a second, they were in his spotlight, and now they're nothing.

No, if only I were so lucky.

Instead, he likes to torment me, see what kind of reaction he can get. I've found it's better not to react at all. I assume eventually he'll grow bored and move on to someone who hits one back his way every now and then. Sometimes, though...

Sometimes I can't help but play his little game.

"Whatever you say, Duchess. This is Sebastian," Indy says as if he's suddenly remembered the man standing at the back of the room. In theory, Sebastian should be the guy I gravitate toward. He holds himself with perfect posture. He's fit and fills out his button-down shirt nicely, but he's not overly muscular. There's not a hair out of place on his perfectly styled head. He has this air of cool indifference about him. I imagine people either want to keep their distance, or they think he's a mystery waiting to be solved.

Sadly, my long-neglected libido doesn't even spark when I study him more closely. He's sort of the male version of me. I'd have to be a complete narcissist to go there, and that's just not who I am.

"Nice to meet you," Sebastian mumbles, already pulling a tablet out of his bag as if social niceties are beneath him. "I'll be setting up surveillance." He pivots on his heel and marches off deeper into my house like he knows exactly where he's going despite him never having been here before.

I turn my focus to Indy, who's watching me again, his stormy gray eyes scraping across my body, and I tense so I don't squirm. Instead, I straighten my back, lifting my chin up high, and meet his gaze. It's one of the hardest things I've ever done, maintaining eye contact like this. I tend to curl inward at direct confrontation and look away, not wanting to encourage people to interact with me. But this time? I refuse to be the first to blink and end this show of dominance or whatever is going on here. I will not be the one to submit.

Eventually, after an uncomfortable amount of time in which I barely breathe, he chuckles and shifts his eyes over my shoulder, and I deflate. Somehow, even though I never backed down, it still feels as if I lost—like he *let* me win.

"You've found yourself in quite the mess here, Duchess, not gonna lie. But don't worry, I've got you." His words almost sound like a caress as he takes a step closer, but I take one back. I'm sure this is another of the ways he intends to play with me, to make me as uncomfortable as possible.

"What's your plan?" I ask, making sure he doesn't hear how I'm the tiniest bit breathless at his proximity, at the scent of his cologne coating my lungs like poison. A poison that causes my knees to go weak and my nipples to pebble. I need to stay more than an arm's length away from him. If he touches me, he might see I'm more affected than I let on, and I can't have that. That's an advantage he would unquestionably exploit at every opportunity.

His grin turns devilish, and that damn dimple on his left cheek deepens as his smile grows. I take this moment to step up onto the stairs, putting the railing between us, so I'm at eye-level with him despite our height difference. "Sebastian's setting up surveillance now, so cameras *everywhere*." He whispers that last word as his gaze darkens, and an involuntary shiver races down my spine, but I lock my muscles to keep it from showing.

"And while he's doing that," he continues, tracing the tip of his finger along the banister as if he's stroking my skin, "I'll be checking the perimeter and getting the lay of the land."

"Why do you do that?" I fold my arms across my chest as armor, but not because he's staring at the way my nipples are definitely poking their way through the thin fabric. I do it because I don't want to let him see me struggle. Indy may joke and provoke and tease, but he's not like the guys at the office who openly leer at me.

"Do what?"

"Attempt to make everything sound sexual? Is it a defense mechanism of some sort? Did mommy not give you enough attention when you were little?" I know it's a bitchy thing to say, and I regret it almost immediately when he recoils like I slapped him and his expression shutters. The playful glint in his eye from only moments ago is gone now, replaced by a cold, calculating creature that stares back at me from within.

"I'll be outside, making sure no one's trying to kill you. Try to stay out of my way," he snaps, turning and stalking out of the room.

When he leaves, I swear he takes all the heat with him despite it being summer in southern California. I pull the cardigan I wear tighter around myself and let out that urge to stomp, slamming my foot down on every step until I get to the top and then hurry into my office. Sebastian is already in here, taking over my space, and my heart jumps into my throat.

I'm suffocating as the walls close in around me, and I don't think there's enough air in here. I need to get out with a fervent desperation that tears at my skin from the inside.

I don't do well with change, and my house being invaded by strangers and adversaries—while necessary—is throwing me completely off. Swiping my tablet up off the desk, I cradle it in the crook of my arm and rush back down the stairs, shoving open the patio doors and hurrying across the grass toward the tree line.

That itch I get underneath my skin to work a problem until it's solved rides me hard as I stick the tablet between my teeth and climb the ladder into my treehouse. Work is my escape from the reality of my life, and I happily give into it.

It might be strange, but I still use my childhood treehouse as my refuge. It's my safe place, the one spot that's all mine where no one else is allowed. I can shut out the world and pretend everything's the way it used to be—back when my parents were alive, when the weight of the company didn't fall on my shoulders and when nobody knew what I was working on.

Back when there were no expectations.

Now there's nothing but pressure and endless questions.

When will the network be finished?

When can we start seeing data?

And the one the shareholders and board ask most frequently?

When can we sell it?

Therein lies the problem. I don't *want* to sell it. I want to create it and unleash it on the world for all the good it can do.

I *will* find a cure even if it takes my whole life, but I don't think it will. I'm close, and this entire business with Fields AI and the Board is yet another obstacle I didn't expect, but don't care to let get in my way.

In fact, I'm happy to spend my days working out here in my treehouse. There's a stocked mini fridge, the comfiest mattress money can buy, and enough throw pillows to make Joanna Gaines jealous.

At this point, I don't really care what Indy and that Sebastian guy do to my house or my property as long as everything is secure and doesn't detract from my work. They're professionals, and even if Indy is irritated with me, I trust he'll do his job effectively. It's why I brought them in, because I have neither the time nor the skills to handle this situation on my own anymore.

I ignore the way my stomach wants to sink through the wooden floor when I think about Indy being mad at me and the awful things I said to him earlier after he helped me out with the Board. I'm a people pleaser, that's all this is.

I fall into the mattress and lean back on the pillows, letting every muscle in my body relax as my eyes flutter closed for two seconds. All thoughts of my earlier interaction with Indy and the Board melt away as I lose myself to the comfort of the numbers and code on my tablet.

There's a new algorithm I've been working on for the last six weeks that I believe will be a massive breakthrough when I get it right. When I was little, my father used to put me on his knee in the office and talk to me about his dreams for the artificial intelligence he hoped to create one day. How the potential for problem-solving in a machine vastly outperformed the human brain in some specific ways.

It's what I was raised to believe. I've seen it with my own two eyes, now that technology has caught up with the vision my father showed me so many years ago. Right now, it's where I should be spending my time, not dealing with wrangling a rogue Board.

It's like trying to herd cats keeping them all in line and on the same page rather than looking solely at how much money Driscoll Tech is putting in their pockets.

Since Dad's gone, my sole purpose is to bring his dream to fruition. No one understands why I work so hard, so I've shut them all out. My uncle tried to convince me to let the R&D team finish the network and take a vacation. I didn't speak to him for a month. I don't need that kind of negativity in my life, and nothing will derail me from my goal.

No matter what it takes, no matter what I have to sacrifice, I *will* finish this program.

My brain settles into a rhythm like a fine-tuned instrument, and my fingers fly across the screen as I work. It's not until my neck has fully cramped that I look up, blinking my dry and stinging eyes to get some relief from the strain. The sun has set, and the darkness presses in, a velvet tapestry of navies and plums. It's so dark, there are already stars twinkling above.

It's not as if this is the first time this has happened, losing myself to my task for hours and hours.

But I hear shouts in the distance—shouts of *my* name.

Masculine shouts with a panicked edge.

Standing, I stretch my fingers overhead, wiggling them to get blood back into all the digits. I tuck my tablet under one of the throw pillows—I can access my work from the cloud server I keep if a random thought strikes me tonight before bed.

The climb down the ladder is slow and methodical. Falling and breaking something isn't on my agenda, and I don't have time for the recovery. When my feet touch the grass, I bend down and slip my shoes off, curling my toes into the cool blades and closing my eyes. Reconnecting with nature isn't something I'm able to do often. It's moments like these that remind me I'm human and not some cyborg destined to live my life hunched over in front of a screen and languishing under the harsh light of fluorescent bulbs.

"Penelope!" Indy shouts from where he's standing near the patio. He's got a flashlight in his hand, and it's aimed in my direction. No doubt he's spotted me by now, so there's no way I'm going to be able to avoid a confrontation with him.

The tiny hairs on my arms stand on end in anticipation of whatever argument is coming, and a cold sweat breaks out along my forehead and down the back of my neck.

He marches across the grass, and if I ignore the fact he's angry with me for hiding out, I might be swept up in the ridiculous fantasy that he actually cares beyond what his job demands him to, which is silly. Indy has proven with every single interaction we've had that not only does he not view relationships with the opposite sex the same way I do, but that he would be a distraction.

A colossal, dangerous, carnal distraction.

A distraction I can't afford to indulge.

I brace myself for the onslaught, curling my fingers into fists and resting them on my hips. My back straightens, and my heart speeds up as if it's sprinting toward an invisible finish line, determined to win at all costs.

"Where the fuck have you been?" he rages when he gets close enough, and I flinch as if his words are a physical blow. I'm not good with negative social interaction—or any social interaction, really—on a good day, and he's *really* upset.

"I—"

"We've been freaking the fuck out, tearing this place apart trying to find you. I thought someone kidnapped you!" he shouts, and I take a step back. I can only imagine what I must look like right now, eyes wide as saucers and lower lip trembling. For all of my bravado, I'm really just a chicken deep down—one with a lot of pride who doesn't like to show how weak I really am.

"I—" I try again, but he doesn't let me get a word in.

"And what would we have had to do then, huh? What kinds of dangerous situations would you have put all of us in because you can't seem to follow some simple fucking safety protocols?" Indy's breathing hard and his eyes are narrowed and unhinged. He looks as if he's about to reach for me—to check me over for injury or shake some sense into me, I'm not sure which—but hesitates at the last second. Instead, he moves to one of the trees at my back and punches it so hard leaves flutter down around me.

He hits it again and again, and I can only imagine what the bark is doing to his knuckles. Finally, with heaving breaths, he stops and rests his forehead against the trunk, but I don't wait to see what else he might say.

My eyes sting, and I'm seconds away from crying, something I've never let anyone see me do—not even at my parents' funeral. I sure as hell am not going to allow Indy to see me at my most vulnerable, not after this.

Instead of waiting for whatever he might say, I take off across the lawn. He must sense what I'm doing because he calls out, "Protocol, Duchess."

I don't know what *protocol* he's referring to, so I don't bother responding. He probably won't let me speak anyway, so I continue on, escaping inside the safety of the house, charging through the French doors, and sprinting for my room.

When I slam my bedroom door, I turn my back to it, sliding down the solid surface until I'm sitting on the floor with my knees pulled into my chest. I sit like that for so long my butt goes numb before my phone pings, and I pull it out of my pocket, shocked to realize I haven't checked it in hours.

And when I do? I understand why Indy's so upset with me.

That protocol he mentioned? It's right there in my inbox, and the number one rule is never going anywhere without clearing it with him first.

Feeling like the world's biggest asshole, I climb into bed, still fully clothed but lacking the energy to do anything about it. Tomorrow can't get any worse, right?

CHAPTER 2
INDY

My knuckles throb as I squeeze my phone. The video is dark but clear as Penelope breathes evenly in her bed. The moonlight hits her creamy skin where her tank top has slipped off her shoulder and if she moves again, her nipple will pop out. If that happens, the last scrap of my restraint will snap. I'll find myself in her room jerking off over her sleeping body until I mark her smooth skin with my cum, rubbing it in so she can walk around all day with a part of me on her. Fuck, I've been hard nearly every minute since I walked into this place yesterday picturing all the ways I want to make her relinquish her control to me.

The only break I got was when Penelope went missing. My destroyed knuckles are a reminder of that. It's my own damn fault for ruining them against that tree last night, but it was either that or go find a person to take out my rage on. No matter how mad at Penelope I am, hitting girls is a line I'd never cross.

My blood is still boiling from last night. How hard is it to follow fucking directions? I searched the entire goddamn house before I finally found her, and by then, I was already mentally making a checklist of the weapons we'd need to go track her down and bring her back. Not going to lie, the idea of getting my hands bloody sounded like a fantastic idea, but then she was suddenly there, and I completely lost my shit.

Even if I could somehow put my phone away and calm my dick down enough to get some sleep, the stupid phone won't stop going off. Some random chick I almost hooked up with a couple of nights ago and made the mistake of giving my number to now thinks I owe her something or she has some claim on me. Her constant texts are interrupting my view of Penelope and a black haze starts to seep into the edges of my vision as irritation pulses through my veins.

I don't owe that girl shit. My stomach lurches at the idea of settling down while my skin goes clammy.

The sun isn't up yet, but there's no chance I'm sleeping tonight. After putting my phone into airplane mode, so it'll leave me the fuck alone—and so I can pretend I have some control over the compulsion to watch Penelope sleep—I untangle my legs from the sheets and climb out of bed.

I've got to burn off some of the anger percolating inside me before I see Penelope again because if I don't, there's a damn good chance I'm going to blow up. If I do, I get the feeling she doesn't forgive easily, and the thought of that fills my stomach with dread. For some reason that I have yet to figure out, the way she sees me matters. Every time she lifts her chin, defies me, or tells me off, I only want to push her harder to see what she'll do next.

Will this be the time I get to see the unshakable and always in perfect control Penelope crack and show me what she keeps buried deep down inside? The true version of herself no one else gets to see?

It never is, and she never does.

I give up and stand, checking the time, focusing on the bright screen in the pitch-black room.

Four twelve a.m.

Black basketball shorts are the first thing I find, and I pull them on stopping only to brush my teeth on my way out of the room. I don't bother with a shirt. I doubt anyone's awake right now, considering having Sebastian on this job with me means every inch of this place is covered with motion sensors and cameras—the perimeter at least. We should be able to sleep easily knowing if someone so much as breathes in this direction, we'll get alerts on our phones.

Looks like everyone else in this house is taking advantage of that fact but sleep never comes easily to me. Especially not with the temptation of an unaware Penelope on live stream twenty-four-seven. She can't hide from me, not when she doesn't know she's being watched.

After last night, I'm questioning whether I need to spend my day scouring all the nooks and crannies and hidden spots around this entire property to make sure that the next time Penelope goes missing, I'll know every place she might try to hide. She won't be able to escape me.

Letting her out of my sight isn't an option. She may get under my skin, but she's *my* problem. If anyone tries to take her from me, they're not going to like what I do to them. Messing with Penelope is like playing chess, and I'm not about to stop until either I trap the queen or get her to submit to me.

When people see the mask I wear, they assume I'm a fuckup who jokes around about everything, but something far more sinister lives inside me now. There will never be a time where Penelope will get more from me than a need to see her break. They say misery loves company, and maybe that's true.

But I do know one thing for sure:

Broken people love to destroy anything pure that dares challenge our shattered view of the world.

There's no one more pristine than Penelope Driscoll, and I want to dirty her up and turn her world upside down. At this point, it's a compulsion that I've lost control of. An obsession. That's why when she disappeared last night, I absolutely lost my shit, and why I'm still trying to pull myself back together.

My cock throbs painfully between my legs at the idea of Penelope dropping to her knees before me, surrendering, watching all her carefully crafted layers fall away. I've never fucked a client before, and I don't plan to start now, but she's got an innocence behind her sweet brown eyes that I want to steal and hoard for myself like I'm a fucking dragon guarding its treasure.

My door creaks when I open it and I freeze, listening to be sure I won't be interrupted on my way down to the gym. I spotted it on my self-guided tour of this palace disguising itself as a house yesterday. When I'm sure I haven't woken anyone up, I dart out into the hall and close the door as softly as I can.

My shoes are cradled between my hand and my chest, their rubber soles pulling at my bare skin. It's like finding my way through a maze getting to the gym in the basement, and after a few wrong turns, I finally make it. The door swishes closed behind me the second I step inside, and the lights overhead flick on by an automatic sensor.

There's a bench lining one of the walls, and I drop onto it, sliding my feet into my shoes and lacing them up. I usually use headphones to avoid anyone knowing exactly what it is I listen to when I'm on the treadmill or lifting, but I'm not in the mood to stifle what I want today.

As a straight guy, letting the people around you know you like to work out to nineties pop and boy bands is only asking for it. But right now, I don't give a shit who figures out my secret love of the Spice Girls or Nsync, so I plug my phone into the speaker system and cue up my playlist.

With all the money poured into this place, hopefully Penelope's had the basement soundproofed because if not, she and Sebastian, and whatever staff she may have living here, are about to get a very loud and fucking fire wake-up.

As soon as the first notes ricochet off the walls, the tension in my muscles starts to loosen. The adrenaline kicks in, and I step on the treadmill and crank it up. I'm not in the mood for any kind of warm-up this morning, so I jam my finger onto the button to increase my speed until I'm sprinting.

This is the release I needed—well, I could think of a more satisfying release that involves climbing between Penelope's uptight silky thighs and shoving my cock inside of her while she sleeps, but I don't want to rock a hard-on while I'm running so I don't let myself get too immersed in that dark fantasy.

I don't know how long I run, lost in the music and the rhythm of my feet striking the belt beneath me. When Sebastian pushes through the door with his face buried in the tablet, sweat drips from my hair, rolling down my chest and back. My lungs burn in the best way, the pain of exertion fulfilling a deep-seated craving nothing else can.

There aren't any windows in here, but based on how Sebastian's put himself together, not a hair out of place or a wrinkle in his standard button-down, I'm going to assume it's after dawn. It's not until my heart rate slows to something less frantic that my stomach rumbles, and I'd kill for some breakfast. My eyes dart to my phone where it'd only take a click or two to catch a glimpse of Penelope as she wakes up. When I think about what I'd *really* like to eat for breakfast, my mouth waters.

With one of the towels stacked on the table that sits in the corner, I wipe my face and chest down while Sebastian stands silently, waiting for me to give him my attention. The only reaction I've seen out of him so far is a grimace when I toss the towel in the dirty bin.

He doesn't even give me a *good morning*.

A lot of the other guys can't stand working with Sebastian. He's sarcastic and a know-it-all asshole, but I'm an asshole, too, so I don't mind. Maybe it's for the same reason I'm drawn toward Penelope—Sebastian's perfect appearance and unshakable attitude tempts me to light fires and stand back to watch them burn just to see what he might do.

It's for that reason I walk right up to him, getting directly in his space, and when he leans back to get away from me, I wrap my sweaty arms around him and pull him into a tight hug. His entire body stiffens up as I wrinkle his perfect shirt and drop an obnoxious kiss right on his cheek with wet lips and sweat dripping out of my hair. "Good morning, Bash!"

He flinches at the nickname, and I can feel it because I'm still clinging onto him like a barnacle chilling out on a rock. "My name is Sebastian," he sneers, finally shaking off his shock and using his forearm—so he doesn't touch me skin-to-skin—to push against my chest and shove me away.

I let him go without a fight and grin widely when he looks down at his ruined shirt and then glares at me. Not for the first time, I wonder if something's wrong with me since I seem to get enjoyment out of messing with people in this way, but I don't really care if there is. Everyone has some part of them that's damaged, and at this point, I'm only glad I'm not a raging sociopath who regularly goes on murder sprees for the fun of it.

"I came to let you know the surveillance feed is set up, so there's no need to shadow Miss Driscoll while she's here at home. This should allow us to avoid any more incidents like the one last night," he yells over the music, his cold gaze locked on mine. Looks like Bash has some backbone in him after all.

I'm impressed.

My music is still blaring over the speakers, and I'm honestly surprised he hasn't gone over and ripped the thing out of the wall. Sebastian rolls his shoulders up towards his ears, and I have to wonder if it's to try and block out the sound without making it obvious that it's bothering him. His weight shifts from one foot to the other, and if I had to guess, I'd say he's about two seconds from turning tail and hauling ass out of the room.

I chuckle when I picture him ripping his wrinkled shirt off and coating his skin in Purell, and that glare he's still got trained on me narrows until his eyes are nothing but slits. *Wannabe* booms over the speakers, so I cross the room and press pause to cut him a break. I take a second to check the cameras, but my Duchess isn't in her bed. My mind switches into predator mode, wondering if I should hunt her down and how she'd react to the shirtless, sweaty version of me.

Goddamnit. I have to adjust my dick in these shorts that hide nothing, and I don't even care that Sebastian is actively shrinking away from me. "Jealous, Bash? We could have a dick measuring contest." I need a fucking distraction from this constant hard on bullshit. Penelope's turned me into *this* and if I can't fuck her, I don't know how I'm going to survive this case.

Maybe I should rethink my rule about fucking clients.

"Tell me what you want," I purr and then lose my shit. It's funny, right? "Tell me what you really, really want," I manage to choke out after I get my laughter somewhat under control.

He looks confused as hell, like he definitely didn't get the joke which is even funnier because he thinks he knows everything, and the music was *just* playing. Hopefully, he doesn't think I'm talking about his cock because I'm a strictly pussy kind of dude. "I already told you," he snaps, more than done with my shit already. Unfortunately for him, it's still early, and the two of us are about to be stuck together for however long it takes to deal with the threat to Penelope.

"What game are you playing at now?" His tablet is held against his chest like a shield, almost like he thinks he can use it to protect himself from me. It's cute.

Finally, I roll my eyes. If I can't tempt Penelope with my body, I'm ready for a shower and some breakfast, in that order. "It was a joke, dude. You know, because of the song that was playing?"

Sebastian blinks at me owlishly, and I open my mouth to start singing as proof when the door swings open and Penelope struts in. She's all swaying hips and bare skin outside of the sports bra and tiny shorts she's wearing. My mouth slams shut and goes dry at the same time as my gaze skips down her body, feasting on the buffet of skin she's got on display, all laid out for my consumption. It's so much better live than on video, but there's something about catching those moments where she doesn't know anyone's watching her.

I don't even think she knows how stunning she really is, which seems insane. How could she not know? If she does, I've never seen evidence of it. My dick is threatening to expose my fixation, so as she takes over the treadmill I vacated and sets her pace without a single glance in my direction—after she said a quiet *good morning* with the barest of smiles at Sebastian—I turn and storm out of the room.

The good mood I worked so hard to gain this morning is gone in an instant, with one look at Penelope, and for some reason, her ignoring me pisses me off. I don't like it when she doesn't pay attention to me and getting under her skin is right at the top of my to-do list for the day.

Scratch that—for *every* day.

I want her to have me on her mind all the time, wondering what I might do next or how I'm going to throw her off, where I'll pop up next, or what I might say.

I want to live rent-free in her mind twenty-four-seven. It's my latest obsession, and once I achieve it, I'm not sure what I'll do. All I know is I'm laser focused to make it happen, so that's why I'm here. I need to get rid of every other distraction in her life so all that's left is me.

It's not because I want to fuck her—which I most definitely do.

This is about so much more than that. She didn't realize it at the time, but back in Bali, she might as well have waved a red flag in front of a bull when she blew up at me for some stupid bullshit reason.

After my shower—and jack-off session starring none other than my sweet, innocent Penelope—I feel ten pounds lighter and still fucking *hard*. Her tits bouncing while she ran on that treadmill... Fuck. At least I'm feeling better and ready for whatever Sebastian's cooked up. I may fuck around a lot, but I know I have a job to do, and when push comes to shove, I always get it done. This time it's even more important given the stakes.

A quick stop in the kitchen for a protein shake and banana has my breakfast covered, so I take the stairs two at a time to get to the office Sebastian claimed as his as soon as we crossed over the threshold. When I walk in, I'm not at all surprised to find that he's transformed it into some sort of epic command center.

I think this is usually Penelope's office, and vaguely I wonder if she's seen this yet. Somehow, I doubt it, considering she seems like she's as big of a control freak as Sebastian here is. If she knew how much he'd taken over her space, she'd probably be flipping the fuck out right now. The thought brings a smile to my face that's so similar to the one the cartoon version of the Grinch gets, it's scary.

Well, at least in my own head it is. I probably look deranged on the outside, but the only one here to see it is Sebastian, and I don't care if he thinks I've got a touch of psychopath in me. Really, messing with him is only more fun that way.

Maybe I should drag her up here and show her what he's done.

Sebastian is standing in front of a large monitor mounted on the wall that's got a list of names on it. I step up behind him, slurping the last bit of my protein shake loud enough that he startles before whipping his head around to cut me with his gaze. Too bad it's as effective as a dull pair of kitchen scissors. I notice he's changed into a new shirt and smirk when he takes a step away to put distance between us.

"What am I looking at?" I ask as I refocus my attention back onto whatever this list is.

He looks like he wants to tell me off for asking such a stupid question. Instead, he takes a deep breath and pushes his glasses further up his nose before he opens his mouth to explain. "This is our list of suspects. As you can see, they all revolve around either Driscoll Technologies or Fields AI. First, we've got the Driscoll Board of Directors—Franklin Moreno, Hannah Salazar, Valerie Silva, Ira Abrams, Nathan Carpenter, and Miss Driscoll's uncle, Collin Driscoll. He's also the acting CFO."

Sebastian uses a fancy laser pointer to gesture toward the list on the left. I read through it and commit each name to memory. We met that group of entitled dickheads yesterday and I want to fucking *cackle* at the reminder of the look on that pretentious prick's face when I put him on his ass.

The list on the right isn't really a list at all. It's one single name: Drew Reynolds, CEO of Fields AI.

I take a minute to think through all the names I'm looking at before I speak up. "Based on the fact the Board had to turn down the competitor's offer in order for him to take it to the shareholders wouldn't that rule out all six of them?" It seems obvious to me, and if

Drew is threatening Penelope, it'll be easy enough to pay him a visit and wrap this up today.

My angry fingers choke my phone like I imagine doing to Drew's neck later today. Too bad this can't end yet. I'm not ready for my fun to be over. I bounce on my toes once, unable to contain the feral energy demanding I go find Penelope and force her to submit. Sebastian's voice pulls me back from my impulses.

"Possibly, but it's early, and we don't know anyone's motivations yet. It's not smart to cross any names off the list until we're certain they're not involved. I'm going to start sifting through the company email accounts of every member of the Board to see if I can find anything useful," Sebastian says. "If I find nothing, I'll move to their personal accounts." He clicks the screen off and walks around the desk before settling into the chair behind it.

He spins and turns his back, effectively dismissing me, but I'm not done yet. "Good talk, Bash, but what shall I do while you're off saving the world?" I make my voice high-pitched and as feminine sounding as I can manage with my deep baritone, and he raises his hand and waves it at me over his shoulder dismissively.

"Stick to Miss Driscoll. One of us has to be the field agent here, and you know it's not going to be me. Report back anything suspicious you see or encounter so we can build a case file. I shouldn't have to remind you of the protocol." He doesn't even bother turning, and I bristle at the way he's ordering me around like he's my boss.

I open my mouth to argue with him but close it again because his strategy is solid and plays right into my plan for my Duchess. I'll find another time to make it clear he's not in charge here, of me or what I do. As I turn to leave the room, I find myself almost giddy with anticipation of finding all the ways I can burrow underneath my stuck-up Duchess's skin. Stick by Penelope? Now that I can do.

CHAPTER 3
PENELOPE

Shivers work their way down my spine from Indy's close proximity. A big, obnoxious red box flashes on the screen of my tablet because once again, I'm too distracted, and the process is hitting snag after snag while I run a test. My fingers get caught in a tangle as they run through my hair again, and Indy catches my wrist and works my hand free. I yank it out of his hold as if his touch burns me, and it does. Just maybe not the way he thinks.

"Would you mind waiting outside the door?" I grit out, the cool composure I always wear like a shield slipping, and I know a hint of my frustration leaks out. Indy doesn't miss it if the self-satisfied smirk he levels in my direction is any indication.

"No can do, Duchess. I've got to keep my eyes on you *at all times*." If anything, he sidles up closer, staring over my shoulder at my mess up. He leans so close that his warm breath brushes across my skin like a caress, and my lower belly clenches. It takes every ounce of control I have not to fidget in my seat or press my thighs together. I refuse to give Indy the satisfaction of knowing he gets to me and that for the past few months, he's been the star of every sexy daydream I've had.

"At least move back so I can concentrate," I snap, jerking my shoulder back so it hits him in the stomach, and he lets out a surprised *oof*.

"Actually, whatever it is you're doing there has me riveted, so I think I'll just—" Indy moves away from me and grabs the comfy chair

I keep in the corner of the lab, dragging it across the room. The sound of it scraping along the floor is jarring and seemingly endless. The vein in my forehead pulses like one of those alien eggs in a bad eighties sci-fi movie, and I rub my temples as he plops down into the chair as close as he can. "Sit here and watch," he says, finally finishing his sentence.

"Aren't you supposed to be keeping an eye out for threats? Someone could sneak up on us," I feel the need to point out, and he chuckles, but it's this low, gravelly sound that rumbles down my entire body. My toes curl and my heart skips a beat because of that sound. Rubbing at my chest absently, I try to focus back on my failed string of code. When he picks up a piece of my hair and starts playing with it, I know it's a lost cause.

"With Bash's systems in place, no one's sneaking up on us while we're here in the palace." I roll my eyes at his disparaging description of my house. "The danger is when we step out into the real world, Duchess, and don't you worry. I can handle anything your little problem throws at us." Somehow his words strike me as completely overconfident and also condescending in a way that infuriates me. I also think that's what he's *trying* to do.

"If I'm not in danger here, then why are you insisting on hovering?"

Indy shrugs, and I watch the muscles in his broad shoulders shift under his t-shirt with the movement. He smirks when he catches me staring, and I quickly look away, but it's too late. He already saw me checking him out.

"Maybe I'm so drawn to you, I can't help myself." He says the words so casually as if we're discussing something mundane like the weather, and a snort escapes me before I can rein it in. But he tugs on my hair, pulling me so close, our noses brush. My heart trips over itself at the intensity in his gaze.

"Right." With a heavy sigh, I realize there's no way I'm going to be able to focus with him sucking all the energy up in the room, so I click my tablet off and pick up my phone instead, checking the time.

I'm supposed to be in the office dealing with the Board and getting ready for a meeting my best—and only—girlfriend set up for me as a favor. Driscoll Tech took a hit, and it's my job to get it back on track regardless of what the Board thinks. Hopefully, this meeting is the start. "I need to be in the office in an hour, so I suggest you be ready to deal with whatever threats may jump in our path by then."

I don't wait for Indy's snarky comeback and instead gently tug my hair free and hurry off to my room. For once, he actually gives me space and doesn't follow right on my heels. When I'm in my room, I close the door and lock it behind me, feeling a little dizzy from the relief of being alone and having some space to breathe and gather my thoughts.

I strip out of my leggings and the oversized hoodie I found on my dresser this morning that suspiciously smelled like Indy. Ordinarily I wouldn't have worn something that I wasn't sure was mine, but it looked so comfortable and after last night I didn't have it in me to deal with confining clothes and heels this morning.

Now it's time to suit up, so I go into the closet to find something more appropriate.

On the way to the bathroom for a quick shower, the back of my neck prickles like I'm being watched. I cover my chest with my arms and look around, but my room faces a private tree line and I'm on the second floor. The paranoia must be starting to get to me.

With the recent chaos upending my life, I'm falling behind on my self-imposed deadline to finish the AI project. There's nothing more important to me than getting it done, but if I want to keep working on it as I had been, I have to right the ship. I can't let it continue to sink to the bottom of the ocean. I refuse to let my parents' legacy be taken over by someone who would wring it for every cent of profit they could before turning it into something immoral like so many other tech companies. It's Fields' track record and I'm not going to let him win.

No, my father had ambitions to make the world a better place, starting with the children, and I'm determined to continue down the same path. Using technology to solve the devastating plague of childhood cancer was a dream he and I shared. We would spend hours with our heads pressed together working out the algorithms to test and best ways to tackle the problem. My father set up Driscoll Tech to make money on other smaller inventions and designs so that the medical AI wing we were developing would never have to make money in order to operate.

It was the legacy he wanted to leave behind, and I couldn't let it be milked for profit. It was why I decided to bring on a team of bodyguards to watch my back while I navigate the shark-infested waters of big business. It's why I'm going to do whatever the PR guy I'm meeting with today suggests, no matter how much I might want to sneak out to my treehouse with my tablet and hide from the world.

I can't let myself get distracted by infuriating and frustratingly attractive curly-haired bodyguards who make me want to forget everything but them. It's dangerous, and I don't have the time or mental energy to deal with what might come of it, so I renew my resolve as I push off the door and hurry into my bathroom to get ready.

After a quick shower, I toss on my usual office attire of a pencil skirt, camisole and cardigan thrown over the top. It's uncomfortable and boring, but it's also what everyone expects of me. I slip my feet into a killer pair of heels—they literally make my feet want to die—and take one last breath. I pretend I'm breathing in strength and confidence, filling myself up starting at my toes. I repeat the breathing exercise until I imagine I'm topped up with the bravery I will need to face the office.

Three loud raps sound against my door, and I tense as Indy's slightly muffled voice carries through. "C'mon out, Duchess, or I'm coming in."

That gets me to rush across the room and twist the lock, flinging the door open to reveal Indy standing there with a devastating smirk on his full lips. It reveals a dimple in his left cheek and he's got his hands tucked into the pockets of his jeans. I have no doubt that if I ignored him, he'd have made good on his threat, and a thrill runs through my body at how easily he could dominate me if I let him. But fixing a broken or dismantled door is one thing I don't need to add to my overflowing to-do list. The idea of him being so desperate to get to me he couldn't help but break down the door is admittedly scorching hot and my belly clenches, but that's not reality, and I berate myself for getting lost in the fantasy of it.

I *just* shored up my resolve and two seconds in close proximity with this man, and it's already crumbling around me, falling at my feet like broken pieces of brick and mortar. Tilting my chin up, I hurry past him, not stopping to look in his direction or bother with saying a word. In fact, I lift my phone and watch where I'm going out of my peripheral vision while I answer urgent emails on the way to the car, pretending my panties aren't wet and my nipples aren't trying to break through my shirt.

Pretending I don't want him to throw me on a bed and make me forget my own name with the massive dick I got a peek of in those basketball shorts he wore to the gym this morning.

Indy catches up quickly, falling into step beside me, and I can feel his attention like a warm blanket that covers me from head to toe —a blanket that gives me butterflies I'm trying desperately to ignore. There's this weird twist of *longing* somewhere in my chest that startles me so bad that when I realize what it is I stumble. Indy's long fingers wrap around my elbow, his strength the only thing that keeps me from falling flat on my face.

He clicks his tongue at me like I'm a naughty child, but all I can focus on is the waves of heat radiating outward to the furthest reaches of my body from where he's touching me. My face flushes, and my nipples tighten even more, and when I look up and our eyes lock together, I feel like I'm falling all over again.

Then, he breaks the spell. "I swear you're obsessed with your phone, Duchess. Does it give you everything you need?" He breathes that last part with his lips so close to my ear that I can't help the goosebumps that inch along my skin.

Coming to my senses, I rip my arm out of his grip and rush ahead, my heels clicking against the marble floor all the way to the front door. Indy's chuckle echoes behind me, and I hate that he can read me so easily. It's one of the things I've always prided myself on, keeping a calm demeanor that's always unaffected and at least somewhat detached so those around me have no idea what I'm actually thinking.

Indy's always seen the things I try to hide. I think he knows the effect he has on women, and unfortunately, I'm not immune. As much as I wish I wasn't sometimes, I'm only human, and I have needs and desires just like everyone else. My body has instincts that take over without my permission despite what my brain may demand.

And my body? It wants Indy Foster like it's never wanted anyone before.

When I slide into the back seat of the car, Indy moves in beside me, ignoring all the other open seats and taking the one closest to mine. He's sitting so close that his thigh leans against mine, the heat of which stops the breath in my lungs, and I have to work to keep my heart rate down. He smells like something smoky and dangerous, like a bonfire on a winter's night you'd dance around barefoot and naked under a full moon. I can't escape him; he's everywhere.

He's assaulting every one of my senses, and I'm so turned on, I have to dig my nails into my palms to keep from climbing in his lap. Indy leans closer as I pretend to scroll through my inbox, but I'm not seeing anything on the screen. Every ounce of my attention is focused on him—on the way his leg's still touching mine, on how he's in my personal space, and his lips are inching closer and closer toward my ear. I brace myself for whatever he might say, knowing no matter what it is, I'm not prepared.

I'll have no witty comeback or smart-ass remark because I'm so out of my depth with this man, it's like I'm sitting on the ocean floor trying to see above the surface.

"I can fix your little problem, Duchess. If you want."

I don't know what he's talking about. Before I can stop myself, I make eye contact, turning my head to look at him without thinking about how it'll put our lips so close together I can feel his warm breath against my mouth.

"What problem?" I ask, meaning for it to come out cold and detached, but instead, I sound breathy and sultry in a way I didn't know I even had in me.

"The one where no one's ever made you come hard enough to show you there's more to life than work." He reaches over, and his fingers trace along the neckline of my camisole right above the swell of my breasts. I can't help the shiver that follows in the wake of his fingers, and my already hardened nipples turn into points of diamond.

My blood turns molten, and a growing part of me wants to melt into him with a heartfelt *yes, please*. But the other part—the more logical part—wants to slap that bitch right back down. Who the hell does he think he is speaking to me this way? He knows nothing about what I've sacrificed and what I will continue to sacrifice for a cause so much bigger than myself or my pleasure. The fact no one has ever given me an orgasm is beside the point.

Some people just have a harder time getting off than others and screw him for making me feel bad about it.

Suddenly, the heat that'd been building inside me morphs into anger, and I push against his chest, shoving him away to get some distance. I ignore how hard the muscles under his form-fitting black t-shirt are against my palms.

"What, and you think *you're* up to the task?" I eye him up and down with a wrinkle of my nose that I hope conveys how repellant I find him at this moment. "You have no idea what I've been through or what I'm working towards, and the very last thing I need is to get distracted by a man who only lives moment to moment with no direction and no thought to how his actions affect others."

I'm really on a roll now, throwing his judgment back in his face. Storm clouds are gathering in his gray eyes, and all traces of flirtation are gone. He radiates a menacing tension that I'm sure he'd like to unleash on me, and I'm relieved. Better that than trying to get into my pants because even now I don't think I'd be able to resist.

"And what would happen if I did give in, huh? You'd sleep with me, get that new notch for your bedpost, and then throw me away like garbage? Yeah, hard pass. Thanks, but no thanks."

We're both breathing hard. My hands shake where they're balled into fists, my nails digging into my palms so hard they draw blood. His close proximity throws me off balance. Every breath of oxygen I suck in is tainted by his spicy-clean scent. I think he finally gets it when he unbuckles and slides over in the seat so we're not so close anymore. I ignore how cold I am now that he's acting like I don't exist. He stares out the window, and my attention drops to my phone. I'm both relieved and disappointed when he doesn't try to talk to me again the rest of the ride into the office. It's almost believable when I tell myself it's better this way.

When we arrive, he gets out before the car even comes to a full stop, but he doesn't stalk off like I expect him to. He waits, not bothering to actually look in my direction, but I imagine he's scanning the area for threats or whatever it is he's supposed to do. At least, no matter what else he says and does, Indy is a professional. Even if he's upset with me or hates my guts, I know he'll do whatever he has to do to keep me safe.

"Thank you," I murmur as I get out of the car, brushing by him as he's holding the door open for me.

"You may think I don't know you, Penelope Driscoll, but you're dead fucking wrong. It's *you* who doesn't know shit about *me*." His words are so quiet I almost don't hear him. Except I do, and the bitterness and despair lacing his voice surprises me into silence. I don't know what to say, and my stomach twists into knots with regret. I shouldn't have let my fear and frustration get the better of me in the car.

Right as we're about to step inside the building, I spin around, coming face to face with my surprised bodyguard, though he quickly covers it up, and the anger seeps back into his hard stare. "You're right. I'm sorry I acted as if I did. Can we forget the whole thing and go back to somewhat tolerating each other?"

His jaw ticks, but eventually, his demeanor relaxes a fraction, and he nods. "Sure, Duchess. If that's what you want."

While he doesn't seem as angry, I'm not sure I've said the right thing here. As much as I want to fall to my knees and beg him for that stupid dimpled smile because I don't like when he's upset, my pride won't let me. I can't worry about it now. I'm about to step into the hornet's nest, and if I don't maintain the image of the Queen, they'll tear me down faster than a billboard in a hurricane.

I take a deep breath, letting the calm, unaffected mask I wear in this building slide over me like a death shroud. I'm as ready as I'm going to be.

"Sebastian is monitoring the building's security feed from home base. He'll let us know if he spots anything suspicious," Indy tells me as we step through the doors. It's a relief knowing I don't have to try and keep track of everything myself. Having Indy at my back gives me an extra shot of confidence I sorely need today.

The office I use when working in the lab is on the first floor, so I don't bother getting on the elevator and head for that instead. Colette, my assistant, knows I avoid the top floor unless I absolutely have to go up there. It's where the executive offices are and where the Board operates from. My uncle insisted when I took over that I take the massive corner office that used to be my father's, so I did to avoid the argument. That doesn't mean it'll ever really be mine. As far as I'm concerned, that office still belongs to my father.

When I step inside, Indy's right on my heels. Harrison Astley, rumored PR genius, already sits in front of my desk, looking perfectly at home. "Mr. Astley, thank you for coming. I hope I haven't kept you waiting long."

He stands up and holds out his hand for me to shake, and when I do, I notice Indy tense up behind me out of the corner of my eye. I'm so attuned to him, even that small movement captures all my focus and my mind spins with possibilities.

Does he not like me touching Harrison?

Is he... *jealous?*

He shouldn't be. From what I hear, the handsome Brit is happily married and he's not really my type. My eyes flick back toward my lickable bodyguard. He may be the worst, but he's blazing hot.

"Not at all, I just arrived. I'm going to keep this short and sweet as we've both got better uses of our time than to drag out a meeting that could've happened by email."

I smile at him, letting the mask crack just a bit. It's always nice to meet another person who appreciates efficiency and respects your time. "Agreed, and if what Montana's told me about your home life's true, I can't believe you even found the time to come all the way out here at all."

He grins and it's so warm it catches me off guard. That smile is so different from the one he gave me when I first walked in. "Yes, well, when Montana Blackwood demands a favor, you don't turn her down, newborn sleep schedules and tour dates be damned."

"Fair enough," I say, getting more comfortable with Harrison by the second. He seems like good people, and I don't know many of those. "Tell me then, what's your plan? How do I fix this nightmare?"

"With all the rumors about the future of Driscoll Technologies, you need to show the shareholders and your clients that you're as steady as you've ever been. So steady, in fact, you're taking time out of your packed schedule to throw a gala for charity."

A cold chill sinks into my bones as I roll my chair out from behind my desk and drop into it. Social functions are at the very top of my avoidance list. Indy moves behind me, a sentry guarding my back and keeping watch, which helps me relax and focus, two things I desperately need more of right now. His fingers curl over the back of my chair and graze against my shoulders every time I move.

"I don't really have time—"

"Nonsense," Harrison says, waving me off. "You'll make time, and if not, that's what assistants are for, yes? This is non-negotiable. If you want to spin the attention you're getting in a positive direction that is. Pick any charity that deals with children and leave the press to me. You've got one week to pull it together. I've already had your assistant send me over a contact list that includes your largest clients, the Board, and all the shareholders. I'll begin pulling strings to make sure everyone you need to attend shows up. You reserve a space and put together a team to do the rest."

All I can do is nod numbly. There is no part of this I want to do. None of it. I hate every word that has been uttered aloud in this office in the last five minutes, but I know he's right. He's an expert for a reason, and Montana wouldn't have sent him to me if he couldn't help. I blow out a breath. I'm going to suck up my discomfort and do whatever it takes to salvage this company's future.

I press the button on my desk phone to call Colette into my office as Harrison stands and buttons his blazer.

"If there's nothing else, I'll take my leave. I'll be in touch via email." Harrison nods at me and then Indy before sweeping out of the room. He really is a force, and once he's gone, I slump in my chair. My elbows are propped up on my desk, and my forehead falls into my hands. I'm completely overwhelmed by everything I have to do, and now I'm going to add a gala on top of it?

One where I have to wear a fancy dress and make a speech and...

"Breathe, Duchess." Indy's strong fingers dig into the tight muscles of my shoulders, and I moan, letting my head fall forward and indulging in the way he kneads the tension out. When he's done, his hand slides down my spine and back up and I wish he'd do the same thing down the front of my body. A quiet groan comes from behind me as if he's as affected by this as I am, but then his touch disappears.

My eyes flutter open and there he is, leaning his ass against my desk and searing me with the intensity of his gaze. "Listen to me, Duchess. You're a badass, and this little party? It's nothing. If you can walk in that boardroom and kick everyone's ass today, you can handle putting on a pretty dress and bullshitting with some backstabbing assholes for a couple of hours." He leans forward and runs his fingers through my hair again—something I'm starting to suspect he's fixated on—and then pushes it out of my face. "And now you don't have to deal with it alone. You're going to make this party your bitch."

There's a terrible stinging behind my eyes and all I can do is give him a watery smile.

Whenever I get overwhelmed, I crawl into the shower and cry until I've released the feelings. No one ever gets to see it, and right now, Indy's on the verge of witnessing my tears. I blink rapidly to keep the stinging at bay, to keep the waterworks from falling until I can get home and into my private space, but one tear manages to slip past my eyelid and streaks down my cheek.

He tracks the movement before reaching up and wiping it away. There are so many questions in his eyes, so many layers I never would've suspected. There's a darkness there I've never noticed before, but I can tell it runs deep. I wonder what put that haunted look in his eyes?

It's not like I get to spend a lot of time thinking about it, not with the Board upstairs pretending like they have control over my fate. They don't. When I said I'd do anything to save my father's legacy, I meant it. Even if that means starting all over.

I'll burn this place to the ground if I have to and rebuild in one of my garages.

Now that I've had my moment of weakness, I push back from my desk and stand. The breath I pull into my lungs tastes like defiance and with my shoulders back and Indy at my side, I'm ready.

We leave my office and head for the elevator. Once we're inside and I've pushed the button for the top floor, Indy speaks. "If you want me to use my knife at any point, just flash your tits at me, Duchess. It'll be our sign," he says with the sketchiest smile I've ever seen. It's part cocky asshole, part violent deviant and I can't say I hate it.

Remember when I said sometimes I can't help but play his game? Well...

"These?" I ask, sliding my hands up until I've got a boob in each one. I throw my head back as I massage them lightly, pinching my nipples through my bra and tank top. Tingles spread across my skin knowing he's watching me but can't touch. I've never done anything like this before, but I don't think I want to stop.

Indy groans as if I'm torturing him and now it's my turn to smile. I look over just in time to see him adjust the massive bulge in his jeans. The sexual tension in this elevator is rising higher than the floor numbers speeding by.

When the doors slide open, Indy curses and I pretend none of that just happened. There's a righteous Board waiting for me, and I don't intend to let them think they can bully me any longer. The time for playing is over, both with Indy and the five members of the board.

I stride down the hall with my chin raised and every strike of my heel on the marble tile sounds like a gunshot. Indy's close behind me, and there's reassurance in knowing that he'd knife one of these assholes for me if I asked him to. I think he'd even do it for his own fun without any word from me, but I don't want to test that theory.

The Board is already assembled and waiting in the conference room when I push through the glass double doors. My uncle sits at the head of the table, but his expression is unreadable. They don't stop talking when I walk in, but that's not surprising. Why would they? They don't respect me, but that ends today.

Indy's watching me. I can feel his attention burning into my side. I'm tempted to have him get their attention, but that's not going to earn me what I need.

"How about we stop wasting each other's time? You want out of this company? Off the board? You've got it," I say and slowly they stop talking and turn to me.

"You're going to sell then? To Fields?" Ira asks, his beady eyes glinting with imagined money signs as he sips from the glass of bourbon in front of him.

"I think you're making the smart decision, honey," Valerie says with the sweetest—and fakest—smile she can manage. I cringe at her condescending endearment, but keep my mouth shut for now. Let them dig their own graves.

"We'll need to know timelines and of course what our shares will be," Franklin adds. I think he's gained weight since the last time I've seen him as his stomach is so round, he can't get close enough to the table to reach his pen.

"This is what your father would've wanted," the traitor Nathan says as everyone else dissolves into excited chatter. Let them.

My gaze flicks over to my uncle who's frowning as he watches me. "Something to add, Uncle?"

He pushes back from the table and moves around it until he's standing beside me. "Why are you doing this, Penny? Because of me?"

"It's what you've wanted, isn't it?"

He sighs and I'm struck with this sudden bolt of sadness for the past year and what's become of our once close relationship. I could really use some family in my corner right now.

"Did I want to be CEO? Of course I did. But to throw this all away because things aren't going the way you want?" He shakes his head. "Why not step down and let me take over? I can navigate us out of this, and you can go back to your little projects."

Every part of me bristles at his words and instead of responding to his attempt to manipulate me, I turn back to the rest of the board. "Since you all are so determined to see this company fall to someone with no morals and no care for what he does with it, rather than sell, I'm going to destroy every bit of tech I've been developing over the last three years. The medical AI that you'd hoped to sell off before you scurried away to your private islands and lavish vacation homes? I'll be deleting it as soon as I step out of this room. Since I own the patents to every bit of technology my father and I have developed—me, *not* Driscoll Tech—I'll be taking them with me."

"Now wait—" Franklin's turning red as beads of sweat gather along his hairline and across his forehead but like he did to me last night, I'm not going to give him a chance to speak.

"The only way this company continues to exist is with me as CEO. Attempt to undermine me, vote me out, or go behind my back and make deals without my knowledge and I will take the nuclear option in one second. My ownership is iron clad, and if you test me, this all goes away." I snap my fingers. "Like that."

Hannah hasn't said anything yet, but her lower lip sticks out in a pout like she's five. I don't care to hear what they have to say, and when I turn to leave, Indy gets close enough to whisper in my ear, "That was hot as fuck, Duchess. The only thing that would've made that better is if you would've flashed your tits and I could've stabbed one of them."

It's my turn to smirk and the shackles of the Board's expectations and the pressure to make them all happy fall off of me. I'm floating even as my feet are firmly planted on the ground.

"Penny!" Uncle Collin calls out as we reach the elevator but when the doors open, I step inside. I've got nothing to say to him.

As the descent starts, my racing heart doesn't slow. If anything, it picks up speed with the adrenaline burning through my veins. Indy looks right at me with those dark gray eyes of his and I'm helpless to look away. I can't. He's caught me in his web and there's no escape.

We're moving closer, the air between us sparking with electricity and I think this might be it. This is when I give in, and I'm trembling as I reach for him.

But then the door slides open and someone steps into the car, breaking Indy's hold over me. I turn away and I hear him exhale loudly from the other side of the elevator. I'm shaking and my legs have gone weak. My entire body is electrified right down to the marrow in my bones, and I don't know what to do with it.

When the elevator finally stops at the ground floor, I walk out first knowing Indy will be right behind me. As soon as we're in my office, his fingers are gripping the back of my neck and he's spinning me, dragging me against his hard body. His thick length is obvious between us as his lips hover over mine.

He doesn't kiss me, and I can't bring myself to kiss him either. My breaths are shallow and so are his. The minty taste of his breath lingers on my tongue. His other hand is at my hip, the fingers digging in so hard I'll have bruises, but I want it. I want to see his marks on my skin, this man that I hate.

This man that I have no hope of gaining the upper hand against. No hope of controlling.

"Duchess," he says with a husky voice that cuts me up inside. I have no idea what I'm doing, but right now I want to do it with him. I'm riding an adrenaline high and the confidence that comes along with what I just did.

With Indy, I don't have to have all the answers. With him, I can let go.

His fingers drift up, and I let them. Eyes closed and head tipped back, I let go for the first time maybe ever, trusting him to catch me. And for one second, I'm weightless.

"Oh! Shit, I'm sorry. I didn't mean to interrupt," Colette says before starting to back out of the door, but I hold up my hand to stop her as Indy backs off enough to stand to his full height. He doesn't take his hands off of me. I don't think he cares who sees the way he's touching me. In fact, I think he *wants* Colette to see.

Her face is partially hidden behind a potted plant she's carrying, but when she sets it down on my desk, she's watching me with renewed interest, and I know she's going to grill me for details later. She's never seen me even go on a date with anyone in the last year, let alone caught me in whatever this is.

"No need to apologize. This is Indy Foster. He's one of the private security guards I brought in after the takeover attempt. Indy, this is my assistant, Colette."

"Hey," he says, looking her over with the sort of interest someone might study a stray dog with, like he's trying to assess whether she's a threat.

I shiver when his hold tightens, and I know he feels it. There's no lying to him about the way he affects me. As much as I don't want to,

I force myself to move away, over to my desk to check out the flowers. "What's this?"

"It was delivered for you just before you got in. Pretty, isn't it?"

Narrowing my eyes, I hook my finger into the top of the ceramic pot and drag it closer to get a better look. "Who sent it?"

"There's a card, but I didn't open it," she says, gesturing toward the tiny envelope sticking up from a plastic holder embedded in the dirt.

I pluck it off the stick and set it aside, the dots finally connecting in my brain on what kind of plant this is, and it's clear this wasn't sent to me as anything other than a threat. I know it before I've even read the note.

"This is deadly nightshade," I announce to the room, and Colette gasps while Indy takes a step forward, his palms hitting the desk as he leans forward to study the plant. The delicate purple star-shaped flowers make it look so non-threatening, but the berries make the plant live up to its name. Unfortunately, all I can manage to do is drool over his muscular forearms. That can't be normal, having more of a reaction to my bodyguard than the very real threat against me.

Indy, though... he's like a safe harbor from the storm. As long as he's around, nobody's going to get to me. I hope.

"You won't be ingesting any of the berries, so you'll be fine. Clearly, whoever sent this wanted to send a message. How about we see what it is?" Indy asks, and I reach for the card, but Indy swipes it away.

"Hey! I'm perfectly capable—"

"Believe me, I know you can handle it, Duchess, but maybe this once you don't have to? This is my job. Let me do it."

I want to argue, but why? Why would I *want* to read some threatening note that's going to stress me out more?

"Okay," I agree while he pulls out his phone and snaps some pictures of the plant. He narrows his eyes suspiciously, but I really don't want to fight about this.

"Get rid of this," he tells Colette and then turns his attention on me. There's something so hot in how he's looking at me right now, all protective and determined. "Let's go, Duchess. There are too many unknowns in this building. You're done here."

It's a demand, an order, and that gruff, bossy tone reverberates straight to my clit. I hate that my body wants him so much. If Colette hadn't interrupted us earlier, I wonder if Indy would've fucked me against the wall or bent over my desk. All the build up from earlier comes raging right back, and Indy shoots me a look that's pure sin. His fingers wrap around my bicep, pulling me out of the room.

With one look from Indy, Colette stammers out an apology and disappears, and I can't blame her. The guy is intimidating on his best day. There's a sense of urgency about him that he didn't have before with this new threat. At least he's taking his job seriously.

It only takes a couple of seconds for my driver to pull up and Indy to usher us into the car, slamming the door behind him and telling the driver to take us home. Whatever's in that note seems to have him on edge, and I regret my decision not to read it.

His phone is in his hands, and his thumbs are flying over the screen as he sends text message after text message, his body coiled like a fine-tuned weapon ready to strike.

My curiosity gets the better of me, and I find myself asking, "What did the note say?"

He looks up at me and can't mask the concern on his face or the rage burning in his eyes. "Don't worry about it, Duchess. I've already got Sebastian reviewing security footage and tracking down who sent the plant. No one's going to touch you."

Those words fall off his tongue with a surprising amount of possession wrapped around them, and I find myself unbuckling my seat belt and sliding into the space beside him. Despite how much we butt heads, there's something about Indy that demands I depend on him. To hand over control and let him keep me safe. He's the one person willing to stand between me and danger. He can't be all bad, can he?

Inside this car, it's just us. For one minute, I want to forget everything except the way Indy siphons all the energy out of the space around him, greedily soaking up my absolute attention. He's intoxicating in the way I imagine staring into the abyss of a black hole would be—the endless mystery tempting even the strongest-willed adventurer to take a step forward.

"How about we have some fun?" Indy asks, and he unbuckles and leans up between the front seats, giving me the most amazing view of his ass in the form-fitting jeans he wears. Luckily, I have plenty of notice when he moves to sit back down so he doesn't catch me checking him out. *Crazy* by Britney Spears blasts through the sound system.

"Baby, I'm so into you," he sings along so loud I can barely hear Britney, "you got that something..."

"What can I do?" I find myself joining in, and I can't help but laugh.

By the time the song ends, we're both grinning and a little out of breath. When Indy said he wanted to do something fun, I pictured a whole lot more blood, mayhem, and sex. But this? It's perfect. I've laughed more than I think I ever have in my entire life messing around with my deadly bodyguard. I sober up as we pull into the drive because, unfortunately, giving in to this need to be closer to Indy, to bask in his comfort, may be more dangerous than what lies in wait outside.

Chapter 4
INDY

My eyes are fixed on the screen gripped in my hands. Penelope's working in her basement lab, and I can't seem to tear myself away. I'm not getting shit done because I might miss something if I stop watching her. Like the way she gets this wrinkle in her forehead as she tries to figure out whatever problem she's working on, or how she's so focused it's like she escapes into her own little world. I want all of those moments collected for me to own. *Only* me.

As much as I don't want to admit it, there's something about her that has me completely captivated, and it's not just this need to break her down so I'm all she has left.

While we're in her house, there's no need for me to act like her shadow, but I find myself doing it almost constantly. I can't seem to help myself, and I don't want to. There's a strange magnetism that keeps pulling me in her direction, and I know it's dark and dangerous. Keeping a detached indifference is necessary to protect myself, but Penelope tempts me to break all my rules.

It's exactly the reason I can't, even if leaving her alone is impossible.

The rules are in place for a reason and breaking them would most likely mean the end. The end of everything I've worked so hard to rebuild into some semblance of a life after I was shattered so completely, I didn't think I could keep living. With a pain so deep, the very act of breathing felt like torture, there was a time that recovery seemed impossible. But now I've found a reason to get out of bed each day.

It's not fair that I'm alive, but then life's never cared about fairness.

My melancholy is interrupted by Sebastian dropping into the chair behind Penelope's desk—the one he's taken over for himself. I reluctantly slip my phone back into my pocket as irritation claws at my insides. I try to manage a cocky grin or a snarky comment to rile him up, but I can't find the energy to do it. The darkness has been unchained for the moment, and until I can shove it back into its box, the mask I wear to make the world feel comfortable around me like I'm normal, just like them, is long gone.

"That pompous bag of dicks Drew Reynolds sent Miss Driscoll the nightshade," Sebastian announces, and when I look at him, his jaw is clenched so hard the muscles are ticking. I want to make a joke about how he just called someone a bag of dicks, which is the least Sebastian thing I've ever heard come out of his mouth, but I don't. I can't. Memories are still battering at my brain, and I'm having a hard time pulling myself back to reality.

Even the image burned into my brain of Penelope bent over her desk working downstairs isn't enough of a distraction.

"You figured that out fast," I note, curling my fingers into fists to keep from reaching for my phone. The need to have my eyes on Penelope is a compulsion I can't ignore. It's ironic, Sebastian, of all people, calling someone pompous. For some reason he wears an expression like Drew Reynolds beat him up and stole his lunch money. Maybe he has some personal beef with the CEO of Fields AI, but I don't really care if he does. Whatever his dislike of the guy is, it's not my problem. Sebastian can handle it himself—he's shockingly capable, considering he basically lives behind a monitor.

There's a reason he's our only analyst, and it's because he's a phantom who lurks behind the screen, destroying people before they have any idea what's happening. In short, there's no one better.

He does another very un-Sebastian-like thing and scoffs. "As if it was hard? He didn't even try to hide the purchase. He used his real name and credit card to pay for the delivery. He all but signed his name on the bottom of the card."

"What does he have to gain by getting Penelope to step down? If she does, I'm sure there's some plan of succession for who takes over Driscoll next," I muse, the fog of the past starting to clear with the challenge of untangling the puzzle of Penelope's mess. "Probably her uncle."

"Perhaps whoever that person is, Reynolds believes he can either control him or get him to push through the takeover."

My palm rubs across the rough skin at my jaw as I consider what Sebastian is suggesting. I flick my gaze over in his direction, and he looks like he's lost in thought, doing some sort of calculations, or running through possible scenarios in his mind.

"You think Drew Reynolds needs a trip to the Basement?"

Sebastian snaps out of wherever he was in his head and his eyebrows pinch together. It's no secret he doesn't have the stomach for getting his hands dirty. "I don't know that we've reached that level just yet."

"Maybe." The idea of dragging Drew down into Connor's basement to play with him for the shit he's already pulled lures out the violence that's always right under my skin. I'm aware my urges aren't normal. Torturing a man because he's hurting someone you're sworn to protect gets results and if not, well... it's satisfying in a way only fucking or bloodshed can be. A release.

This is who I've been forced to become to survive my rebirth by blood and fire. There's no guilt.

It's not like I don't act this way with all my clients. I did it for Montana, so Penelope's no different. Except I know that's a colossal fucking lie. Penelope is mine and *no one* threatens what belongs to me. The Fields AI CEO sending her a poisonous plant that could kill her has the monster inside me raising his head and baring his teeth while he claws his way to the surface. He wants to tear the world to shreds.

Or at least turn Drew Reynolds into steaming meat ribbons atop a mountain of bones.

The intensity of my obsession with Penelope is so fucking disastrous. Attachments aren't something I allow. For my sanity, or what's left of it, this is the only way. I have no heart left to lose, but the sliver of saneness I managed to recover hangs by a fraying thread.

Her hooks are already rooted deep in my chest, the tissue scarring around the bloody wounds as they settle into permanence. They demand I get closer. Demand I let her peel off the mask and see the nightmare underneath. Getting under her skin started as fun, but her getting under mine was unexpected. But fun is the persona I've crafted, and it's who I have to keep being no matter what comes my way.

If I show what lurks inside me now, there will be no reining it in a second time. The world looks different when you've lost everything. It turns you into something indestructible, forged in brutality and hardened by circumstance. It's why I'm no good for her; why I'm no good for anyone.

Why it's unfair for me to keep her, even though it won't stop me from doing it anyway.

"What do you suggest our next steps should be?" Sebastian asks, steepling his fingers and pressing them against his mouth as he watches me, waiting for my verdict. He's good at collecting data, but strategizing is more my forte.

"We start to dig, or more specifically, *you* start to dig," I tell him. "We need more information. What is Drew Reynolds up to? And is anyone helping him from inside Driscoll?"

"That segues nicely into my next topic. I already started sifting through the Driscoll Board's communications and came across an email I think you'll find interesting." Sebastian slides his tablet across the desk like an old mobster pushing an inked-up napkin with too many zeroes my way.

Picking it up, I scan through what looks to be an email, though I can't tell who it's from. The more I read, the more my vision tints red at the edges.

"What the fuck is this?" I growl, standing up so abruptly my chair topples over. I need to pace because this feral energy inside me makes it impossible to sit still.

"It was buried deep in some obscure archive, forgotten and re-routed through so many servers and a VPN it's impossible to tell whose inbox it ended up in." His voice lowers, and if I didn't know any better, I'd say his cold and indifferent tone has heated up a fraction. "We can see who it came from, though."

"Drew fucking Reynolds." I toss the tablet back down on the desk in disgust, and Sebastian winces, grabbing it and checking it over for damage. He cradles it to his chest and glares up at me.

"You don't have to take it out on the technology."

I stop and turn slowly to look at him, tilting my head to the side. He shifts under my scrutiny, and a savage grin spreads across my face. "I'm sorry, did I hurt your girlfriend, Bash? Want me to get down on my knees and apologize to her?"

Stretching my arms in his direction, I start to round the desk, reaching for his beloved tablet, but he jumps up and hurries away from me, so we're on opposite sides again. I fall to my knees and clasp my hands together. "I'm *so* sorry, precious tablet. I didn't mean to hurt you. Don't blame Bash. It wasn't his fault."

Sebastian is seething, his face red, and if he was a cartoon, little tendrils of smoke would be wisping up out of his ears. For a second, some of the tension breaks, and I want to laugh, but then I remember what I read. Sobering, I pick myself up off the ground and dust off my jeans while the anger on Penelope's behalf starts to coalesce all over again.

"Are you finished?" Sebastian bites out, and I nod, no longer in the mood to fuck with him.

Wordlessly, I pick up the chair I knocked over, and we both sit back down. "I'm going to have to tell her."

"No need to do it now, not without all of the information. I'm already working on getting around Fields' security systems now, and I'll be in by the end of the day. When I sort through the CEO's inbox, I may find more incriminating evidence or at the very least get some clarity on the situation and who he might be working with."

My jaw tightens as I grind my teeth together. Knowing I'm going to have to hurt her slices into the hollow space in my chest where my heart would be if I had one left. "If you were Penelope, wouldn't you want to know right away? Holding this back feels like a betrayal."

I might want to tear her down and watch as her perfect composure falls to chaos, but not in this way. Hurting her was never part of my plan. I want her to shed her rigid, sheltered persona and embrace the wilder side I know she's got buried somewhere underneath her sensible cardigans and extreme ambition.

This right here is something different altogether.

I pull my phone back out of my pocket and click the screen on, checking on Penelope again, but she hasn't moved. A lurch in my chest surprises the hell out of me. The relief is palpable when I have eyes on her again. It's way past dinner time, and she hasn't stopped since we got back this morning, not to eat or rest. She's not taking care of herself and the grip on my phone tightens until it creaks ominously.

Why the fuck do I even care?

Penelope is nothing to me—a client, a friend of a friend who I barely know. She doesn't need me to take care of her or tell her what to do. So, what the hell's wrong with me? Why does some primal part of me want to take her choices away so I know she's thriving like she deserves? That part wants to throw her over my shoulder and force-feed her before tucking her into bed—*my* bed.

Distant memories threaten to float up from the depths where they're submerged, and I force them back down, piling rocks on top of them to make sure they stay buried where they belong. Back when I used to be someone else, I cared about the people around me, but I don't have that luxury now.

Not since my heart burned up in my chest leaving nothing but an empty space and a pile of ashes behind.

Abruptly, I push back from the desk, shoving my phone back in my pocket where I don't have to look at Penelope, and there's no chance her existence will threaten the tiny bit of peace I've managed to find. I start to walk out of the room before I turn back to Sebastian. "I'll deal with this tomorrow."

When I'm back in my room, and the door's firmly closed behind me, I pull my phone back out of my pocket. It takes every ounce of willpower I have to avoid looking at the security feed and checking on Penelope. I'm not used to denying myself, but I need some space. Maybe I'm kidding myself because Penelope and I feel inevitable.

I need to blow off some steam, but Sebastian isn't a field agent. He can shoot and fight, but I don't want to risk him freezing up because he's out of practice if something happens. I'm the only one that stands between Penelope and whoever has it out for her, so I can't take off.

Right about now, a dive bar that serves cheap beer and some no-strings fucking sounds like my last hope for derailing the collision course I'm on. But I'm stuck. So, I do the next best thing and click open the internet browser on my phone, navigating it to my favorite store.

I kill an hour and my credit card balance, but by the time I'm done checking out, I feel better than I have all day.

My willpower runs out and I check the damn feed one more time before I pass out. Penelope's still in her lab as she stretches and yawns, revealing a sliver of skin that hardens my cock so fast I get dizzy from the rush of blood down south. I'm sprawled out in bed, stripped down, and when I think about running my tongue along the soft, pale patch of skin on her stomach, I go completely hard.

My mind conjures up a fantasy, and I'm lost to my imagination. If I was down there in her lab with her, I'd grip her by the throat, spinning her around and pressing her face down on the table. I'd slowly tug the zipper of her curve-hugging skirt down and yank it off of her.

She'd protest, but she wouldn't mean it, and I'd shut her up with a kiss so consuming, the only thought on her mind would be how badly she wants me to sink inside her tight little pussy.

She wears these stockings with the seams down the back that drive me insane, and they're held up by garters that I run my fingers underneath, making her shiver. I might pull one of the clips, snapping the elastic against her thigh while she gasps. Her body would be a work of art, one only for my admiration as she's bent over, her sweet pink cunt on display.

Here in my bed, in real life, my fingers slip into my boxers and wrap around my shaft. I stroke myself to the fantasy, losing myself in the idea of running my palm up to the middle of her back and then down her spine before slapping her ass for tormenting me for so long.

My strokes are coming faster now, and I let out an obscene groan. I swipe my thumb across the slit at the top of my shaft, collecting the pre-cum that's leaking out and use it to lube up my hand. While my other hand plays with my balls, I imagine burying my face between Penelope's parted thighs.

Her flavor would explode on my tongue, coating it in heaven. No one's ever made her feel like I would. A low growl rumbles through my chest at the idea someone else has tasted her. If anyone's ever had their face between her legs, I'll have to hunt them down and kill them because I can't have anyone else alive knowing how my Duchess tastes.

Her face would be splashed with pink while I tasted her for the first time. She'd writhe and shift at the invasion of my tongue against her pussy. The sensation foreign and new while I'm lapping at her like I'm starved, fucking her with my tongue like I'm about to with my dick.

She'd clench around my tongue as she comes with a desperate plea for more spilling from her lips. I'd play with her clit and lick up the mess, savoring the quick and dirty orgasm on my lips. When I picture her coming apart, I lose it, and cum erupts out of me, coating my abs as I try to catch my breath. As I come down from the high, I'm left wondering what the hell that was. The illusion dissipates like smoke blown away in the wind, and a rush of need to go make it play out for real overwhelms me. I've been inside women and not come that hard, but my Duchess?

She's in a whole new league.

Before I lose the battle with myself, I click off the screen and set my alarm, grabbing my t-shirt and cleaning myself up before tossing it on the floor. Forgetting about this whole thing is the best way to deal with it.

Distance.

It was a lapse of judgment and won't happen again. I'll add another memory to the ones I refuse to acknowledge and call it good. Maybe someday I'll be better at telling myself believable lies. Thankfully for once sleep comes easily after that, but I toss and turn all night.

When my alarm goes off the next morning, I jerk awake, and what I have to do this morning hits me like a mallet to the skull. Penelope deserves the truth, and I know if it were me, I'd want to know. It has to be me who tells her. I don't trust anyone else with my Duchess.

I throw the blankets off, hurrying to shower and get dressed. We'll need time before Penelope's supposed to be at the office, and I'm not giving her any excuses to get out of the conversation we need to have. Plus, she didn't eat lunch or dinner last night, so I'm damn well going to make sure she eats breakfast. Knowing she doesn't take care of herself pushes my protective instincts into overdrive. I'm about to climb the goddamn walls.

By the time I get downstairs, Penelope's fully dressed, and it's obvious immediately that she barely slept last night. Irritation coils inside of me. If I'd gone and forced her into my bed like I wanted, we both would've slept better. She doesn't really wear makeup, so the dark smudges underneath her eyes are glaringly obvious. She gives me a tired half-smile, barely able to muster the energy to mumble a *good morning,* and I almost lose it and demand we forget the outside world today and go back to bed—preferably together. I'd even forgo fucking her to let her get the sleep she needs.

Penelope has other ideas.

"I need to be at the office in half an hour," she informs me, and I grip the edge of the counter. Memories from last night's daydream replay in my head. I shift so the semi starting to tent my jeans is hidden by the counter and try to ignore the desire pulsing straight to my cock.

It takes me a second to shake off the lust saturating every fiber of my being, but then her words register.

"No can do, Duchess. I happen to know you didn't eat lunch or dinner last night. I'm not taking you in until you eat an actual breakfast." I fold my arms across my chest and glower down at her, daring her to test me.

She waves me off like she doesn't know the depths I'm willing to sink to in order to take care of her. "I'll have Colette grab me a bagel. It's fine."

"I'm not asking, Duchess. Besides, we need to talk." I drop those ominous words, and they have their desired effect. Her eyes cloud over with confusion, and I take that as my opportunity to push my agenda forward. "C'mon, I'm taking you out."

Shockingly, Penelope doesn't argue and follows me out to the car. She falls into the passenger seat as soon as I open the door, looking lost in thought. I don't bother interrupting as I close the door and jog around the hood to slide behind the wheel. There's so much tension between us it's like an electrical current, snapping and popping, ready to erupt into sparks and flame any second.

By the time we get to the restaurant, we haven't spoken two words to each other, and I'm ready to throw her in the back seat and fuck the stubborn out of her. I want to crack a joke, tease her about how uptight she is, flirt with her—*something* to get her to talk to me. Her silence is grating. The Penelope I've come to know should've been peppering me with ten thousand questions all the way here, demanding to know what we needed to talk about.

But she didn't. Why?

I have to assume it's because she's exhausted and overwhelmed. The way she's nibbling on her thumbnail as she gets out of the car and follows me into the diner is a dead giveaway that I'm right. She's got so much shit on her plate right now, I hate being the one who's about to pile more on, but it has to be me. She's going to fall apart and I'm the one who'll be there to pick up the pieces. If I could save her from this, I would.

Once we've found a booth and looked over the menu, Penelope tries to order some bullshit fruit bowl while staring down at the screen of her fucking phone.

"You need to eat more than fucking fruit," I growl, glaring at her as I snatch the phone out of her hand and stick it in my pocket. I'm probably not helping her stress level, but I can't sit by and watch her wither away to nothing. I look up to the server. "She'll have pancakes and sausage and hashbrowns. Oh, and eggs. Lots and lots of fucking eggs."

I pluck the menu out of her hands as we have a stare down. Finally, she relents, tiredly smiling up at the server. "Scrambled, please."

I'm so surprised she isn't fighting me, I even manage to hold back from making a joke about her eating my sausage.

She leans back against the booth, cradling the steaming mug of coffee the server poured between her hands. For once, her attention isn't split in a hundred directions. It's intently focused on me, the way it should always be. There's a possessive tightness in my chest I don't like. I don't know what to do with my desire to keep her knowing it's an impossibility.

"You know kidnapping's illegal, right?" she muses, blowing across the rim of her mug before taking a tentative sip.

"Only if you get caught."

She eyes me. "Fair enough. Now, what was so important you had to drag me to a public place to talk about it?"

I look around again, checking the door and the windows. Satisfied there's no one about to interrupt us and no immediate need for violence, I turn back to her. "Haven't I made it clear that the last place I want to be with you right now is in public? Breakfast in bed is more what I had in mind, but I can't cook for shit, and you need to eat. So, here we are."

Leaning across the table, she mirrors me until our faces are only inches apart, and I can see every fleck of gold in her deep brown eyes. The connection between us pulses beneath my skin. I swallow hard, knowing the magic of this second is about to expire like a clock striking midnight with what I have to tell her. I close my eyes because as much as I like to torment her, I don't want to see her expression when this news leaves my lips. My heart drops down to the floor as I open my mouth and let my eyes open, knowing if she has to face the pain, I'll have to share it with her.

"Your parents were murdered," I whisper, and just like that, her world shatters again.

CHAPTER 5
PENELOPE

I blink at Indy. There's a wall inside my brain protecting me from the words he uttered. They launch themselves at the blockade, attempting to penetrate the safe cocoon inside my head. He's watching me with concern, tense and ready to jump into action should I break down.

Every time the words circle in my mind, they chip away a little bit more.

Murdered.

Murdered.

Murdered.

The demolishing of that protective barrier happens so fast that I can't even stop the choked sob that comes from deep inside me, from a place where the tatters of my soul struggle to hold together. I slap my hands over my mouth to try to hold the agony in, but it does nothing to slow the tears rolling down my face.

I'm trembling with the trauma of it all and if I'm not careful I might just splinter apart. I hardly register Indy moving out of his seat and into mine, dragging me into his lap so that I'm completely surrounded by him. He holds the fractured parts of me together with his unrelenting strength.

But this is Indy. I shouldn't feel safe to fall apart in his arms with the way he likes to torment me. He'll probably use my weakness against me later. But right now, I'm crashing hard and he's the only soft place to land.

"I've got you, Duchess. Let go," Indy soothes, murmuring soft words into my hair as my entire reality and all the truths I thought I knew are washed away with the force of a flash flood.

Our food sits cold where the server dropped it off, neither one of us touching it. It doesn't matter; I couldn't eat it anyway with the bile burning at the back of my throat. By the time my tears slow and my shuddering breaths even out my eyes are swollen, and I'm wrung out.

If it weren't for Indy's arms banded around me, I'm positive I would have fractured apart and be laying in pieces on the dirty diner floor.

"Who killed them?" I croak out. Now that I'm thinking more clearly, it's the only thing I want to know.

"We don't know yet." There's a hard note of determination fortifying his words. "But I promise you I'll find out." The underlying threat of violence in his voice settles something in me as he uses his thumbs to wipe the lingering tears from my face.

"I want to help." I sit up with a new resolve taking root deep down where nothing will be able to dig it up until I get answers. Indy's grip on my waist tightens, and it's at this moment I realize I'm still in his lap. His muscular arms are still clutching me to his body as he holds me in a bruising grip. I wiggle to try and loosen his hold and his head falls back while his jaw clenches, but his arms stay firmly in place.

When something hard presses against my thigh I don't wait anymore and push against his chest, practically throwing myself onto the seat beside him. My cheeks burn at my body's reaction to his arousal because a responding heat pulses between my thighs, and between the fresh grief and my confused feelings around this man, I don't know how to handle it.

He clears his throat, the sound breaking through the awkward tension that now sits between us. "Sebastian is already on it. If he needs any help, you'll be the first to know. I promise."

I don't think I have much choice but to go along with whatever he thinks is the best plan. This is his domain and as long as we're on the same page trying to figure out who killed my parents, I'm okay with taking a backseat.

"I want to know everything you uncover as soon as you find it," I say, leveling him with a look that promises I'm not going to go easy on him if he hides anything from me.

"You got it, Duchess." Indy looks down at our spoiled food and then back over to me, a crooked smile tilting his lips in a way that nearly coaxes a smile out of me. Right now, I'm not sure I'm physically capable but he's tempting me. "I'll order us a replacement to go."

I nod and when Indy goes to leave the booth my hand snaps out and catches his wrist. "Thank you for telling me," I murmur, hoping he knows the thank you isn't just for sharing what he found but also being here as I fell apart.

A gasp slips past my lips when I gather my courage and look up at him. There's such pain and heartbreak in his tumultuous gray eyes, and it hits me that he can relate. He knows what I'm going through, because he's been dragged bloody and beaten through a hell of his own and survived.

"I hope you understand that when I find the piece of shit who took them from you, I'm going to make them suffer," Indy vows, his tone drenched in malice and violence. His turbulent eyes darken to charcoal, and it makes me shiver. I want that. I want whoever took them from me to feel every ounce of pain they've forced on me over the last year plus interest.

I've never been prone to violence—even on TV or in movies I avoid it. Yet when that promise left Indy's full lips, it settled into my bones with a certainty that it would happen. Justice would be delivered.

"Thank you," I whisper, trying to gather myself back together after dropping my defenses and letting him see every second of vulnerability. Now I'm unsure how to act. Indy hasn't moved from where his thigh presses against mine and we're squished in the booth together, and I'm still holding his wrist. My senses are on overload between the fresh wave of grief pouring through my veins and the electricity that vibrates between us.

I don't know Indy that well, but that glimpse into the bottomless well of pain that he hides inside bolsters my confidence about what kind of fate lies in store for the monster who took my parents from me.

Hopefully, Indy's imagination is better than mine when coming up with inventive ways to make someone suffer. While I might not have it in me to hurt someone, that doesn't mean I don't want it to happen. The taste of vengeance on my tongue is bitter, but I swallow it down anyway. By the time our server drops the bag of our takeout onto the table and Indy's paid the bill, I'm ready to face whatever lies in store for me at the office.

My defenses are back in place, and when Indy grabs my hand and laces our fingers together on the way out to the car, I can't help but take strength from this new connection between us. For once, there's no teasing or prodding, no pushing me to do something I'm not ready for. Right now, he's my mirror and his willingness to shoulder my pain, to shelter me while I navigate my new reality means everything.

He's giving me what I never knew I needed, someone to help carry the weight for a little while. I can't help but wonder if we've reached some sort of new normal in our relationship—not that we have a relationship, but I hesitate to call what's between us a friendship. Maybe this morning means that we're there, that I can lean on him if I need to and I can be there for him, too, if he ever wants to unbury whatever skeletons hide deep down inside.

This new information weighs me down. My body is sluggish, heavy with grief and wrung out from emotion. The burning behind my eyes is a reminder any second this hard truth could wreak havoc on me. I've barely managed to stuff everything back inside, and heat strokes across my face when it occurs to me how Indy's now seen me at my lowest.

Anger surges up replacing the anguish, a dichotomy I suspect

I'll struggle with for a while. I'm mad at myself for giving him ammunition to use against me. Any weakness I show is an opportunity to be exploited. I didn't used to be like this but stepping into my father's shoes has taught me many lessons, one of which is that everyone is a possible enemy and to always keep your guard up. Indy's proven more than once he's all too happy to play the villain in my story.

Most days I miss who I was before my parents died. Back then, I could focus on my projects and not worry about anything else. There was a lightness to my existence, a carefree naivete that I wish I could get back. That girl died right along with them.

There's no going back, no resurrecting my parents. Accepting that this is my life now is the only way. Every day I wake up and accept who I've been forged into by circumstance and today is no different.

Despite this new knowledge, I must continue on.

Indy holds the door open for me as I slip into the passenger seat of his car before he passes me the bag with our breakfast in it. My stomach gives a halfhearted growl before he closes me in, and my attention sticks to his form as he rounds the hood of the car. His movements are smooth and confident as he slides behind the wheel. His strong forearm flexes when he grips the steering wheel and presses the button to start the engine.

When he insisted I fire the driving service I normally use, I wanted to rebel but enjoying this view is worth giving him the victory.

"I only want to check in with Colette and make sure there aren't any fires to put out this morning," I tell him and he side-eyes me while he shifts into drive.

My head tips back against the seat as I stare out the window. "Fine, any new fires that are in danger of turning into a raging inferno between now and tomorrow," I amend.

"Why? Have a date this afternoon?" His tone is teasing, but there's something darker edging just underneath.

"Actually, I do." He's always riling me up, and I can't resist the opportunity to do the same to him.

When his grip tightens on the wheel and the muscles in his forearm flex, excitement flutters up inside me. He's got me running through a full panel of emotions this morning, and I can't remember the last time I felt so much in such a short period of time.

"With who?" His voice is frosty, like it's dripping liquid nitrogen and I shiver.

"Stick around and you'll get the chance to find out," I say, enjoying getting under his skin for a change.

Indy must be done with the conversation because he leans forward and cranks the music up so loud, I can barely hear myself think. That's fine by me; I've had so many twists and turns flying at me lately, not being able to hear my thoughts is a welcome reprieve from the usual never-ending mess in my brain.

With my head tilted back against the seat, I close my eyes and let the music permeate my body until it's all I can feel—my skin humming with the bass, my ears aching as the lyrics wrap themselves around my soul. Behind my eyelids, I can picture the story playing out, and a tear slips free and carves a hot path down my cheek.

I don't get a lot of time for the emotional release of it all before the car jolts softly to a stop and I'm forced back to reality. Indy turns down the music and I open my eyes, wishing I could skip this next part. Any appetite I had is long gone now, and I ignore the food sitting at my feet.

It's not like I ever wanted to be a CEO, and if there was any other way, I'd leave it behind and let someone else who's more qualified take over. Uncle Collin would do it in a heartbeat. The problem is this was my parents' dream, and I'm the only one who wants the vision they had for what Driscoll Technologies could become enough to sacrifice everything to make it happen.

I'm the only one who will see it through no matter what it takes and who cares more about the vision and the good we can do than about the money we can make. *That's* what I'm fighting for, and now that I know my parents didn't die in a tragic accident but were very deliberately stolen from me, I'm more determined than ever to see this through.

Even if it means sacrificing the things I want, their vision is bigger than me. It's bigger than any one person, because the potential help our technology can bring to the world is worth more than any of it.

We can save lives—no, we *will* save lives—and there's nothing that will convince me to throw in the towel and give up now. Especially not a couple of threats from pissed off rivals. I trust Indy and Sebastian, and anyone else who may work to protect me and my mission, to keep me safe while I carry on with what needs to be done.

Someday, when the technology is fully developed and out helping those who never would've had a chance without it, I may step back and live my life for me, but that day isn't today. There's still work to be done.

Lost in my thoughts, I don't notice that Indy's gotten out of the car and swung my door open. He leans against it like he's got all the time in the world as he waits for me, and I can't help drooling over him. As much as I hate to admit it, the man is sexy as sin. He's wearing black jeans that hug the muscles in his thighs and a black t-shirt that looks like it was made just for him. When I finally lock eyes with him, his are amused and filled with heat that melts away some of my resistance to stay away from him. The arrogant smirk he wears is infuriating and I quickly look away as heat burns my face before I push up off the seat.

He doesn't move back to let me by. Oh, no. That would be too easy.

Indy fills most of the space I need to pass through to get out with his broad frame, so I'm forced to brush my body along his, and everywhere we touch tingles explode under my skin.

"Shouldn't you be looking around for threats or something? You know, doing your job?" I finally mutter, trying to get my racing heart under control so he doesn't see how much I want to reach out and shove my fingers into his wild curls and yank him closer.

His low chuckle is dark and wicked as he steps up behind me, the heat of his body blanketing my back as his finger trails down my spine. "Don't worry, Duchess. I'm aware of every single thing happening right now," he purrs right near my ear, and I know he doesn't just mean the people coming and going around us. My thighs squeeze together involuntarily as his voice twists down and settles between my legs. His words leave my knees shaky and my nipples tight inside my bra.

Whatever's happening right now, I know I can't be the only one affected, not when the evidence of Indy's interest in me brushes against my hip. That monster he's got in his pants has got to be a health hazard. If I let him anywhere near me with that beast, he'd tear me in two. I want to smack some sense into myself for even imagining what it'd be like to let him get that close. This is *Indy Foster*. The grade-A jackass who loves to mess with me for his own amusement and sleep with anyone who'll let him inside her.

The reminder is like a bucket of ice water to the face, and I snap out of whatever lust-infused web he managed to weave me into, side-eyeing the hell out of him as I come to my senses. "Good, so you can deal with the fact one of the security guards isn't at his post while I meet with Colette," I let my tone turn frosty as I march inside the building without a backward glance. If I threw a little extra sway into my steps, well, I'm entitled to a little payback.

By the time I get to my assistant's desk, I'm feeling more like myself, but a wave of exhaustion sweeps over me, and I close my eyes to take a breath.

"You okay, Pen?" Colette asks. I open my eyes to her staring up at me with concern.

She's worked for me for almost two years and is probably the closest thing I've got to a friend in this building.

I wave her off, brushing my hair off my face. "Fine, but I need you to cancel all my meetings for today. I'm out of the office. Is there anything that can't wait until tomorrow?"

She glances at her computer screen and then shakes her head, her shiny blonde waves falling over her shoulder. "No, everything can wait. Is there anything I can do to help? Or we could go grab a coffee and you can get what's bothering you off of your chest. It's been forever since we played hooky for scones and caffeine."

I try to force a smile, but after the morning I've already had, it probably looks more like a grimace. "I know, and I promise when I get a second to breathe, we'll catch up, okay? You're already doing enough by juggling my schedule. If anything catastrophic comes up, call me, but otherwise I'll see you tomorrow."

She nods, flashing me the bright smile that she seems to effortlessly wear. "I'll hold you to that catch up date." This time I do manage a small laugh as I leave her to it, sweeping into my office and making sure there's nothing that requires my immediate attention. There's not, so I don't stick around. The longer I spend time in here, the more likely someone from either the research and development team or the board will demand my attention. Today, I don't have the energy. I bail. Indy's waiting in the lobby for me, leaning against the wall by the elevators, his gaze focused on me.

I arch an eyebrow at him. "Everything sorted out?"

He jerks his head in a quick nod and I take that to mean we're good to go, so I take off towards the entrance, my heels clicking on the tile.

Where I'm going next is the best reminder of what I'm working towards, and I'm anxious to get there.

Indy catches up to me only a few steps outside the doors of Driscoll Tech and his hand finds my elbow, pulling me to a stop. The heat of his fingers through my silk sparking the flames of my desire to life all over again. "Where do you think you're going, Duchess?"

"I've got a date, remember?" He shoots me an icy look as I pull my elbow free. I'm under no illusions I wouldn't have broken his hold unless he let me. I stop outside his car so he can unlock it and let me in.

That stare of his burns into me while he hits the button on the fob. He's waiting for me to tell him where we're actually going, and I relent. I'm too emotionally exhausted to keep up with our games right now. "I need you to take me to the children's hospital."

Indy's reaction is instantaneous and shocking. He jerks as his whole body goes stiff almost like he's been shot. His gaze fills with this devastation that freezes the breath in my lungs when I take a step forward to reach for him. He goes blank, like his soul is no longer present in his body. He's just a shell.

"I'm not taking you there," he finally says. His voice lacks any emotion, and his eyes are empty.

I look around before turning my attention back on him. "Yes, you are. It's your job, and I don't see any other bodyguard here who can take your place."

Without another word, he rips the door open, all of his earlier flirtatiousness long gone. I slide into the seat and buckle up while he slams the door so hard, I flinch. When he walks around the front of the car and gets in, he doesn't look in my direction. The car is silent as he pulls out onto the street, and the air between us is thick with tension, but not the usual playful kind. I want to ask what his problem is, why he's acting this way, but he's putting out all kinds of don't fuck with me vibes and I'd be an idiot not to listen.

So, I sit with my hands folded in my lap looking out the window with only the occasional glance out of the side of my eye in his direction. His rigid posture doesn't change, and he doesn't say one word to me the entire drive.

When we pull up into the drop off lane, he doesn't bother parking or saying anything. The other night he was completely pissed off about me going off protocol, but here he is dropping me at the door without checking the place out first. All the tiny hairs on my body lift as unease slithers down my spine. This is a bad idea, but I've made a promise to be here, and I will not break it.

His dead gaze flickers over to me for the first time since we left Driscoll but still, he says nothing.

"Aren't you coming in with me? Isn't that what I hired you for?" I bite my lip as I glance over at the people streaming in and out of the automatic doors. As much as I try to pretend the threats don't bother me, they do. I called Connor and his guys in on this because I don't want to face this alone. I don't want to be a victim of greed, corruption, and entitlement. There's important work to be done, and I'm the only one that can do it, so I won't stand for having that cut short if I can do something about it. Indy expects me to go inside unprotected and I don't know how to change his mind.

"I told you, I'm not going in there."

"You have to," I argue as my heart tries its best to pound out of my chest.

"No, the fuck I do not. Now get out. I'll keep an eye on the entrance from here," he bites out, and I jump at the hostility in his voice. With trembling fingers, I reach for the handle, steeling myself for the dangers that could be lurking just outside this car. I don't know why Indy's reacting this way, but a sliver of hurt works its way into my chest, feeling like it's stuck between my ribs. As my eyes burn, I blow out a fortifying breath. If I thought we had a moment earlier at the diner, I was obviously wrong.

Like every other time something hurts me, I stuff it down inside and lift my chin, glaring defiantly at him even while I shove the door open. "If I die in there, so help me, I'll haunt you until the day you die, Indy Foster," I threaten as my feet hit the concrete.

And as I'm slamming the door closed, I could swear I hear him say, "Yeah, get in line," and I don't know what to do with that.

CHAPTER 6
INDY

My phone screen blurs as I stare at it with unfocused eyes. Thundering in my chest, my heart pounds out an unsteady rhythm that fills my ears with nothing but the rushing of blood through my veins. Panic claws at my insides, tearing them to shreds with torrents of adrenaline while I fight to catch my breath.

Leaving Penelope to go into that building alone could get me fired—or her hurt—but I *couldn't* go inside. Blindly I stab out a message on my phone, hoping I opened the right contact before succumbing to the onslaught of memories bubbling to the surface. No matter how hard I fight them back, they're pulling me in, relentless in their desire to drag me down to a place I never want to revisit.

I no longer see the midday sun out my windshield or the sliding doors at the hospital entrance, and instead pictures from the past skitter across my vision like spiders erupting out of a nest. The world around me melts away and I'm helpless to relive the worst moments of my life as they play out again and again. Slamming my eyes shut did nothing to stop the visions, and it's not until fingers dig into my shoulder that I'm ripped from the past.

Clinging to the almost painful grip, I use it as an anchor to ground myself here in the present.

"The fuck's wrong with you?" a deep voice barks from somewhere above me, but I can't respond when air isn't getting down into my lungs.

Spots replace the fucked-up memories behind my eyes, dancing as if they're taunting me but I blink until they fade.

"Shit," the voice hisses, shifting his grip from my shoulder to lay a couple of fingers across my carotid feeling for my pulse. A string of curses pierces my panic-induced haze and then I'm being dragged out of my car and shoved against the warm metal.

"Snap out of it," he barks.

I almost want to laugh at how fucking ridiculous that order is. Doesn't he know if I could, I would? Shit, mentally I'm in the very last place I ever wanted to come back to and it's like I'm drowning, sinking to the bottom of a dark and murky lake as my lungs scream for air with no idea how to find the surface.

"You better not start shit for this," the voice mutters before pain explodes across my face and I gasp, heaving air into my lungs for the first time in what could've been an eternity. The throbbing in my cheek helps clear my mind and my vision, and I blink like I'm coming out of a bad hallucination, which I sort of am.

When I lock eyes with Asher who's shaking out his hand and watching me with a shit ton of concern etched across his face, I hunch over with my hands on my knees and gulp down air. Relief courses through me as the memories and despair fade away, retreating to the darkest corners of my mind where they belong.

My hands tremble as I drag them down the clammy skin of my face and my heart still crashes around in my chest.

I open my mouth to thank him for pulling me out of my panic spiral as I straighten up, but nothing comes out. Licking my dry lips, I try again. "Thanks."

Asher looks me over again before slowly nodding. "Want to tell me what the hell that was? And where Penelope is?"

No way in hell am I telling him what triggered me, or why I'd be triggered in the first place. "Fuck this, I'm out of here. She's inside so you should probably go track her down."

Asher's eyebrows lift. "You can't just leave. I'm not even on this case."

"You are now. Congrats," I say, sliding past him and back into my car. When he doesn't move, I let every inch of raging violence and chaos swirling inside of me show behind my eyes and level him with a glare that promises pain if he doesn't get out of my way.

For a second, it looks like he wants to challenge me but then he runs tattooed fingers through his shoulder-length hair and shakes his head at me while he steps back. I waste no time slamming the door and turning over the engine, and it's only seconds later I'm tearing out of the parking lot desperately trying to leave the ghosts of my past in the rearview mirror.

I have no idea where I'm going. My mind and body are both such a fucking mess right now that I'm operating on autopilot as I haul ass down the road like the hounds of hell are snapping at my heels. It's not until I pull into a dive bar on the other side of the city that I feel like I can breathe again.

It took me years to peel myself up out of the self-destruction of my past, but now I feel myself slipping right back into familiar old patterns and habits that kept me somewhat sane when the world around me burned down. For a second, Penelope flashes in my mind, the look filled with fear and confusion she gave me when I ordered her out of the car, and guilt roils in my gut. It's an emotion I can't process right now while I'm fighting like hell to not slip back into my head.

All I need is to forget.

To bury myself in distractions until it all disappears.

It's still early afternoon, so when I step inside the dimly lit bar, there's hardly anyone here. The ones I'm assuming are regulars are posted up on one side of the bar and the bartender lifts his head away from a conversation he was having with one of them and spots me.

"Welcome to *Brew Lounge*. What can I get you?" he asks as I slide onto an empty stool with a tear in the cracked leather.

"Whiskey," I say as he drops an empty glass down on a coaster in front of me and turns to grab my drink. As he finishes the pour, I wave my hand. "Leave the bottle."

He arches an eyebrow at me, and I dig in my pocket, grabbing out my card and tossing it onto the bar. "The bottle," I repeat as he takes the card and leaves the mostly full bottle of some shitty whiskey behind. Quality doesn't matter today. As long as it burns the memories from my brain, it'll work.

Before my first drink is done, my phone starts buzzing in my pocket. I'm surprised it took them this long to start calling after I bailed on a client, and for a second a new panic starts up. Maybe something happened to Penelope when I took off on her, but I can't deal with that right now. I'll add her to the growing list of people I couldn't save.

A familiar self-loathing I thought I put behind me starts whispering lies in my head about how I'm not strong enough to protect anyone from anything, but this afternoon they feel threaded with truth.

I'm not proud of running out of there, but I had no choice. Shame burns me up inside hotter than the liquor sliding down my throat, so instead of facing up to my own bullshit, I switch my phone off. A fucked up voice inside my head taunts me with the need to have my eyes on my Duchess, but I ignore it.

Tomorrow, post hangover, I'll talk to Connor and Asher and, fuck, maybe even Sebastian and see if I still have a job. Right now, the memories are too fresh, the pain lashing at me too close to the surface. Forgetting is all that matters.

Hours crawl by as the level of brown liquid in the bottle gets steadily lower and my body and mind start to numb. I can't remember why I ever thought sobering up and returning to regular life was a good idea, and at this moment I'm positive I could stay here on this barstool forever living my best life.

I'm about to demand a fresh bottle from my new friend behind the bar when I get distracted thinking about Penelope. I wonder if she's safe, if she's home.

If she's in her bed staring up at the ceiling thinking about me.

As if I deserve to be on her mind after what I did today.

The alcohol swirling in my system shuts up the smarter side of me that knows my obsession with watching Penelope on my phone isn't healthy, so I tug it out of my pocket and click into the app. I've never been great at telling myself no, and when it comes to her, I've given up trying.

Like I imagined, she's sprawled out in her bed, her blanket kicked mostly off so her creamy skin is on display. She's only wearing a t-shirt that hits the top of her thighs leaving her long legs bare, and I wonder if it's one of mine that I snuck in her room and left so she'd wear my clothes. Even with whiskey burning through my veins, my dick hardens at the sight of her. It shouldn't, especially knowing how I fucked everything up today. But my body doesn't care. Penelope's mine even if she doesn't want to be.

The bottle empties as I pour the last dregs into my glass, never taking my eyes off of my phone where it sits on the bar in front of me. Penelope shifts in her sleep as if she's restless and I wonder if it's because of what happened between us. Or if she dreams about me.

The urge to leave this place and crawl into her bed even if only to hold her while she sleeps is overwhelming, and I lift the glass to my lips, finishing off my drink to keep myself from doing exactly that. She doesn't need me, not when all I'll do is let her down.

Besides, there's a bigger chance she'd kick my ass out of bed than welcome me in if I tried it.

Someone takes the stool next to me, but I don't bother looking away from the screen I'm fixated on. Not until the man leans closer, his shoulder bumping up against mine and his stale tobacco sent assaulting me as he stares down at Penelope vulnerable in her bed.

"Fuck, what I wouldn't give to slide between those legs," he says, and my head whips around just in time to see him adjusting his pathetic dick in his pants. Rage like I've never known before ignites inside me, and I click the video feed off, slipping my phone into my pocket as I let the darkness consume me.

"The fuck did you just say?" I ask in a low voice filled with malice as I move off my stool. I tower over the man who's about to feel the anger that coats my skin unleashed on him. No one gets to see my Duchess like that but me, and I can't even hear his response over the sound of blood rushing in my ears.

His bloodshot eyes crinkle at the sides when he grins up at me. "Bet that pussy's real tight, too." He sighs almost wistfully, and I fucking lose it.

Before I even realize I'm doing it, my fists are balled and flying toward this fucker's face. We're both drunk, but the buzz in my veins comes purely from violence and the need to erase the memory of Penelope's body sprawled out on her bed from his mind. When I hit him the first time, he flies off his stool with wide eyes. The alcohol slows down how fast he reacts and processes what's happening but not for me.

I'm suddenly stone fucking sober and my rage has only one focus point—this piece of shit who dared look at my girl and imagine his tiny dick would ever be good enough to go near her. Over and over my fists collide with anywhere I can reach as I fall to my knees to be able to keep hitting him. He's curled in a ball, arms thrown up over his head to protect himself, but I don't give a shit. As he begs me to stop, I only hit him harder.

His words roll around in my head, circling again and again as I stand and kick him in the stomach and the ribs to get them to stop. I can't catch my breath, but I don't fucking care. Let my lungs burn to ash with the exertion. The only thing that matters right now is making him realize his mistake. Penelope is *mine*.

Completely lost to the savagery of the moment, I don't notice right away when hands reach out and grab me, dragging me off the man who lies still on the ground. His effort to cling to consciousness as I rearranged his face was futile, and if he's dead I won't even be sorry. In fact, I hope he is because then I'll know no living man besides me has seen Penelope so vulnerable.

"Ambulance is on the way. You better hope he's not dead," the security guy grunts as he tries to toss me outside, but I rip my arm from his grip. I'm tempted to hit him, too, as the rage inside me still simmers below the surface, but the room spins as the adrenaline starts to fade and the effects of the shit ton of alcohol I drank today hit me like a sledgehammer.

"I'm going," I tell him while I push out the front doors, but maybe I was wrong because he doesn't seem to want to let me go. He's following me and I think he's trying to get me to stay, to stick around and wait for the cops but fuck that. I don't care what happens to the guy. If he's breathing, there's a good chance I'll be tempted to finish the job. I can't say I've never killed anyone before, but this would be the first time I do it in a possessive rage, and I'm usually smarter than that. Fucking liquor and bad decisions.

I fumble with my phone, managing to call a ride and I lean back against the side of the building to wait for it, breathing the cool night air down into my lungs. Eventually the security guy decides to back the hell off and goes back inside. I try to sober up and talk myself out of having the driver drop me at Penelope's so I can climb into her bed instead of going home to my empty one.

She'd let me in, and I could crawl between her legs and slide inside her. It'd be so easy to get her to bend to me, to cry out my name. Fuck, now my dick's hard. It would be so easy to give in and beg for forgiveness for the bullshit I pulled today. But I can't. I can't drag her into my mess when I know I'm too fucked up for her. My fingers delve into my hair, yanking on the ends in frustration.

As the ride I ordered pulls up, and I let the driver know my address and clench my teeth together to keep from spewing out Penelope's address instead.

The entire drive home, my body is rigid as I keep myself locked down, and eventually the driver lets me out and I stumble up into my apartment. I maybe get half of my clothes off before I face plant into my bed and drop out of consciousness.

After a blissfully dreamless night, I wake up full of pain and regret. It's like my early twenties all over again, and to be honest that's not a time I ever care to relive. Not only was I a total asshole, but I was also running from ghosts in any and every way I could think of. It took me finally realizing that you can't really outrun ghosts to start to grow up, but yesterday's reminder of why I'd tried to escape in the first place just goes to show I haven't really grown as much as I thought.

Case in point, the gazillion messages and calls waiting for me when I look at my phone. I'm still not ready to deal with them, so I ignore them and steal a few minutes to watch Penelope in her lab before I head into the shower to scrub off last night's many mistakes. It's not until I'm dressed, have downed a cup of coffee and a whole fuck ton of pain meds that I can even think about tackling the mess I made all over my life yesterday by running out on my responsibilities.

Shockingly, I don't have a single message from my boss, and most of the calls and texts I *do* have are from either Asher or Sebastian. I figure one or both of them must've covered for me, so I let out a tiny sigh of relief that I still have a job. Working for Connor might've started as a way for me to let out some of my aggression, to try to prove that even though I haven't kept everyone important to me out of harm's way, I still had something to offer.

Now the guys at Hollywood Guardians are like a sort of family to me, and if I lost that I don't know what I would've done. Thanks to Asher having my back, it looks like I don't have to find out—at least not today.

That doesn't mean I'm not going to have to face my fuck up this morning, so I swallow the last of my coffee and call a ride back to the bar where I left my car last night. I practice some bullshit meditation thing I used to use that I don't think ever really worked for the entire ride back to the bar to try and keep my thoughts from degrading into useless predictions about what I'm about to walk into.

Getting into my own car, some measure of control seems to snap back into place and while I'm not looking forward to having to explain my behavior to Asher or Sebastian, I do feel more grounded than I did yesterday. I don't let myself think about Penelope and what I might say to her. Abandoning Penelope the way I did reinforces how much I don't deserve her. How I'm not ready to give myself to her even as I demand she be mine.

She could've gotten hurt—or worse—because of me and my damage. Even the idea of having to face her and own up to leaving her like I did has my stomach roiling like a stormy sea all over again.

I'm starting to regret the coffee I drank this morning as I pull into her driveway—which still looks more like a damn castle to me than a house. My hands shake as I turn off my car and get out, jogging up the steps. With all the security cameras and alerts Sebastian has set up around this place, I have no doubt they're already well aware that I'm here, but my heart thumps at an uncomfortable pace while I stand on the porch and wait for them to let me in.

I'm tugging my phone out of my pocket to send a text to Asher when the door swings open, and I come face to face with the man himself. He looks me over with concern before his expression darkens to something more violent. "Well, at least you're not dead… yet. Can't say you'll come out so unscathed once you talk to Penelope, though."

I wince internally, guilty as fuck about leaving her like I did, especially after the revelations from breakfast yesterday. I'd ignored my better judgment and given in to the obsessive need to protect her when she broke down, and then I walked out on her like an asshole. I doubt there's anything I can say that will ever make leaving her like that okay, and my throat tightens as I try to swallow down the regret.

Out of everything shitty that happened yesterday, Penelope thinking I'm an unreliable dick is near the top of the list.

Asher spins on his heel but leaves the door open for me to follow him inside. I do, turning to shut the door behind me before heading deeper into the house. Asher stops in the kitchen and pours himself a cup of coffee, eyeing me over the rim. He doesn't offer me shit, but I can't exactly hold it against him and if I were him, I'd probably be a mixture of worried and pissed off, too.

Rubbing the back of my neck, I decide the only way out is through, so I jump in the deep end. "Thanks for covering for me yesterday with Connor."

"You gonna tell me what the hell that was about?"

The words creeping up my throat burn like acid, so I swallow them down and shake my head. "No."

"Right, well, you still have a job, but you pull that shit again and I'm going to run my ass straight to HQ and spill like I'm having a damn tea party."

"Fair enough, and for what it's worth, I'm sorry to dump everything on you like I did."

He lifts a shoulder and lets it drop. "Seems to have worked out. Sebastian had already put in a request for an extra man on this one anyway, so Connor assigned me to stick around."

Penelope picks that moment to walk into the kitchen, her soft, wavy hair falling over her shoulders as she stares at the tablet in her hand. My chest constricts because for this brief period of time before she notices me, I can pretend she's still starting to give in, that if I turn on the charm, she'll roll her eyes but her kissable lips will quirk up in a tiny smile just for me.

Instead, she looks up and we lock eyes. I open my mouth to try to say something—anything—to get her to look at me again like she did yesterday morning before everything went to shit.

But I don't get the chance. Without uttering a single word, she turns and storms out, but not before I got a flash of hurt on her face before she could hide it away. Knowing *I* did that? It has me stalking across the room to the liquor cabinet and reaching inside for the first bottle I touch.

Asher lifts an eyebrow as he watches me but says nothing. It's not like he or I are strangers to the way the world can fuck you over, and while I don't know his specific history, and he doesn't know mine, in this moment I know he gets it. It's why he covered for me last night, and why he'll do it again today if he has to.

It's never been clearer that I'm fucked up, and Penelope? She doesn't need my bullshit tainting her life, even if I'll never be able to let her go.

"I fucked up, Ash," I whisper as I bring the glass to my lips with a shaking hand and throw it all back at once.

"She'll come around, man," he says, coming over to where I'm bracing both hands on the counter and breathing heavily through my anguish.

"That's the problem, though. I don't know if I want her to."

CHAPTER 7
PENELOPE

A CONSTANT LOW-SIMMERING rage has taken up residence as my main emotional state over the last week. Between having my team of bodyguards constantly lurking around, and the Board and my competition both trying to undermine me and take what's rightfully mine, my temper has been running on a short fuse.

This isn't me. I'm the quiet, docile girl who doesn't snap at people or make waves. But it's the space I exist in now and I'm not sure how to get out of it.

There's a hurt there, too, one I wish I could ignore. Somehow, Indy got under my skin. It's something he's always trying to do—or at least, something he *did* try to do before he turned into whatever he is now. My eyes flick over to the half-empty bottle of scotch on the liquor cart across my office with irritation.

It's not like I care that he drinks the expensive liquor since I'm not going to. After he abandoned me at the hospital last week, he's been like an entirely different person. Sullen, reserved, and almost constantly drunk. He doesn't even bother going home, just stumbling around my house staring at me and pissing me off.

Whenever our eyes happen to meet, he looks away like he can't stand the sight of me and I have no idea what to make of that. For a second, in that diner booth, I thought Indy was someone I could open up to, that I could lean on at the very least as a friend—even if my body craved more. Even now, with his wild curls, bruised knuckles, and rumpled clothes, my heart speeds up and my panties are drenched.

I don't have time for his breakdown, though. Maybe if he was willing to open up and let me in, I'd think about changing my mind but so far all I get are looks filled with pain, guilt, and longing so intense, when they happen it steals the breath from my lungs.

I'm not stupid; I know there's something seriously wrong. The guy with the confident swagger and mischievous glint in his eye has been replaced by this drunken husk.

I don't even know why he's sticking around at this point. It's not like he's coherent enough to fight off someone making an attempt to get to me. But he's here lurking in the shadows like some horror movie stalker while I try to get on with normal life.

This is all too much. I'm so overwhelmed, rage tears prickle the backs of my eyes. I've been pushing them back all week, but this time it doesn't feel like that's going to work. Luckily, right now I'm alone, so I drop what I'm doing and rush for my room.

What I really want to do is sprint across the house and dive into the shower so the sound of the water running will drown out my sobs, but if I do that, I'll draw too much attention to myself and then I'll have to stop and answer questions about what's wrong. Since that's the last thing I want to do, I take my time getting there, even though I have to drop my chin and keep my blurry gaze focused on the marble floor the entire way, so no one sees me cry.

After Indy dropped the bomb about my parents being murdered, it's like the scab has been ripped off the grief of their deaths and I'm trying to pick up the pieces all over again. Maybe that's why I'm so upset with his cold shoulder act. I thought he understood how difficult all of this is for me, that I didn't ask for any of it, and I could have someone else to lean on for a change instead of having to shoulder everything myself.

It's not like I'm unfamiliar with carrying a heavy burden alone, but just this once, for just one second, I thought things were different.

That tiny sliver of hope was crushed nearly as fast as it sprung up, like a tiny seedling that's been stepped on before it could ever bloom. I think it would've been better to not have it at all then to have lost it.

Agony spears through my chest as I fight to breathe through the coming emotional hurricane. Right now, the walls I've spent months constructing are crumbling as if made of sand, and I can only imagine the breakdown is going to be a big one. My throat is choked, constricted closed so air wheezes through on its way to my desperate lungs.

My door stands partly open, and I push through, not bothering to close it behind me as I stumble towards the bathroom, stripping off my clothes as I go. Blindly through the tears, I reach for the handle and turn the water on, letting it cascade toward the drain while it heats up. When steam finally billows out of the stall, I hurry inside, tilting my chin up to let the hot water mix with the tears already streaking down my cheeks before washing them away.

This is why my favorite place to let go, to have a good cry is in the shower. There's no one to judge whether you're strong enough, and once the water runs over your skin, there's no evidence left of your moment of weakness.

My sinuses ache by the time I'm done, and my body is trembling from the emotional release, but I take a shaky breath and steel myself. I don't have the luxury of crawling out of the shower and into my bed to nap the day away and hope tomorrow's better. People are depending on me—*lives* are depending on me. I can't ignore that, as much as I want to sometimes.

Whatever Indy has going on in his life, I don't have the room in mine to take it on unless he's willing to open up, and I think this week he's made it clear that he's not. As much as he's drinking, I'd even venture a guess to say he's not willing to face up to it himself, let alone let someone else in.

The demons he's running from are powerful, and I can't help him unless he wants me to. That means as sad as I am to have lost a friend

—and maybe someday more—before I'd ever really had him, I have to move on. I have to look at the loss of my parents and Indy pulling away as another test of my strength and my resolve.

My strength may be questionable at times, but my resolve is ironclad and can't be shaken. I've already sacrificed everything for the cause, and I won't stop until the project is finished and I can sit back and watch my creation do its work. Unfortunately, no one ever tells you being a revolutionary isn't all it's cracked up to be. Fame and glory don't exist in the trenches, and right now it feels like I'm fighting a war.

It's me against an entire army of people who'd like to see me fail so they can swoop in and pick at my carcass for any scraps they can exploit for profit. It's sickening, and sometimes I hate the world we live in.

Children are one of the best things about this world, before it sinks its claws into them and turns them into jaded, greed-filled, cynical adults. They're innocence and light and balance us all out, and it's why saving the ones who'd be lost without cutting edge treatment drives me. It's hard to get lost in your bad day when you look into the sunken eyes of a child losing their battle with cancer.

It's with renewed determination, and a reminder of my favorite little patient's grinning face, that I pull on my big girl panties—literally and figuratively—and leave my breakdown behind as it drips off the tile walls and swirls down the drain.

When I step out of my bedroom, I'm better in control of my emotions. My grief is back under lock and key and my perfected resting bitch face is in place as I stride toward what used to be my office but now is the place the security team operates from. Sebastian took it over, and while I do miss having my work organized in one place, as long as I have a tablet or a laptop, I can really work from anywhere. At least this way I know where to find the guys if I ever need to.

When I step inside the office, Asher is leaning over Sebastian's shoulder pointing at something on the monitor with one long, tattooed finger. They're murmuring quietly so I can't make out what they're talking about, but when he notices me, he straightens. Sebastian's gaze barely flickers in my direction before settling back on the screen as his fingers fly across the keys.

Indy's nowhere to be found.

I cross over to where Asher's now leaning his hip against the desk while he folds his arms over his chest, his leather jacket crinkling with the motion, waiting to hear what I'm about to say.

"Harrison Astley suggested that to get some positive press, I need to throw a charity gala. I need a distraction, so you and me are going to plan it," I say, not bothering to tell him I'd originally planned to force Indy into the job to punish him for messing with me.

"Don't you have an assistant for that shit?" Asher asks, looking mildly annoyed as he picks up a letter opener and starts flipping it around between his inked fingers like a knife.

"I do, but like I said, I need a distraction. Besides, she's going to handle a lot of it, but I need to write a speech and you need to deal with how to keep me safe."

Asher grumbles under his breath but I can't make out the words. Sebastian looks up from his monitor. "Incoming."

With that one word, Asher's entire demeanor changes from casual boredom with a hint of annoyance to badass bodyguard protector. He stalks past me out of the room, his shoulders tense and body alert. I follow behind him as he hurries down the stairs on surprisingly light feet, his hand wrapped around the grip of his gun in the holster he wears under his leather jacket.

Approaching the front door, he pauses, pulling his gun out and clicking the safety off while he leans over slightly to glance out the curtained window beside the door. My heart is thrumming in my chest as a cold sweat trickles down my spine. I'm not expecting any visitors, so I don't know what to make of whoever might be at my door.

The logical side of me thinks that if someone wanted to hurt me, it's unlikely they'd stroll up to the front door, but my nerves are so on edge that any change of routine has me practically climbing out of my skin.

Asher's posture doesn't relax, but he does swing the door open, and I have a second where I think I might pass out before all the breath escapes from my lungs and I sag in relief. "Uncle Collin! What are you doing here?"

My father's brother—Collin Driscoll—my only remaining family member, strides into the house like he doesn't even see the hulking bodyguard holding the door open. His brown hair is sprinkled with salt and pepper and he's wearing a white polo shirt tucked into slacks like I've seen him do so many days at the office.

I've always loved my uncle, and he's worked side by side with my father on the business since my father created it. Until the last year, we'd always been close. I was honestly surprised that Dad didn't leave Driscoll Tech to Uncle Collin considering how closely they worked together, and he was just as surprised if his reaction and cold shoulder are any indication.

I expected him to be my biggest supporter when I took over as CEO, answering my questions and taking as much off my plate as he could. But that wasn't what happened, and he's been practically ignoring me for a year, leaving me to handle everything alone.

"I can't check up on my favorite niece?" he asks, slinging his arm over my shoulder as we walk back toward the kitchen. I stiffen and shoot him a scathing look.

"Oh, I'm your favorite niece now? Since when?"

"Since I've seen how over your head you are. I'm here to help. Thomas would've been so disappointed in the way we've handled things since his death."

I raise my eyebrow, walking around the kitchen island to put some distance between us. "We?"

His eyebrows pinch together. "Yes, we. We've both made mistakes."

I close my eyes and take a deep breath. "Sure, I've made mistakes because I was thrown in the damn deep end without knowing how to swim. You could've helped me at any time, but you've been happy to let me flounder on my own." It takes every ounce of willpower I've got to keep my voice level, even as it shakes while I spit out the words. Hostility coats each one, lacing it with venom that I hope takes root.

"You could've asked me to step in at any time," he says, crossing his arms as he leans his hip against the counter.

I laugh then, this hollow-sounding thing. It's either that or slam my fist down onto the counter. "So that's what this was about? You sitting back and hoping I'd fail so you could swoop in and take over? It's good to finally know what's most important to you, *Uncle*."

"To be honest, Penny, I never thought you'd last this long."

I ignore him, pulling open the fridge for something to do. "Are you hungry? I could put together some sandwiches or something," I offer blandly, wondering if he'd notice me sprinkling dish soap in his —or rat poison. Too bad I have to keep the peace for the sake of the business.

"No, I'm not staying. I just wanted to see if I could talk some sense into you after this Fields fiasco. Clearly, you're not ready to see reason yet. I wonder what it's going to take before you do. How much are you willing to lose before you finally realize you're never going to be him? You're never going to make this company what he wanted it to be. It's not your fault, but you're just not cut out for business." His voice softens at the end as he steps closer, reaching out almost gently before he pulls his hand back.

Asher has followed us into the kitchen and is leaning against the wall tucking his gun back into its holster under his leather jacket. His eyes never once leave Uncle Collin, and the frostiness in his stare surprises me. Ordinarily I'd tell him to back off, but right now I'm raw and scared and I'm not going to blindly trust anyone no matter how long they've been in my life.

Letting him know I'm good, I give Asher a tiny smile before returning my attention back to my uncle. For a second, my thoughts drift to Indy and I hope whatever drunken hole he's got himself set up in he stays there. I don't want my uncle thinking I'm not handling my security issues on my own. For whatever reason, now that my dad's gone I need him to see I've stepped up just fine without his help.

His deep brown eyes—that are so familiar my chest aches—settle on me before his lips quirk up in a smile. "When that point comes, know that I'll be here waiting and ready to step in. I just hope you don't wait too long. There are some things even I won't be able to fix."

My mouth tips into an unforgiving smile. It's all I can manage right now as I shake with barely controlled rage at the audacity of this man. "For my dad's dream—for *our* vision of the future, Uncle, I'll risk everything so I wouldn't hold your breath while you're waiting in my shadow. Oh, but do keep next Friday open on your schedule. It's short notice, but we're holding a gala to smooth over the Fields situation. My PR rep suggested it and it's very last minute, but it's important that we present a united front to our employees and shareholders. I'll expect you to be there."

My uncle frowns as he leans against the counter. "Do you think now's the best time to be throwing a party when people are questioning our business? We need to get the AI code finished so we can announce a new product to sell, a *revolutionary* product. That'll be what turns this around."

A shooting pain from my jaw to my temple clues me into how hard I'm gritting my teeth together. Why does every single person in this company question my decisions? I want to scream and rip my hair out and destroy something, but I don't. If I did, I'd be labeled as unstable or crazy and replaced in the blink of an eye. I love everything I've worked for, everything my parents worked for, and I can't let that happen. So, I take a steadying breath before I explain what I shouldn't have to.

"We need to show we can do both at the same time, that we're a pillar of the community and also creating cutting edge tech. Taking time out of our busy schedules to raise money for a worthy cause demonstrates that we are so on top of our business that we have time, energy, and money to spare. It's also raising funds for a cause important to not only me, but the company in case you've forgotten my father's original intention. I don't think there's much more important than that. I can't believe I have to explain this to you"

Uncle Collin bristles and I look at him through slitted eyes but hold my tongue—barely. "You do remember we're running a business, don't you? I don't know why I expected you to understand. You're still a child."

His dismissal stings and I jerk back like he slapped me.

Until I see him shift out of the corner of my eye, I forgot Asher was in the room with us. His movement catches my attention and I glance up, but he's distracted with something across the room. I can only imagine. With my luck, it's Indy stumbling around drunkenly and that's the last thing I need my uncle to see. He already thinks I'm some stupid kid who knows nothing, who's standing in the way of everything he thinks he deserves.

I don't know why it still surprises me when I get a glimpse at a side of him that lurks underneath that doesn't seem satisfied at all with his lot in life. He hasn't exactly been subtle about it.

"I'm well aware of your opinion, Uncle Collin. Now, you're welcome to stay but I need to get back to work. You know, running the business."

He pushes off the counter and waves me off. "No, I have other matters to deal with this afternoon. Let me know if you run into any more trouble this weekend you need me to bail you out of. Otherwise, I'll see you at the office."

Nodding, I watch him walk away, letting himself out the front door. It's not until he's gone that I fully exhale, the end of which turns into a groan of frustration. My hand shakes as I bring it up to my clammy forehead and swipe at my bangs, needing them off my face. Dealing with everything on my plate right now is too much. I've reached my tipping point and fallen over the edge, and now my blood thunders through my veins as a numbness spreads across my brain.

I need a break before I go insane.

A shadow falls across the floor beside me and I look up to Asher watching the front door like he's waiting for Uncle Collin to come back so he has an excuse to throw him out. "You okay?" he asks, tearing his gaze away to stare down at me with concern.

"Oh, sure. I'm just peachy."

Lifting the phone in my hand, I send a text to the only friend I have, hoping like hell she can drop everything in her own busy life and save me from myself.

"I'm gonna need details, babe," Montana says, some of her frozen margarita sloshing over the side of her glass. Steam rises from the surface of the bubbling water as I sink further down into the hot tub. I'm submerged nearly to my chin and I'm considering never coming back up.

"Do I have to?"

She gives me a *look* and I scrunch up my nose.

"Fine, but remember you asked for my mess."

"I did. Now tell me everything."

I open my mouth to start, and she cuts me off. "Start with Bali."

Months ago, I took a trip with Montana and her husband, Ronin, to Bali. Unfortunately, Indy came along, and as our first official meeting, it went horribly.

"There's not a lot to tell. Indy proved what a royal asshole he is."

She shakes her head and clicks her tongue. "I'm gonna need more than that."

Rolling my eyes, I sip my drink and let the sweet iciness roll over my tongue while I consider how much to tell her. The business side of things, I can handle. What I need Montana's help with is untangling my feelings for a certain bad boy who soaks my panties and twists my heart into knots.

"He's always been sort of flirty, you know? It's not just with me, it's with every girl in his orbit. I didn't take it personally or anything, but it's hard to resist when he focuses all of that directly on you."

She sips her margarita and gestures for me to continue.

"In Bali, I let myself relax a little, thinking it might be fun to give in. He was constantly hounding me to put down my phone, to let go for a little while and after you and Ronin disappeared, I did it. I set my phone down and let him drag me onto the dance floor." That moment replays through my head, a flash in time where I couldn't have wiped the smile off my face if I tried. Being held close, swept across the dance floor by this gorgeous man as if nothing else mattered in the whole world but moving our bodies to a sultry rhythm in the steamy tropical night. His focus was one hundred percent on me and for an instant, I was drunk on Indy.

"At the time, I was in the middle of some pretty intense negotiations with a contractor we desperately needed to secure for a component of the artificial intelligence we're building, but there was a bidding war between us and Fields. When I set my phone down, I missed a time sensitive message, and we lost the contractor to that walking, talking dick otherwise known as Drew Reynolds. I may not have reacted very well."

Montana arches her eyebrow. "What did you do?"

I take a second to sip my drink, cheeks heating at the memory. "I'm completely embarrassed about the way I acted. I lost my temper and blamed him for costing me precious months waiting for a replacement. There may have been some shrieking and I think I stomped my foot... more than once."

"Yikes."

"Yeah. It gets worse."

"Please tell me you didn't punch him in the face or something." She says it like she doesn't mean a word and actually wishes I *would* have punched him, even though I happen to know he's one of her best friends.

"Sorry to disappoint, but no, I didn't resort to physical violence.

When I said it got worse, I didn't mean that I did anything worse. I meant that *he* did."

Montana sits up straighter, eyes narrowing, and I'm suddenly staring into the face of the badass band manager who's admittedly pretty terrifying. "What did he do? I love the guy, but I'm not above a well-placed knee to his balls."

I blame it on the slight buzz I've got going on when my eyes get misty, and I try to cover it up by taking another drink. "He did what he always does. He tempted me, made me think that spark I feel around him wasn't just on my side. Then he stomped all over it, grinding any hope I might've had that he actually liked me, or cared about me at all under the heel of his boot. He found the nearest girl in the skimpiest bikini I'd ever seen, set his sights on her, and told me he was going to go spend his time with someone who quote *knows how to have fun.*"

Montana gasps and then her eyes narrow into deadly slits. "He did not."

"Oh, he did, and then he left with her. The next time I saw them was breakfast." I wasn't about to admit that his insult cut deep, so deep that I'd spent the night huddled in the shower sobbing my eyes out and convincing myself no one would ever love me. Good times.

"And now he's, what? Being a mega dick all over again? Hold my drink, I'm going to drag his ass out here and demand answers," she says, standing up as water cascades off of her stupidly fit body. Seriously? Didn't she just have twins?

She thrusts her glass at me. It's almost empty but whatever was left in there spills into the water.

"Please don't. It's already embarrassing enough that after Bali I even let him get remotely close again. He's like my freaking catnip or something. Now that he's essentially gone off the deep end and won't talk to me about what's going on, I'm done. I have more important things to focus on anyway. Let's just have another drink and pretend men aren't all garbage for a little while."

I can tell she wants to protest, since her husband is actually a great guy, but she doesn't. Instead, she splashes back into the water and reaches for her glass, clinking it against mine in solidarity.

"Fine, but I'm talking to him when I sober up for sure. He may be a total manwhore, but you deserve better than to deal with his bullshit."

"Don't even worry about it. I'm done with Indy Foster for good."

Even as I say it, the words taste like a lie.

CHAPTER 8
INDY

THERE COMES a time in every man's life where he has to wonder what the fuck he's doing. As my head's being split in two by offset throbbing on either side of my skull, now's my time to reflect. My phone buzzes again having done it so many times this morning, this last one topples it over the edge of my nightstand. It hits the rug with a muffled *thunk,* but I don't bother reaching for it.

I know what I'll find and it's more disappointment than I can take this early and this hungover. Groaning, I roll over and blink blearily at the ceiling. Okay, so the light filtering in from outside tells a different story, one that says maybe it's later than I think in the day. Doesn't matter; I'm not going anywhere.

It's the precarious time of day I've come to hate the most. The one between when the alcohol flows back into my bloodstream, and I forget and when the memories assault me. It's been a near-constant cycle of PTSD-style bullshit and getting blackout drunk enough not to face it.

All in all, I think I'm coping. I'm handling it. Surviving. Am I hiding out from the real world? Fuck, yes. Do I feel like an absolute piece of shit over the way I left Penelope outside that hospital? Also, yes. Do I feel nearly blinding rage when I think about the man at the bar who saw my Duchess nearly naked and vulnerable?

Yup.

Since that night, I've been laying low at home so I don't fuck up even worse. I've been in this cycle before, and it eventually ends. The memories start to dull, if not fade, and I can ease off the drinking and get back to the half life I'm destined to live now that the best parts have been stolen away.

Jesus, I'm a depressing motherfucker when I'm hungover. I almost can't stand myself. Slowly sitting up, I grasp for the nearest half-empty bottle I can find and tip it back. It takes seconds to burn its way to my stomach, and then the numbing warmth starts to spread through my gut and out into my limbs. For the first time since I woke up, I can take a deep breath and the throbbing in my head starts to fade into the background.

I'm tempted to dive back under the blankets, to let unconsciousness claim me again. My fingers scratch at the rough beard I've grown this week, not caring enough to shave it. I can't even remember the last time I changed my clothes, but there's no one to see my downward spiral, so I don't care.

There's a freeing sort of apathy in my current state. With the pain threatening to suffocate me every minute of every day, to tempt me to end it all so I don't have to experience it anymore, nothing else seems important enough to worry about.

Flopping back into my pillows, I throw the blanket back over my head blocking out the sunlight. That shit burns like my eyes are melting out of my skull when the buzz wears off, so the darkness is a welcome relief.

My phone starts to vibrate across the floor again as someone hammers on my front door like a fucking maniac. I curse Asher for making me come home last night. If I was still at Penelope's palace, someone would answer that for me. For a minute, I think about ignoring it and pulling my phone under the blanket to spend more time watching Penelope on the cams. There's a perverse satisfaction in feeling close to her without tainting her with my toxic bullshit.

But the pounding starts up again. I knew the guys wouldn't let me wallow forever, but I figured I had another couple of days before they came and knocked down my front door. I fully expect to be dragged out of here whether my heart's broken and bleeding out on the floor or not.

Asher? Connor? Ronin? They're not going to put up with my bullshit much longer. They don't know what it's like to go through what I have. To have the best parts of you ripped away by a power beyond yourself. To feel absolutely helpless to stop it from happening. To discover how truly small you are in the grand scheme of existence.

I throw the blanket off with a huff, sitting up and grabbing the bottle off the side table. The bigger swig I take this time burns less on the way down. My feet hit the floor and I dig my toes into the rug trying to ground myself before I stand up. Whatever's on the other side of the door isn't something I want to deal with. I know it. They know it.

Like everything else fucked up in my life, it doesn't change the fact I have no choice.

For a brief second, as I set the bottle back down, I wonder if I might find Penelope standing on my porch. Fuck, I hope not. I don't have the mental energy to spar with her, and she sees too damn much.

No matter how fortified a shield I may put up around her, somehow when she looks in my eyes, I know she *sees*. She sees down inside me to the dark and twisted and ugly pieces that are broken and scattered but gathered back together into some semblance of a person. I'll never be whole again, and somehow, I think she knows it.

More than all of that, I'm a fucking mess. It's not a secret but knowing it and seeing it are two different things. Her seeing me like this? Looking like a homeless alcoholic who spent the last week sleeping in a dumpster with only bags of trash as a mattress?

It's not a good look.

Too bad I don't care enough to do anything about it.

"Open up, you asshole!" Montana's muffled shout carries through my entire condo as she pounds on the door again. "Don't make me call Ronin."

She probably means it as a threat, and maybe I should take it that way, but out of the two of them, she's the scarier one—and I've seen the dude torture someone.

I flip the deadbolt and fling the door open. Montana's standing in front of it with her red hair tossed up on her head and a scowl on her face that could melt metal.

"Move," she snarls as she pushes the twins' stroller into my place. I barely jump out of the way in time. She absolutely would have run me over.

My fingers curl around the door before I breathe out and then back in trying to steady myself before I swing the door shut.

"God, you smell like a fucking brewery that's been condemned and lit on fire. Go take a fucking shower," she tells me with a glower that means business. She's not fucking around, and I'm under no delusion that she'll call in the whole fucking cavalry if I don't do what she says.

I can't say if this little intervention was her idea or if the guys decided to send her first to see if it would shake me out of this hole I've found myself at the bottom of, but of all people who I want to stay on the good side of, she's at the top of the list.

"Fine, but order something to eat," I mumble as I shuffle off to my bedroom. My eyes shoot to the bottle beside my bed and for a second, I think about swiping it on my way into the bathroom, but I don't. Montana's already pissed enough, and if I come out showered but drunk, she might have the guys throw me in the Basement until I sober up.

Fifteen minutes later, I'm out of the shower, dressed, shaved, and feeling more human than I have in days. Speaking of, I have no clue what day it is. There's an incessant throbbing in the center of my chest that hurts with every beat of my heart. It's why I drink to numb it away, and the agony is white-hot as if no time has passed at all.

I'm distracted by the fussing of one of Montana's twin boys— they're identical and I have no fucking hope of telling them apart— and the smell of Chinese food.

The sight of my best friend with her boys tightens something in my chest and when I swallow, it's around a mountain-sized lump. I can't handle it, so I turn away and dish up, not paying attention to what I'm scooping onto my plate.

It's all going to taste like ash anyway.

I sit across from Montana on the couch, shoveling food in my mouth to avoid having to talk. Well, that and I can't actually remember the last time I ate so despite not feeling hungry, the second that first bite hits my tongue it's like my stomach roars to life all sorts of pissed off I've ignored it.

Montana levels that unsettling green gaze on me while I eat, but outside of little murmurs to her boys, she doesn't say shit to me. I don't know what she's waiting for. I'm not about to start spilling all my bullshit to her. I don't care if she is the only person I feel comfortable talking to, that's about everyday crap. Hookups, movies we like, making fun of her husband. Shit like that.

Real stuff? The stuff that fucks you up inside beyond repair? The stuff that haunts you both when you're awake and asleep? The stuff that squeezes your lungs until it's impossible to breathe sometimes?

No one gets to see that part of me.

Somehow, it's like if I were to open up and share it, to speak it out loud, it would diminish. I know that sounds crazy because it hurts so fucking bad, but if it started to go away, that would mean letting go. I won't ever let go.

I can't.

So, I keep that part of me tucked away where it slices at my soul with a razor blade, but the pain means what happened matters. It's not lost to time or fading memories. The pain means the memories live on inside me.

It's like she's been waiting for me to finish eating because the second I set my plate down, she's on me like a fucking vulture on a fresh carcass. I can't even protest when she thrusts Hudson at me—or is it Hayes? Either way, if I don't grab him, he's going to drop, so I pull him into my arms.

Fuck.

Fuck.

That pain in my chest? Yeah, it's split wide the fuck open and all the food I just ate is swirling around in my gut threatening to make a re-appearance. That new baby smell is crippling, but I still close my eyes and breathe him in deep.

"I should kick you in the balls for being such a fucking *guy* to Penelope," she starts, spinning the other twin—I think that one's Hayes, maybe—on her lap so he's looking up at me while he shoves a chubby fist into his mouth and drools all over the place.

Hudson blinks up at me, grabbing with his pudgy fingers for my shirt. Ugh, my eyes are fucking *stinging*, goddamnit.

Instead of giving in to the misery, I decide to focus on anger instead. "What the fuck are you talking about? I didn't do shit to Penelope."

"Oh?" She raises one red eyebrow. "You didn't ditch her in Bali to go be with someone who *and I quote* knows how to have fun?"

I open my mouth to defend my shitty actions, but she holds up her manicured finger like she's about to make a list, so I shut it again. I'll let her get it all out because it's easier to hash this out than talk about what's really wrong. Besides, I'm an asshole. It's not like it's a revelation to me.

"How about when you told her about her parents, practically held her together while she broke down, and then left her on the steps of the fucking hospital while her life may be in *fucking danger?*" Her voice gets all high-pitched and shriek-y there at the end, and yeah, okay, she has a point. I have been a dick to Penelope. I know it, my Duchess knows it. I never pretended to be a good guy.

Tormenting her is one of the few things that make my day better, as messed up as that sounds. Watching her, obsessing over her has been the highlight of my year.

"What do you want me to say?" I shift Hudson to my other arm and get up, going into the kitchen to grab a bottle of water.

"I want to know why you think you can treat my friend like one of your skanky hookups. She's not like that. If all you want to do is fuck with her, find someone else. I think she actually likes you and it's not fair of you to string her along like you give a damn." Montana pulls out her keys and dangles them in front of Hayes's face.

My world stops spinning as my heart stalls in my chest. Penelope *likes* me?

Hayes's whole expression lights up as he reaches eagerly for shiny metal with both hands and fuck do I want them the hell out of here. I blink a couple of times and focus on whatever she just said.

"I want Penelope, Red. So fucking bad. But I'm broken as fuck inside. There won't ever be a time when I'm going to be able to be more for someone like her, and she's the kind of chick who wants more. Who *deserves* more. She just can't get it from me, and I can't let her think there's false hope." I rake my fingers through my hair, that constant knot in my chest tightening painfully only for a different reason.

Maybe in another lifetime, or if this life had shaken out differently for me, I could've seen myself with Penelope. She's the kind of girl you fall in love forever with, and I can't let that happen. I'd destroy her.

Montana tilts her head as she studies me. "Tell me what broke you." The *so I can fix it* is unspoken but there all the same. Too bad she can't fix me like some problem with one of her bands. It's what she does. She's a fixer through and through and damn good at it, but it won't work this time. There's nothing left to fix.

"No."

She blinks at me as if she's entirely unfamiliar with the word. "No?"

"I'm not talking about it."

After a long, awkward stretch of time where we stare at each other, her willing me to submit and me giving off an aura of *fuck off*, she finally sighs. "Are you going back to work?"

"I don't know if I'm in a place to be responsible for someone else's life right now. I can't even keep mine together."

"Do you think there's anyone in this world that can protect Penelope better than you can?" she asks.

I want to say yes. It's on the tip of my tongue to suggest *anyone* would be better than me for the job, but the words stick in my throat. They're a lie, because as much as I want to keep my distance and not let her in, Penelope's already burrowed inside of me and claimed the hollow place in my chest as her own. Knowing she's been in danger this week and not being there to see with my own eyes that she's safe has been torture. If it hadn't been for the alcohol and stalking her on video, I would've caved a lot sooner and gone back only to find out how she is.

"No," I mutter, letting my head fall so I'm looking down at Hudson in my arms. He's gnawing on my shirt with his single tooth and drooling all over me like a maniac, but he fits like he's meant to be here. I fucking hate it.

"Good, so I'll tell them you'll be back tonight." Montana stands up, tucking Hayes back into the stroller. "Might want to get a new shirt," she smirks, lifting Hudson out of my arms. "Actually, I'll send you over a tux. They're going to need you at the gala."

I groan and let my head fall back against the couch. "Can't Ronin go? You know you love it when he dresses up in a tux."

She gets a gleam in her eye that I really don't need to see, but then blinks it away. "No, he's working on something else. If you don't show, Asher's going to have to cover Pen all night by himself."

Fuck Sebastian and his lack of field training.

"Fine, I'll be there."

Maybe focusing on someone else's problems will give me a night off from the relentless torment of mine.

SHADOWING PENELOPE AT THIS GALA IS FUCKING TORTURE. FOR the first time in days, I'm focused on something other than the demons that stalk me, so most people would think I'd be relieved.

The problem is the most beautiful woman I've ever seen in my entire life is so pissed off at me, she won't make eye contact. It's driving me out of my mind with jealousy, how she gives her attention to everyone else in the room but me.

Her attention belongs to *me* but she's denying me what's mine. Soon enough, she'll learn that she can't shut me out.

In fact, outside of her gaze flashing over me in my tux once or twice, she's pretty much acted like I don't even exist. Have you heard of kids pretending like you're dead to them? Like they can't see you or hear you? It's like that, only colder and for some reason fucking *hurts*.

My favorite hobby used to be getting under Penelope's skin, but now she won't acknowledge me long enough to let me have my fun. It seems like the tables have turned and now she's managed to claw her way underneath mine.

The pale pink dress she wears hugs every single curve like it was sewn onto her body. Who knew she had a banging body like that underneath the cardigan sweaters she usually wears? Fuck, it's enough to make me want to drag her into a back hall and bury my tongue between her thighs to see if she tastes as good as she looks. My cock gives a very enthusiastic twitch at the idea.

"Watch the doors," Asher says. "I've got the windows by the podium."

His irritated voice snaps my gaze up and off of Penelope's ass as she walks right in front of us. Ever since I showed up here tonight, he's been pissy with me, but I can't really blame him. I may owe him a free punch to my face later to make up for it, but I'm kind of hoping he doesn't take the shot.

I already feel like I've been through a meat grinder emotionally, and I'd rather not feel it physically, too.

My eyes dart over to the doors, scanning the area for any potential threats but I see nothing out of the ordinary. The sky outside is dark, but I can't make out any stars with the inside lights reflected in the glass. There are people in black tie formalwear all over the place stuffing fancy hors d'oeuvres down their throats and chasing it with champagne that costs more than my rent.

I'm still unclear on how spending so much on a party like this earns money for a charity, but on my list of shit to worry about, it doesn't even make the top fifty.

"All clear," I tell Asher, as he echoes the same from his end. Penelope comes to a sudden halt and Asher and I both almost run into her back.

"Penny," Collin Driscoll says in the smarmiest voice I've ever heard, and I want to punch him in his fucking face for the way he talks down to my girl. "You look beautiful." Her uncle holds out his arm for her to take, and she does, giving him her first smile of the night even though there's tension in her eyes. I don't know if anyone else notices, but it puts me on alert. There's something about the guy I can't stand, and I'm guessing it has to do with the way he treated her the other day in the kitchen.

Was it fucked up to lurk outside in the hall and listen in? Maybe, but I have no regrets.

Asher leans over and whispers, "What a dick." His laughter surprises me, but it feels good. It's been a long time since I've heard it, and while I didn't expect anything about tonight to put me in a better mood, it breaks a lot of the tension between the two of us.

We act as sentinels on either side of Penelope while Sebastian occasionally checks in on the earpieces we both wear from somewhere in a back room. He's got eyes on most of the party via his camera feeds and will let us know if there's anything to worry about.

Collin leads Penelope around the room, introducing her to people. It's boring as fuck, so I tune it out and watch the waiters and waitresses spin around the room with trays of alcohol. My hands shake as I fight off the urge to grab a drink or two and throw them back. Having the gala and my job to focus on helps, but the pain I was drinking to numb hasn't gone away.

Being near Penelope, in her orbit, helps, too. Her shutting me out gives me something else to focus on. I'm going to figure out how to break through, because the thought of being on the outs with her is depressing as hell. I won't tolerate it.

I have enough depressing shit in my life, and she's the one bright spot.

"It's not happening," Penelope snaps, dropping her uncle's arm like it's made of poison and knives. I wouldn't be surprised if it is.

My attention immediately fixates back on the two of them and I unconsciously step closer. I may have fucked up leaving her at that hospital, but I had my reasons. I've never left a client vulnerable like that before, and the circumstances were extenuating. Now that we're in a different situation, in a different time and place, if Collin Driscoll is about to strike out at his niece, you can bet your whole fucking savings I'm going to rip his head from his body and shove it up his ass, before he has a chance to hurt her.

"You're under too much stress. You could go back to doing what you do best and working in the lab. I don't understand why you're fighting so hard to save a company you don't even like." Collin throws his hands up, stalking off into the crowd.

Penelope reaches out blindly for a passing waiter and grabs a glass of champagne, tossing it back in one.

"Are you okay?" I ask, reaching out to brush my hand against her back but she stiffens the second I make contact, cutting me with a glare so sharp I'm practically bleeding out *feelings* all over the ground.

"Nevermind," I mutter, stepping back.

She laughs then, but it's not a pretty laugh. It's caustic and mean and filled with pain. I recognize it because it's the kind of laugh I'd let out if I could do such a thing anymore.

"I need some air," she says and then takes off. There are a fuck ton of people in here, and I don't know if they made an announcement or something but there's hardly room to move. Penelope doesn't let that stop her as she pushes her way through the masses, but as soon as she passes by, people step into our path making it impossible for Asher and me to follow as quickly as we'd like.

"Where the fuck did she go?" I yell over the noise. The panic is starting to bubble up in my chest as adrenaline spikes into my veins. My heart pounds against my ribs so hard it hurts as I scan every face looking for Penelope.

"Find her," Asher snaps as he presses his hand up to the earpiece he wears touching the sensor to turn on the microphone.

"I'll check outside," I say, remembering how at the palace Penelope calls home, outside is her safe place. The place she runs when she's feeling overwhelmed with the pressures of the world.

Before I can take more than a few steps, a loud scream from outside tears through the constant buzz of conversation from the crowd, and I'm no longer patient as I elbow and shove my way through the bodies, flinging people out of my way.

When I step outside, my pulse is so loud it's all I can hear, but I don't see Penelope. For a second, I'm relieved. There are a group of younger people—probably interns—fucking around near the fountain and one has her shoes off and is soaking wet like she got tossed in. That scream wasn't from my Duchess.

The relief is instant and breathtaking, but Penelope's still missing.

"No sign of her yet," Asher's voice carries into my ear.

"Nothing," Sebastian echoes.

A flash of pale pink catches my eye and as I lean over the stone railing looking down into the grass, I see her. Her shoes are off as she runs, her dress billowing out behind her and I'm taking off to follow before I register what I'm doing.

I only catch a glimpse before she disappears into the gigantic hedge maze, but I'm not about to let her vanish on me again.

Like it or not, Penelope Driscoll is mine.

CHAPTER 9
PENELOPE

THE GRASS IS cool against my feet as the blades pop up between my toes. Now that I'm out of that stuffy ballroom, I can breathe. I tilt my head back so there's nothing but millions of stars in front of my eyes, letting them flutter shut while I breathe in the still air of the night.

Out here, it's like the rest of the world stops existing. It's just me, the plants, and the sky. Every path I walk down leads me somewhere. Sometimes it's a dead end, and sometimes it's another passage. There's a certain pattern to it that's comforting. I'm not worried about getting lost in the maze. Eventually, someone will come for me, or I'll find my way out.

My thoughts are a chaotic mess. As if I don't have enough to deal with between the hostile takeover, my parents being killed, and finishing the AI system I'm building, now I'm worried about my uncle pressuring me to step down and let him take over Driscoll Tech.

I'm not even going to let myself think about how much of a mess Indy's presence here tonight has me in. He looks downright edible in his tux but I'm so angry with him I can't even enjoy it.

My hand drifts out from my side, my fingers brushing against the rough and smooth contrast of the leafy walls on either side of me. An earthy smell hangs heavy in the air as if the grass was mowed earlier today and I inhale as much of it as I can while I try to ground myself to admit a hard truth.

And make no mistake, he's the alphahole type, the kind that you'd hate yourself for if you couldn't resist him.

The truth is as much as I don't want to accept it, I can't seem to stop thinking about Indy Foster. I've officially become one of those stupid girls who loses all sense of her worth when a hot guy pays attention to her—even if that attention is just him being an asshole.

Indy leaving me at the hospital the way he did was just the final straw. Him getting drunk constantly and walking away from me when I needed him most? Well, that was him fulfilling my expectations of the person I figured he was. Maybe he's going through something. If so, I get it. I do.

Sometimes I *wish* I could tell the world to shove it and lose myself in drugs and alcohol and forget. Unlike him I don't have that luxury.

Maybe I'm a little bit jealous of his coping mechanisms, but I don't think that's it.

I think him showing up tonight looking like temptation in a tux and acting like it's just another day is what's bothering me most. I can handle everything else. I have been for months. What's throwing me off is Indy Foster and his reappearing act. There's a crushing hurt I don't want to acknowledge making it hard to breathe or eat or sleep. I feel so stupid because I knew. I knew we'd end up here if I let him have even a peek into my heart.

What am I supposed to do with him now?

It's not exactly like he's going to open up to me, but the more I think about it—okay, stupidly obsess about it—the more I want him to. I want him to come to me and share the darkest parts of himself. The parts he doesn't think should ever see the light of day. The parts even he can't admit to himself.

The problem is I know he never will.

I'm setting myself up for an epic sort of heartbreak if I let him in. I know it. I can see it coming from a mile away, but it feels impossible to stop. His dark, wild eyes and that dimpled crooked smile suck me in and I don't know how to escape.

If only it was as simple as chewing off my own foot or something. Somehow, I think letting Indy into my heart is going to be more painful.

So why can't I stop thinking about him? Wishing things were different? Wishing just once he'd look at me like I'm the only other person in the universe?

I round another corner, swiping at a stray tear that's broken free and runs down my cheek. I've reached the center, but I've been in this maze a hundred times, escaping out here any time my parents dragged me to an event when I was a child.

It has secrets, ones that I've worked hard to discover.

The center isn't actually the center. There's a hidden compartment, but you have to crawl through the bushes to get to it. I reach down and grab a handful of my skirt, hiking it up as I'm about to crawl inside just as Indy rushes around the corner and nearly runs into me.

He's breathless, panting like he ran the whole way. Those savage gray eyes frantically run over my body and leave goosebumps in their wake. The way he looks at me feels like a physical touch and I barely suppress a shiver.

He reaches up and presses against his earpiece, his eyes never once leaving me even to blink. "Found her. We're in the maze."

He lets go and then his whole body language changes. He shoves his hands in his pockets and finally looks away, scanning the area. "Would you believe this is my first time in one of these?"

Up until now I've been giving him the silent treatment, but the relief in his eyes changes my mind. I don't *want* to shut him out. In fact, what I really want is the opposite, even if I'm not ready to say it out loud. I want Indy Foster to let me in. I want to dig into his soul and carve my name so deep it'll scar.

"Want to see the best part?" I give him a small smile and try not to think too hard about the surprise on his face when I do.

I turn and duck right into a section of the leaves, only here there are no branches. The leaves give easily and on the other side is a space big enough for only two people. The walls are lined with white moonflower blooms, and the ceiling is open to the starry night sky.

Indy pushes through behind me, and I sink to the ground. He follows my lead, dropping to the grass beside me. It's silent here away from the party, so quiet I can hear both of us breathing. There isn't much light, only tiny pinpricks from the moon and stars but the walls are so high it feels like a whole different world in here. One where only we exist.

"I thought you weren't talking to me, Duchess," he says in a quiet voice, and if I didn't know any better, I'd say he sounds sad about it. Maybe he did notice.

"I wasn't."

"What made you change your mind?" He reaches over to the hedge wall closest to where he sits and plucks off one of the white blossoms, handing it to me.

I take it and tuck it behind my ear before biting my lip. It's unexpectedly sweet, him giving me this flower as all his attention settles on me expectantly.

I don't know if I want to confess everything to him, but there's something sort of magical in the air right now. It feels like we've been transported to another place in another time where there's nothing but him and me. It feels safe to confess my deepest buried hopes and wants, but there's still the fear that he'll reject me. Maybe he'll laugh or tell me again how he's not the kind of guy who does serious.

Still...

If I don't take a chance, I'll never know.

"I don't like not talking to you." I pluck at a nonexistent piece of lint on my dress, but eventually gather my courage to look up at him.

He blinks at me as his lips turn down into a frown and his eyebrows pull together like he doesn't understand what I said. Maybe he can't believe I actually admitted it.

My heart picks up speed as I decide I'm going to go for it. I'm going to ask for what I want to know. "Why did you run away?"

His expression shutters and he turns away, clenching his jaw. "We should get back."

"You're never going to tell me, are you?" Like I said, I knew this would be the result, but I had to try. It doesn't stop the twisting in my chest or the blurring of my eyes as tears gather. The last thing I want is to let Indy see me cry again—especially not when he's the reason I'm upset.

"No." One syllable, so final in its utterance I swear it echoes through the stillness of the night like a death knell.

"I can't do this anymore," I say, jumping to my feet. "I want you off my security team. Now," I tell him before lunging for the opening to get out. Suddenly the space is too small. His cologne is everywhere, his body heat warms my side, and I need to get away with a desperation that surprises me.

Indy has other plans, though, and when I rush for the exit, he grabs me around the waist and hauls me into his lap. I scream and try to throw myself off, pounding my fists against his chest and struggling but his strong arms are locked tight around me. It's a waste of energy to keep struggling, but rage courses through every atom of my body as hot tears slide down my face.

"Stop struggling, Duchess."

"Let me go," I growl, digging my nails into his forearms. I don't even stop to admire how sexy they are, which is a testament to how hurt and angry I am.

"No."

I huff out a breath that blows my hair away from where it's tangled in front of my face. "Is that your new favorite word?"

I'm so damn annoyed with him. He won't talk to me, but he won't let me go. I guess I should be grateful he made me angry because my tears have dried up.

"No," he says and his lips twitch. Asshole.

We sit in silence while I breathe hard and by the time I catch my breath, I want to jump up and run for it again. He hasn't said a word and I don't know how to get past this messed up stalemate we're in.

I'm finally willing to admit—at least to myself—that I want more from Indy. Even if that's just sex, I'm willing to take it.

Okay, maybe not because let's be honest here—I'm already catching feelings and we haven't been together like that.

Still.

Why won't he talk to me?

The silence is oppressive and when I move to get up again, he tightens his arms around my waist. I have no choice but to lean back into him and press up against all the ripples of his abs and sculpted planes of his chest. My only regret is that my dress isn't made of thinner material so I can feel it all better.

Or maybe that we don't have clothes on at all.

"I have a son," he says so quietly it's nearly a whisper and I swear I stop breathing. A million questions flash in my mind but I bite my tongue to hold them all back, sensing if I utter one single sound, I'll break the spell and he won't tell me anything else.

"Had," he corrects, choking on the word and my heart breaks for him. I move, twisting around. As soon as he sees I'm not about to take off on him after that bombshell, he loosens his grip and lets me spin so I'm straddling him. I wrap my arms around his neck and pull him to me, hugging him tight. All I can do is try to hold together his broken pieces while he tells me about the worst thing that I could imagine.

Worse than losing my parents.

He lost his *child*.

He's breathing hard and something warm and wet hits my shoulder. I don't dare look, but I think he might be crying.

"I'll tell you, just... don't go." His fingers dig into the hair at the back of my neck while his arm wraps around my waist, clinging to me.

I tighten my grip on him, pushing my fingers into the hair at the back of his head and playing with the strands. It seems to calm him down because his breathing slows and evens out a bit. It takes him a long time before he speaks again.

"He was three when I... lost him."

"Will you tell me about him?" I ask. Picturing Indy as a dad seems impossible. Yet I've seen glimpses of how he cares for the people in his life, and somehow, I'm not surprised that he'd be good at it. He protects people for a living—it checks out.

I feel him smile where his cheek rests against mine. I can imagine what it looks like, probably tinged with sadness at the edges, but there's love there, too. An aching kind of love for what's been lost. The kind that takes something with you when it goes.

A whole lot of pieces are clicking into place with this new information. Indy Foster suddenly makes sense.

"His name was Chase. He was so good, Duchess. Everything good in me he got, same with his mom. We were in high school when she got pregnant and I was nowhere near ready to be a dad, but when it happened, he became our whole world. He used to wake me up by escaping his crib and jumping on my bed making these horrible screaming dinosaur noises."

We both laugh, but his dies off and I keep playing with his hair as his body relaxes more and more against mine.

"When he was two, he had his routine appointment for shots and shit. He'd been unusually tired for a couple of weeks, so the doctor wanted to run some tests." He has a full body shudder and his arms tighten around me as he buries his face in my neck. "It was cancer. Leukemia. He fought... hard. But he lost. He was just gone."

If I thought my heart broke for him before, now it was laying in jagged pieces scattered all over the grass underneath us, dripping blood on the vibrant green blades.

There's nothing I can say. *I'm sorry* doesn't seem enough, but no words can change this. No words can take back what happened or make it better. So, I do the only thing I can. I lean back until he lifts his head and the broken and empty look in his eyes calls to the grief inside of me. Then, I brush my lips against his.

It's not meant to be heated, only comforting. When he kisses me back, my cheeks are stained with tears as they fall from both our eyes and mix together between us. I pour everything I'm feeling—the sorrow, love, comfort, understanding, and anger—into this kiss. It's everything and nothing, a salvation and a damnation, a re-opening of old wounds and a healing.

As we cling to each other and our lips connect again and again, his taste on my tongue and his body pressed against mine heals something in me, too. I'm lost to Indy, to his grief and agony, as his hand shoves further into my hair and grips the strands, angling my face so he can deepen the kiss.

I'm dizzy, my head spinning and the only thing I can breathe in is him. A branch cracks on the other side of the hedge and we pull apart, but Indy doesn't go far. He rests his forehead against mine while we breathe in the same air. My lips are tingling, and I want to chase his kiss, for it to never stop. I'd happily drown in Indy, never coming back up for air.

In our own little world in the secret hideaway in the middle of a hedge maze, I think I've fallen a little bit for Indy Foster.

My hand falls from his hair to rest over his heart. It's beating as fast as mine, strong and perfect in his chest. "I won't tell anyone," I whisper, needing him to know I'd never betray his confidence like that. It's more than clear he doesn't talk about Chase, but my heart wants to shoot up into the sky and explode like a firework because he chose to tell me about him.

"Indy?" Asher calls out, and his heavy footsteps walk the length of the hedge just outside our secret escape. "Penelope?"

I start to untangle myself from Indy, but he leans forward and presses a lingering kiss to my lips before letting me go. My legs shake as I stand up, both from the intense emotion of what just happened and also because kissing Indy sent waves of pleasure crashing through my body.

"Coming!" I call out, not wanting Asher to start to panic all over again. I finger comb through the tangle of my hair and push out of the hidden leafy door. Asher eyes me as I straighten my dress and try to make myself presentable.

There's only so much fingers can do, though, and I'm sure I look an absolute mess.

Indy follows out of the hedge seconds after I do, and Asher's eyebrows shoot sky high. He doesn't say anything about finding the two of us together hidden away from the world. Smart man. Instead, he turns to level his gaze on me. "They're waiting on you for the closing speech."

I shoot a panicked look at Indy because I can't go on stage like this. I look like a wreck. I'm sure my mascara has run down my cheeks, my hair is in tangles, and I bet if my lipstick isn't completely rubbed off, it's definitely smeared all over my face.

"You know what? My uncle thinks he can do a better job at running Driscoll than I can? Let him make the speech," I decide, pulling my phone out of the pocket on my dress—yes, pockets are a must in all dresses—and text him letting him know I'm going home. He can do whatever he wants with that. I fulfilled my end by throwing this damn thing and I don't want to be here anymore.

I'm actually sort of giddy making this call and a laugh slips out before I can slap my hand over my mouth. The corner of Indy's mouth curves up. "What's so funny, Duchess?"

"It feels so good to say no. I can't remember the last time I said it."

"Maybe you should do it more often," Asher drawls, leaning against the firm wall of the maze as his tattooed fingers tuck a stray piece of hair behind his ear. That cannot be comfortable.

"Maybe," I agree. I glance over at Indy and the way he's watching me is so intense, my cheeks flame. It's predatory and his eyes are practically burning. I think if he could, he'd light my dress on fire with his gaze so he could look his fill of what's underneath. Maybe I wasn't the only one who didn't want that kiss to end.

"Which one of you knows how to get out of this thing?" Asher asks, pushing off the wall and looking in the direction he came.

"I've got this," I say, striding forward feeling more confident than I have in a while. I may look a disaster and my messed up heart may be in tatters, but when Indy takes my hand and laces our fingers together, it's like he heals something inside me I didn't know could be repaired.

We walk out in silence, making turn after turn, and I know we're getting near the exit when the sounds of the party start to filter in. I hate things like this, having to be social with people who are judging everything you do. There's no perfect for them. No way to win them over, because every single flaw will be picked over and discussed at length, and if you have none, you're *too* perfect and something must be wrong with you.

It's exhausting.

"Can we go straight to the car?" I ask, not having the mental energy to go back inside and deal with any more people.

"You got it, Duchess. Ash, can you have Sebastian meet us there?" Indy squeezes my hand and then does one of those guy head nod things at Asher.

"Yeah, I'll be right behind you," he says, taking off inside.

"What's he doing?" I ask, watching him go.

"Going to get Sebastian and help him carry out whatever gear he's got. We'll come back tomorrow to take down all the cameras."

Indy leads me to the parking lot and into the car. The whole night is catching up with me and I start to nod off in the back seat as soon as I sit inside. I can barely keep my eyes open, but then the door opens and Indy's hopping out of the driver's seat, Asher's taking his place, and Sebastian's jumping into the passenger seat. Indy climbs in the back beside me and slides as close as he can get, wrapping his arm around me so I can lay my head on his shoulder while he buckles me in.

"Close your eyes, Duchess," he orders as his lips press into my hair and I can't help feeling like something's unlocked between us. Everything feels changed and sinking into him is the most natural thing in the world.

"We have to tell her," I hear distantly as I try to fight sleep pulling me under. It's Sebastian, I think. "She needs to know someone's stealing their tech."

"We will. In the morning," Indy snaps. "Look at her. She's fucking beat. It can wait."

He's right. Whatever it is will still be there to screw up my life in the morning. For now, I want to revel in the best feeling in the world—being pressed up against Indy Foster.

CHAPTER 10
INDY

"We need to talk," I say, cringing at how fucking wrong those words sound coming out of my mouth. Penelope must think so, too, because her eyes get wide and then narrow to slits. I'm not about to say anything she's probably imagining right now, but she doesn't know that. The last time I uttered those words, I told her that her parents were murdered, so I can only imagine what she's thinking right now.

"It's not like that," I say, needing to reassure her. "Sebastian found something in his crawl through your company servers."

"What? Someone's stealing my work? Was that what I heard last night?" It's almost funny how mad Penelope looks after dropping that on her. She's got this adorable wrinkle between her eyebrows that I want to reach out and smooth with my fingers or maybe kiss until it disappears.

Penelope wakes up before the fucking sun, so it's still dark out as I drop this on her, but I felt guilty about not 'fessing up immediately last night. I'm not some sort of tech genius like Bash. I don't know how much someone could theoretically take in one night if they discovered we knew what they were up to.

She looks better rested this morning, more herself. Even I have to admit I slept sober and through the night for the first time that I can remember in years. Maybe there's something to this whole talking about Chase and what happened thing. I don't know what compelled me to confess to Penelope last night, but the thought of her walking away from me again, from her throwing me off her security team because she didn't want to see my face again... it fucking crushed me.

I'm so fucking tired of hurting.

"Where's Sebastian?" she asks, hurrying to pour herself some coffee. "We need him and to get to the DT offices."

"What, now?" I ask, noting that it's still dark as fuck outside. It's maybe five a.m. If I'm up this early, it's usually because I haven't slept yet or I'm hitting the gym, not going into the office and starting some fucked up corporate espionage bust.

This is some Post versus Kellogg shit right here.

I pull my phone out of my pocket. "I'll text him and Ash."

It doesn't take long for the two of them to come down, and within minutes we're loading back into the SUV and barreling down the road towards the Driscoll Tech offices.

The doors are locked when we get to the front entrance, but Penelope enters a code into a keypad underneath the lock and gets us in. "The research servers are down here, and the corporate servers are upstairs," she tells Sebastian. I don't care what Bash and Asher do; I'm sticking to Penelope like my ass is fucking superglued.

"I'll go upstairs to check the corporate ones. They're in a room on the other side of my office," Penelope says, and Sebastian and Asher break off to check the ground floor.

I have no idea what we might be looking for, but I'll stick nearby to help however I can. We step onto the elevator and it's like all the oxygen has been sucked out. I know Penelope's stressed about this, but she sucks her full bottom lip between her teeth and the air crackles between us.

I haven't kissed her again since last night, but I'm transfixed watching her mouth, wanting desperately to taste her again. She's addictive and like an addict, I want more. One hit will never be enough. Penelope, though... She deserves to know she's more than just sex to me.

Every girl I've been with after Chase's mom—and admittedly, even before her—never meant anything to me. I never wanted more, not until Penelope fell apart in that restaurant booth and trusted me to hold her together.

My tongue drags across my lower lip as I imagine her taste. My dick is actively protesting this whole taking it slow thing, but it's important to me Penelope knows she's different. I'm not going to tell her. I'm going to show her that she's more. I'm done fighting my obsession. If I'm going to ruin her, I'll make sure it's worth it for both of us. I won't let myself sink inside her tight little body until I'm sure she understands who she belongs to now. Until she begs me for my cock.

The elevator doors slide open, and we both breathe an audible sigh of relief. My jeans are tight as hell, and I don't even try to hide it when I adjust myself. Let her see what she does to me. When she looks, I smirk at her. I've got nothing to be ashamed of or hide. Wait until she sees what I'm packing when I start walking around her palace in gray sweats. I wonder how pink I can make her blush when she gets an eyeful of my dick.

Fuck, now I'm getting even harder. I blow out a breath as she jerks her gaze off my crotch and down the hallway further into the office. There are lights on and...

"Did you hear that?" she whispers.

"Yeah, someone's down there," I say, confirming that the voices I just heard weren't in my head.

"The conference room's that way." Penelope starts to take off, but I grab her arm and pull her behind me, putting my body between her and whatever danger might be down the hall. Sometimes she's so fucking reckless I want to shake her.

With one hand on Penelope and the other wrapped around the grip of my gun, we stalk down the hall. The lights in the conference room blaze and it's obvious there's a meeting going on.

A meeting of the board Penelope wasn't invited to.

At five thirty in the morning? Sketchy. As. Fuck.

"Are we busting in there or what?" I whisper, keeping one eye on the fucks making Penelope's life harder.

She shakes her head and holds her finger up to her lips to indicate I should stop talking. Her gaze flicks to the five people betraying her and I hate the lack of surprise I see in her eyes when she takes them in one last time, before we sneak away.

When we're back in the elevator, fury radiates off her and the only thing I can think to do is pull her against my chest and hold her tight. It takes almost the entire ride down for her muscles to relax, but bit by bit she does until she's practically melted into me when the doors open.

Luckily neither Sebastian nor Asher are around when we step out of the elevator, so I don't have to explain anything I'm not ready to. We catch up to them pretty quickly and fill them in on what we saw.

"We need to get out of here before they end their meeting," I say, looking down at my watch.

"Indy's right. Employees are going to start showing up soon and I doubt they'd want anyone to catch them together like that off hours. It'd look suspicious," Penelope says, winding a stray piece of hair that fell out of her ponytail around her finger. My fingers twitch with the need to take over for her, but I won't. Not with an audience. Not yet. Soon enough that won't matter once she understands.

"It *is* suspicious, especially in light of what I've found," Sebastian says, pushing his glasses up his nose and hiking the messenger bag he brought in up higher on his shoulder.

"So, you found something in here then?" Penelope asks.

"Not yet. I'm good, but I'm not a magician."

I bristle at Sebastian's dickish tone, but Penelope doesn't seem to mind. I imagine in her business, she's used to dealing with people like Sebastian all the time, so it doesn't faze her.

"Let's go back to the house and figure out next steps," Penelope says, taking charge in a way that sets me off more than I expect. I can picture bending her over that boardroom table and showing her who's really boss of her in all the ways that count, so I file that away for when shit is less chaotic and she's aware of where we stand now.

It's a short ride back to the house and when we get inside, we all instinctively move towards the kitchen. It's the warmest place in this castle of a house and we gather around the island counter.

"I want the board gone," Penelope says, setting the tone for how this shitfest is about to go down. I know some hard decisions are going to have to be made, and it looks like she's up for the challenge. A spark of pride lights up somewhere in the vicinity of my chest, but it's so out of character for me, I don't even know how to process it.

I don't care enough about other people to feel proud of them. It's not in my makeup anymore, yet that jolt says otherwise. What the hell is she doing to me?

"How do you propose we do that without dragging them out of there and making things bloody?" Asher asks, leaning lazily against the counter like it was specifically put there to support his weight.

I chuckle. "Why's your go-to always getting your hands dirty?"

"First, who said anything about my hands? I've got a whole arsenal of weapons I'd rather play with," Asher says, pulling a knife out of his pocket and flicking it open, scraping it under his nails as if to demonstrate. "And second, I said *without*. Not that I'm ever opposed to going that route," he quickly adds, turning his gaze onto Penelope. "I just figured it wasn't really your style."

She pales and shakes her head. "It's not. Keeping things... clean is preferable."

I wonder if she knows just how much blood stains my hands and what she thinks about it if she does.

"Cutting off your board is never going to be completely clean. There will be backlash," Sebastian states like it's fact.

"No shit, but at least we have a goal," I say, moving up beside Penelope and bumping her shoulder with mine. I hope it looks like an accident, but really there was too much space between us, and I couldn't *not* touch her. This is one of the hardest things she's had to face, and I don't want her to feel like she has to go through it alone. "What do we do to make it happen?"

"I'm going off the books with this. We have a corporate attorney my father used to use, but I wouldn't be surprised if he reports to the board. I'll have to find someone new and get them to look at what my options are." She nibbles at her lip, and I have to curl my fingers into fists to keep from reaching up and rubbing my thumb across it to smooth out the indentations from her teeth then replacing them with my own.

"I might know someone," Sebastian says, pulling out his tablet.

He looks like he's already lost to the task and about to walk off when Penelope calls out, "Wait."

Sebastian looks up, his perfectly gelled blonde hair reflecting some of the morning sunlight starting to come in through the kitchen windows. "I need you to figure out where the stolen code is going and who installed the program that's siphoning it. That's your top priority. I can deal with the lawyer."

"We'll help," I offer, feeling all at once completely useless. This is not even close to my area of expertise. I'm on the same page as Ash—I'd rather hit something and make it bloody than deal with corporate politics and having to tiptoe around bullshit.

Chess isn't really my forte. Sweeping my arm across the board and scattering the pieces into mayhem is much more my style.

"Thanks," Penelope says, giving me a small smile that spackles over another one of the millions of cracks around my heart. Maybe—eventually—they'll all be healed enough to resemble something solid again.

"C'mon, Duchess. You need a break," I say, reaching around where Penelope's huddled at her desk and closing her laptop.

"Hey, I wasn't done!" She turns and glares up at me, but I lean down and kiss the tip of her nose which turns her cheeks pink and melts some of the fury out of her eyes.

"Don't care. You've been holed up in here for days. This isn't a request. You need to have some fun and remember that there's more to life than hostile takeovers and duplicitous board members."

I grab her hand and tug her up out of the chair. "Go change into something you don't mind getting dirty."

She eyes me for a second but then decides to listen for once and moves towards the door. Before she walks out, she turns and looks back biting her lower lip and my eyes drop to stare at how her teeth indent the soft flesh. Shit, now I want to fuck her mouth. "Is this a date?"

"You bet your sexy ass it is. Now go."

The surprise in her eyes shouldn't piss me off as much as it does, but my teeth grind together anyway. I get that I have a reputation, but Penelope's different. The fact she doesn't understand that entices me to bend her over her desk and prove it. She's strong and smart and capable in a way that most women aren't. In fact, I've never met another one like her and it's fucking me up inside.

The weirdest part is that I don't even care.

I *like* that I'm all twisted up.

If you'd asked me a week ago if I'd feel this way, I'd have told you to go fuck yourself. But after the gala, everything changed.

I'm not the guy you date. I'm not the guy you bring home to your parents. I'm not the guy you marry and settle down with and have three kids and a dog and a white picket fence.

But for her?

For her I might try.

It's been a hot minute since I've been out on a date with anyone. Anytime I've taken a girl out, it's always with the sole intention of fucking her and leaving before she falls asleep. In so many ways, this is different. At the end of tonight, I won't be getting any. It's not because I think Penelope would hold out on me. I see how she looks at me like she'd give up her entire fortune to take a peek inside the gray sweats I strut around this place wearing just to taunt her.

The heat in her eyes and the way she sucks that bottom lip into her mouth to try and hide how I affect her tests my resolve every fucking day.

But I won't give in. Not until I'm confident I've proven to her that she's more. Not until she begs.

It's not going to stop me from getting another taste of her, though.

While Penelope gets ready, I head out to the garage and pack up the supplies I gathered earlier. When I go back into the house, she's already coming down the stairs and I'm impressed by how fast she's gotten ready.

She's wearing a pair of jeans and a crop top that shows off the tiniest sliver of her stomach. Her outfit is nothing special, and yet it's probably the sexiest thing I've ever seen her wear. All I can think about is stripping her out of it. My dick is fully onboard with this plan as I fight to keep her from noticing. There's something about Penelope letting her hair down, letting me see a side of her that no one else gets to that fucking kills any desire I have to wait to strip her bare and fuck her raw.

My heart pumps harder with every step closer she takes until she's standing right in front of me staring up at me with the same lust swirling in her eyes that I've got in mine. Every pulse echoes down to my dick and I'm so hard it hurts. A tiny kiss is all I let myself have because if I don't hold back, we'll never get out of here. I'll be buried balls deep inside her tight cunt in the next ten seconds.

Now that I've decided she's mine, I never want to take my hands off of her. "Ready?" I ask when I've pulled away, claiming her hand and threading our fingers together.

"Where are we going?"

"It's a surprise." I hold open the passenger side door and wait for her to climb in, checking out her ass as she does. "But I promise you're going to like it."

She raises an eyebrow. "And if I don't?"

Fuck, I need to spank the defiance out of her. My palm itches to do it, but I'm not so sure she'd be cool with that on the first date. "I'll spread your legs apart and suck on your clit until you lose your voice from screaming my name to make it up to you."

After that, she tries to hide how she can't seem to sit still in her seat and how her nipples are poking through her t-shirt, but I don't bring it up again. I like her flustered and turned on for me.

While I drive, I decide to let all my freak out to play and turn on my pop playlist, singing along to break some of the choking sexual tension. If I want to make Penelope agree to be mine, she's going to have to not only accept the dark and broken pieces of me, but the weird ones, too.

I sing along to Justin Timberlake and the Spice Girls at the top of my lungs and after laughing her ass off, Penelope actually joins in. I'd have never guessed she listened to music like this, let alone knew the words. She's blowing my mind.

When we step out of the car at our destination, her shoulders are loose, and she's got an easy smile on her face that *I* put there. That's right. I'm fucking *awesome* at this whole boyfriend thing, even if that word doesn't feel like enough and she doesn't know it yet.

"What are we doing here?" Penelope asks, looking around the empty alleyway we're standing at the mouth of. We're on the edge of downtown in a more run-down area. There's nothing unusual about this spot. A dumpster at the end and a couple of doors lining the brick walls that lead into places that are either closed or out of business.

I don't bother answering her. Better if I show her what we're going to do, so I move around the back of the SUV and grab out the duffel bag I loaded up. I toss it on the ground at her feet and bend to unzip it, pulling out a canister and shaking it.

It clicks with every shake making a satisfying sound and I step closer to the wall, ripping the cap off and tossing it aside. Then I press down on the nozzle and spray paint the biggest dick I've ever drawn onto the side of the building complete with proportionate balls.

"What the hell are you doing?" Penelope hisses, cutting her eyes to the mouth of the alley. I parked so no one can intrude on us, blocking anyone from being able to catch me off guard.

"Uh, wallpapering the fuck out of this building with a whole bunch of dicks? Grab a can and help me."

She shakes her head and folds her arms across her perfect set of tits, hiding them from me. I scowl at her for ruining my view, but all she does is lift her eyebrow in challenge. "I'm not doing that."

I'm tempted to bend her over the back seat, yank her jeans down, and spank the shit out of her until her ass is pink from my palm and she submits to me completely.

Instead, I tilt my head and ask, "What, you want to paint something other than dicks? Why?"

She reaches up and pinches the bridge of her nose like I'm exasperating the fuck out of her. My lips twitch because it's hard not to bust up laughing my ass off, she's so fucking cute.

"I'm not vandalizing someone's property!" she whispers but it's projected like she's yelling it.

"C'mon, Duchess. Be naughty with me," I purr, sauntering towards her slowly.

"No."

"Yes," I say, up in her space now. Wrapping my fingers around her throat and tilting her chin back, she glares at me with her eyes full of defiance.

"Maybe I should bend you over the back seat and spank the attitude out of you," I murmur, watching as her pupils blow and cheeks turn pink. I run my finger down one to see if it's as warm and soft as it looks.

Penelope leans into me like she can't control herself and a tiny whimper falls from her lips. I can't help my sinful smile. She's so fucking responsive, when we finally fuck, it's going to be explosive.

"Or maybe," I murmur, leaning close to her ear so my lips brush against the sensitive shell. "I should tell you I know the building's owner, we have permission to do whatever we want, and I already paid for the clean up to take care of whatever we do."

She jerks back and blinks up at me as the haze of lust clears. "Really?"

"Really. Go crazy, Duchess. Paint all the dicks you want. Make a mess. No one can see you and no one cares. Let all the bullshit out and be a little wild for once." I reach down and grab a can of paint and toss it at her.

She fumbles but catches it at the last second, looking down at it like it might spontaneously combust in her hands. Eventually, though, a tiny grin forms on her face and she starts to shake it up. I try not to put pressure on her, so I turn away, going back to my wall of dicks and deciding to go more anatomically correct, adding veins and hair.

On my next set, I make the balls uneven and on the next the dick's got a curve. My dick is picture perfect thank you very much, but not all cocks are created equal. I'm lost in my art but eventually I get bored of the dickscape and check on Penelope.

She's gone in the opposite direction I have, painting all sorts of landscape shit like mountains and beaches. She's not an artist, so it's not very good but she seems really into it. Her hands are speckled with different colored paints, and she's got a couple of blue streaks across her face. Her face is flushed, and her bottom lip is swollen from where she's got it trapped between her teeth as she paints. She's never been sexier, and I can't help but want to get closer. She pulls me into her orbit just by existing.

I toss my almost empty can back into the bag and move in her direction, not stopping until my chest presses against her back. I snake my hand around her waist, flattening my palm between her breasts. Her heart's racing under my hand as she breathes hard, but when I touch her, she drops the can to her side and leans back, letting me hold her. She fucking melts like she knows I'll catch her and it's almost too much.

The way Penelope trusts me when I haven't earned it blows my mind. The second I touch her, it's like the whole world disappears and it's only her and I. All the stress and tension disappear like some sort of magic.

I spin her around and crowd her space, pressing her back

against the still-wet wall as my fingers wrap around her throat. She opens her mouth to protest, but I don't let her. I kiss her like I'll die if I don't, digging my fingers into her hair using my hold on her throat to tip her head so I can taste her better. She opens her mouth to let me in and I waste no time burying my tongue between her lips. This isn't the only set of lips I want to bury my tongue between and tasting her this way only provokes my cravings for her.

I'm destroying her mouth with mine, ruining her for any other kiss from any other person. I'm the only man she'll ever kiss again, now that she's mine. This kiss is endless and yet not nearly long enough when we break apart, covered in paint with bruised lips and empty lungs.

"I think I've got paint in my hair," she says, laughing as she reaches back to check.

"My dirty girl," I murmur, stealing one more kiss while I drink in the happiness flooding her eyes. "Sounds like you need to get cleaned up then," I tell her, bending down and throwing her over my shoulder while she shrieks.

Across the street from the alley is a park with a huge fountain in it that's famous for throwing pennies in to make wishes. Supposedly, if you throw in a quarter, you'll get your wish guaranteed.

I'm about to find out what happens when I throw Penelope in it instead.

She cracks up laughing, alternating with slapping me on the ass and kicking her feet the whole way across the street, but when she realizes when I'm about to do she starts begging.

"No, Indy! Stop! Don't you dare! Please don't," she pleads and I only grin bigger before tossing her in.

It's not very deep so I'm gentle about it but she splashes into the penny-lined fountain and comes up spluttering. Her hair's soaked and plastered to her head and her clothes are clinging to her curves. I glance around for anyone who might be checking her out ready to throw down, but it's just a bunch of kids and their parents.

They look at us in shock, and then they shake it off and some of the kids start to try to climb in, too.

When I'm satisfied it's only moms and their kids here, I follow her in, ducking under the stream and kissing the hell out of her all over again. My hands wrap around her back, pulling her into me so our bodies are pressed together. There's no space between us, and if I could, I'd freeze time and live here like this with her forever. Under the artificial waterfall, the water runs down between our lips, sticking to our eyelashes and dripping down our bodies but neither one of us cares.

If I could, I'd strip her bare and fuck her right here but even I'm not that much of an asshole. Besides, she's vulnerable like this so we can't stay.

When some little shit throws a penny right at the back of my head, it snaps me out of my Penelope-induced haze, and I realize she's shivering, and we've already been here too long. We're both completely drenched, but I toss my arm over her shoulders as we step out of the fountain and pull her into my side while we walk back to the alley.

She looks the most relaxed I think I've ever seen her, and I've gotta admit it's a good look. Almost as good as the one I'm going to put on her face when I make her come for the first time.

"Ready for the last part of our date, Duchess?"

"Does it involve getting dry?"

I toss her a towel and watch as she wraps it around herself, shivering. "I think you'd like it if I kept you wet," I say, letting my gaze roam hungrily over her body. I don't even try to hide how I'm staring at the way her clothes are sucked against her skin. I have to adjust myself when I start to think about what Penelope might feel like when I slide inside her with damp skin pressed against mine. Why the fuck did I decide to be a good guy again? My dick feels like it wants to stage an intervention.

The truck has heated seats, so I pop the door open and start the engine, turning on the heaters while I towel myself off and pick up our mess. After the duffel bag is stuffed back into the back of the SUV and I toss her one of my sweatshirts, I hold the door open for Penelope and then climb behind the wheel.

She sighs when she settles into the seat wearing my hoodie and a soft smile I don't think I've ever seen on her, even on the cams when she thinks no one's watching.

With perfect timing, her stomach rumbles and I chuckle. "Hungry?"

"Starving. The next stop on this date wouldn't happen to involve food, would it?"

"What kind of gentleman would I be if I helped you work up an appetite and then didn't feed you?"

She chokes on her laugh. "You're *not* a gentleman."

I gasp mockingly and then give her my most depraved grin. "Not with all the things I'm imagining doing to you, no. I'm sure as fuck not."

Penelope shifts in her seat and rather than let her get away with pretending she's not as turned on as I am, I put my hand on her thigh, inching it higher. Pushing her to her limits is one of my favorite things to do.

"Um, well, I really do need food," she chokes out as she lets her legs fall open.

I slow down as I turn into my favorite sweets spot, Midnight Cookie. When I shut off the engine, I unbuckle and turn in my seat to face her. "How do you feel about dessert for dinner?"

Those must've been the magic words because Penelope lights up like a damn supernova. My chest tightens knowing I put that look on her face, and fuck if I don't want to do it again.

"Seriously?"

"Yup." I jump out and walk around to open her door, grabbing her hand before she can even think of denying me. "I know cookie is in the name, but they have a little bit of everything."

We buy enough dessert to last us a week but we're not sticking around here to eat it. Obviously, we're both starving because the amount of sugar and fat weighing my arms down right now is obscene. I'd buy this a thousand times over if it keeps that relaxed smile on Penelope's face.

The drive back to her house is quiet, but not in an awkward way. When I pull through the gates and into the garage, she surprises me by taking my hand and leading me across the lawn and over to her childhood treehouse. The same one she hid from me in on the first day.

I had to admit, I haven't given it a lot of thought since that day other than to contemplate lighting it on fire so she can't escape from me again. If I didn't think it would hurt her to burn it down, I would in a heartbeat. I never want her to have an escape from me. She can hide from the world but never me.

When we get inside, we strip out of our wet clothes and fall into the nest of blankets and pillows spread out on the mattress that's set into the floor. We both keep our underwear on but having Penelope's bare skin pressed up against mine is a test I think I might fail. As much as I want to take things with her a step further than we did earlier, I somehow manage to hold off. My dick hates me for it, but I need her to understand this is more.

What's between us isn't going away, and neither am I.

We get high on sugar and each other while we escape the outside world for a few hours. We could exist in this moment forever and I wouldn't trade it for anything.

Eventually, she curls up beside me, resting her head on my chest and before I can even think about how perfect this whole day was, I'm slipping into unconsciousness without an ounce of pain.

CHAPTER 11
INDY

"How could no one have come?" Penelope practically yells into her phone. We've been inseparable for the past few days since we defaced a building together. Being with her this way without my bullshit or a screen between us soothes the monster that lives inside me. I'm damn near docile when I'm with her. Now that I've gotten attached to her, the idea of something happening to Penelope is triggering all sorts of fucked up scenarios to play on a loop in my head and the only way to keep them at bay is to have my eyes—or hands—on her at all times.

Healthy?

Fuck, no.

I also don't care.

I'm hypervigilant and will end anyone who even looks at her wrong.

We're down in her lab while I watch her work. It's boring as fuck and I don't understand any of what she does, but I can't bring myself to leave her side. Anytime I leave the room she shoots me a panicked look like if I walk out, she might never see me again. The feeling is mutual.

"I'm coming. No, don't keep calling them. I'll be there in a few minutes." Penelope ends the call and then slams her phone down on the table.

"Something the matter, Duchess?" I probably shouldn't tease her right now considering how pissed off she looks, but I can't help it.

That part of me that loves getting under her skin is still alive and well.

She looks like she wants to tear me a new asshole, but then all that anger seems to vanish and her shoulders curl inwards. "I'm sorry for bringing up a sore subject, but do you remember the day you left me at the hospital? How I said I had a date?"

Something real fucking uncomfortable twists in my stomach, and surprisingly it's not about the hospital. My fingers twitch at my sides, ready to pull out my gun and hunt someone down. "What are you trying to say?"

"I wasn't lying when I said I had a date. It just wasn't what you're thinking," she explains, as she hurries to pack up her tablet, close out the windows on her computer, and grab her sweater and purse. She shoves the laptop in her purse which I guess doubles as a bag for the thing.

"Care to elaborate?" I'm leaning back against the desk and my fingers wrap around the edge, squeezing so hard the joints ache. If I let go, I'll be tempted to stalk across the room and fight dirty to get answers. I'm trying to be better.

For her.

"There's a little boy. His name is Rory, and he has leukemia. He's been undergoing chemo for months, and when I started volunteering, we hit it off."

I try and fail to swallow past the lump in my throat, ridiculously grateful I never loosened my grip on the desk. Now it may be the only thing tethering me to reality as my mind threatens to splinter off into flashbacks of the past. I don't even get to enjoy the relief of knowing she's not with anyone else.

"He's a foster kid and he deserves so much better. He told me once that sometimes his foster mom forgets to pick him up when they bring him in for chemo. Sometimes they can't be bothered. His social worker has to pick him up half the time and the other half his foster mom drops him off but doesn't stick around."

Penelope's words penetrate my panic and when they register, I shove off the desk, no longer capable of holding still. My muscles are tense and my pulse pounds in my ears. How the *fuck* can anyone leave their kid, even a foster kid, to go through that alone? I've seen firsthand how horrific the experience is and you have to be a special kind of piece of shit to not give a fuck.

"Anyway, I gave the nurses my number in case they ever forgot to pick him up again once I cleared it with his social worker. She isn't always available, and while they can't tell me anything about his treatment, I did manage to convince his social worker to let me pick him up if they don't by submitting my application to foster. I really think Rory's only a monthly check to them and they don't care what happens to him." Penelope's eyes are watery and she's blinking fast like she might cry, and fuck if I want to take away her pain.

"What do you need from me?" I ask, both dreading the answer and hoping I can help in some way. As much as the thought of walking into that hospital again or seeing the tiny bald head that comes from putting poison in a little body that's fighting for their life scares the everloving fuck out of me, I can't do nothing.

Penelope's eyes soften as she grabs her phone off the desk and tucks it into her purse. She moves closer to where I've stopped pacing and puts her hand on my chest over my heart and looks up at me. "I have to go get him, but you don't have to come. I don't expect you to. Will you call Asher and ask him to meet me at the car?"

As I look down into her warm brown eyes so filled with understanding and compassion, it hits me that I actually *want* to face this. Okay, so I don't actually want to go in and see all the suffering or be reminded of my trauma, but I also need to move on with my life. For the first time, I think I might be ready, but only with Penelope by my side, holding my hand and looking at me like she is now.

Like it's okay that I'm broken because she is, too, and we can use our broken pieces to build something new together.

"I... want to go."

She looks as surprised as I am to hear those words coming out of my mouth. "Are you sure?"

I nod, afraid that if I try to speak again, I might tell her no. That I'm not sure and that I'll never be sure and that I can't do this.

"Okay, but if you need to wait in the car I'll understand."

We rush out of her office and take off for the hospital, making good time. My heart is pounding so hard in my chest I'm convinced it's doing permanent damage as we approach the automatic doors to the bottom floor of the children's hospital.

The same fucking hospital where Chase took his last breath.

I don't think I can do this.

In my chest, my lungs seize up and I have to bend forward and rest my hands on my knees against a wave of dizziness. My heart's beating too fast in my chest, and my hands are tingling. It's like the ground is tilting beneath my feet, the world is rocking on its axis and the only way to get it to stop is turn around and run far the fuck away from here.

Why did I want to face this again?

"Go back to the car, Indy. I'll get him and meet you there," Penelope says, tugging on my arm.

I stand up, swaying before regaining my equilibrium. "No, I can do this."

I go to take a step forward, but she puts her hands against my chest, gently holding me back. We both know I could overpower her if I want to, but I hear her out instead.

"You don't *have* to do this. Not all at once. It's a huge win that you even willingly came back here today. It's enough."

It's enough.

Two words have never meant more to me in my life.

I deflate and reach down, gripping her hand and pressing a kiss to her knuckles. She gives me a small smile and then leaves me where I am so she can hurry inside and get Rory.

I don't want the kid to have to walk because he might not be feeling so hot, so I focus my energy on getting in the car and pulling up to the front. I wonder if the floor they do the chemo infusions on is still the fourth one, and then I hate that I have that knowledge at all.

No kid should ever have to go through cancer and the ugliness that comes along with it. It's fucked up.

The steering wheel groans under the tight grip of my fingers, but I don't dare loosen it. If I do, I'm not sure what will happen. Maybe I'll float away. Maybe I'll lose my mind. Maybe I'll let Penelope down.

Not one single scenario running through my head ends in anything good if I let go of this leather wrapped wheel.

The back door opens, and a kid hops in with more energy than I'd have thought he could have after getting treatment today. He's wearing a black beanie and a smile that's got a couple of teeth missing.

He's studying me and I'm watching him right back while Penelope climbs in the passenger seat. I'm back to near blinding panic, but then the little shit says, "So, you're the one who's been stealing all of my Penelope time."

I bark out a laugh at the balls on this kid and miraculously I start to calm down. "Yeah, I guess so. Sorry, kid."

He scoffs. "You owe me. Pen's like the only one who'll watch YouTube and play Roblox with me. Do you know how hard it is to play Jailbreak single player? All the other in-game assholes gang up on me."

I pull out of the parking lot and then cut my gaze back to Rory in the back seat in the mirror. "Sounds like you need to play a different game."

"Sounds like you need to learn how to play Roblox. I've missed like four whole hours the last couple of weeks since the only time I get to play is during treatment."

It hits me then how shitty this kid's life must be and how grateful I am for Penelope and the huge heart she has. What would this kid have right now if not for her?

"Tell you what," I say, surprising the shit out of myself by how my anxiety has melted away and how much I've warmed up to this kid in the last few minutes. "If you feel like you can eat, how about we do pizza? We can start there, and maybe you can explain to me just what the hell Roblox is."

Penelope reaches over and pries one of my hands off the wheel and grips my fingers in hers, shooting me a grateful smile. I've been avoiding anything having to do with sick kids for so long because of my grief and trauma that I figured those would always be triggers for me. But here I am with Penelope and Rory, and I think it's doing more to heal my wounds than anything ever has. A part of me that's been festering since Chased died is starting to scab over as I think about how I can help this kid.

Maybe I've been going about this all wrong and the key to fixing the jagged remains of my heart is facing what I fear most head on.

"Yes!" Rory says, pumping his fist in the air before narrowing his eyes back on me in the rearview like he's daring me to argue with what he might say next. "But only if there's pineapple on the pizza."

"Gross, dude." I fake gag.

"No way. Pineapple and pepperoni are the best toppings."

"I can't take you seriously if you're going to say things like that," I tell him and then glance over at Penelope. "What do you think, Duchess?"

"I've always liked the contrast of sweet and salty of pineapple on pizza." She shrugs and I let my head fall back against the headrest while we wait at a red light.

"Not you, too," I groan while Rory laughs his ass off in the back seat. My own lips tilt up because you can tell by looking at him this kid's been through some shit, but he's never let it dim that light he has inside.

We get to the restaurant and order a couple of pizzas, one of which has the gag-worthy pepperoni-pineapple combo Rory swears is the best. Penelope even humors him and eats a slice even if she looks like she'd rather light it on fire and throw it in the trash.

There's an arcade off the main restaurant and Rory kicks my ass at every game we try, and by the end he's walking like he's ten feet tall and talking so much shit I can't help laughing at him.

"Dude, you need to learn a little thing called humility," I say after losing to the little shit for the third time in a row. He's making a whole thing out of some victory dance he saw on Fortnite, and people are starting to stare. I flip them off because who gives a fuck if the kid looks ridiculous? He's having fun and they can fuck off, even if he looks like he's about two seconds from passing out.

"I hate to say it, but we've kept you out long enough, bud. I bet they're wondering where you are at home," Penelope tells him when we head back to the table for drinks.

A strange sinking feeling settles in my gut, and I don't know what to make of it. If you would've asked me yesterday if I thought I could spend the entire afternoon with a kid who's actively fighting cancer I would've told you to go fuck yourself for even bringing it up.

But now that I'm here... I don't really want to take him back.

Maybe it's some fucked up sort of misplacing my grief onto this kid who's a couple of years younger than Chase would've been if he was still alive, but Rory's cool as fuck and I've actually had a lot of fun with him.

"Aww, do we have to? I told Indy I'd kick his ass at pinball," Rory pouts and I can't help but snort out a laugh at his casual use of supposedly inappropriate language. I'm not about to correct him, and the kid's been through enough shit in his short life. If he wants to call me an asshole or say fuck? I'm not going to tell him he can't.

"Next time," Penelope promises. We clean up the table and load into the car. The mood has shifted from one of lightheartedness and fun to something heavier and more somber. Rory drags his feet like his body physically doesn't want to carry him out of here and away from Penelope, and maybe even me.

Something uncomfortable clenches in my chest and I don't like it one fucking bit.

When we drop the kid off at his house, I don't want to let him go inside. The place is in one of the shittiest parts of town and it's falling apart. When he gets out of the car, no one comes out to ask where he's been or who's had him this whole time.

Worst of all, the kid looks underfed, and his clothes and shoes are falling apart.

"They're not taking care of him," I say as he disappears through the front door.

"No, they're not." Penelope's voice is quiet and carries a sadness I feel down into my scarred soul.

I tear my eyes off the front of the house to look at her. "What can we do?"

"I don't think there's anything we can do except be there for him. I've got an application in to foster but it takes time to process. For now, I've tried to be the friend that's there when he needs me. The solid presence he can count on since I don't think he's ever had that before." She reaches up and swipes at a stray tear that runs down her cheek.

Her heart is so fucking *good,* and I know my next words are probably setting me up for an epic disaster, but I can't help it. "I want to be that for him, too."

Penelope stares at me as if I told her I just grew a second dick. "You do? Is that... okay?"

I want to tell her it's fine, that I can handle it, but I don't know if I can. I don't know if I can watch another kid lose this fight. If I go along for this ride that might drag what's left of my soul down to the depths of hell for an eternity of misery.

But.

I have to do this.

I *have* to.

This kid—Penelope's right. He deserves so much more than this shitty life he's been given so far, and no one else is waiting in line to give it to him.

Blowing out a breath, I nod. "I can't do nothing."

She reaches over and grabs my hand, twisting our fingers together. "If you stumble, I'll hold you up," she promises and it's sweet but also corny as fuck.

I can't help it—I laugh my ass off.

"If you tried to catch me, I think I'd crush you under my massive muscles."

She rolls her eyes but when she looks back over at me the melancholy of a minute ago is wiped away. "Massive? Hardly. If anything, you've got more of a swimmer's body."

"Fuck, no. Look at this," I tell her, flexing my biceps. Her eyes drop to check me out and I don't miss the heat in them before she blinks it away.

"Let's go on an adventure," she suggests instead, pulling out her phone. I want to tell her it'll be an adventure when she comes all over my cock, but I keep my mouth shut. "It's not going to fix anything to sit out here all night."

"I didn't know the word adventure was in your vocab, Duchess."

"Shut up and drive. That way," she says, pointing down the road. She doesn't tell me where we're going or how long it's going to take, but she's right that getting on the open road and out of the city helps my mood. If it wasn't for her, I'd have sat outside Rory's house all night looking for an excuse to go in and take him away.

There's something about the rhythm of the road rolling by under the tires that melts all my tension away. I guess I can see the appeal of Connor's love for motorcycles because add the wind whipping by and there's not a lot of places you can be except fully in the present.

The sun's already lightening the horizon by the time we pull into our destination, and I've been so lost in my thoughts and the stories Penelope's been sharing about her childhood I didn't see this coming. We pull into a parking lot and there's nobody else here.

"Have you ever been here before?" Penelope asks as she stares at me with a huge goofy grin on her face and bright eyes. She's so fucking excited, I can't help but catch the vibe, even if we should both be exhausted.

"No, never."

"Me, neither, but I've always wanted to watch the sun rise over the canyon."

We hike down to an observation platform as the first hint of the burning sun crests over the walls of the Grand Canyon and I sit on the rocky path, pulling Penelope down to sit between my legs. She rests her back against my chest, letting her head fall back while I pull her tighter against me.

"What do you think?" she whispers after the sun is fully up, as if using her full voice will break the spell.

"I think we'll be okay, Duchess."

I've never been someone who shies away from risk, and I think giving into my obsession with Penelope might be my biggest risk of all.

CHAPTER 12
PENELOPE

It took an entire day of driving and sleep to get to a place emotionally where I could handle being back in the lab. This whole place feels tainted now thanks to my uncle and the Board. They've pushed and made their feelings known about having me in charge, but that doesn't mean I'm going to stop or give up.

This is my legacy, and I will fight with everything I have in me to preserve it and to accomplish what my father set out to do.

I don't care what happens to Driscoll Tech as long as my research and this project stay with me. I was serious when I took off the night of the gala and left my uncle to clean up the mess. Let him.

He wants to push me to step down? Well, that's not suspicious at all, is it?

I've been trying to focus, to make progress on the string of algorithms I'm building, but I keep rage-tapping the screen so hard I've actually managed to crack it. Colette had to go out for another one, so while I wait, I order in for lunch using the company card.

I guess I'm just going full rebel now.

It's hard to care when the world is crumbling around me.

I'm blaming my bad mood today on having to be in this building and not on how sexually frustrated I am *or* on the fact that Indy's gone for the first time in a week. Asher's on guard duty today, and while I like the guy fine, he's not Indy. He's been my constant companion and while being codependent isn't healthy, it's us. I don't want it to change. I'm safe when I'm with Indy—safe and more alive than I've ever been.

It wasn't like he wanted to leave, but the guys staged an intervention and told him he needed to go home, get some errands done, pack a new bag. Basically tend to his life. He's spent all his time tending mine, so I guess his has taken a back seat. That's fair, even if I hate it. I don't want to share him.

It's not like I can expect him to be by my side twenty-four hours a day, seven days a week. But I crave it like chocolate when I'm PMSing. There's never been another man in my life who's occupied my thoughts like Indy does. As soon as he confessed about his son's death, it was like all the walls I'd erected around my heart came crashing down.

Think of one of those Las Vegas hotels being demolished. That's how it felt.

New tablet in hand, I try to tread more carefully this time, channeling my focus into the numbers. It's never been difficult for me to escape into them before, and I have to wonder if that's changed now because I don't actually want to escape from my entire life.

Sure, there are parts that I'd rather not experience like running this company, but even though I'm in danger and have had a death threat, things don't actually feel that bad right now. I know Indy has a lot to do with that, and the spontaneity I'm learning to embrace for the first time in my life is addictive. *He's* addictive.

Asher's sitting in the corner with his gaze darting back and forth between the windows and the door. "I don't like how exposed you are in here," he finally says after watching both for the last half hour.

"And *I* don't like holing up to stare at a screen all day without natural light."

"It's not safe."

"The property is secure and anyone on the grounds has to go through security," I remind him.

He's still scowling in the corner when his phone goes off. It's already late in the evening, so my argument about natural light doesn't really count since all I can see outside are the artificial lights that illuminate the garden. My father insisted the garden be built outside my lab so I'd have something to look at while I work.

Something to ground me and remind me of home.

"I've got to take this. I'll be right outside the door. Don't go anywhere and stay away from the goddamn windows," Asher says before rushing out and leaving me alone in the room. It's not often I don't have one of the guys with me, usually either Indy or Asher, though Sebastian does play babysitter occasionally at the house when we're locked in.

Finally, my mind engages with the numbers, and I sink into the work, letting my thought processes carry me into my project. When it happens, I tend to lose sight of what's happening around me. Whether the sun has set or risen, whether I'm hungry, whether people are speaking to me.

Or whether one of the giant windows in my lab has shattered and someone is climbing inside.

It would've been helpful to notice that last one, and it becomes clear when someone grabs my throat and tightens their hand, I should've been paying better attention. I have no idea how much time has passed since Asher left the room or why he hasn't come bursting back in.

Surely someone shattering a window as big as the one in here would've drawn his attention, but I'm here alone. The man with his fingers wrapped around my throat and the mask over his face so I can't see who he is glares down at me with empty, emotionless eyes so cold, goosebumps rise on my skin.

I can see it in his eyes.

He wants me hurt—or dead.

Hard to say which, but too bad for him I've been working on my confidence and I'm not about to let him come in here and hurt me. My pulse is frantic as I drive my elbow up into his stomach. He grunts but his hand barely loosens. I claw at his forearm, trying to dig my nails in but he's wearing long sleeves and it's tragically ineffective.

Black spots dance at the edges of my vision and I know I've probably got one last move in me, so I quickly pull up a memory of something I saw in a movie once. I relax my entire body, going completely dead weight on him. As I fall, his fingers rip away from my neck and I suck in a lungful of air, trying not to cough at how raw and sore my throat feels as the air scrapes down it.

I'm only now noticing that the lights have gone out and I don't know if it's only in this room or the entire floor. Where the hell is Asher? I open my mouth to scream for him, but no sound comes out. The man looms over me, kicking me once in the stomach and knocking the air out of me all over again. My lungs are useless, completely empty of oxygen and I think I might actually die here.

A flash of the devastation on Indy's face as he loses me, too, pushes forward and I kick back using the last of my energy to fight like hell.

His hand wraps around my hair, twisting the strands around his fist as he yanks me up, and I make a choked sound at the fiery burn of my scalp.

"Word of advice?" he says and it's so casual, like he's out for a walk and greeting a neighbor. "Stop fighting and it'll go faster."

I want to tell him to go to hell. That he's got the wrong girl if he thinks I'm going to just let him take me or kill me.

But I can't.

Fear coats my body like toxic sludge and instead of listening to his deranged logic, I redouble my efforts, even as tears leak down my cheeks from the pain. The hand not wrapped in my hair comes slamming down across my face and I think something cracks, but I can't know for sure.

Blood pours out of a cut either on my cheek or forehead, I can't tell which. That doesn't stop me from kicking and clawing and thrashing around. I'll never stop fighting, not until my very last breath.

Kids like Rory? They need what I'm working on as much as their next precious moment of life. I will *never* give up the fight. Not until it's out in the world and giving them the cure they deserve. Indy flashes before my mind and he's managed to worm his way into my heart enough that I don't want to give up for him, either.

He's already lost the most important person to him once. I know I'm not the same, but I don't want to be another person he's lost. I won't do it.

This asshole? He's not going to take my life from me. Not today.

As I'm thrashing around, I see a glint of something metal only for a second, but it's enough to send a fresh wave of terror coursing through me. Now's probably the time I should start begging for my life, but something tells me he's not going to care what I have to say.

"Who the hell are you?" I ask instead, feeling like I'm able to form words for the first time in forever. They sound like I've smoked ten packs a day for the last fifty years.

"The last face you'll ever see," he says, and the tip of his knife presses into my side. I never stop moving, thrashing around but I can only see out of one eye because the other is swollen partway shut and coated in blood.

As he pushes the knife into my torso, I shift again and I don't know if he hit anything vital or not, but something warm and sticky soaks into the fabric of my skirt before it starts to run down my leg. He pulls the knife back out and looks as if he's ready to stab me again, but with a last rush of adrenaline, I lift my knee and ram it into his balls as hard as I possibly can.

He falls, and I fall right beside him.

My head spins and my heart is beating both hard and slow at the same time as I try and press my hand to the wound in my side. Warmth pumps out through my fingers with every slowing beat of my heart. I blink once, then again, only I think I might've lost consciousness.

I'm not deluded enough to think I managed to take down my

killer, but maybe he'll give me the mercy of letting me bleed out on the floor so I can spend my last moments in my head with the people I love most.

An incessant tugging on my hand pulls me from a blissful unconsciousness. I want to go back, back to the blackness where nothing hurts and there's no awareness of the real world where it's harsh and unforgiving.

The bright overhead lights make me blink a few times when I peel my eyes open, and when I look down at my hand, I find a nurse adjusting an IV. I close my eyes against a sudden bout of vertigo, and when I open them, I'm looking straight into Indy's cataclysmic gray gaze.

"Jesus, Duchess. Do you have any idea how much you scared me?" He looks haunted with dark circles under his eyes, wrinkled clothes, and his skin is an unhealthy pale color like he hasn't seen the sun in too long. His curly hair is unruly like he's been running his fingers through it for days.

"Sorry," I mumble, and it's like I've poured hot coals down my throat.

The nurse shoots Indy a disapproving glare when he gets on the bed beside me and gently slides his arm over my shoulders, pulling me into his side. I do my best to snuggle into him even though my entire body feels like it's been dragged a couple of miles behind a car.

"If you don't like it, you can get the fuck out," he snaps at her, and I let out a small gasp. His gives no fucks attitude really shouldn't be as hot as it is, but the violence in his voice induces a shiver down my spine.

She looks like she wants to destroy him with her eyes, but she tells me she's going to find the doctor now that I'm awake and disappears from the room.

"Water?" I manage to get out and he reaches over and passes me a cup. After I've had a couple of sips, I feel like maybe I can speak.

"What happened?"

Indy's jaw clenches and he radiates anger but when I shift against him, he takes a breath and brushes his fingers through my hair being extra gentle with my abused scalp. "It was a fucking ambush. Ash got a call from someone saying his father had been arrested, which if you knew anything about his family, would be a huge fucking deal."

"Wouldn't that be a big deal for anyone's family?" I ask, whispering the words because it's easier that way.

"Good point, but for his family it would mean some serious shit had gone down that he'd have to step in and handle." He looks thoughtful for a second and then shakes it off. "Anyway, the second he stepped into the hall three guys were on him. Asher's a badass at basically a John Wick level, so he handled it, but it took him longer than it should've, and we still don't know how they got past security."

"Should I know who John Wick is?"

"He's got all these action movies. If you're going to be laid up recovering, we can watch them."

I try to shake my head, but it hurts, and I wince. "Ouch."

The only way to describe the look in Indy's eyes is murderous. I wonder what happened to the man who attacked me.

"What happened to the guy who did this?" I ask, gesturing with my somewhat less sore arm to the rest of me.

"Asher's handling it."

"Do I want to know what that means?"

Indy's body is tense against mine. "No, I don't think you do."

"So, Asher found me and called an ambulance or something?"

"Or something. The point is, you're here, the guy missed your kidney by less than an inch but other than blood loss there shouldn't be any permanent damage. The same can't be said for him."

The fingers on his hand curl into a tight fist, the knuckles whitening. He wishes he could punish the man who did this to me. It's written all over his face.

"What do we do now?" I ask, letting my head fall onto his shoulder and working my fingers between his to get him to relax. One by one, I manage to pry them apart and thread them together with mine.

"I never should've listened to Asher and Sebastian. If I'd been there, this wouldn't have happened. I'm not taking any more time off, even if it's only a couple of hours, until we can be sure it won't put you in danger."

"Do you think as long as I'm running Driscoll Tech there will ever be a time I'm actually safe?" I've been tossing this question around in my head for a while now. Having such a high stakes job and being the face of a multi-billion dollar company on the edge of developing world-changing technology is a much riskier lifestyle than I ever considered it would be.

"I don't think life works that way. You could have the safest job in the world and run into the wrong person at the wrong time and end up in a bad situation. It's more about doing whatever you have to do to mitigate the risk. To make sure you're accounting for things that could happen and planning for them. That's why you have us."

His words aren't really reassuring in the way I think he intends and a profound exhaustion seeps into every muscle and bone in my body. "It's not like I can pay you to stay with me like this forever, though. Other people need you, too."

He stiffens as his eyes darken. "I'm not only here because it's my job, Duchess. Not anymore."

Indy closes the distance between us with a kiss so world-tilting, I'm dizzy when it's over. "Now rest while I convince the doctor to let you out of this nightmare factory."

I close my eyes and let the knowledge Indy's watching over me lull me to sleep.

"What's it gonna be, Duchess? *She's All That*? *Varsity Blues*? Oh!" Indy claps his hands together shooting me a way too excited grin. "*Clueless*?"

"Should I know what any of those are?"

His mouth falls open. "How the fuck have you never heard of the greatest teen nineties movies ever made?"

"How are you this badass bodyguard but sing along to Backstreet Boys and Britney Spears and love teen angst rom coms?" I counter, grabbing my fluffiest blanket and dragging it back with me towards the headboard.

The glare Indy levels me with is filled with savagery and I shiver, hoping despite the bruises littering my body he might make good on the unspoken promise.

"*She's All That* it is," he says, clicking the buttons on the remote until the intro starts to play. He grabs the bowl of popcorn he made earlier and sets it on the nightstand, crawling in bed with me before tugging the blanket over both of our legs.

I'm pressed right up against him, and it's hard to focus on the movie when every nerve ending under my skin is hyper-fixated on the places we're touching. It's distracting and the story becomes impossible to follow. By the time Laney is getting a makeover, my heart is racing, my nipples have been rubbing against the soft material of my t-shirt for over an hour, and there's a tingle between my legs that demands attention.

Oh, and Indy. Freaking Indy knows exactly what he's doing because he's only making it worse. His fingers have been tracing circles into my bare thigh right below my sleep shorts for at least a half an hour, drifting closer and closer to where I'm dying for him to touch me before dodging away at the last second.

I'm ready to scream in frustration, to grab his hand and force him to relieve the buzzing need under my skin, but if I do that, he'll know exactly how wound up I am. Everything is a battle of wills with this man, and while I may not have realized it before, I enjoy the game.

Sparring with him is fun and distracting in the best way, and so I can never make it easy.

It's not in my nature to let him have his way.

By the time the credits roll, I'm contemplating reaching into my nightstand drawer and digging out the toy I keep there, showing Indy exactly what he's missing out on by not giving me what I'm desperate to have.

I've made the decision, turning to reach for the drawer feeling like I'm going to explode, when Indy's arm comes around my waist and he tugs me back against his firm body. He's hard as he presses against me, and I have to bite my tongue so I don't moan.

"Where are you going, Duchess?"

I nearly scream, crazy out of my mind with lust and practically writhing against him. My skin is so sensitive, and I want him to touch me everywhere all at once.

"Since you're not giving me what I want, I figured I'd take it for myself," I tell him, glaring pure defiance at him that he laughs at before leaning over and pulling my lip between his teeth.

"That's not how this works," he murmurs, his lips dropping against my neck so I can feel the words against my skin. "Take off your shorts."

"Make me." I don't know why I'm fighting him, but it might have something to do with how frustrated I am. It's a culmination of all the other times where Indy has kissed the hell out of me, gotten me close to the edge and then left me hanging. I *really* need the release of coming all over him.

I don't even care which part he uses at this point—tongue, dick, fingers.

As long as it's attached to his body and inside mine, it's going to be catastrophic.

At my resistance, his eyes flash and I know he likes the fight just as much as I do. His strong fingers wrap around my wrists, bringing them up together over my head. His face is close to mine, our noses almost touching while he stares down at me with a feral look in his eyes. One I want him to unleash on me.

"Remember you asked for this," he says, using his free hand to dig in his pocket. He pulls out a knife, flicks it open, and uses it to slice down the sides of my shorts and panties. He tosses the knife aside and then rips the ruined fabric from my body, leaving my lower half totally bare.

"Since you decided to defy me, I'm not going to let you come until you beg," he says, letting go of my hands while he moves down my body.

He stares down at my exposed pussy like it's the holy freaking grail, eyes half-lidded while he drags his tongue along his lower lip. It's like he's imagining what I'm going to taste like before he dives in, and I've never seen anything sexier.

"Why would I beg when I can just get myself off?" I ask, running my fingers down my body but the second I make contact with my clit, he's smacking my hand away.

Then he slaps my pussy, growling, "Don't touch what's mine."

I'm so wet, I've got to be dripping onto the sheets underneath me, but that slap? Hottest thing that's ever happened to me. My back bows off the bed as his fingers spear into my core. It's not gentle, not like I thought it might be because of my injuries.

But Indy isn't treating me like I'm breakable or delicate. He's taking everything he's been waiting for and yanking me along for the ride. When he licks me, he's everywhere, devouring everything. His tongue drags across where his fingers are moving inside me and up to my clit, lapping and circling and lightly scraping his teeth across it.

I cry out his name, punching my fingers into his hair and twisting the strands into my grip so I can pull him closer and hold him tighter. I'm barreling towards the abyss, towards a release that's been weeks in the making and one I don't know if I'll be able to withstand.

There's a good chance what Indy Foster is doing to me right now will destroy me.

What a way to go, though, right?

I'm so close, my insides tighten around his fingers when he pulls back. He gives me a manic smile, his lips glistening with my wetness. It coats the entire lower half of his face like a savage.

I growl in frustration because I know what he wants.

"Beg."

My glare could turn sand to glass. "No."

He grips my hips in his big hands, holding me down against the bed and stroking his tongue across my entire pussy one time before looking up at me from between my legs. "Beg me."

"Never." My heart is practically jumping out of my chest it's beating so hard and every time it does, my clit echoes the pulse with a throb of its own.

His grip tightens and he flips me over pulling me up so I'm on all fours. "If you want to come, Duchess, you're going to have to do a better job of convincing me I should let you."

Shit, my resolve is wavering because I really, *really* want him to get me off. In fact, I don't think there's anything I want more.

"Not happening," I say from between clenched teeth as his fingers stroke along my opening but don't quite push inside. It's maddening.

I jolt forward as his palm comes down across my ass in a hard slap, one he immediately soothes by stroking my clit with his long fingers. I can't help the moan that slips from between my lips as everything clenches in response. I'm *right* there on the edge and he knows exactly how to keep me on the wrong side.

"All you have to do is ask me to let you come."

Thinking maybe he can't see me, I balance my weight on one arm and sneak my fingers down between my legs finding the little nub and giving it a solid rub before he notices and smacks my hand away again with wet fingers.

Three hard slaps sting across my ass as he punishes me for defying him. "My Duchess wants to be a bad girl tonight, hmm?" Indy says, pressing his denim-covered bulge right up against me. I could cry for how good it feels having him pinning himself against me like this and if he would only move a little, maybe unzip his jeans and push inside me...

I'm definitely going to give in. I know it like I know my own name.

"Please," I whisper, hating that I'm going to lose this battle, but knowing that the pleasure will be worth it.

"Please what?" Indy asks, stroking his fingers along my clit lazily before pushing them back inside me.

"Please make me come," I cry out, my muscles trembling from the prolonged torture. The skin of my ass is sensitive and the brush of rough denim against it has me pressing back against him wanting more. The fight has completely gone out of me and now I'm a mess of unfulfilled desire and weeks-old lust ready to hurtle me into a whole other reality.

"Hold on to something, Duchess," he demands, and I feel the bed shift behind me. The sheets are bunched in my fist and when I look down between my legs, he's turned onto his back and slipped his head between them.

His firm hands grip my hips and pull me down onto his face where his tongue is like a tornado, sucking and swirling in a vortex of pleasure. It takes next to nothing before I'm clenching around the fingers he's got inside me and screaming his name. Tears run down my face from the intensity of it all and my arms collapse, unable to hold my weight while the pleasure thrashes around inside my body.

He never stops the assault on my clit, sucking and flicking his tongue against it until I'm shuddering and trying to crawl away from him because it's so intense. When he's ready, he finally pulls his fingers out of me and slides out from underneath me, licking the digits clean.

"Fuck. You're my new favorite flavor," he tells me, looking smug as hell with half-lidded eyes and a messy face.

I'm worn out and relaxed, basking in the afterglow of the best orgasm I've had in my entire life—and there haven't been many—but

I want to experience everything with Indy. I want not just his fingers and tongue inside me, but his dick, too.

I've felt it pressed against me and I know I'm going to like what's inside those jeans of his. I don't think it'll take much convincing if the prominent bulge at the front of his jeans is anything to go by. I can't stop staring.

When the trembling in my limbs has subsided a bit, I start to crawl forward towards him, wanting to curl my fingers around his length, see what he tastes like, feel him moving inside my body.

But when I get close, he wraps his fingers around my upper arms and drops a soft kiss to my lips before pulling away. This isn't the first time he's put space between us like this, and a shock of insecurity jolts through me.

I find myself blindly grabbing the sheet and tugging it to cover up, suddenly needing the protection. Indy runs his hand through the mess of curls on top of his head and blows out a breath, eyeing me warily.

"Why don't you want me?" I ask him, hating how my voice cracks and shakes.

He moves closer so his knees are touching mine and wraps his hands around the sides of my neck, his thumbs stroking either side of my jaw while he tilts my head up so I have no choice but to look at him.

Like this I can't hide any part of myself, and I hate him a little bit for it.

"Why the fuck would you ever think I don't want you, Duchess?"

"Maybe you've forgotten Montana is my friend. I've heard about your manwhore ways, Indy Foster. But you won't go there with me. I must not meet your suddenly impossible standards." I try to look away as tears threaten to fall but he won't let me.

His thumbs stop their gentle movements, and he rests his forehead against mine with a sigh that I breathe down deep into my lungs. Maybe if I get the air from his lungs deep enough into mine, I'll be able to keep him.

"You've got it all wrong. You're different."

"Right, which is why you don't want to sleep with me."

He groans. "Fuck, you're infuriating."

"Right back at you."

"Yes, it's true that I used to hook up—"

"A lot," I add.

"A lot." He lifts his head from mine so he can stare into my eyes again, stormy gray clashing with muddy brown. "But that's not you."

I open my mouth to tell him that *could* be me. I could be the kind of girl that opens her legs for Indy, has some fun, and then moves on. I know even as I think it that it's a lie. Especially when the thought of letting him inside my body and then having him walk away like it means nothing would kill me. I think I'd have to crawl into a hole in the forest and die from the ruin of the last part of me that survived the loss of my parents. I can hardly stand it when he leaves the room, and I haven't even had all of him yet. What would the agony be like if he slept with me and walked away?

"No, it's not." Decision made, and proud of myself for being honest, I try again to shift away from him, readying myself for his rejection.

"Good." I blink up at him sure I've heard him wrong. "Can't you tell you're more than that to me? Haven't I been obvious as fuck about my feelings for you? Even when I'm giving you shit and picking on you, it's only because you make me fucking crazy. I'm obsessed with you, Penelope. Absolutely fucking wrecked. If I fuck you now, you might think all you are to me is another hookup. But you're not, and I'm going to prove it to both of us."

"By *not* sleeping with me?" My head is spinning with his idiotic but sweet logic. It makes a certain kind of Indy sense, I guess.

The massive boulder that'd settled in my stomach shatters into shards now that I understand why he keeps stopping things between us.

"So, you want me." I need to clarify.

"More than I want the air in my lungs."

"But you're not going to sleep with me."

"When we fuck, it'll be because you know you're more than one night for me. When we fuck, it'll be because we're endless. Ride or die." He leans forward, pressing a gentle kiss to my lips. "Make me earn the privilege, Duchess."

My heart skips at the look in his eye and I don't know if there's any saving me from my fate.

CHAPTER 13
INDY

Ronin slaps me on the back a little too hard, the dick, but he looks good. With the two of us on different cases and his twins being born, we haven't had a lot of time to hang out lately. He's got dark circles under his eyes that I remember like they were yesterday—the telltale mark of how fucked your sleep schedule is when you've got a baby—or in his case *babies*—at home.

"You sure you've got this? I can cancel," I tell him. My stomach is practically revolting at the idea of leaving Penelope here while I go out. I promised myself I wouldn't leave her side until I know she's safe, but here I am breaking the fucking thing at the first chance.

I can't seem to help myself, though. The other day when I spent the afternoon with Rory and Penelope, something fractured inside of me started to heal. I haven't been able to stop thinking about that day or the kid. The same obsessive need to protect Penelope now includes the kid and I've been climbing out of my skin to get eyes on him and make sure he's okay.

I don't know whether it's the fact that he reminds me of how I imagined Chase would be at his age or if it's something else completely unrelated. Maybe the haunted look in his eye like he's seen way too much shit for a kid his age.

Whatever it is, he's somehow managed to burrow down inside my brain and I can't ignore this compulsion to erase as much of that look as I can.

I'd trade almost anything to give him his childhood back, at least the parts that I can. Cancer has already stolen so much from him; his family most of the rest. Seeing how resilient he is, how much life he still has in him pushes me to be better. I can't ignore it. I have to act, but despite all these feelings swarming around like angry bees, I'm not ready to tell Penelope yet.

What if I can't do it and I let the kid down? The look of disappointment I know will be in her eyes isn't something I can take on top of my self-hate and guilt. For now, the pull I've got towards the kid is going to stay between him and me. If I can't handle being around him and getting attached, I'll set up cams and watch him from afar.

Ronin stares hard at me. "You don't think I can handle guarding the princess in her tower for a couple of hours?"

"I don't know. I seem to remember your wife's stalker getting a little too fucking close on more than one occasion."

A shadow passes over his eyes as they narrow. "And what happened to him in the end?"

"He got what he deserved, but maybe this time let's not have the close calls with my Duch—" I swallow hard and shift my gaze to the floor. "With Penelope."

All animosity shucks off of him and Ronin grins this stupid fucking knowing smile at me that I don't like one goddamn bit. "Sure, boss. I won't let her out of my sight."

Ronin's giving me shit, but I can take it. If it was Asher standing here saying the same thing, I might have a problem, but I happen to know Ronin is straight up hooked on his wife like a junkie. When we were guarding Red months ago, I could never have imagined understanding where he was coming from with that shit. No fucking thank you.

Now, things are different, and Penelope has peeled back the layers of my existence and settled herself right down inside me so deep I don't think I'll ever be able to carve her completely out. The way Ronin's watching me right now? He knows just how fucked up over her I really am, even if I'm not ready to deal with it.

I don't like it. Not one damn bit.

"Yes, shit with my wife may have gotten out of hand," he finally says, crossing his arms. "But nothing's going to happen to Penelope. We've learned from our mistakes. She'll be fine holed away in her office for an afternoon. I think Asher, Sebastian, and I can handle it."

My jaw clenches at his sarcasm, but he's right. I'm being overbearing and I know it, but I can't seem to stop. I don't *want* to stop. When it comes to protecting Penelope, nothing is off limits. There is no line I wouldn't cross to keep her safe.

I hold up my hands. "Fine, I'm trusting you but if anything happens while I'm gone, I'll rip your spine from your body and use it to beat Asher and Sebastian into matching bloody piles."

He huffs out a laugh that only pisses me off more. "Get the fuck out of here before I go tell Penelope what you're up to today."

I turn to leave and throw both my middle fingers up at him as I walk away but his voice stops me in my tracks. "Oh, Elias wanted me to tell you he got the medical records. He'll have an answer for you later today."

My shoulders tense but I nod once and keep walking, trying not to let the crushing anxiety overwhelm me over what he might find. I called in a favor to Elias, our team's resident doctor, to have him look over Rory's medical records. Even though it's too late, I want to know what I'm setting myself up for by getting involved with this kid. There's no way I can go in blind.

Not this time.

If there's more heartbreak in my future, I want to be prepared.

With a deep breath that inflates my lungs and drags out my courage, I push my worry over shit I can't change out of my head. Before I'm out the door, I've forgotten about everything except what I'm about to do. Well, that and Penelope. She never leaves my head, like a beautiful song I can't stop singing. Rory has had a shit life so far, and if I can make even a day of it better for him, I'm going to.

Even if my stomach is doing backflips.

Even if my skin is cold and clammy.

Even if my heart wants to dive down inside my gut and pretend I'm not setting myself up for more fucking devastation.

Shit, I must be a masochist.

I can't help it. The kid calls to me on some primal level that's impossible to ignore—sort of the same way Penelope does. It's unexplainable, but then feelings usually are. I'm not even going to attempt it. For some reason, I think he's supposed to be mine.

But not before one last check on my Duchess. I pull my phone out and watch her in her office for a few minutes, hating the distance between us already. I'm so fucking gone for this girl.

The drive to his house takes far too fucking long, and I'm a whole ball of nerves when I climb out of the car. The walk down the broken sidewalk that leads to a front door that's seen better days seems endless and not long enough.

My jaw tightens but I try to keep my irritation in check. The last thing the kid needs to see on a day that's supposed to be a break from the hard shit is me going homicidal on his foster parents. That shit is next to impossible to contain, though. Especially when I lift my hand to knock and the door flies open before I can make contact, and there he is—Rory looking like something out of the first Harry Potter movie.

The kid's clothes are a couple of sizes too big and should've been thrown out two owners ago. They're stained and I see no less than five holes. But what stops me from barging into the house and demanding answers for why these assholes aren't doing even the basic level of taking care of him is the bright look in his eyes when they land on me.

"Indy!" he shrieks and throws himself against me. He's small for his age but his enthusiasm has me backing up a step from the momentum. Rory's small arms wrap around my waist, and he squeezes tight and I just fucking melt. I'm a goner and I don't think I ever had a hope of being anything else.

He's just so full of life and so *pure*. He and Penelope are the same in that way—the light in their eyes matches. The darkness in me craves it. Maybe that's why I'm so attracted to Penelope, and why the attachment to the kid has already sunk its claws into me and twisted. The only way I'll be able to get him out now is to rip out pieces of myself in the process.

No one comes to find out what's going on or who's at the door, and as much as it pisses me off that Rory's foster parents care so little anyone could walk off with him, right now I'm ecstatic. If they showed their faces, I'd have to demonstrate exactly what I think of their failures as parents to this sick little boy, and I don't know if I'd be able to hold back even knowing he's standing right here.

"Hey, bud. Want to get out of here?"

"Yeah, dude. This place sucks," he says, letting me go long enough to bump his fist against mine like he suddenly realized he was too cool for the hug he gave me. As soon as his feet hit the ground, he tears out the door yelling, "Where are we going?" behind him as he runs to my car.

"You like baseball?"

He spins and levels me with these huge eyes that are practically glittering with his excitement. "Hell, yes!"

Rory's little body vibrates, and I can't help but laugh at his enthusiasm even when he's trying hard to act like he doesn't care. It's contagious and when I open the back door for him, he climbs inside and right into the booster seat I grabbed for him yesterday. It's like nothing phases him and he reaches for the seat belt as I close the door and get into the driver's seat.

My chest loosens knowing I've got him and he's safe even as thoughts of Penelope consume my attention and threaten to steal my momentary peace. The compulsion to pull out my phone is nearly crippling, and I feel like I'm being torn in two. But Rory chattering about where we're going pulls me back from my destructive thoughts.

There's a bag on the passenger seat with a baseball hat in it and I toss it back to him. It matches the one I'm wearing and when he sees it, he lights up like this is the best day of his life. For all I know, it might just be, and knowing I put that expression on his face is like filling in the cracks of my heart with molten gold.

Rory goes on and on about some new YouTuber one of the kids at school showed him and how he wishes he could watch them at home. The kid actually looks forward to his treatment time because of the iPad the hospital lets him use while he's there. It's a fucking gut punch how little this kid actually has and how he looks at life like it's a gift. How he's just happy to exist and every tiny scrap thrown his way is like a full buffet.

It turns me murderous, knowing a soul as innocent as his keeps getting dealt the shittiest hands. But now he's got me, and shit is going to change.

We hit traffic on the way, and I introduce Rory to some of my favorite songs, belting out the lyrics while he scrunches his nose.

"This music is garbage," he yells over an Nsync song. A wide grin splits across my face. He just needs to learn to have better taste in music. I glance in the rearview mirror and notice Rory's replaced his beanie with the baseball hat I bought him. Warmth radiates out across my chest and for the first time in years, I realize I'm relaxed. As relaxed as I can be while I don't have eyes on my Duchess.

I'm not worrying about work shit, or my horror show of a past. I'm in the moment, enjoying taking a kid to a game. Something I would've done with my own son had he lived long enough to do it. The usual jagged stab of pain that accompanies thoughts of what might've been with Chase is duller somehow here with Rory like he's a magician who can cure me as much as I wish I could cure him.

When we pull into the parking lot and I help him out of the car, he grabs my hand and drags me up to the wide gates of Dodger Stadium with its bright blue signs everywhere. His earlier cool facade has melted away in the face of this experience. The scent of popcorn and fried meat hangs in the air and my stomach growls.

"You hungry, kid?" I ask, knowing full well I'm about to load Rory up with as much junk food as his tiny body can handle. Anything he wants today is his. There's no way I can deny him when he flashes me that dimpled grin missing a couple of teeth. If Penelope had any idea what I'm up to, she'd give me so much shit for being a total sucker for this kid.

I'm struck with a bolt of longing so fucking intense, I have to suck in a breath and rub at my chest. As much fun as I'm having, I want Penelope here with me—with us. She never lets her hair down and just has fun. Maybe I should have kidnapped her for the day, too. It'd beat trying to ignore the urge to spend the afternoon staring at her on my phone.

Rory distracts me from my impulse when he bounces from one foot to the other and yanks my hand down with both of his, so I'm forced to bend forward. "I'm so hungry, my stomach is eating itself."

His eyes are darting around at all the concessions inside, wide and untamed, and I almost suspect he drank a couple cups of coffee before I picked him up, he's so hyped up. I laugh at his dramatic bullshit. "Then let's get some food, bud. What sounds good?" I ask, letting him tug me over to the line for giant hot dogs, pretzels, and popcorn.

My arms are loaded down when we find our seats, and the excited grin and wonder never leave Rory's face the entire game. We're both stuffed and maybe a little sick by the time the game ends, and I know I've pushed the limits of his energy because he's got shadows underneath his eyes that weren't there this morning.

His tiny body is maxed out and as much as I wish I could bring him home with me and watch over him while he sleeps, I'm not a kidnapper so I have to take him back to his foster family. A pang of sadness hits me that I didn't expect. It's like the loss of Chase is right there under the surface all over again, and maybe it's fucked up for me to use Rory as a way to deal with my loss but being around him is the first thing in years that's kept the pain at bay.

"That was *so* much fun, dude! Can we go again next weekend?" Rory asks in a sleepy voice as he slides down off my back and the piggyback ride I'd used as an excuse to carry him out of the stadium when he insisted he could walk. He looked dead on his feet, so instead of arguing, I tried to make it fun, and it worked like a charm.

Outsmarting an eight-year-old is suddenly my greatest accomplishment of the day and I wish I could go home and tell Penelope about all of this.

I don't know how she'll take it, though. Me messing with this kid, getting involved when I don't know if I can stick around to see it through. Even as I think the words in my head, I know there's no way I'm going to be able to walk away now. I'm drawn to Rory like he's meant to be mine, the same way I'm pulled toward the brunette beauty who's set up residence in the hollow center of my chest like no one else ever has.

"I don't know, bud. We'll have to see how you're feeling, but if not next weekend, then for sure soon, okay?"

"Okay," he agrees while rubbing his eyes. This time I strap him into his booster as his head lolls to the side. He's out before we even hit the freeway, and I keep the radio to a low murmur so it doesn't wake him up. The drive gives me time to think, to process. All day I've been trying to ignore my phone, both desperately wanting and not wanting to know what Elias might've found in Rory's medical records. Not to mention check in with Penelope on the cameras. Watching her is my addiction.

The kid has to be on some sort of government healthcare, right? What if he's not getting all the treatment he needs? What if his prognosis is grim? What the fuck will I do then? The pounding of my heart is hurried and uncomfortable while a cold sweat breaks out across my forehead. The steering wheel protests under my white-knuckled grip as my thoughts spin out with all the scenarios I never let myself think about before attaching myself to this kid.

I could walk away now and survive it. I know I could. But could he? Even if he survives childhood cancer, his lot in life has been shit so far. He's in the foster system and I don't know anything about his past or how that came to be. With the way his foster parents don't seem to give a single shit about him or what he's going through, I'm going to say there's only a small window left before life completely sucks the innocence out of him and spits out someone hardened and jaded. Someone who could've done great things if they'd only been shown love and stability.

The car rolls to a stop outside the small, rundown house and I glare at it through the windshield wishing it'd burst into flames so I'd have an excuse to just keep driving and never bring Rory back to this place. Unfortunately, it doesn't happen, so I throw the door open like it's personally offended me and stomp around to the other side of the car.

A few deep breaths help me gain some much-needed calm before I grip the handle and open the back door. Outside of his eyelashes fluttering against his pale cheeks, Rory doesn't move a muscle as I reach over and unbuckle the seat belt.

"Hey, bud. You're home," I murmur as I lift him up and haul him out of the car. His small arms come up around my neck as he clings to me even in sleep and my heart seizes like it's being shocked. I'm in so much fucking trouble, but I don't know how to save either him or myself. How could I possibly step back knowing what Rory's going through? He needs me as much as I need him.

I carry him up to the front door and knock, but no one answers. Someone's yelling inside, a woman, I think, but they don't bother worrying about me standing out here with this little boy they're supposed to be responsible for. They don't know me, and yet I was able to come take him for the day without coming face to face with anyone inside. It's fucked up and the rage starts to ignite in my veins.

So many alarm bells are going off inside my head, it's ridiculous. My whole identity centers around protecting people and everything in me is screaming to turn around with Rory and walk back to the car and take off. Too bad I'm not looking to get charged with kidnapping right now because it's tempting as fuck.

I lift my hand and rap my knuckles against the door harder this time, hoping it'll be heard over the yelling. Rory flinches in my arms with the noise but he doesn't wake up. Finally, the door is flung open and a hugely overweight woman with a cigarette dangling from her lips and holes in her shirt that I imagine are burns from said cigarette stands in the doorway shooting me a dirty look.

"What?" she barks before her gaze darts down to the sleeping boy in my arms. The precious boy I can't believe I have to hand over to her.

"Hi, ma'am." I grit my fucking teeth against all the things I really want to say. "I'm just dropping Rory off but he's asleep." I want to lay down the law, fight, yell, blackmail, maim. Whatever I have to do to make sure this bitch takes care of Rory the way he deserves. "If you get out of my way, I'll put him down in his bed."

Admittedly, I'm dying to see what kind of horrors are in this house. Not that I won't come back and break in to set up cameras. Because I will, the first chance I get.

She scoffs and flicks the long ash from the tip of her cigarette onto the floor. Her hand comes out and flicks Rory on the arm before I can shift him out of striking range and he jerks awake, blinking sleepily in her direction.

"I'm not going nowhere, and it's about damn time. We've been waiting for dinner. Get your ass in there and make something," she snaps at the little boy in my arms—the *sick* little boy who's fighting for his fucking life—and his eyes widen while he starts wiggling in my arms so I'll put him down. Instead, I tighten my hold.

"You can't be serious," I say through clenched teeth as pain shoots through my jaw from the force. "You're going to make an eight-year-old cook your dinner? Knowing he's sick and exhausted?"

She takes a drag of her cigarette and at first, I think she's not going to answer. I'm starting to reconsider my earlier stance on whether or not I'd be willing to go down for kidnapping charges. "No one stays here for free. He does his part, or he's gone."

"It's not fucking free when you're cashing a check every month to take care of him," I snap right back. Who the fuck treats kids like this?

"Let him down or I'll call the cops," she threatens, clearly over my challenging her parenting skills. Not that she has any.

"It's okay, Indy," Rory says in this quiet, resigned voice and something inside me dies. He's reassuring *me* right now, and I can't deal with it. I'm an absolute asshole. I fucking hate this life for him, but my hands are tied. As much as I don't think I can do anything for him right now, I *know* I can't do shit if I'm rotting away in a jail cell. I'll be back with cameras, though. Make no fucking mistake. I'm not about to let this shit go unpunished.

Rory trudges inside and as he walks under this beast of a woman, she flicks her cigarette, and the ashes fall onto his baseball hat and his t-shirt. His shoulders stiffen and she glares down at him. "Hurry up, boy, or I'll find another use for you that you're not gonna like." She's got a sadistic look in her eye as he takes off deeper into the house, so far I can't see him anymore.

Done with me, she tries to shut the door in my face, but I wedge my shoe into the door frame. The way she looked at Rory as he walked into that house has every single hair on the back of my neck standing on end and I may not be able to walk out of here tonight with the kid, but no way in hell am I about to stand for whatever torture she thinks she can subject him to.

"We need to get something straight," I say as I scowl at her. I try to make myself as menacing as I possibly can, using my height and muscles to my advantage as I loom over her. "If I find out you've harmed one single hair on that boy's head, I'll become your worst nightmare. I won't stop until I repay every hurt, every harsh word, every scar or wound you've ever inflicted on him with fucking interest. And then, when that's finished, I'll destroy everything you care about. I don't care what it takes, your life won't be worth living when I'm done."

She laughs, and it's this wet thing that turns into a hacking cough, as if she doesn't believe me, so I take a threatening step forward and let the darkness inside me rise to the surface and shine out through my eyes. Maybe she'll get a glimpse of what I'm truly capable of. I think it works because the half-burned cigarette between her fingers falls out of her shaky hand and hits the carpet and the amusement from a minute ago disappears.

The blotchy skin on her face has paled and her mouth opens and closes a few times as if she wants to say shit back to me, but nothing comes out.

After I've waited a couple of minutes with nothing but silence between us, I straighten from where I was towering over her. "Glad we understand each other."

Finally, she seems to get her voice back. "You can't come in here and just take him. I could call the cops right now and force you off my property."

"You could," I agree with a cold and twisted smile. "But if you do, I promise you'll regret it."

I step back to the end of the porch, the old wooden planks under my feet groaning under my weight. "Your time of treating that kid like shit is up, so get used to seeing my face."

She manages to get her fear under control and levels me with a glare as she slams the door closed. Her voice echoes around the small front yard as she yells at someone inside like she didn't just hear my threats. I have a feeling I'll have to show her I'm serious. You can get away with threatening some people—the truly cowardly ones—with words alone, but then there are those like Rory's foster mom.

She's been around the block and seen some shit. It's going to take more than poison-laced words to get her to fall in line, but I don't mind. In fact, as I slide behind the wheel of my car, the desolation of having to leave the kid here to suffer whatever fate that bitch has in store for him fades and it's replaced with a vicious determination to show her I'm not to be fucked with.

When I threaten someone, I mean every fucking word. She's about to find out what that looks like.

As I'm merging onto the freeway, I dial Sebastian. "Sebastian," he says when he answers, and I can't help myself.

"Dude, how many times do I have to tell you your name isn't a greeting? You sound like a douche when you answer that way."

He sighs, sounding more tired than I think I've ever heard him. I just sort of assume at this point that he's a robot since he never seems to need sleep. "What do you need, Indy?"

"Are you okay?" I may not be close to the guy, but we're a team and I take that shit seriously.

"I'm fine," he huffs. "What do you need?"

I decide to let whatever's bothering him go for now. For all I know, he's just tired from digging through an entire corporations' worth of computer and business bullshit. If that's the case, I almost hate to ask this of him, but I can't sit back and do nothing while that woman treats Rory the way she does.

"I need you to do me a personal favor. I'll owe you."

He pauses before speaking slowly, as if considering whether he wants anything from me in return. "Yes… you will. What is it?"

"There's this kid, Rory Hamilton. I need you to find out who his foster mom is and dig into her life. I want to know where she spends her time and her money. Anything you can dig up on her, any family she has, any weaknesses to exploit."

"So, the usual then?" he drawls, sounding bored. "For a second, I thought you were going to ask me for something challenging."

"Nah, but I do need something else."

"Of course you do."

I choose to ignore the sarcasm dripping from his voice. "Cameras. Enough to wire up an entire house."

He pauses. "Is this sanctioned by Connor?"

"Not exactly, but I need you to do me this solid. I'll owe you."

"I thought we'd already established you were going to owe me for the research."

I lower my voice and let all the teasing and bullshit drop out of it. "I'll owe you double. Please, man. I'm begging."

He lets out an exasperated sigh. "Fine, since you've begged, I suppose I can assist. I'll have a bag waiting for you when you get back. If Connor asks, I'll tell him you stole them."

I let out a quiet laugh. "Go right ahead. How long until you've got something on the foster parents?"

"Give me a couple of hours."

"I'll catch up with you when I get back," I tell him before I hang up.

Ronin has been texting me obnoxiously all afternoon, every couple of minutes updating me on everything Penelope's doing. Eating a sandwich. Working on an equation. Pulling her hair back into a ponytail. While I know he's trying to push my buttons and act like a dick, right now it's a relief to look back at her day since I couldn't be there with her. All her moments belong to me—no matter how mundane or insignificant they may seem.

It's also how I know she spent ten minutes eating lunch and another twenty playing a stupid game on her phone she thinks none of us know about.

I'm too wound up to go right back into work mode, so I take the long way home, driving over by the beach and rolling down the windows to breathe in the salty air. By the time I pull through the iron gates leading to Penelope's ridiculous palace-like estate, the wild fury coursing through my veins has reduced to a more manageable simmer, as long as I don't think about the kid or what he might be going through right now.

When I step through the front door, I don't immediately go for Penelope despite everything in me demanding I do it. I know once I take over for Ronin, I'm not going to want to leave my Duchess. Instead, I head for the office where I know Sebastian's holed up in the hopes he'll have found something I can use to torment Rory's foster mother. It's only been an hour or so, so I don't have high hopes.

He looks up when I walk into the room, pulling his glasses off and pinching the bridge of his nose. I've never seen Sebastian look less than perfect. Even when he's been working on a case nonstop, his clothes are usually wrinkle-free, and his face is smooth. I swear the guy doesn't grow facial hair.

Right now, though... he looks wrecked. Dark circles under his eyes almost look like bruises and there's a wrinkle in his forehead that looks like it's on the verge of becoming permanent.

"Dude, you should get some sleep."

He ignores me and instead pushes a folder across the desk in my direction. I move to grab it, flipping through the pages. What I read as I'm skimming over everything is better than I hoped. I drop the folder and pop my ass out, twerking against Penelope's—well, Sebastian's—desk doing a happy dance.

He looks at me with disgust written all over his face. "Stop that, you look ridiculous."

"Whatever, my ass is amazing," I tell him, straightening up and jogging behind the huge wooden desk, bending down and grabbing his face between my palms and smacking his cheek with a wet kiss. "You have no idea the difference you just made."

No way could I have gotten this info without Sebastian's help. There's a reason he's the only analyst we've got—he's all we need. Though, to be fair, he's looking pretty rough so maybe I need to mention it to Connor. The guy could use a vacation.

"As long as you take the folder and the cameras and get out of here, that'll be thanks enough," Sebastian says, lifting his eyes off of his tablet long enough to make eye contact. "For now." The reminder that I owe him is clear in the words and his stare, but right now I'd give him almost anything for what he's given me.

I scoop up the dropped file and the cameras he pointed out on the corner of his desk and head out in search of Asher. The pull to find Penelope and wrap her up in the tightest hug I can is strong, but I'm going to resist until everything's in place. Ash is out back, standing on the patio with his arms crossed glaring out into the woods behind the house.

My gaze shifts between him and the tree line, back and forth because I'm trying to figure out what he's looking for or staring at, but it's nothing obvious so I give up.

"Hey," I say as I move up beside him. Asher tears his gaze off the forest long enough to side-eye me before looking back out into the distance.

"Hey."

"Sorry for disappearing today, but there was something I had to do," I say, realizing I should've checked out with him before I took off and left Ronin here in my place. He knows how shit is, though. Sometimes you get caught up and forget to do the responsible thing.

"We handled it." He turns towards me this time. "Where'd you go?"

A cold sweat breaks out down the back of my neck when I think about explaining everything to Asher. We might be close, and we might have tortured people together, but this is too much. Saying it all out loud again is too much.

"I don't even know where to begin," I admit, and it's probably the most honest thing I've ever said to him.

"At the beginning?" he suggests with the hint of a wry smile, and I take a deep breath in an attempt to inhale some courage.

"I... had a son," I say, rushing the last three words out so fast, I don't know if he even really hears them. But then he tilts his head and studies me.

"I never would've guessed that," Asher says without giving me bullshit platitudes that mean nothing. I appreciate that he doesn't ask me what happened because I sure as shit know I'm not ready to get into it.

"It was a long time ago," I tell him, even though the wound still gapes and gushes blood every day. "But I've avoided anything to do with kids or hospitals since. Until Penelope introduced me to Rory."

"Rory?"

"A little boy who's battling leukemia. That's where I was today, out with him."

Asher's eyebrows lift towards his hair, and I don't think I've ever actually seen his surprised face before. It's almost comical. "You left your job to go spend time with someone else's kid today?"

"When you put it like that, it sounds like I'm not right in the head."

He gives me a flat look.

"He's not just someone else's kid, bro. He's a foster kid. One who's going through chemo alone and who lives with half a dozen other kids in a tiny shitty house that's falling apart and a foster mom who forces him to cook meals for the family and threatens to use him as a human ashtray." I'm breathing hard by the time I finish, and my fingers are curled into fists. If only I could go unleash some of this rage on that poor excuse for a woman who's got custody of Rory.

"Fuck. Talk about a shitty hand. Anything I can do to help? Have you asked Penelope to get involved?"

I know he's implying her connections or money might make a difference, but this feels important for me to handle on my own. "She's close with him, but I haven't told her I picked him up today."

"Why not?" Asher asks, lifting his hand to block the fading sunlight from his eyes so he can stare back into the woods.

"What are you looking for?" I ask.

"Earlier I thought I saw movement on one of the cameras back this way," he says as if it's no big fucking deal and suddenly my eyes are locked on the tree line, too.

"Shit, any sign of anything?"

"Not in the last twenty minutes," he says, and I relax a fraction. He's got it covered.

"I was afraid if I started to get attached, I'd freak," I admit and for a minute Asher doesn't say anything. Maybe he forgot he asked me a question and is trying to figure out what I'm talking about.

"Makes sense," he finally says. "Anything I can do?"

He's not the type who offers that shit without any follow through. If Ash is volunteering his assistance, he means it.

"Actually…" I start, knowing he's going to hate this next part. "His foster parents, Trisha and Wayne, like to play the tables at an underground casino I happen to know is run by a certain West Coast gang leader."

"No." Asher shakes his head, the tree line completely forgotten. "No fucking way."

"I'll beg," I say, getting down onto my knees to prove my point.

"Get up, asshole," he snaps, unfolding his arms to reach down and grab me so he can yank me back to my feet.

"What's it going to take?"

Ash's whole body is tense, his back rigid and his jaw ticking. "You realize every time I have to ask him for something, it pulls me back in that much more, right?"

"I wouldn't ask if it wasn't important. He's an innocent kid, Ash."

He scrubs his hands down his face looking entirely too exhausted for someone in their late twenties. "Fuck. Fine, but you'll owe me so goddamn huge I'm not sure you'll ever be able to repay the debt."

"I don't care," I tell him, and I don't. "Do it."

Asher stares at me a few more seconds before giving me a sharp jerk of his head. "It'll be done."

"One more thing," I say and then I lay out my plan for getting cams into Rory's house. Asher assures me he'll handle that, too.

For the first time in hours, a tiny bit of the knot in my gut loosens. When I get the hell out of Asher's vicinity before he can change his mind, I get a call that blows the knot to smithereens.

"Elias? Tell me you've got good news," I say as I lift my phone to my ear. I'm already halfway to Penelope's home lab but I stop walking in the middle of the hall. It's like my entire body freezes, every muscle, the breath in my lungs, the voice in my throat. The only thing still working is my heart and it's beating furiously while I wait to see what he's going to say.

He doesn't know it, but the next words out of his mouth have the power to destroy the cracked foundation I've been working to rebuild or set something inside of me free for the first time in years.

And he doesn't disappoint. "He's going to be okay, Indy. He's responding to his treatment well, and it's almost finished. His counts look good. I'd say his long-term prognosis is excellent."

I reach out for the wall to steady myself, sliding down it as my knees go weak and give out. My eyes sting and suddenly everything crashes back in like the world was muted. *He's going to be okay.*

I'm almost dizzy with relief as I thank Elias and hang up, holding my head in my hands while I catch my breath. This bit of news sparked something in me, and I spring up, feeling like I could take on the entire world. I run the rest of the way to Penelope's lab and when I get there, Ronin glances up looking bored as fuck, but I ignore him.

Instead, I run over to my Duchess and scoop her up off her stool and into my arms, twirling her around while she laughs and digs her fingers into the back of my neck to hold on.

"Put me down!" she yells but it's through laughter, so I know she doesn't really mean it. I slap her ass before dropping her tiny body to slide down across mine, so I get the pleasure of feeling every curve rub against me on the way down and she shivers when her feet hit the ground. I'm immensely proud I have that effect on her.

I can't help myself, I'm so fucking excited and relieved, so I kiss her hard, slipping my tongue inside her mouth at her surprised gasp. She doesn't make me wait long before she's kissing me back with just as much intensity. She tastes like summer desserts and home, and I'd rather pass out from a lack of oxygen than stop kissing her, but she pulls away before I'm ready, pushing up on her toes to rest her forehead against mine.

"What's gotten into you?" she whispers and my gaze flicks over her shoulder to find Ronin gone. Smart man. I'd have had to punch him for watching me make out with my Duchess.

"I have a confession," I tell her, and she stares up at me with her wide, innocent eyes so full of hope and trust. I've hurt her, I've acted like a complete jackass and yet she still looks at me like this. I don't know what the hell I could've done to deserve her faith, but I'll fucking take it and I'll dig my fingers in and never let go.

"What did you do?" A wariness creeps into her gaze, but I grin anyway. It's understandable she'd be hesitant to hear what I have to say.

"I spent the day with Rory."

Her eyes widen even more as she leans back and stares at me in shock. "You did?"

I nod. "And I convinced Elias to look over his medical records because I had to know. I had to know..." I can't finish, and I find myself blinking back emotion I in no way want to show on the outside.

But Penelope? She gets me.

Her soft palm slides along my jaw and she gently tilts my head so I'm staring down into her bottomless brown eyes, so rich and full of life I want to dive in and never come out. "I'd want to know, too. How is he?" she asks, curiosity sparking in her eyes. Her body is stiff, and I know she's probably more invested in the kid than I am. The fact I just broke all kinds of privacy laws to get this info doesn't even phase her.

"He's going to be okay, Duchess," I say, and she collapses against me, throwing her arms around me and holding me while she trembles. I don't know if she's crying or laughing, or maybe she's just overwhelmed with relief. Whatever she's feeling, I'm fucking floored that she's leaning on me to hold her up right now.

I hold her closer, pulling her as tightly against my chest as I can while I rest my cheek on top of her strawberry-scented hair. "Go on a date with me."

"Now?" she asks, and her words are muffled because her face is pressed up against my t-shirt and she hasn't bothered to move even an inch out of my hold.

"Tomorrow."

"Okay," she says, and I think I might've just had the perfect day.

CHAPTER 14
PENELOPE

WHY DOES time always seem to move so slowly when you're looking forward to something? I try to keep busy by burying myself in work, and that's usually all it takes for me to find hours have passed in the blink of an eye. Sadly, that doesn't seem to be working today as I wait for my date with Indy.

The last time we went out, it was spontaneous, and I didn't have time to overthink or worry about what we might be doing. He's refused to tell me anything, and to be honest, I don't think he even knows himself. I wouldn't be surprised if there was no plan and he just whisked us off somewhere random. As much as I've gotten to know him in the past several months, I already know he's not in any way a planner.

His carelessness and maybe carefree-ness rubs up against my rigid need for schedules and order, but I'm trying to embrace it. To let go a little. To make the most of the time we have now that it's been brought sharply into focus just how little of it there really is.

I hardly get anything done the entire day, and when there's only an hour left until the time Indy told me to meet him downstairs, I close my laptop with a frustrated groan. Butterflies explode in my stomach and my blood hums with anticipation. I have no idea what to expect from Indy, and the prospects of what might happen tonight unfold in the minefield of my mind.

A giddy sort of rush consumes me then, and I step into the shower taking extra care to shave everything. While I may not know what he has in store for tonight, I do know I'm not about to be caught stubbly and gross if things get heated. A furious blush sweeps over my face that I can't see since I'm still under the hot water, but I feel it, knowing what might happen tonight. What would've already happened if it was up to me.

The memory of Indy's hard body pressed up against mine, the taste of his kiss on my tongue, his scorching touch against my skin sparks my nerve endings to life. A throb pulses between my legs that I don't want to relieve. For once, I don't want to be the one to alleviate that particular ache. No, this time I think I'll wait and see what the charming playboy with the dirty smile might do about it.

I have less than zero experience dressing for a date, so I spend the next ten minutes rushing through outfit changes and texting Montana mirror selfies to get her opinion. We finally settle on a floor-length deep purple dress that I bought for a charity gala last year but never wore because it was so far out of my comfort zone it's laughable. There's a plunging neckline that practically hits my belly button and a slit up my left thigh that shows so much skin I can't wear underwear.

If Indy hadn't given me the vague instruction of dress up, I'd be in jeans and a cardigan or maybe a skirt. This fabric, though... it's lighter than it looks and the swish of it against my skin is silky and cool. It almost feels like I'm not wearing anything, and when I walk down the stairs and find Indy waiting below, I laugh at the way his eyes practically bug out of his head.

That stormy gray gaze of his sweeps down my body, and I shiver from the heat of it. A path of fire under my skin is left in the wake of his perusal and that ache between my legs pulses back to life. When I step up beside him, his fingers press into my lower back, pulling me into his hard body and his soft lips brush across my cheek.

"You look supremely fuckable in this dress, Duchess," he purrs into my ear so Asher, who's standing beside the front door waiting for us, doesn't hear. I pretend his words don't make my knees shake or my nipples hard but based on the way his focus drops to where the thin fabric covers my breasts, I'm going to go ahead and say I'm not doing a very good job.

I decide to be bold and brave and lower my voice to match his, looking over at him from underneath my mascara-coated lashes. "So, what are you going to do about it?"

His sharp intake of breath has a smug smile pulling at my lips. Somehow, I think it puts him off-balance when I play with him this way, and I'm pretty sure I like it. I'm going to have to remember that for future use when Indy's annoying me to no end.

Before he has a chance to get the last word, I move out of his hold and towards the door at the same time Asher pushes off the wall to go out first.

Hands grab me and pull me back against a hard chest before Indy's lips brush my ear. "I've always been a dessert before dinner kind of guy, and with you tempting me like this, I'm going to have to indulge."

Before I can react, I'm being spun and swept up, tossed over Indy's shoulder. His palm smacks across my ass before his arm bands over my thighs and holds me down.

"Stop!" I squeal, trying to kick my feet. One of my heels slips off Cinderella-style while Indy jogs up the stairs. It's clear he's not going to listen to me, but it's not like I'm fighting that hard. If he wants to act like a caveman and have his wicked way with me, I'm not exactly opposed. In fact, goosebumps have broken out over my entire body and my lower belly has tightened in anticipation of what's to come.

I only meant to tease him a bit, maybe get him riled up, but I guess I did too good of a job because my head hangs only inches above his firm and bitable ass, and I can't help but lose myself in him.

"We're going to be late," Asher calls out from somewhere behind us, but Indy doesn't even pause. His boots slam down on the final couple of steps, and he stalks towards my bedroom, clearly on a mission, tossing me onto the bed and moving back to slam the door. As if he thinks I might try to escape.

As if I'd want to.

Heat slashes across my cheeks, and for a second, I wonder if I should be embarrassed that Asher and probably Sebastian know what's about to happen behind these closed doors, but I'm not. Indy brings out my confidence in a way no one else ever has.

No. I want to own the way he lights me up. I want to revel in it, enjoy it. Life over the last year—and if I'm honest, before that—has been a grind that has stolen so much from me. This moment right here? I'm stealing it back, making it mine. Right now, it doesn't matter what I *should* be doing.

Doing what's expected got me into this mess, and for just this moment I'm going to surrender to what's been building between us. I'm going to jump in with both feet and embrace the mayhem.

Indy's dark, tempestuous eyes scrape across my body like a physical touch, and I can't help but want to put on a show. I've never been this girl—the wanton one who flaunts her sexuality, but he brings it out in me.

When my back arches, he leans over me. His fingers run teasingly between my breasts and down to my bellybutton along the exposed skin my dress leaves on display. "You know," he says slowly, almost lazily. "I've been watching you."

My eyes lift from where his hand is drawing lazy circles around my flat stomach to clash with his. "What do you mean? When?" My heart beats faster at the secret thrill of his confession.

"When you think no one's watching," he says, kicking off his shoes and crawling onto the bed. He straddles my thighs with his, trapping me between his muscular legs. He leans forward, drawing a path along my collarbone with his tongue that shoots sparks straight between my thighs. "When you lay in this bed and toss and turn because I'm not here to fuck you until the world disappears."

He drags his teeth along the curve of my neck, so his next words are a whisper in my ear, and I shiver. "When it's dark and you let all your fantasies of my cock inside of you play out in your head because you think no one can see you, but I can. I *do*."

His clean and spicy scent encases me, filling my lungs with

nothing but him. When I breathe, I breathe him in and the look in his eye as he hovers over me and ensnares me in his gaze says he knows it.

He's so close now that my lips brush against his when I speak, the tips of our noses touching. Maybe it should bother me, knowing he's been watching. But it doesn't. "Did you like what you saw?"

I know this is waving a red cape in front of a bull. I'm taunting him, desperate to see what he'll say next. The predatory look in his eye raises all kinds of doubts about whether I'm the one in control here, or if he's got me right where he wants me, like a mouse tossed into a cage with a python.

"Enough that I pulled my hard dick out and made myself come while I pictured being choked by your perfect cunt."

I gasp at his dirty admission and how easily he owns up to his stalkerish ways. I don't know if it's his confession or the way he slams his lips down on mine and demands entry with his tongue, but I'm coming apart at the seams, unsure who I even am anymore. My head spins and my heart thrashes against the cage of my ribs as he pours his need into me with every stroke of his tongue. Every time he's held back, every time I've teased him with flirty words or lingering looks, it's all built up into the storm he's unleashing on me now.

And I hope it blows me away.

I hope I drown in it.

I hope I'm ripped apart and remade as something new.

Some*one* new.

Because after this I can't go back to pretending there's nothing here between us. I'm burning for him as he devours me, dying to let him take anything and everything he wants. I know it's not healthy, but I can't think logically right now. I've devolved into pure feeling, at the mercy of nothing but my senses and Indy's controlling them all.

Without him, I'm nothing. Lost to emptiness, a life without color.

When he pulls back, my lips are swollen and his glisten. His eyes are dark and lust-blown, hungry and intense in a way I've never seen from him before. His body presses against mine, pushing me into the mattress and making his hard, thick length obvious where it digs into my lower stomach through his slacks. I shift, wanting to alleviate some of the pressure building between my legs but he's got me trapped.

His fingers trail along my side, up across my chest until they skim over my nipple. I'm sensitive and jump a little at the sensation and he chuckles. It's this dark, sinful sound that curls around my chest and tightens, grabbing hold of my heart and lungs like he's their master.

"I've relived how sweet you taste on my tongue a thousand times," he says, wrapping his hand lightly around my throat one finger at a time. "Imagined how tight your pussy would feel spasming around my cock." He squeezes for a second before loosening his hold again. "How I could dirty up the good girl and make her scream my name while she comes all over my dick."

He's staring at me again, not blinking and the intensity is almost too much. "Is that what you want, Duchess? Me to fuck you so good you can't help but finally admit who owns you?"

His hand is still wrapped around my throat, but I nod anyway, unsure what might come out of my mouth if I try to speak. If I begged, the humiliation might kill me, but I think that's what'll happen if I part my lips to try to form words.

He sits up then, looking me over as if trying to decide what bite to take first in an endless buffet. The moment he decides it's clear on his face. He moves off of me, the cool air where the warmth of him used to be tightens my nipples under the thin silk of my dress.

His eyes drop to my chest even as he holds out his hand to help me up off the bed. When I stand, one of his hands goes to my waist and the other lifts to my breast, his thumb stroking across my nipple, and my thighs push together in response. He turns me to face the floor-length mirror and I don't recognize the woman staring back at me.

Her eyes are bright, and her cheeks flushed. Her lips are bruised and swollen from Indy's kisses, and she looks sexy.

I look sexy.

It's a bit of a shock, but I don't get the chance to linger in it as

Indy's fingers skate along my waist. He moves behind me without saying a word. When he looks over my shoulder at the two of us reflected in the mirror, a dirty smirk lifts the corner of his lips and a hint of the dimple in his cheek pops out.

He doesn't speak, but his eyes dare me to stop him as his fingers climb up my thigh. Higher and higher they slide against my skin until his hand is shifting aside the fabric of my dress and slipping inside. He inches across my leg until he reaches my inner thigh. My breath catches as he pushes the tips of his fingers inside me.

I'm practically dripping so he finds no resistance and my eyes roll back at the exquisite feeling of his rough fingers filling me up. My head falls back against his shoulder as he pumps his digits slowly in and out, a profane noise filling the air from how wet I am.

"Open your eyes, Duchess. I want you to watch while I make you come."

I do as he says, fluttering my eyes halfway open as I stare at us reflected in the mirror in front of me. The picture before me is erotic, the way his hand disappears inside my dress and at the same time, his other hand creeps up my body, between my breasts, and grips my throat in a possessive hold.

"Good girl," he purrs in my ear as his palm rubs against my clit with the perfect amount of pressure to coax a moan from between my lips. As I climb higher, my body shakes from the pleasure building between my legs. With every stroke of his fingers and press of his palm, he watches through dark eyes the way he's making me crumble with only a touch. My legs threaten to give way as I fall over the edge, lost to the pleasure pulsing through my body, but Indy catches me.

"Beautiful," he murmurs as he releases his hold on me slowly, as if he's not sure my legs will hold me up. He brings the hand that was just inside me up to his mouth and holds my gaze in the mirror while he licks his fingers clean. A blush heats my chest and face, but he looks like he's enjoying every filthy second. "Every orgasm from now on belongs to me, Duchess." A flash of possession in his eyes heats my blood all over again.

When I'm standing on my own, there's tugging on my zipper. It's my only clue as to what Indy's up to. His fingers brush against my spine as he lowers the zipper so slowly, I itch to take over and do it myself so I can be free of the layers between us.

Finally, the fabric falls to the floor, pooling at my feet and I stand before him completely bare while he's still in his button down and slacks, though I can't see him except for his reflection in the mirror.

"Are you just going to watch me or are you going to strip down and actually do something?" I ask, knowing it's provoking him, daring him to make the move we both want. But I'm vulnerable like this, unveiled for his judgment and I'm not sure how to handle it. I've never allowed myself to be this open with anyone before, and suddenly I want to wrap my arms around myself and hide as much of my skin as I can, sure I'm not up to his usual standards.

His eyes glint with darkness, but other than that, he doesn't show any signs of taking the bait. He's completely controlled and unshakable, and it's such a contrast to everything I see swirling in his eyes.

Not to mention what a wreck I am after that breath-stealing orgasm. I'm still panting, trying to catch my breath after Indy stole it away with his magic fingers.

"Get on the bed," he says, but it's clear by the way he says it that it's an order and I better obey.

A shiver races down my spine at the dominance in his voice, something I never would've imagined liking before this moment. Yet, my core clenches like it's desperate for more and I find myself scrambling into the bed and falling onto my back to stare up at this gorgeous specimen of a man as he strips his clothes off.

Even in this, he tortures me, moving as slow as he possibly can while he undoes each and every button. My eyes track every movement, every flick of his wrist and press of his fingers until he speaks and my attention snaps right back up to those chaotic eyes of his.

"Lay back and spread your legs for me, Duchess. Let me see how drenched your pussy is." His voice is raspy and deeper than usual.

Until he speaks, I'm not aware I've leaned forward, my body pulled towards his by an invisible string hooked beneath my skin.

I do what he says, my usual desire to defy every word that leaves those sinful lips absent while facing the prospect of seeing him fall in the same way he's made me.

"Good girl."

His eyes trail over my skin, taking in every inch like he's drinking me in, desperate to memorize every scar, every flaw, every imperfection. When they finally come to a stop between my thighs, his hands move to his belt, tugging it open and sliding it out of the loops. Briefly, his gaze flicks up to meet mine and it's burning with lust and mischief.

But then it drops back down as he unbuttons his slacks and steps out of them and his boxers. The second his cock springs free, my mouth goes dry. It's huge and thick and all I want to do is get a closer look.

Or maybe a taste.

Or get it inside me as soon as humanly possible.

Indy doesn't give me the chance, though. Instead, he climbs onto the bed and up my body until his face rests just inches from where I'm aching for him to touch me. His eyes are locked on mine as he lowers his head and kisses my inner thigh and then moves to the other. Goosebumps break out across my skin and my nipples tighten. I can't look away, transfixed by this powerful man between my legs.

He breaks eye contact first when he suddenly dives in, and I gasp at the feel of his mouth on my clit. His strong hands grip my thighs, and he pushes them further apart, giving him better access to lick more of me.

And he does.

He wastes no time tasting every single part of me, and all I can do is grip his hair and hold on for the ride. His face is buried between my legs and instead of pushing his head away like I might've done in the past, my fingers are tangled in his hair and I'm pulling him as close as I can get him, grinding all over his face. His fingers grip my hips so tightly I'm going to have finger-shaped bruises in the morning, but I'll happily wear them if he just never stops.

Finally, he gets tired of teasing me and sucks my clit into his mouth, drawing circles with his tongue and that's all it takes for me to detonate. The most brilliant sensation bursts through my body, leaving tingles in its wake. I scream incoherently so loudly that when I start to come back down, my throat actually aches.

He chuckles as he wipes his mouth off and sits up. "Next time, make sure you enunciate, Duchess. I want them to know whose tongue you're coming on."

If I wasn't floating somewhere above my body right now, I'd have kicked him for that, but I can't find it in me to toss his banter back at him. I think I'm the most relaxed I've ever been, so close to boneless I might as well be a puddle on the bed.

Indy crawls up my body and drops the softest kiss onto my lips, but then he rolls over, taking me with him so we've switched positions and I'm draped over the top of him like a blanket.

It doesn't take long for me to start to come out of my stupor when I feel his massive cock pressed against my thigh. Indy helps me move, grabbing my legs and positioning them on either side of his so I'm straddling him. I push up on my hands, suddenly more than ready to experience everything he has to give, even if I'm a little terrified he won't fit.

When I rock my hips against him and throw my head back, I feel a sharp sting where he's pinched my nipple. I can't believe I'm doing this, putting myself on display for this man. It's one of the scariest things I've ever done.

He must see the mixture of fear and desire in my eyes because he takes over then, reaching over to grab a condom and rolling it on. He moves his dick to my entrance and I'm dying to know how it's going to feel when we finally give in to everything that's been building between us.

Before I can protest and ask for us to change positions, he pushes inside me with a thrust of his hips and any argument I was about to make melts away.

In its place is intense pleasure. I'm so full of Indy and it's everything and I never want it to end. Even though I'm on top, there's no mistaking who's actually in control here. Indy thrusts his hips up, finding a rhythm for both of us while I grip onto his hard chest and go for the ride of my life. Watching his body flex underneath mine while he hits spots inside me I never knew existed is so hot, I wish I was taking a video so I could watch it again and again later. I never want to forget how he looks in this moment, his eyes half-closed and burning with need so scorching I might actually combust.

"You're doing perfectly, just like that," Indy murmurs as he picks up speed, gyrating his hips so he somehow rubs the perfect spot and fills me completely at the same time. "You look so beautiful with my cock inside you."

Those divine fingers of his find my clit and once they do, it's game over. As soon as they brush against that sensitive bundle, my walls clench and I'm powerless to stop the way he's expertly working my body. I don't want to think about how he got so good, so instead I focus on the way he's turning my blood into liquid fire with every touch, and every stroke of his cock inside me is just adding gasoline to the inevitable explosion.

"Gorgeous, Duchess. Now, let me see you come," he demands, and his husky voice is like a detonation switch. I want to rebel, to fight, but the second the command wraps around my insides it sparks the inevitable and lights up every nerve in my body. Flashes of color shoot off behind my eyes and for a second, I don't recognize the voice screaming his name as my own.

Indy never stops thrusting into me, and when he finds his own release, he yanks me down on top of him, gripping onto me like he's trying to crawl inside my body with more than just his cock.

It's like all of the walls between us have come down leaving us both raw and exposed for the first time and neither of us know how to handle it.

But we don't have to, because before Indy's even pulled out of me, there's a banging on the door.

"Hurry the fuck up, we're going to be late," Asher's slightly muffled voice booms through the wood.

I didn't know he'd be coming with us ahead of time, but it's not surprising. I'm still in danger, and while Indy has the skills to protect me, if he's focusing on our date, he won't be as alert as he should be in watching my back. Knowing Asher will be there for an extra layer of security helps me relax.

Indy and I break apart and hurry to get dressed. I run a brush through my hair in the bathroom and reapply my lipstick. As soon as I'm finished, Indy's stepping behind me in front of the mirror and I get a flashback to twenty minutes ago and a different mirror and feel my face heat.

He spins me and his fingers go under my chin and tip my face up so I'm looking him straight in his calm gray eyes. For once, there's no storm raging.

"I can't stop picturing the way you looked coming all over me," he says, leaning forward to brush his lips across mine. "And if you think we're done here, you're so fucking wrong it's insane. So, be good and don't close off again."

I can't help but want to defy him. He brings it out in me. "And if I do?"

His eyes heat, that same desire sparking to life again inside them. "You're going to get an up close and personal introduction to the way my palm feels imprinted on your perfect ass, Duchess. It's up to you how this plays out but know I'm not going to let you walk away from me."

He steps behind me and drags the zipper of my dress up before he leaves the bathroom, but his eyes are locked on me when I follow and fling open my bedroom door. He walks out behind me, the heat of his body warming my back as I move down the stairs and out the front door, feeling the imprint of him inside of me with every step.

Chapter 15
Penelope

"Are either of you planning on telling me where we're going?" I ask as I slide into the back of the SUV and Indy follows behind me. Asher gets behind the wheel and shakes his head.

"This assface made me promise I wouldn't ruin the surprise," he says, but based on the tone of his voice, he's not happy about our destination.

Indy grabs my hand and threads our fingers together, pulling our linked hands up and pressing a kiss to the back of mine. The way he's so casually touching me now throws me off. I wonder if he really has let his defenses down for good. Maybe it's tenuous, but something about that knowledge excites me and my heart speeds up in line with the car accelerating. "Don't worry, Duchess. You're going to love what's coming."

"Better be worth it," I think Asher grumbles from the front seat, but it's so quiet I'm not completely sure that's what he actually says.

"It will be," Indy replies with a gleam in his eye I haven't seen before. The sun set a while ago, so when the streetlights light up his eyes as we drive past them, I catch a glimpse of the savage excitement he's not even trying to hide, and my curiosity goes into overdrive. The power radiating off of him is intoxicating.

I'm not sure how long the drive takes because Indy distracts me with dirty talk whispered in my ear, promises of everything he wants to do when we get back home. Asher's silent in the front seat, but there's an anger filling the space around him that's so strong it's almost corporeal.

When we pull up to an upscale restaurant, my eyebrows shoot up. I never took Indy for the plain dinner and a movie date kind of guy, and even less so at a fancy restaurant.

As if he's reading my mind, he flashes me a sinful smirk and says, "It's not what you think."

I glance back out the window, but it just looks like a restaurant to me. At least until Asher's words, mumbled from the front seat, ramp my curiosity up even higher.

"I can't believe I'm back here. This place has a way of getting its hooks into you and dragging you back kicking and screaming no matter how far away you get or how long you hide. There's no fucking escape." His tone is bitter and resigned as he pushes open his door and gets out, slamming it behind him. I don't know if his words are aimed at Indy or me or both of us, but neither of us moves to get out of the car, sensing maybe he needs a second to himself.

It's Indy that opens the door and gets out next and I follow behind him, grabbing onto his outstretched hand so I don't break an ankle in my heels. When the door's closed behind me, the three of us stand in a sort of makeshift huddle with my back to the car and my two bodyguards penning me in. They're not paying much attention to me, though. Asher's glaring at the burly guy near the front door and Indy's watching his friend.

"I'm sorry I had to ask you to do this, but trust me when I say it's necessary, for the best cause. Wait until you meet the kid you're helping, dude. You'll see."

What Indy says only confuses me more about what we're doing here. "What are you guys talking about? What kid? Rory? And what is this place?"

Neither of them bothers to answer a single question, so I open my mouth to demand answers. I don't like surprises, and my eyes narrow as Indy lays a finger over my lips before I can speak.

"All in good time, Duchess. Just let me be your arm candy and fetch your drinks while you enjoy the show." The bastard is so charming when he gives me his crooked smile, the one where his dimple pops out. His eyes sweep over me, and I can hardly remember my own name when he looks at me like this as if he's replaying every filthy second of what we did earlier. Forget about the questions I'd just been so determined to find the answers to. What can I say? I'm picturing it now, too.

When we step up to the front door, my arm's looped through Indy's and Asher greets the big guy wearing a suit like he knows him. The guy is obviously some kind of hired muscle, as tall as Asher and Indy, but bulkier. I think I hear the guy call Asher sir which is odd considering this is a restaurant and he doesn't work here.

Maybe he comes here a lot? Or brings his clients? Or maybe the guy at the door works as a bodyguard at Hollywood Guardians?

My inquisitive nature won't let me relax and let this stuff go, but Indy does a good job of distracting me whenever he catches my mind spinning with possibilities, trying to put the pieces together.

"How does Asher know those guys? Does he come here a lot?" I finally whisper, leaning into Indy's shoulder. I take the opportunity to breathe him in and I hate to admit it, but his clean and increasingly familiar spicy scent mixed with mine helps me calm down.

"Duchess... Asher's family owns this place." My mouth falls open as I look around the opulent interior with this new information. It's dripping elegance with low lighting, expensive decor and crystal chandeliers scattered throughout. "It's just one of many like it, plus a shit ton of other illegal bullshit they're caught up in. You know his last name is Mason, right? Like *the* Masons?"

Asher swipes a card he pulls from his pocket against a reader, and the second the light flashes green, elevator doors slide open, and we step inside. We had to pass security before we got to the elevator who were dressed similarly to the man outside the front door, and the mention of illegal bullshit suddenly makes sense.

"Isn't that a secret society or something?" My stomach flips as the elevator starts to descend.

"Maybe, but also they're the most prolific mafia on the west coast. Think of them as a gang or a crime ring or whatever, only massive. They stretch the whole coast and Asher's dad, Nicholas? He's at the very top. His grandfather built it, his father expanded, and since our Ash is the first-born son, he was expected to take it over. The heir apparent."

Asher stands beside us silent and tense as Indy recounts his history to me as if he's not right here, but he doesn't make any move to stop the conversation. I figure he's okay with me knowing as long as he doesn't have to fill in the blanks himself.

"He obviously didn't since he's here with us," I say, and admittedly, it's weird talking about the guy like he's not standing three feet away.

"You want to take this one, Ash?" Indy turns to his friend and asks, but Asher shakes his head once and the muscle in his jaw flexes like he's clenching his teeth.

Indy grins like that's what he expected before he turns back to me. "No, he made a deal with his father that bought him his freedom, but it's tenuous at best. Personally, I think the old man's letting him blow off some steam before he yanks him back in and no matter what Ash does to get out, it won't matter. But what the hell do I know?"

Asher scoffs. "No way in hell am I letting him pull me back in. I already gave up everything to get out, there's nothing left for the bastard to take."

My heart hurts for my stoic bodyguard. How could a father be as cruel as his seems to be towards his son? Suddenly, I'm angry and I don't want to be here. Heat scatters across my face as my heart rate picks up. "Why would you ask him to bring us here? We could've done anything else. It's not fair of you to ask him to come here."

"This is the only way, Duchess. Like I said, we're here for a show and sadly, there was no other option to make it happen. It had to be here. Once you see what's coming, it'll make sense." Indy's eyes soften as he rubs his thumb along my cheek, and my irritation starts to melt away. I still hate that we're here, and I can't think of anything worth putting Asher through coming to this place, but I trust Indy.

The history lesson ends when the doors open, and we step out onto the floor of what looks to be a casino. A very, very illegal casino.

The whirring of slot machines and laughter are the first things I notice, followed by the acrid scent of tobacco smoke hanging in the air. I want to cover my face so I don't have to inhale it, but I resist. I don't want to draw attention to myself. For now, I'll endure it even if I hate the way I can feel the lingering nicotine seeping into my clothes and hair.

As we move further inside, I notice how crowded it is. There are tables set up all over the place, and most of the seats are full. It's loud —both with cheers and the mechanical sounds of slot machines perpetually spinning around and around. Like I imagine a casino in Las Vegas would have, there are scary-looking security guards stationed throughout the area, but unlike Vegas, they wear violent expressions and carry weapons threateningly out in the open.

Indy's hand finds mine and threads our fingers together, keeping me between him and Asher as we make our way through the gamblers. Somewhere in what I'm guessing is the middle of the room, Indy plops down seemingly at random at a table, pulling me onto his lap and tossing some money onto the green felt surface in front of the dealer.

"I thought you said we were here for a show," I say as he reaches around me and picks up the cards the dealer's just set down for him.

"We are." He taps the table, and the dealer flips over a new card.

"I'm confused because you're clearly gambling, not sitting in front of a stage."

"Relax, Duchess," Indy says as he scoops up his chips and slides them back in front of him. "Give it a few minutes. It's not that kind of show. The timing didn't match up perfectly, but I promise this will be worth the wait."

I glance over to Asher but he's busy scanning the room, doing his job. For a few minutes, I do the same, trying to figure out what I should be watching for but without more information and with so many people in here, it's impossible. Eventually, I decide to trust in Indy and do what he says—relaxing back into him and watching a few hands play out.

One of his arms is wrapped around my waist, his big palm splayed possessively across my stomach. He's holding me close, and it helps me unwind in such an uncomfortable environment. After a little while, I actually start to watch him play what I've now learned is Blackjack. When he beats the dealer, I can't help but cheer and the answering grin he gives me is infectious.

Flashes of what we did in my bedroom earlier hit me as I sink into his lap, and I can already feel the blush working up my chest and into my face. Indy leans into me, his nose brushing the sensitive skin behind my ear, and I shiver.

"I'm thinking about it, too," he murmurs as his thumb stokes my lower stomach through my dress. "I can still smell you on my face." His length thickens underneath my thighs, and my body clenches in response. I want him more now than I did before I had him. Like an addict, the craving has only gotten worse.

"Then why are we here and not home doing more of... that?" I ask as my eyes dart around the table, to the dealer and the other players. I don't want them to overhear our conversation.

"Soon, Duchess," Indy murmurs in my ear, and I'm sure it's not by accident his hand brushes across my nipple as he moves to throw in some more chips. It's so sensitive that the sensation shoots straight to my clit. I bite my lip to keep from moaning because that would be incredibly embarrassing, but my blood is on fire and everything between my legs tingles for more of what I now know he's capable of.

After another couple of hands, Indy collects his chips and his hand falls to the small of my back like he can't go another second without touching me as we both stand. There are cocktail servers circling the gamblers, but Indy ignores them all, instead leading me to the bar in the back of the room. While he orders our drinks, I spin and take in the artificial glitz and glam of this place. Beneath the shiny exterior is a thread of violence and greed that's hard to ignore once you notice it.

I'm distracted by Indy passing me a drink, which he hands me with a smirk. "Matches your dress," he says about the purple drink in a martini glass with a blackberry garnish. The tart liquid slips down my throat and helps relieve the burning that's developed there thanks to all the smoke.

"Thanks," I say, bumping my shoulder into his. I can't help but touch him. It's like we're drawn together and even though sometimes fighting it is fun, tonight I don't want to. Not after what happened earlier. Not with that infectious excitement bordering on mania shining in his eyes. I want to know what he has in store, and I have no problem sticking close to him to find out.

"Where's yours?" I ask and he holds up an amber-colored bottle.

"I'm still technically working, and nothing is getting past me to get to you tonight." His words quiet the underlying fear inside of me. I've been tense since we walked in here despite having Asher with us. Knowing Indy's still got my back helps me relax.

Marginally.

I still don't like surprises and not knowing what I'm about to experience has me on edge. I sip my drink, but like Indy I don't plan on gulping it down. Losing my wits right now seems like a bad idea, especially when we don't know who's after me or when they'll strike next.

My fingers are wrapped around the glass, clutching it to me like a lifeline. Asher has melted into the crowd so I'm suddenly more vulnerable than I've been all night. That's probably not true, but that's how it feels. Indy's all cocky confidence and I'm sure if I mentioned it, he'd tell me I'm perfectly safe with only him.

With this many people—and guns—around, I don't think he'd be right on that one.

"Calm down, Duchess. Ash's family owns this place. Nothing's going to happen to you unless Asher wants it to."

I jerk my gaze up to his face where he's wearing an arrogant smirk. "He wouldn't—"

Indy laughs like I just said the funniest thing he's ever heard. "Oh, he would. Well, not to you because I'd fucking kill him, but you think Ash wouldn't get violent if he needed to? Or wanted to?"

I don't know what to say to that, so I say nothing. Instead, I take a small sip of my drink and scan the room for the fiftieth time. "Why do people love this so much?" I finally ask, waving my hand around at all the people throwing their money away. "Casinos obviously stack the odds in their favor. I mean look at this place." Indy slides his arm around my waist and tugs me closer into his body as he follows my gaze out into the crowd. "Don't people wonder where they get the money to make it so nice?"

He's thoughtful for a second, those gray eyes I could get lost in sweeping across the crowds of people all dressed up for a night out who'll walk out of this place with much smaller bank accounts.

"It's the hope you'll win that attracts people and keeps them coming back. It's why they get addicted. It's the rush when you win and the hope that when you lose, you'll win it back. Behind all the glamor, it's ugly and tarnished, but you already knew that."

Choosing to ignore his last comment, I make one of my own. "It sounds like you're speaking from experience."

"Not me personally, but I've seen gambling destroy people's lives. It's fucked up how it can eat away at you. Speaking of..."

"Speaking of being fucked up?"

He nods. "And ruining lives. Look." Indy takes my half-empty glass and turns to set it on the bar behind us before he points out onto the casino floor.

Two of those massive guards that honestly terrify me a little bit are moving through the crowd. The patrons are parting for them like one of those ships that breaks up icebergs as they carve their way to a disturbance closer to where Indy and I stand.

There's a couple who didn't get the memo about the dress code arguing with one of the dealers. They'd stick out even if they weren't actively yelling at the poor man who looks like he'd rather duck under the roulette table than stand there and take this for another second.

At this point, a crowd has started to form around the table, and people watch—some with their phones out—as the security guards arrive and drag the couple from the table. Their chips are left behind as they're hauled towards the elevators, something the man is screaming about so loudly I can hear him over all the other chatter and casino noise.

When the elevator doors close behind the foursome, Indy grabs my hand and pulls me along with maybe the biggest grin I've ever seen on his face. His dimple is out in full effect, and women are struck speechless as we hurry towards the elevators. A sense of excitement starts to build inside me knowing that for some reason, right now, this man wants me of all people. It's like he doesn't even see those other women in dresses skimpier than mine who are perfectly groomed and look like they'd be willing to do anything he wanted them to, right out here in the open.

I shake my head but go along for whatever it is he thinks is about to happen. At least I'll finally get some answers.

As we step up to catch the elevator once it comes back down, Asher materializes out of the crowd and takes his place beside us. The wait isn't long, and when we walk back into the restaurant, I'm amazed at how quiet it is. Indy doesn't give me a second to catch my breath before he's hurrying me out the front doors.

When we get outside, I stumble in my heels as we come to an abrupt stop. Indy's fingers wrapping around my elbow are the only things that keep me from falling on my face on the marble front steps.

"What am I looking at?" I ask as I watch the couple from downstairs try to get aggressive with the two burly guards. The man is tall but rail thin with almost no hair, but what's left is combed over like he's trying to hide the whole top of his head. He's wearing faded jeans and a t-shirt that's wash worn and stretched out so it's boxy on his frame.

The woman—who I'm assuming is his wife—pulls out a pack of

cigarettes, lights one, and blows the smoke into the face of one of the guards. The guy pushes her away and she laughs before throwing the lit cigarette at his face. I cringe as he bats it away, and my nose wrinkles in disgust.

"That," Indy says, wrapping his arms around my waist and resting his chin on my shoulder. "Is Trisha and Wayne McNeely." Smug satisfaction rolls off of him in waves but I'm still not sure what's happening here.

"Why do those names sound familiar? I feel like I should know who they are."

"They're Rory's foster parents, Duchess," he explains, and I gasp, focusing on the couple with a whole new level of interest. "This is why he never has clothes that fit and why he's underfed." Indy's voice gets harder and angrier with every word. "Why their house is falling apart. They take those checks they get every month for the house full of kids they're supposed to be caring for and bring it here to lose it. Rory suffers because these pieces of shit come here and waste every cent they get their filthy hands on."

A rage I've only felt one other time starts to build inside of me knowing how unfair life has been to Rory. It didn't have to be. These people could've chosen to love him, or at the very least taken care of him properly. But they didn't. My fingers curl into fists and my face is already on fire.

The way my heart's racing, I have to breathe harder just to keep up and my muscles are tense with the need to strike out and hit something.

Or someone.

I'm not the kind of person who resorts to violence. I've always been able to keep a level head, but when it comes to my family all bets are off. When my parents died and I found out their deaths weren't an accident, I wanted someone to pay. And now? Now, Rory's just about family and those same protective instincts Indy has are rearing up in me.

Before I can talk myself out of it, I take a step forward and then another with Indy right behind me. The walk to the McNeelys doesn't take long and Indy never once stops touching me the entire way here, so I know he's right beside me even if I can't tear my eyes off the pathetic couple. I watch as Trisha throws her fist at one of the guards and they knock her and her husband to the ground. She glares up at us as we step into their space.

Trisha's eyes narrow even further as she swipes at her lip where a split is welling with blood. When Indy and I were talking, these two were trying to fight their way back inside screaming about the injustice of being tossed out on their asses. Obviously, Asher gave the security guys the go-ahead to get rough with these two because their clothes are torn, and they're bruised and bloody where they sit on the sidewalk.

Asher stands on one side and Indy on the other. Indy kneels down in front of the disgraced couple while Asher nods at the two security guys to give us some room.

Rory's foster mother shoots daggers at Indy with her eyes. "You," she spits, and I'm left to wonder how they know each other. When did they have the chance to meet before this moment? Was it when he spent the day with Rory?

"Yeah, me. This is my friend Asher," Indy says, gesturing up to where my other bodyguard is standing stoic with his arms folded across his muscular chest looking down at these pathetic excuses for human beings. "His family runs the place, and guess what? Your welcome's been revoked. You're not allowed back here. Ever."

The smile that lights up Indy's face is equal parts diabolical and angelic, and I'm totally captivated by it.

Indy holds up his hand in Trisha's direction and I reluctantly tear my eyes off of him to find Trisha with her mouth open like she wants to argue but she smartly closes it when she sees the expression on his face.

"In case you get any stupid ideas like trying someplace new, every other casino in this county is run by his family, so consider yourself banned from them, too. Who's taking care of the kids right now while you blow all your money here? Hmm?"

"You gonna let him talk to us like that?" Trisha snaps at her husband. Wayne's face turns an angry shade of red as he splutters out an attempt at placating his wife, but in the face of four men who could break every bone in his body without a lot of effort, he's a whole lot of bluster and not much else.

But part of what Indy said to them is festering inside of me, growing my anger like a disease. Where is Rory while these monsters are here throwing away the money that should be buying his food? The more the thoughts twist around my mind, the harder my nails dig into Indy's arm where I'm gripping onto him and trying to pull him back up. I need his steady presence, because right now I want to launch myself at the McNeelys. It's so out of character for me I don't even know what to do with myself, but thankfully he stands and pulls me into his side, giving me the support I need to pull in a deep breath and steady myself.

"It's time for you to go," I say, surprising myself with the cold tone in my voice.

"And don't think we won't be watching,' I add, knowing instinctively that Indy will back me up on this. Especially since he went to all this trouble of setting this whole thing up. "If Rory doesn't have clean clothes that fit him and a healthy meal three times a day minimum, this will look like fun compared to what we'll do next."

"You can't do this!" Trisha shrieks, pushing herself up off the sidewalk. Her husband doesn't even attempt to help her, and she turns her ire on him next, shoving him with both of her hands to his chest. She puts her weight behind it and he's no match for the force, so he stumbles.

"Actually, it's already done," Asher says, his jaw clenched as he watches these two lose the small amount of composure they had up to this point. Now that they realize their beloved gambling is going away for real, they're getting desperate.

"We'll report you," Wayne says, lifting his chin and attempting to look menacing but between the way his eyes keep darting down to his wife and the shaking in his hands, it's a pretty pathetic attempt.

"To who? You're gambling at an illegally run casino. What do you think the police are going to do?" Indy says, tightening the grip he's got on my waist until his fingers are digging into my skin. As much as outwardly he's calm and in control of this situation, inside I know Wayne and Trisha are probably testing the limits of that control. If I had to guess, he's picturing all the ways he can make them bleed and as much as I've always believed violence isn't the answer, I can't help but join him in that fantasy. These people are the worst, and that's proven all over again by what comes out of Wayne's mouth next.

"We'll keep you from seeing Rory."

Indy laughs while I scoff. "Yeah? I'd like to see you try." I'm still not sure where this confidence is coming from, but when Indy's thumb rubs encouragingly along my skin, I straighten my spine and focus my best CEO icy stare on the McNeelys. "Give it your best shot, but remember I have his social worker on speed dial, asshole. I will use every penny in my sizable bank account to make sure you regret it if you try. You can't keep us away, but we can make sure you don't hurt him any more than you already have."

Wayne's shaking hands ball into fists at his sides. "You bitch," he hisses before lunging for me, but in the smoothest move I've ever seen, Indy pushes me behind him completely and then steps menacingly forward towards Wayne. He's radiating don't fuck with me energy and I can't even pretend that I'm not inappropriately turned on by it. My thighs clench together as a shiver races down my spine when Indy speaks.

"Don't even think about taking another step towards her. In fact, don't even fucking look at her. You want to deal with someone, you deal with me. Understand?"

I'm peeking around Indy's broad shoulder, so I see the moment when Wayne's bloodshot eyes cut to me.

Indy must see it, too, because he stalks forward and grabs Wayne's chin in a bruising hold, forcing his gaze away from me. "I said don't fucking look at her. Not unless you want me to pluck your eyes out of your skull and feed them to you for dinner. You feeling hungry, Wayne?"

"He looks like he could use a couple of meals," Asher muses from beside me, looking as if this type of thing is completely normal. In fact, I think I saw his lips twitch like he was enjoying this. He's totally unphased whereas I'm pretty sure my heart's about to beat right out of my chest.

"Go home, McNeelys," Indy finally says, releasing Wayne from his hold and wiping his hand on his slacks like touching the man disgusts him. "Don't fuck up or you'll be seeing my face again and it might just be the last thing you ever have the pleasure of experiencing."

"This isn't over," Trisha says before backing up and taking off with her husband hot on her heels.

"So, who's hungry?" Indy asks and slaps his hands together, rubbing them gleefully. "Because we're only getting started on this night."

CHAPTER 16
PENELOPE

THE ADRENALINE COURSING through my veins like fifteen shots of caffeine starts to fade and it leaves me euphoric and feeling like I'm floating. I giggle—something I never do. When the sound escapes me, I slap my hands over my mouth and look wide-eyed at my maybe-boyfriend who's wearing the biggest grin I've ever seen. His dimple graces his stubbled cheek and I'm hypnotized by how happy he is at this moment.

He rushes over to me and wraps his arms around my waist, scooping me up into his arms and twirling me around a couple of times before letting me drop back to the ground with a hard kiss that leaves me breathless all over again.

"I can't believe I have to tag along on your date," Asher grumbles from somewhere behind me and when I look around, I notice the two security guards have disappeared—whether it's back inside or to make sure the McNeelys really leave, I'm not sure.

"Sorry, dude. That's the job. You know it as well as I do. If the roles are ever reversed, I'll happily be the third wheel."

Indy grabs my hand and tangles our fingers together before pressing a kiss to the back. Right when we turn to walk away, one of the two security guys moves to stop us. Guess they were following the McNeelys after all.

"Your father wants to see you tomorrow," he says, staring right at Asher.

Asher sighs loudly but nods once. The guy backs off and nothing else is said until we get into the car. Once we're all shut inside, Asher growls and punches the steering wheel a few times in rapid succession. I jump at the sudden outburst, my pulse shooting sky high, but when I look to Indy with wide eyes, he shakes his head.

"You owe me so fucking big for this, Foster."

"I know," Indy says, reaching forward to grip his friend's shoulder and squeeze. "Anything you need, I'm there."

Asher seems to calm down at Indy's reassurance, and we head out onto the street.

"Can you fill me in on where we're going now? I really don't like surprises," I tell Indy, sitting back against the seat and letting him pull my hand into his lap and hold it there.

"Dinner, Duchess. After all of our earlier... activities," his eyes carve down my body like he can see right through my dress. "I thought you might've worked up an appetite."

The way he says that last word has heat pulsing straight to my core, and like he knows it, he smirks wickedly down at me as we pull to a stop. When I look out the window, I can't say I'm surprised. This place is far more where I'd imagine Indy taking someone for dinner than a stuffy Michelin-starred restaurant.

We're stopped outside of what looks like a neighborhood park on the outskirts of the city. It's almost suburban and a little bit quieter than I'd expected from somewhere so close to the casino-slash-restaurant Asher's family owns. I've got a million questions about that and how Indy pulled off what he did tonight—and how he knows Rory's foster parents—but with everything else going on right now, for tonight I'm going to let them go and try and enjoy my time with him.

I can't even deny that seeing Rory's neglectful foster parents suffer the consequences of their actions wasn't incredible, and knowing Indy did that not only for Rory but for me? Well, I can't help but fall a little more.

Asher gets out of the car and opens the back door for us like a chauffeur, but I know he's just doing his job because while he's waiting for us to get out, his eyes are sweeping the sporadic crowds of people eating and laughing at the picnic tables scattered throughout the grassy area.

As soon as I step out of the car, the scent of dozens of foods clash in the air and I sniff, trying to sort out everything I'm smelling. Between something fried, roasting meat, and the cloying sweetness of vanilla, the task is impossible.

Indy takes my hand and guides me under the fairy lights strung up in the palm trees and crisscrossing the makeshift dining area. I'm assuming Asher is behind us, but when I look back, I don't see him. It's awkward having him along on the date, but he's good at blending in so I can attempt to forget he's crashing. At least he's trying to give us some semblance of privacy, and it's not like Indy can't handle anything that might directly threaten me.

It's with those thoughts that I let myself relax and lean against him while he guides us slowly towards the trucks parked front to back in a long semi-circle. There must be at least a dozen in every cuisine you could think of.

"Have you ever stooped so low as to eat food off of a truck, Duchess?" Indy asks with a mischievous glimmer in his eyes.

"You should know by now I'm not a snob." I only just manage to contain my eye roll.

"I don't think you know yourself very well if you think that's true. Maybe in your elite circles you can pass for not being a snobbish asshole, but here among us common folk the fact you don't have a butler doesn't mean you're not stuck up or used to the finer shit in life," he points out.

I put on my most sickly-sweet voice as I bat my eyelashes up at him. "Why do you want me to hate you?"

"Maybe it's more fun that way. I like that fire that burns in your eyes when you're pissed off. And there's nothing better than hate sex."

Something uncomfortable twists in my stomach that feels a whole lot like jealousy mixed with a healthy dose of uncertainty. I've been so caught up in Indy's magnetism I've forgotten the way he uses women as entertainment. Am I just another number he's going to toss aside now that he's gotten what he wanted? I drop his hand and step away enough to put some space between us, suddenly not so hungry anymore.

"I bet you have lots of experience with that," I mutter, hating the insecurity that I know he can see written all over my body language right now.

He runs a frustrated hand through his hair. "Look I don't actually want you to hate me, okay? I just have all these fucking feelings I don't know what to do with. It's scary as shit and it's easier for me to push you away than face up to what they might mean."

Ugh. When he opens up to me and actually gives me a peek at the real stuff going on inside his head, I can't stay mad. With a deep breath to fortify myself, I take his hand.

"How about we play a game?" I suggest, wanting to drop the heaviness of our conversation and get back to the somewhat relaxed and maybe fun place we were in before I was reminded of his manwhore-ish ways.

The relief in his guarded gray eyes tells me I've made the right decision. "I've gotta warn you, Duchess. I don't have any issues with public nudity, but if you want to get into my pants, there are families here and they might not be as impressed as you are with what I'm packing."

"As tempting as that is, that's not the kind of game I had in mind."

His lip pops out in a mock-pout that's so adorable, I want to kiss him until I'm seeing stars. My growling stomach has other plans, though, so I try to rein myself in.

"How about you pick my dinner for me, and I pick yours for you?" He opens his mouth to no doubt add something dirty, but I keep going so he doesn't get the chance. "The goal is to choose the weirdest meal you can find."

His dimple pops out as his lips stretch into an impish smile. "What will be my prize when I win?"

"When I win, I'll get to choose where we go on our next date."

His smile widens at my casual mention of a follow up to what's happening right now and my cheeks heat.

"And when *I* win, I get to have my wicked way with you anywhere and anyway I want." His eyes are fiery and challenging, daring me to tell him no. The problem is I already know he's going to get his prize whether he wins or not. When his attention drops down my body, he observes all the little tells that give away how turned on I am by that thought. It's obvious he knows it, too. He can read my body like an open book.

He squeezes the hand he's already holding and moves up and down in a shaking motion. "Deal. No take backs."

Now that the deal's been struck, I turn to scan the trucks parked around us, paying careful attention to their names and aesthetics. I immediately spot the one I want, but for this to work, Indy can't come with me.

Lucky for me, I have a backup bodyguard. "Where's Asher? I need him to come with me to get yours."

Indy's eyebrows furrow. "Why? I'll be with you."

I shake my head. "That'll ruin it. Just trust me. Can we find Asher, please? While I'm getting your food, you can get mine and we'll meet at that table," I say, pointing to an empty table closest to where we're parked.

He studies me for a second, weighing whether or not winning this game is worth it, and then sighs. He looks out into the crowd for only a second before tilting his chin towards me and in seconds Asher appears at my side. Indy knew where he was this whole time, and I can't help but be impressed by his awareness of our surroundings even when it seems like he's not paying attention.

"What's wrong?" Asher asks, looking between us with concern etched onto his face.

"Nothing, dude. The Duchess here is *demanding* you take her to buy my dinner."

Asher looks at me with raised brows. "You two are fucking weird," he mutters before shaking it off. "Alright. Lead the way."

I shoot Indy a wink before leaving him to figure out what he's going to get for me. When we're out of earshot, Asher asks, "So, what's the deal?"

"The deal?"

"Yeah, the deal. Why am I taking you to buy dinner for Indy? Shouldn't he be the one doing that?"

I laugh. "He's buying mine. I'm trying to find him the strangest food I can and he's doing the same."

Asher gives me a sly smile. "And what'd you pick for that shithead?"

I point to the truck on the far end with a grin. "Whatever they have at that one."

Asher laughs, like full-on belly laughs at the vegan truck they've somehow shaped into an eggplant, and I can't help but join in. It looks like a giant penis emoji with wheels.

When we get into the line, I start scanning the menu and now that Asher's been caught up on our fun, he seems to be all about joining in because he's studying their offerings just as closely as I am.

"How about the curry dog?" Asher suggests and I lean forward to better read the small print description but then I wrinkle my nose.

"Ew. Kissing Indy after he's eaten garlic dill sauerkraut on top of curry seems like the worst kind of torture. How about something a little less... odorous?"

Asher laughs and strokes his chin. I don't think he's noticed the group of women in line behind us ogling him because he's having so much fun at the idea of torturing his friend.

"What about this one?" I ask, pointing out the pulled barbecue jackfruit sliders with slaw.

"Really? That one actually doesn't seem that bad."

"That's the point," I say as we step forward, moving up in line. "I don't want him to know it's vegan until he's eaten it and likes it. He'll get overconfident and think he's won when he sees it, but what are the odds Indy's ever eaten jackfruit before? I don't even know what it is but fruit that tastes like meat sounds like a bad idea."

"Diabolical," Asher says, holding out his fist for me to bump. "I like it."

After we place the order, and Asher studiously ignores the women that are not-so-subtly moving closer to him and pushing out their breasts and giggling loudly in the hopes he'll pay attention to them, we collect the food and go in search of Indy.

"You know, I would've waited if you wanted to get a phone number or two," I tell him, and he scoffs.

"No thanks. There's nothing special about women like that. They all think they can get their hooks in you and make you into something you're not. They're all the same and I'm not interested. Besides, I'm working. If I fuck around when I'm supposed to be paying attention, people get hurt."

Well, okay then. Thankfully, it doesn't take long to find Indy still waiting in line at a truck with a huge scoop of what looks like ice cream on top called Kitchen of Cones. Ice cream for dinner? That actually sounds kind of delicious.

"Hey," he says as he slides his arm around my shoulders and eyes the food cradled in my hands. It smells like authentic barbecue, and knowing what it actually is, I don't know how they pull it off. "I thought we were meeting back at the table."

"Yeah, but someone took it, and you were still in line, so I figured this would work."

His eyes are alight with mischief as he leans in to kiss my temple. We step up to the window to order and he tightens his hold when the pretty brunette behind the window looks at him like he's her next meal.

That coil of jealousy and insecurity twists in my chest and my instinct is to curl into Indy and then try and back away slowly. This girl is gorgeous and compared to her I'm plain and uptight. She's got colorful tattoos and shows off a ton of skin, and if I were a guy, I'd probably be into her.

"Hey, handsome. See something you want?" she purrs, the innuendo clear in both her words and the tone she uses to say them.

Indy, though... he surprises me. He tightens his hold, looking down at me when he says, "Yeah, I do." He gently takes the food I got him out of my hands. "Cover your ears so you don't ruin the surprise."

He waits until I do what he says before ordering, but even though I can't hear him, I see the cold look in his eyes, how hard they've gotten as he speaks to the woman inside. From the way she flinches as he speaks, I don't think he's flirting back with her and something about how he flipped the switch from warm and caring with me to cold and borderline mean with her calms the jealous part of me right down.

Asher reaches out and grabs my wrist, tugging me in the direction of the tables. I look back and Indy is reaching out for his order, so I let my hands go and Asher leads me to a spot where I sit.

Indy's right behind us, and he sets the jackfruit sliders I ordered in front of himself and then hands me what looks like an ice cream cone... except not. "What..." I start before looking up at him. "Is this?"

Asher laughs and Indy looks thoroughly impressed with himself. "An ice cream cone."

My eyes drop down to the ice cream, which I guess technically it is. "But it has lettuce on it. And are those tomatoes?" I ask, poking at the shiny red squares.

Both of the guys have lost it, laughing so hard I think I see a tear sliding down Indy's cheek. But I'm a good sport so I dig a little deeper and find the actual ice cream. It's weirdly black. What foods are black? I wrack my brain trying to figure it out, but honestly... I have no idea. Squid ink? I hope it's not licorice flavored. Not only is it disgusting on its own, but with lettuce and tomatoes... and cheese... it'll be vomit-inducing.

When Indy finally stops laughing long enough to catch his breath, he gasps out, "It's a taco cone with black bean ice cream."

Okay, I can handle this. The flavor profile shouldn't be too bad, even if the idea of frozen beans is the most disgusting thing I can imagine at the moment. He holds out a plastic spoon for me and I take it, poking it into the black substance and scooping up a bite that includes all the toppings.

Which I now notice includes not only cheese but sour cream and salsa, too. I'm about to spoon it into my mouth when I notice Indy hasn't so much as looked at the food I got him.

"Aren't you going to try mine?" I ask and his eyes heat as if he's going to say something dirty, then they drop to the food in front of him.

"You couldn't get more inventive than this, Duchess? Why am I not surprised?"

I fight off the urge to kick his shin under the table and wait for him to pick up the slider. "At the same time?" I ask and he nods.

I slip the spoon into my mouth at the same time he takes a bite of the sandwich. Admittedly, now that I've seen how out there food truck food can get, I probably did go a bit safe only picking something vegan. I really should've looked around more.

The cold bean ice cream mixes with the toppings and while the texture is horrible, the flavor isn't bad.

"Well?" Indy asks as soon as I've swallowed the last bite.

"It wasn't as bad as I thought it'd be," I offer, and he nods like he knew that's what I'd say. "How about yours?"

He shrugs. "It was fine for a pork sandwich. I really thought you'd do better than this, Duchess. I've gotta say I'm disappointed."

"Except that wasn't pork."

His forehead wrinkles as he studies what's left of his dinner. "It wasn't?"

"No," I bite my lip to keep from laughing at the confused expression on his face. "It's vegan. Something called jackfruit."

"You're lying. No way is that anything other than meat. It's okay if you only know how to pick boring foods. That's why you've got me to help drag you out of your beige world."

I don't know if I should be hurt or flattered by that last statement, so I choose to ignore it. "How do we decide who won?"

Indy looks at me like I'm being dense. "Isn't it obvious? I won."

I set down my taco ice cream cone, folding my arms under my breasts. "How is that obvious?"

"Taco ice cream, baby. Taco. Ice. Cream."

"He has a point," Asher unhelpfully adds from beside me where he's taken a spot and grabbed a spoon, digging into the ice cream. "This is horrible, but it's the weirdest."

"See?" Indy says, pointing at Asher. "He knows what's up."

I throw my hands up. "Fine, but you owe me a rematch sometime." Preferably after I've had time to research every food truck in the area and find the one with the strangest foods.

For a second, he looks like a little boy as he pumps his fist, but then he levels me with a look so filled with heat it's like the very air around me has risen in temperature. Asher clears his throat, obviously noticing the sudden tension sparking to life between Indy and me, but the moment is actually interrupted by the crying of a baby.

Indy flinches and then blinks a few times. His body tenses and he pushes up from the table. He looks like he wants to run, and Asher and I glance at each other with confusion. He doesn't even say anything before taking off in the direction of the car. "Indy?" I call after him, but he doesn't stop.

I knew he still had unresolved issues when it came to the loss of his son, but I didn't know he was still so triggered all these years later. My heart cracks for him, knowing but not able to understand the pain he must face every day. The loss of my parents hasn't gotten any less devastating over the last year. I've just learned to compartmentalize the pain better. Seeing Indy have moments like this where the grief is still so fresh even years later is a frightening look into my future.

Asher and I gather up the trash and get rid of it before we walk back to the car. I climb in the back where Indy's leaning against the window on the far side of the back seat. He's breathing hard and his leg is bouncing up and down.

"Hey," I say, sliding in next to him. I don't bother asking him what's wrong or if he's okay because I already know the answers to both of those questions.

I'm not sure if I should touch him or not, but my instincts are begging me to grab his hand, to try and ground him with my touch, so I do. As soon as my skin brushes his, he turns those stormy gray eyes on me and they're filled with such devastation, my soft gasp fills the quiet car.

"I'm fucking broken, Duchess. Ruined and wrecked and I don't know if I can ever be whole again. You deserve everything that's good and right in this world, and I'm neither of those things. I can't be what you need or give you what you want." His voice breaks as he speaks, and my eyes fill with tears at his pain so openly on display.

Still, the version of me that loves to get under his skin can't resist. "And how do you know what I want? Or what I need?"

"You don't think I can read you like my favorite story? That I see every time you go to those kids in the hospital that longing in your eyes? Or how hard you're working to take away their suffering?"

"I don't—"

"I can't have kids, Penelope. I just fucking... can't."

Asher finally climbs inside the car, starting it up and pulling away from the curb without saying anything. I'm grateful he gave us a few minutes to ourselves, but even more grateful to be moving towards home.

"Okay, well, it seems early to start talking about that, don't you think? You're not even my boyfriend." There I go, pushing his buttons again. Plus, the insecure girl that lives inside of me really wants to know where we stand after sleeping together. It may not be a big deal to him, but it's huge to me.

I bite my cheek to keep from grinning like an idiot at the way he growls at me, "The fuck I'm not. You're mine, Duchess."

"Am I? I don't remember you asking." I think my sass is bringing him out of his sadness because now he's getting all possessive alpha male on me, and things are taking a decidedly hotter turn.

"You agreed the second you let me sink inside your body. The minute you came on my cock and cried out my name. *My* name. You know there's no one else better for you than me." His fingers are wrapped around mine so tightly it's starting to hurt but I don't dare pull away.

"Weren't you just trying to convince me you're not the one for me?" I ask him.

"Fuck. The idea of you with anyone else... I'd kill him. I'd wrap my hands around his throat and choke the life out of any other man who touches you." He's trembling and I can't tell if it's from his earlier freak out or rage. For a few minutes, we sit in silence.

We're having this intensely private and heavy conversation in front of Asher, but this isn't one of those things you can plan ahead of time. It just happened, and if it had to happen this way then I'm good with it. It's not like he didn't hear everything that happened before we left.

"I don't want to disappoint you," he admits in such a quiet voice I almost miss it. "After Chase, I got a vasectomy. I *can't* have kids."

I swallow back the sadness his words bring. He sounds so sure of his decision, and right now I know there's no talking him out of it. "That doesn't make me want you any less. There are other ways for me to fulfill my desire to be a mom, Indy. Like my work and the kids I visit. If we get to that point, we'll figure it out, but we don't have to do it tonight."

"What do you mean if?" When the streetlights shine in his eyes this time, the intensity in them shows how serious he is. "I told you you're mine. That means forever. That means I'm not letting you go. That means you'll have to kill me before I walk away because I'm all in. It scares the everloving fuck out of me, but you ripped my chest open and burrowed down inside. There's no saving me now."

He's not saying the words, but I hear them underlying everything he's confessing and it's terrifying and exhilarating to have this monster of a man drop every wall he's ever constructed around himself and show me his vulnerability.

I reach back to unbuckle my seat belt, the need to be as close to

Indy as I can, overriding every safety rule I've ever heard, but before I can, Asher's voice cuts through every thought running through my head.

"What the fuck—"

He doesn't even finish the sentence before the sound of crunching metal and breaking glass surrounds me, and I flash back to the call I got about my parents' accident. As the realization that I may suffer the same fate just as I found something worth living for sinks in, I reach for Indy's hand again, tangling our fingers together long enough to squeeze once.

Then, everything goes black.

CHAPTER 17
INDY

A HARD AND fast thumping in my chest is what gets my eyes to open. My heart thrumming against my ribcage reminds me I'm still alive. I'm disoriented, unsure where I am or what happened until I realize I'm still in the car.

The blood rushes to my head and the seat belt digs into my shoulder and chest as I hang upside down. I'm vaguely aware of the fact there could be someone outside waiting to finish the job if any of us somehow manage to walk away from this wreck, but there's more pressing shit to worry about. Warm liquid drips down my face and I have to assume it's from where the side of my head smashed into the window beside me as the SUV rolled from the impact. The very spot that's throbbing like a bitch.

I don't have time to worry about it right now. A soft groan from beside me has all of my focus as I turn my head, wincing at the soreness in my neck. Penelope hangs upside down just like me, her seat belt keeping her suspended in the air. Her hair falls around her like a waterfall, messy and tangled enough that I can't see her face to determine if she's conscious. It doesn't matter—I'm getting her out either way, but it sure as hell would calm the erratic beating of my heart if her eyes were open.

"Duchess?" I call out. I have to yell because the horn is blaring in an endless note that might as well be drilling down into my skull. The adrenaline is starting to pour into my system now and it helps me focus and dulls the pain all over my body.

Panic for Penelope explodes into my veins when she stays silent. Getting her free of her seat belt and out of this situation is the only thing I'm thinking about. I've got no idea what or who might be waiting on the outside for us, but we can't stay here. It's my job to protect her, and I can't do that from my current position.

She doesn't respond, so I fumble around trying to reach the release for my seat belt so I can get free and help her down. Glass falls out of my hair as I move, and I look down at the roof and see the small amount of light from the streetlight outside shimmering off a whole sea of broken glass. It's going to fucking hurt when I have to drop onto that.

The seat belt doesn't budge, so I dig in my pocket for my knife, cutting myself right out of the strap. Gravity is a real dick when I fall, and I have no choice but to throw my hands out in front of me onto the jagged glass pieces to keep my face from slamming into them as I fall.

My palms are sliced to shit, but I barely feel them. "Dude, you alive?" I ask Asher who's already working to free himself from his own confinement. The airbags have deployed all over the place and I watch as he pulls out a knife and slices into the one in front of him to get it out of his way.

His answering grunt is all I get, but he's moving and that's good enough for me right now. I'll let him handle getting free while I focus on Penelope.

Her wide brown eyes look right through me, and I swallow hard when I catch sight of the fear in them. They're glassy and unfocused and she's breathing fast, her chest rising and falling quickly with each shallow breath she manages to suck down. If I had to guess, flashbacks to her parents' accident are playing through her mind right now and she's stuck in the memories, so it's on me to help her escape.

I'll deal with her mental shit once she's free.

"Hang on, baby. I've got you," I say, trying to be reassuring even if I have no fucking idea how I'm going to manage to cut the seat belt and catch her at the same time. She doesn't seem to be hearing a word I'm saying. I don't know how much she's even really here with me so I can't assume she's going to help me get her free.

I'm murmuring whatever bullshit pops into my head to comfort her as I try to figure out a plan. Sirens wail somewhere far off, but I can't think about that now.

"Fuck," I mutter, running my ruined hand through my hair. There's a sharp sting from my cut up palm when it rubs across with my bruised head. Despite the rush of adrenaline, the pain is starting to slice through causing my thoughts to scatter.

A glance in Asher's direction shows he's almost free and halfway out the destroyed windshield, gun already in hand. Without having to say a word, I already know what he'll do next. It's the benefit of working together for so long and training so goddamn hard. I used to get annoyed when Connor made us repeat shit over and over, but now I appreciate his meticulousness. Ash and I won't need to say a single word to be on the same page.

Once he's outside the car, he'll trust me to handle Penelope while he secures the accident site. Even as I'm calling it an accident in my head, the pain and fear are turning to rage as I look at Penelope again. There was nothing accidental about this, and I need to get her out of here and home where it's secure, and we can regroup.

An unfamiliar face pops into the open window beside Penelope and the man first makes eye contact with me and then his gaze runs over Penelope. I grit my teeth, wanting to snap at him to take his eyes off of her, but the way he's looking is more clinical than anything.

Before I can ask him who the fuck he is, he's ducking inside and reaching for Penelope. "Don't touch her!" I bark, but he's not listening. She whimpers as he slices through her restraints, and she drops into his arms.

A horrible feeling twists in the pit of my stomach and I fumble behind me, trying to reach the gun at my back. My fingers are bloody and slip over the grip, so I can't get a good hold on it. By the time I finally do, he's pulled Pen out of the car and all I can do is scramble out after them.

If he hurts her, I'll kill him.

As soon as I'm free of the wreckage of our SUV, I crawl over to where the man is kneeling over Penelope with his hands wrapped around her throat. Fury like I've never known before rises inside me like a tsunami, and I intend to unleash its full force on him. My pulse pounds in my ears as I pull myself free of the destroyed SUV. Penelope's skin is so pale it's nearly translucent and there's a blue tinge to her lips as she claws at his hands.

Her movements are slowing even as I rush over to them, pulling my fist back and slamming it into the side of his head. I'm woozy from the wreck and stumble right along with the man, but at least his hands are off of my Duchess now. She's gasping and breathing hard while she tries to fill her starved lungs with air.

I land hard on top of him and with the jolt of extra adrenaline in my veins, the pain in my knuckles as I rain down blow after blow on his face doesn't even register. I'm in a dark tunnel and the only thing at the end of it is this stranger's face as I pummel it into a bloody mess. Bone and cartilage shatter under my fists but I don't stop until he's still and the blood on my hands mixes with his.

Penelope's soft cries somehow penetrate the haze of murderous rage, and I sit up and find her curled in on herself with her knees pulled to her chest and her head resting on her knees. The sight of her so broken tempts me to keep hitting the man until he stops breathing, but she needs me right now more than I need vengeance. The time will come for that later.

I crawl over to her and pull her into my lap, wrapping as much of my body around her as I possibly can. She slumps against me, still with that dazed look in her eye and I brush the tangled mess of her hair out of her face.

"Come back to me, Duchess," I say, the command light but firm even though I know she hates being told what to do. I don't dare hope she'll respond with her usual fiery bite, but all she does is blink up at me slowly.

Asher stalks over towards us with his hair falling out of its usual bun and blood running down the front of his face. He looks like Death himself and with the dark energy billowing off of him like smoke, if I were the guy sprawled out on the ground with Asher towering over him, I'd be shitting myself.

I'd have probably laughed if this wasn't so fucked up.

"I've already called Elias. There's a crowd," Asher says, gesturing over to the other side of the SUV and up the hill we somehow managed to roll down. "They're keeping their distance for now, but cops are almost here and there are phones pointed down here."

He gives me a meaningful look and it hits me just how fast we need to get Penelope out of here. With everything else going on, if anyone catches her on camera like this it'll be a fucking disaster—one she shouldn't have to deal with right now on top of everything. We need to get her somewhere safe before her attackers find out she's still alive.

I might not have been able to keep our car from being hit but I can stop any more damage from being done.

"Can you crawl back in the car and find my jacket?" I ask Asher and for a second, he looks like he's going to tell me to fuck off, but then he must catch on to the plan because he hurries over and climbs inside.

It's dangerous as fuck to go back in because you never know if a spark might light the whole thing up, but we can't let Penelope's face get caught on camera. The second this gets posted on social media, it's game over.

"Duchess," I murmur, pressing my lips into her hair. Her body is trembling, and I tighten my grip. "We're going to get you out of here and to the hospital, okay? Just hang on a little while longer."

Her shaking fingers curl around my shirt as she holds onto me so tightly they turn white. "No hospitals," she whispers, and I don't know whether to be pissed off that she's arguing with me about this or relieved that she seems to be coming out of her shock.

"You're hurt. You need to—"

"No." Her voice is more forceful this time. "If I go to the hospital, the Board may find out. Whoever attacked me could find me there. I'd be trapped. Either way, it'll only give them more reason to think I'm not fit to run this company."

Movement at the car catches my attention as Asher crawls out with my jacket clutched in his hand. I glance up the hill and there are red and blue lights flashing brightly now. A few people stand near the edge with flashlights, or the lights attached to their phones, trying to see the wreck below. It's not a big hike up, and it won't take them long to get down to us.

"We need to get Penelope out of here," I say and Asher nods, yanking the elastic out of his hair and swiping it back up into a neater bun to get it out of his face.

He kneels down so he's on the same level with Penelope and me. "Can you walk?" he asks her.

She bites her lip and then nods, and the knot in my chest loosens. "I think so."

He holds out his hand and helps her up. Her legs shake and she looks unsteady for a second, but then she seems to get her balance and holds her own. I follow her up, scanning the area for the best way out. There's a grouping of trees to the north that would make good cover for the hike out, and it's only about a hundred yards away.

"That's going to be the best way, I think," I say, pointing to the trees so Asher knows where I'm talking about. "Can you text Elias and let him know to pick us up north of the crowd?"

Asher nods, already pulling out his phone. "Done. I've got Julian on the way to help. We'll see if anything useful got left behind during this clusterfuck and deal with the cops. Then we'll take this fucker to the Basement," he says, kicking the unconscious man in his ribs.

I grab Penelope's hand, and she's holding on so tightly, the tips of my fingers start to go numb, but no way will I let go. It only takes minutes for us to get to the trees, and when we do, I turn back in time to see rescuers hiking down the hill to get to Asher and the SUV. Hopefully, Julian's there too because they'll have to explain their captive.

Penelope's still crushing my fingers with her grip, and even though she's keeping up and walking beside me, her breathing is shallow and fast, and she hasn't said a word. She trusts me to lead her through this, and I'm relishing how she allows me to take charge. Her faith means maybe I'm not as broken as I once was.

She's everything to me.

The despair that seems to have become a permanent fixture inside of me over the last several years is starting to peel away, and in its place, I'm left with something much warmer. It's so goddamn terrifying. My heart thuds in my chest so hard, it's like a hammer trying to crack through my ribcage and escape.

The hike up the hill is thankfully less steep here so it's not as difficult to climb up as it would've been where we rolled down. Penelope's heels do get tangled in some brush and she trips, but I manage to catch her before she hits the ground. I hold onto her longer than I need to, taking a second to breathe in her sweet scent and remind myself she's still alive. The fact she could've died tonight is starting to sink in, and that familiar punch of panic is seeping through the cracks in my focus. Now isn't the time to lose my shit, so I grit my teeth and try to push it away.

With any luck, I'll be able to bury it down so deep, I never have to deal with it. If I pretend tonight didn't happen, if Penelope's not seriously injured, we can move on and I won't have to face it.

It's not realistic since we'll have to go on the hunt for the fuckers that did this after tonight, but right now I'm happy to lie to myself.

Whether or not I want to deal with it, the reality is someone is trying to kill her. It's literally my job to make sure that doesn't happen, sure, but she's *mine*. If someone hurts her, I'm going to fuck them up.

When we finally get to the top of the hill, we're far enough away from the crowd dealing with the accident that no one pays attention to us. There are so many police cars, the flashing lights hurt my eyes, so I turn, and when I do, I almost collide with Penelope as she collapses against me.

She buries her face in my chest as she shakes while she clings to me. I hold her as tightly as I possibly can while still keeping my senses trained on the area around us. I'm dizzy and a steady stream of blood drips down the side of my face, but I'm the only thing between Penelope and the threats that lurk in the darkness. It's dark and the only source of light is from the moon and the police, so it's a bit disorienting watching for movement in the heavy shadows blanketing the trees.

Every second we spend out here vulnerable in the open puts me more and more on edge, and by the time Elias pulls up beside us, I practically throw Penelope in the back seat and dive in after her. It's not like me to be paranoid, but when someone attacks you so blatantly, you have to think they're going to stick around to make sure they finish the job. No way was that man working alone.

I've seen it time and time again in this business, and I have no doubt that's the case now. Someone's out there watching, and I'd bet my favorite pair of Jordan's they know Penelope managed to walk away from their attempt to end her.

Now the pressure's really on. There's no more opportunity to play around, no more chances to sit and wait and see what might happen next. It's time we go on the offensive, but first, I have to make sure Penelope isn't seriously injured. She looks okay on the outside, but I'm not going to be satisfied until she's checked out. If anyone understands how healthy you can look on the outside while you're slowly slipping into death, it's me.

Once we're buckled in and Elias has taken off, I move so I'm touching as much of Penelope as I possibly can. I wish I could take the seat belt off of her and pull her into my lap, but after what we've just been through that'd be a stupid-ass move.

"Head to the hospital, Eli," I tell him as he drives away from the red and blue lights.

"Already on our way."

"No. I already told you I'm not going to the hospital. You're going to have to drag me out of this car while I kick and scream and fight like hell. I'll be sure to aim for your balls," my defiant little Duchess says while glaring up at me.

"It's cute you think that would stop me."

"I'm serious, Indy. This is bigger than me getting a Band-Aid for a couple of scrapes. If I step foot in a hospital and somehow it gets out I was there, the Board will move against me. I can't go." The hardness in her eyes has faded and now she's pleading with me. Her voice is husky and raw from that fucker choking her, and I want to argue and tell her it's not just scrapes and bruises. She almost died.

But one look in her eyes tells me she's not going to give in no matter what argument I make, so I swallow it back.

It goes against every single instinct and alarm bell going off in my head, but eventually I nod. "But Elias is checking you over the second we get home and if he thinks you need the hospital, I don't give a fuck what you do to me, you're going."

She eyes me warily before nodding. "Fine."

"You good with that, Eli?"

"Do I have a choice?" he asks, staring at me in the rearview.

"Nope."

"Then sure. I'm happy to check you over, Miss Driscoll."

"Thank you, Elias," Penelope murmurs and then settles back in against me as if she can't get close enough. I hold her tighter, letting go of our stupid argument. In time, she'll eventually see that I'm always right and stop challenging me, but her fighting spirit is something I admire. I don't want her to lose it, but in times like this, I need her to let me take control. I crave it as much as I crave her.

Her head falls to my shoulder as I gently stroke her hair, careful to avoid the tangles. Her breathing evens out and I don't know whether she should be sleeping or not. What if she got a concussion? People aren't supposed to sleep with those, are they?

I'm about to wake her up when Elias catches my eye in the mirror again and shakes his head. It relaxes me to have his approval. If something were wrong, he'd be here to fix it. Still, I don't like not knowing whether or not she's seriously injured. The uncertainty is like a knife twisting in my stomach, puncturing my organs with every turn, and poisoning me from the inside out until I've convinced myself she's about to die.

By the time we pull into the driveway, I've broken out into a cold sweat and my heart's racing. The car jolts to a stop and I gently shake Penelope awake. I'd carry her into the house, but even with the burst of adrenaline I'm dealing with right now, my muscles and joints are sore as hell. It looks like none of us got out of the wreck unscathed.

Penelope blinks her eyes open, and her soft lips start to tug up into a smile as she looks up at me, but reality sinks in and I watch as the warmth drops off her face. "We're home, Duchess. Get your sexy ass inside and let Eli look you over."

Mutiny shines on her face clear as the damn night sky and I know she's going to try to fight me. I'd rather not have to haul her over my shoulder and carry her inside. If she's got internal bleeding or fucked something up in her body, that'll only make it worse. I look her over, weighing my options but she beats me to it.

"I keep telling you I'm fine."

"And what do people say about when women tell you they're fine?"

She narrows her eyes and crosses her arms.

"You gave your word, Duchess. You're not one of those people who go back on their word, are you?" It's a low blow but I'll use anything I have to right now to get her in that house and looked at by our resident doctor. I think I need the reassurance more than she does, and I'm not going to back down from this fight.

She must see that in my face because she sighs, and the resistance goes out of her. It shouldn't, but Penelope surrendering to me this way turns my cock to granite. It's not even close to the damn time, but he doesn't give a shit.

"Let's get this over with," she says, and I crawl out of the car, waiting just outside the door to help her out. She takes my hand, and I'm sure she's going to let it go the second she's on steady ground, but she doesn't. That's how I know she's not really mad at me.

Or maybe she is, but not enough to put any distance between us. She's still got to be shaken up over the parallels between tonight and her parents' deaths. If I were her, I would be. I'm not about to abandon her when she needs me, so I tighten my grip as we walk inside.

Elias waits in the entryway, and as soon as we step through the door, he gestures for Penelope to go upstairs to her room. When we walk past him, he puts his hand on my chest and stops me. I've got no choice but to let Penelope go as she keeps walking and I scowl at my co-worker.

"What the fuck, Doc? You can't possibly think you're going to keep me out of that room." I'm ready to throw down right here, my jaw clenched so hard my teeth ache. My fingers curl into fists and just like that I'm ready to tear him apart for standing between me and my girl.

"Protocol says—"

"Fuck protocol," I snap.

He just blinks at me, his expression blank. "Protocol says you need to update the rest of the team and lock this place down. There's an active threat. You can't ignore that, even if it means you let me do my goddamn job without your overbearing ass hovering over my shoulder."

"Like I said—" I start again and this time he steps closer and stares me down, and I'm reminded why he's not just a doctor. Why he spends a shit ton of time in the field, too. This motherfucker isn't intimidated by me.

"We follow protocol for a reason. Your judgment is off, which means you need to listen to what I'm saying. Go find Sebastian, get him doing his thing. When Ash gets back, we'll have a meeting, but until then, you're going to deal with what happened tonight and I'm going to handle Miss Driscoll."

I move towards him so our toes are touching, and I can reach my thumbs into his eye sockets and pop them like grapes if I want to. "You better not handle anything with Penelope outside of making sure she's not hurt. Keep your fucking hands off of her."

He smirks. "Jealousy looks like shit on you, dude. Calm down, I'm a professional."

"Hasn't anyone ever told you telling someone to calm down is a surefire way to get punched in your fucking face?"

Normally, I'm an easy-going guy. Mostly. But with the accident tonight I'm fucking rattled and I know Elias is just pushing my buttons to throw my emotion from out of control to focused rage, but if he doesn't shut the hell up, he really will get a face full of my fist.

All he does is smile at me and step back, turning on his heel and walking up the stairs. I'm tempted to go after him, to take out all my fear and frustration on him, but that's not fair. I know he's doing me a solid right now, even if he stoked the fires of my anger like a damn expert.

He's right about one thing—I am focused now. I go in search of Sebastian, surprised he didn't come find us when he heard us come in the door. No doubt he saw us approaching on the cameras, but he's not really a joiner so he must be back in the office. Considering the way this evening has gone, I wonder if he's made any headway into who the mole at Driscoll is and who might've been behind Pen's parent's accident.

I walk into the room with purpose, ready to get to work but Sebastian keeps his head down, the moonlight pouring through the windows glinting off his gelled blonde hair. I take the chair in front of the desk, kicking my boots up on the surface. I know it annoys him to no end for my dirty soles to be touching his work surface, but he's so engrossed in his laptop that he doesn't even give me a disgusted curl of the lip.

When I get tired of waiting for him to start the conversation, I speak up. "I take it you heard what happened tonight."

He doesn't look at me as his fingers fly across the keys, but it's obvious he heard me when he responds. "Asher called and updated me, yes."

"And? Have you found anything yet?" Normally, I'd give him shit for keeping his nose buried in the screen while we talk, but I know he's as stressed out as the rest of us. I can tell because his tie is loosened and there are wrinkles in his shirt. Plus, I didn't notice it when I walked in, but I think a couple of hairs are out of place like he's attempted to run his hands through it a time or two.

I've never seen him look so disheveled. Any other day, it'd be funny as fuck. Being sly, I slip my phone out of my pocket and sneak a picture. None of the other guys will believe me when I tell them Sebastian, the most uptight guy I've ever met, had wrinkles in his shirt unless I show them proof.

He stops typing as I'm sliding my phone back in my pocket and looks at me like I'm an insect he wishes he could crush under his polished loafer. "Do you have any idea how much data I'm having to sort through? No, of course you don't because you wouldn't know a variable from a function."

I can tell he's disgusted with me by the lifting of his lip and downward slope of his eyebrows as he looks down his nose at where I'm slouched in my chair. Too bad I don't give a shit. "Why would I know that shit? That's why we have you."

His pristine fingers glide along the edge of his laptop, moving it a quarter of an inch to the right to line it up perfectly with some invisible mark he's got in his mind. "Yes, well, I haven't found much yet, mostly superficial nonsense that doesn't serve our cause. However, I did find a chain of messages exchanged between two people who had access to Driscoll email accounts that raised all sorts of flags. Whoever it is knew what they were doing and not only encrypted it, but also set it up to bounce off so many servers it's nearly impossible to trace."

"So, what you're saying is you've got nothing."

He takes his glasses off and glares at me before rubbing his eyes. "I said it's *nearly* impossible. I'm following the trail now and I'll sort it out. It's just going to take time."

"Well, time ran out tonight. Whoever's doing this is stepping up their game. They're getting more aggressive with every attack, and when they figure out this didn't work—something they probably already know—they're only going to come harder."

"Despite what you may think, I'm not a robot. I'm working as fast as I can." He reaches up to adjust his tie and runs his palm down his shirt, smoothing it out. "I did uncover another problem, though."

I let my head fall back against the seat and close my eyes. A headache is starting to throb behind my eyes. "What?"

"That message chain I discovered, it's written in code."

That gets my attention and I sit up, letting my feet drop to the floor. "What the hell? Let me see."

Sebastian's lips thin into a flat line. "You think if I haven't been able to decipher it yet, you can?" He scoffs but turns his laptop in my direction.

I stare at the lines and lines of absolute nonsense and my headache only gets worse. "Fuck," I say, leaning back and closing my eyes again. Maybe I need to have Elias check me over, too.

"My thoughts exactly. I'm already working on decoding it, but like I said before, it's going to take time."

"Fine. For now, I'll talk to Ash and Eli, and we'll figure out whatever else needs to be done. In the meantime, keep working on that and let me know if you find anything."

He doesn't even acknowledge I've spoken, instead turning back to his screen but something else occurs to me. "Oh, and can you see if there's any traffic cam footage of the wreck? It's a long shot, but maybe they got sloppy, and we'll get a plate number or description."

"Unlikely, but I'll look into it." It's a dismissal if I've ever heard one and between the adrenaline crash I've got going on, the accident earlier, and worry about Penelope, I don't have the energy to give him shit about it.

I leave the room and go upstairs, ready to find Penelope whether Elias wants me there or not. He's had enough time with her alone, and I need my fix. I find him stepping out of her room and gently closing the door, so I stop and wait for him to turn around. When he does, his lips quirk up into an annoying smirk. "She's fine."

I reach out and brace myself against the wall, my palm digging into the hard surface as my knees threaten to buckle with the relief of those two words. I knew I was worried, but I guess I hadn't realized how heavily it weighed on me until this moment. "You're sure?"

"You're doubting my skills?" He raises a challenging eyebrow. "I'm positive. She's got some minor scrapes and bruises, nothing a little over the counter pain reliever won't fix." He eyes me, the way I'm squinting my eyes because of the throbbing pain that's starting to evolve into stabbing.

"Looks like it's your turn. Sit," he orders, pointing at the ground. I don't even argue, sliding down and dropping my head against the wall.

Elias drops his fancy doctor bag beside me and gets down on his knees, so we're eye to eye and then shines a bright-ass light in my face. He asks me a bunch of questions and makes me repeat things back to him before having me lift up my shirt.

When he's done poking at my ribs and listening to shit in my stomach and chest, he puts everything back in his bag. "Well, the good news is you don't have a concussion. Nothing is broken, but you've got some nasty bruises. Take one of these now and another in a couple of hours," he instructs, handing me a bottle of pills. "I suggest you get some rest."

"Can't. I'm taking a trip to the Basement, and it can't wait."

His lips flatten into a line as he pulls a pill bottle from his pocket and tips a couple into my palm. "I figured that's what you'd say. Take these before you go. They'll help."

I open my mouth and toss them in, swallowing them dry. Before I can ask, he tells me, "I'll be on guard duty tonight with Sebastian."

My gaze drops to the gun strapped to Elias's side. Sometimes I forget that he's just as capable as the rest of us with a weapon, even if his first instinct is to fix injuries not cause them.

"Okay, Doc." I leave him to it and let myself into Penelope's bedroom. She's already asleep, so I strip out of my clothes and crawl under the blankets. I'm still covered in grime and blood from the accident, but all I need is Penelope's body pressed against mine, skin to skin contact to reassure myself she's still here.

As soon as I reach out and wrap my arm around her waist, tugging her back against me she lets out a soft sigh. Everything else falls away. It's dangerous how attached to her I am. There's a moment of panic where I almost want to push her away. My heart thrashes in my chest with the last remnants of adrenaline I've got left after this hellish day knowing if something happened to her, I don't think I would survive it. Sometimes, I can still feel Chase's hand in mine as he holds tight while we say goodbye, and it fucking crushes me to know I've let myself get into a situation with the potential to experience that a second time.

How did I get here? I never wanted to be in this position again. Now it's too late. I'm crazy about her—insane, actually. God, I'm a fucking idiot. I can't believe I let this happen with someone who's actively in danger. I must be a masochist to put myself through this bullshit, and yet I know it's already too late. There's nothing I can do but my job. Keeping her safe is my singular goal at this point, because if her attackers succeed, it'll destroy me.

Catastrophic scenarios run rampant through my head. All I can think about is what comes next and how to stop it from happening. Eventually, I slip out of bed and throw on some clothes.

It's time to torture some answers out of a dead man.

As gently as I can, I get out of bed. I can't help but stop and look down at this incredibly infuriating woman who's definitely the most beautiful person I've ever seen, inside and out. Her messy hair falls across the pillow and her hand slides across the sheets like she's searching me out. It's almost enough to entice me back into bed.

I hurry and throw my pants back on, not wanting to stick around and chance waking Penelope up. The second those big brown eyes look up at me, logic will disappear, and I'll do more than just slipping back into bed. I wouldn't stop until I found myself nestled right between her thighs, my cock buried inside her as deeply as it can go just to reassure myself she's really here and with me.

Barefoot and shirtless, I silently leave the room.

CHAPTER 18
INDY

"Fuck, man. I don't know anything," the man strapped to the chair groans before spitting one of his teeth out with a mouthful of blood onto the floor.

"Yeah... here's the thing. I don't believe you." I drop the brass knuckles back onto the table and run my fingers along all the tools laid out for my pleasure. "And even if I did, you tried to kill my girl. I can't exactly let that go, you know?"

He screams when I stab him in the thigh with a long-ass screwdriver. It takes a bit more force than I expected, but I'm happy to burn off some of my adrenaline buzz. Asher leans against the wall shaking his head at me but grinning like a psychopath. I raise my eyebrow silently asking him if he wants a turn, but he waves me off. He'll let me have my fun for now.

"I don't think I'm getting my message across." I grip the man's hair and yank his head back so he has no choice but to look up at me through swollen eyes. "I was never going to make your death easy on account of you hurting what's mine. But I might've gone easier if you'd opened your mouth and spit out something useful. Since you claim to not know anything, I guess I can stop playing around and get to the good stuff, huh?"

I let him go and walk over to the table of torture tools like I don't have a care in the world. Inside, I'm seething. The guy strikes me as a professional and he's not about to beg for his life. He knows better than to waste his breath. The only thing that'll prolong his life now is information.

I want to tear the skin from his body but keep him alive while I do it. He put his fucking hands on Penelope, and for that he's going to suffer. But it's a delicate balance. He knows something, and I need him to admit what it is before I take it too far. That's why Ash is here, to keep me in check.

A pair of pliers catches my attention and I grab them, twirling them through my fingers as I approach my prisoner. "Where should I start? Fingernails or toenails? Maybe teeth," I say, tilting my head to study him. He's trembling from the adrenaline or maybe shock from the pain he's already endured.

"Save me the eyes," Asher says, pushing off the wall and walking over to grab what looks like a melon baller. The dude's fucked up, but I can't really judge. Down here, we're all unhinged when we need to be. You leave your judgements and morals at the door.

The man's eyes widen—well, as much as they can when they're nearly swollen shut and black and blue.

I let out a heavy sigh like I'm doing him a favor, but honestly? Squishing eyes skeeves me out. Watching them pop makes me puke without fail. "Fine, but only if I get his tongue."

"Stop! You can't do this," the man pleads, and I cut my gaze down to him, hoping he sees the fire burning there. The unrestrained fury that's taken over. How little I care about the damage I'm doing to what's left of my soul.

He jerks away from me the best he can, restrained like he is, as I drop down and pull his shoe off, tossing it aside. Then I peel off his sock. "Are you going to use your tongue for more than pointless begging? Because the way I see it, you've got no use for it anymore if you're not going to tell us what we want to know."

The pliers are firm in my hand as I pinch them on his pinky toenail and yank, ripping it off while he screams. The smallest nail always seems to hurt the worst. I toss it aside, wiping the blood off on his jeans before gripping the next nail. "I'll give you until I'm done with all your toes to decide. If you've still got nothing to say by then, well, I'll skip your hands and go straight for your tongue. Sound good?"

I don't wait for him to respond before tearing off the next nail and then the next.

"Fuck! Okay, okay," he pants. His breathing is shallow and fast, and I wonder how close he is to passing out. "I don't know much," he says, and I go to take his next toenail. "Wait!" he yells, and I pause, looking up at him from the mess I've made of his foot.

"You've got three seconds."

"I get these texts. They're coded, but they tell me where to be and what needs to be done. When the job's done, I let them know and money appears in my account. I haven't met the person sending the messages so I c-can't tell you who they are."

Asher moves into the guy's space, gripping his throat and squeezing. "How do you know what the messages say if they're in code?"

He tries to speak, opening and closing his mouth as his face turns red but no sound comes out. I have to think it's because of Asher choking the life out of him, but I'm not inclined to interrupt. Ash won't kill the guy, not before we get what we need. Besides, we're on the same page. He knows this death belongs to me. The second he attempted to take Penelope from me sealed his fate.

Finally, Asher lets him go and he gasps in a breath that's choked and desperate. He coughs and splutters as I stand and set the bloody tool down on the table. "Well?"

"M-my phone," the man chokes out and I look him over, frowning when I realize I'm going to have to dig in his pockets to find it.

"If I stick my hand in your pocket and feel any part of your dick, I swear to Christ I'll cut it off," I say, unhappy about this bullshit. While this may not have been the first hit or sketchy job this dude has worked, he's no elite hitman. He's unkempt, smells like shit, and his clothes are too tight and dirty.

And I'm about to have to stick my hands inside of them to find his fucking phone.

Awesome.

He's bloody and sweaty and shaking and I'm disgusted as I reach my fingers down into his pocket and pinch his phone between them, dragging it up and out. I toss it to Asher while I wipe my hands off on my jeans, but there's no cleaning the filth of this night off. Even a shower won't be enough to scrub the blood from my hands when I'm done here.

"I can help you guys," the man starts to say and Asher punches him in the face to shut him up.

"Dumb fuck," he mutters as the guy's head lolls to the side. "They never learn."

"Facts," I say with a grin before I lift my boot and kick this asshole straight in the ribs. His body jolts from the impact but he's out cold and doesn't make a sound. After a couple more kicks, he starts to come around with a whimper, but he doesn't regain consciousness.

"Hold up," Asher says, holding his hand out for me to stop my assault. When I do, he grabs the guy's hand and presses his finger to the screen when it lights up. With the phone unlocked, he steps back and starts scrolling.

I take the opportunity to walk back over to the table, knowing that if his phone holds the information we're looking for, there's no reason to prolong this anymore. Asher can have his turn at the guy and then we need to end it. Now that I know he's suffered and the answers are within reach, I'm ready to get out of here and back to my Duchess. I trust Elias and Sebastian to keep her protected while I'm gone, but there's still nothing like having my own eyes on her.

I'm about to pull out my phone and check the cameras when Asher curses, drawing my attention to him instead. "What?"

"There aren't a lot of messages but the ones that are here are still impossible to read. There has to be some kind of key. Wake his ass up."

I reach behind Ash to the little bowl of smelling salts, grabbing a packet out and stalking over to our captive. I crack it and wave it around under his nose while he jolts awake. It takes him all of one second to become a frantic, crying, begging mess I have no patience for. The pliers are in my hand again in the blink of an eye and I'm back on the floor at his feet, his ankle gripped in my hand, poised to start taking more of his nails off when he screams at me to wait.

Something in his voice convinces me to hear him out. "I failed and they'll know by now. I didn't check in, so they'll send someone else."

Asher and I exchange glances, knowing our time down here just got cut infinitely shorter.

"Who?" I ask.

"I don't know," he cries, shaking his head. "We work alone." I turn back to his foot, and he kicks out. "But! But I can give you the key. If I give you the key, will you let me go?"

I stand up and he looks up at me with the last fragments of hope in his eyes, and I revel in crushing it when I give him my answer. "I'll do you one better. How about that? I'll set you free from the pain." Then I pat his cheek and stand back, giving him the illusion of choice.

Either way, he's not walking out of here.

And now that he's given away that he has the key to break the code, there's nothing but pure, white-hot agony in his future unless he spills his guts.

He whimpers but then, as the hope fades from his eyes, resolve takes its place. "Go into my cloud folder," he says, his voice shaky as he nods his head in Asher's direction. Ash does what he says and then looks up at him expectantly.

"Click into the *elements* folder," he tells Asher and then rattles off a password when prompted.

"What am I looking at?" Asher asks as his eyebrows pinch together. He's staring at the screen but it's obviously not making sense, whatever he's looking at. I move over beside him so our shoulders are pressed together, staring down at the screen in his hand.

"It's a periodic table," I tell him, still not understanding how this works with the code.

Asher shoots me a look like *no fucking shit, dumbass* and I smack him lightly on the face with a grin.

"Not just any periodic table. Look closer at the numbers and letters," the asshole strapped to the chair in the middle of Connor's basement says in a quiet voice. It's one hundred percent filled with defeat, just the way I like it. He's been thoroughly broken, and it wasn't even that hard. Honestly, I'm a little bit disappointed.

"Not gonna lie, dude, it's been a hot minute since I took chemistry," I tell Asher and he lets out this commiserating chuckle.

"Same. I'm going to shoot this shit off to Sebastian and let him sort through it." He messes with the screen while I turn back to our captive.

"So, this is the key?" I ask, gesturing back to Asher. The guy's nodding like a bobblehead and I lean back against the table of tools, folding my arms across my chest while I wait for Asher's confirmation.

The itch to check my phone is getting stronger by the second. Up until now, the adrenaline consumed me to the point I wasn't thinking about anything but how much pain I could inflict on this fucker before he took his last breath. But now that I'm stuck waiting around and the edge of violence has eased off, the need to check on both Penelope and Rory is surging back up.

I reach into my pocket and pull out my phone, letting the compulsion win. It's going to take Sebastian at least a couple of minutes to scan what Asher's sent him and verify it's the real deal, which means I've got time to kill.

The man in front of us seems to have passed out again, his breathing shallow and labored as his chin rests against his chest but I don't care to wake him up. At least this way I don't have to listen to his whimpers and crying. At least take your punishment with honor, for fuck's sake.

Asher's still hanging out tapping on the phone screen, so I pull up the first video feed, the one that's on Penelope. She's sleeping peacefully in the middle of her bed, her dark hair spread across the pillow and the blanket kicked off, so I get a prime view of all kinds of skin on display like she knew I'd be watching.

Hell, she probably did.

The thought of her playing with me like that gets me hard, and I shamelessly adjust my dick in my jeans. The second I'm done with all this bullshit I'll be inside her and I'm not going anywhere else until my cock falls off or she begs me to stop.

God, I can't even think about how close I came to losing her tonight. Fuck, just remembering how she looked with this asshole's hands around her neck triggers that murderous darkness to swirl up inside of me all over again. I need to remember to cut off his fucking fingers for what he did before the end.

Boner officially deflated.

I'm glaring at the soon to be corpse as I click out of Penelope's feed and into Rory's. Asher wasted no time setting the cams up and when the live stream loads, I'm grateful for how seriously he takes his job. What I see stops my fucking heart as my fingers clench so tightly around the phone, it's on the verge of shattering.

Just like the control on my fucking rage.

The control I only now got a grip on.

Trisha McNeely's gripping Rory by his hair holding a cigarette to the skin of his arm while his mouth is open in a silent scream and tears stream down his face. I only imagine it's silent because I don't have the volume up on my phone, but I don't turn it up. I can't. If I do, I'll break.

There are five other kids huddled nearby, towered over by Wayne who glares down at them threateningly, a half-empty bottle dangling from the fingers of one hand and a belt wrapped around the other. They're all clinging to each other with tear-streaked faces and sad, empty eyes no child should ever have.

"Sebastian for sure has a hard on for this code breaking bullshit," Asher laughs, shaking his head as he still looks down at his phone. I'm trembling, on the verge of a full-on rage out but he has no idea. Not yet. "We're all good, though. He thinks he can figure it out with this last piece."

Asher finally looks up at me and any amusement that was on his face drops off. "Shit, what now?"

"Rory. Can you finish this?" I ask, already moving toward the door.

"Yeah, go," he says, putting the phone into his pocket to tie up this loose end. "I'll be there in a bit."

I want to tell him he doesn't have to rush, but I don't know what kind of fuckery awaits me at the McNeely's and there's a good chance I'm going to unalive at least one of those two shit for brains before the night is over. I might need Ash to bail me out of jail... or bury some bodies.

Maybe both.

As soon as I'm out the door I'm running, and I don't stop until I get to my car and peel out of Connor's driveway. I call Penelope on the way, knowing I don't want her to see me at my darkest but also understanding she's the link to Rory's social worker. No matter how things turn out tonight at that house, he's not staying there another second.

"Indy?" Her voice is raspy from sleep, seductive enough to slow the wrath in my blood.

"Hey, Duchess. Sorry to wake you, but I need your help." I throw on the blinker and merge onto the freeway, darting around cars while I push harder on the accelerator. Every second wasted is another Rory has to endure the torture of those meant to protect him.

There's a rustling like she's sitting up and when she speaks, she sounds much more alert. "With what? Tell me what's going on."

"I put cameras in Rory's house," I tell her, laying it out bluntly. I don't feel even a sliver of guilt over doing it, especially not now that I know what's going down tonight.

"Why would you do that?" She doesn't sound accusing, only curious. Some weight lifts off my shoulders knowing that she's not judging me for my need to have eyes on the two of them at all times.

"I didn't trust the McNeelys, and I had to know he was okay. But Duchess? He's very fucking not okay."

"What do you need me to do?" This is one of the things I love most about this girl. She's a problem solver and doesn't hesitate to fix what's broken. Maybe that's why she's drawn to me.

"Get his social worker on the phone and tell her I need her to meet me at their house. It's bad, Duchess."

"How bad?" she asks quietly like she doesn't really want to know the answer.

"They'll be lucky if they have their lives by the end of the night," I say, trying to avoid having to give her any details.

She blows out a breath. "I'll be there as soon as I can. Try not to kill anyone."

"No promises."

"Indy."

"You didn't see what I did. No. Promises."

"You can't go to jail. I need you," she tells me, but it sounds like it pains her to admit it. My girl's not the kind to admit her weaknesses, and in her eyes needing anyone is weak. Her admitting this to me? It's huge—so huge, I almost forget about my anger for a second. Almost.

"I won't go to jail, Duchess. The only ones making that trip tonight are Rory's foster parents. I've gotta go," I tell her and end the call. Normally, I'd deal with the McNeelys myself down in Connor's basement. They'd disappear like the scum of the earth they are, and no one would ever miss them.

The problem is they're part of the system, responsible for other kids, too. If they disappeared with no trace, people would ask questions. And what would I do with the four kids? My usual methods aren't going to work this time, and I have to play it smart. I've got Penelope now, and Rory. I can't leave them unprotected if I get caught with blood on my hands.

So, I dial a new number, and then I drive like hell.

When I get to the shitty little house, I throw open the door and storm inside without knocking. Glass shatters somewhere and the sounds of kid's sniffling and crying softly throws my temper into overdrive. The room is in chaos, chairs tossed over and the broken shards of what remains of Wayne's bottle of liquor scattered across the ground.

"What the fuck are you doing here? Get out of my house!" Trisha snaps as her glassy, unfocused gaze lands on me.

"Where's Rory?" I demand, taking a step towards her with every intention of wrapping my fingers around her thick neck and choking the answer out of her if I have to.

Her eyes cut to somewhere over my shoulder before snapping back to me, and an unholy, malicious smile curves across her cracked lips. "You can't do shit here, so fuck off out of my house."

I'm focused on Trisha, so I don't see Wayne come out of nowhere and slam into my side. He reeks of cheap alcohol and sweat, and he's so pathetically weak his hit barely budges me from my spot. I don't miss a beat, elbowing him right in his face, feeling his nose break as blood spurts all over the place.

"What kind of sick fuck hurts innocent children?" I ask the room, knowing neither of Rory's foster parents are going to answer the question.

Trisha pulls a cigarette out of her pocket and lights it up, and I step forward with every intention of snatching it out of her hand and using her skin to put it out... over and over again.

"We had to find other ways to entertain ourselves," she sneers, looking all too fucking happy with this turn of events. This bitch thinks she got one over on me. "They're *my* kids. I'll do what I want with them, and you can't do shit about it. Now get out."

"I'm not leaving without Rory." I'm standing in front of her now, and I snatch the lit cigarette out from between her lips ready to do some serious damage. Her eyes widen with fear for a split second before I hear it.

"Indy." The whimper is so quiet, I'm surprised I picked it up over Trisha's shrieking and Wayne's sobs.

I spin and see him huddled behind the overturned table in the dining room, his back pressed against the wall. His knees are pulled up to his chest, and he looks up at me with red-rimmed green eyes that are haunted in a way I've never seen from him before. My fingers curl into fists as the itch to make Trisha and Wayne pay for stealing my boy's innocence crashes over me.

Red and blue lights suddenly flash off of the walls and I know I've only got seconds. "I'm going to get you out of here, okay, bud?" I tell him and he blinks up at me slowly. I don't know if he's hearing me, but if this is going to work, I need him to understand. "When the police ask you, I need you to tell them you called me. Can you do that?"

He nods and then moves so fast I barely have time to catch him. He throws himself at me, his tiny arms wrapping around my neck. He's trembling and squeezing me so hard I think he's afraid if he lets go for even a second, I'll disappear. Little does he know I'm not going anywhere. Not now. Not ever.

The cops are storming into the house, and I watch as they take in the scene. Trisha and Wayne are handcuffed while the kids are pulled outside. I know they're going to ask me questions, too, and I'm shocked I'm not in handcuffs myself. The way Rory's clinging to me probably helps my case that I'm not the bad guy here.

I don't wait for them to question me. I know it's coming, but Rory's been through enough in this house of horrors. The sooner I can get him out of here, the better.

We step out into the cool night air and the lights are more intense out here. Rory's buried his face in my neck, and I tighten my hold on him. My body is like a protective shield around him, and no one's getting through me. I spot Penelope and Lucy, Rory's social worker, huddled together at the edge of the yard talking with one of the police officers.

As if she knows I'm watching her, Penelope lifts her warm brown eyes and they connect with mine, assessing me before they slip over to Rory. The relief as she looks him over is palpable, and I cross the lawn to join them.

"Indy, this is Lucy Davis, Rory's social worker, and Officer Hernandez," Penelope says. I mutter some polite bullshit out but honestly? I want to take Rory and Penelope and get the hell out of here.

I gesture for Penelope to move away from the two of them so I can talk to her out of their earshot, and she follows me a few steps away.

"How is he?" she asks, keeping her voice down so our conversation stays between us.

I rub his back and he doesn't budge. He's become deadweight in my arms and he's not shaking anymore. "I think he's asleep. Passed out."

Her eyes soften and then take on that determined glint that gets me hard as stone. "We're taking him with us, so what do you need me to do?"

I lean forward and kiss the hell out of her, loving that we're on the same damn page. "Whatever it takes, Duchess. Throw your fortune around. Bribe the fuck out of anyone you need to. I don't care. If you want me—"

She narrows her eyes and lifts her chin. "Do not finish that sentence, Indy Foster. I'm perfectly capable of acting like a stuck-up pain in the ass when I need to, and I think I've already proven that I'm willing to stray from the straight and narrow when the occasion calls for it. So, you take our boy home and have Elias check him over and I'll finish up here."

I open my mouth to argue, to tell her there's no goddamn way I'm leaving her here without me. That it was dangerous as fuck for her to even come here in the first place, but then I see Asher leaning against her car. The smug bastard gives me a knowing smirk looking chill as hell even though he killed someone less than an hour ago. He must've gone straight to pick up Penelope and bring her here instead of coming straight after me.

I grip the back of her neck and pull her closer so my lips hover over hers as I make my demands. "Stick to Asher. Don't go anywhere out of his sight. Promise me."

She shivers and even though I'm fucking wrecked from this day—the longest day of all time—I'm still going to sink inside of her the second she gets home just to prove that I can.

"I promise, but only if you wait up."

"Duchess? You've got yourself a deal."

CHAPTER 19
PENELOPE

I think my heart might explode.

No, really.

And if it goes, it's taking my ovaries with it.

I'm staring down at Indy curled up behind a sleeping Rory like he's trying to keep the world from touching him. I have a feeling my bodyguard is more attached to the kid than he's let on. There's this picture in my mind, one where the three of us are a family. One where Rory won't have to worry about where his next meal comes from or whether anyone in this world loves him. One where Indy's free from the demons of his past, loving without conditions or restraint or deep-seated fear.

One where I never have to let either of them go.

They're both still fully dressed with Indy on top of the blankets and Rory tucked cozily inside. It's after midnight and this day has stretched on so long, it might as well have been a year. I can't fault Indy for crashing even if he reneged on our deal. Rory's more important than my need to be close to my boyfriend.

That's what we are now, but it doesn't seem like enough. The way my world has come to revolve around Indy and his presence in my life is scary at best, but also like a freefall where for an indeterminate length of time you're floating, completely weightless and free. You never know when the crash might happen—or if it will come at all. And it's only more exciting because of the unknown.

Elias pops his head in the room, and I take that as my signal to duck out. I want to hear what he found when he examined Rory. The little boy was clutching onto Indy like a boa constrictor, squeezing like his life depended on it, so I didn't get to check him over myself.

The door clicks behind me as I pull it closed, twisting the handle so it's almost silent. Elias waits for me near the stairs and I walk over to him, sitting down on the top step. The weight of everything that happened today is heavy, nearly crushing my bones into dust under the exhaustion.

He sits beside me looking as tired as I feel. There are dark shadows under his eyes as they lift to settle on me. "How are you feeling after the accident? Sore?"

"A little, but considering how bad it could've been, I'm doing alright. How's Rory?"

Elias sighs and looks away. "Physically? He'll heal. But the shit he went through tonight, that leaves a scar. He seems like a resilient kid, so I have every hope it won't hold him back, but we won't know until he gets some rest, and he recovers from the burns."

A cold chill cuts down my spine. "Burns?"

The doctor looks like he's been through a lot in his young life, but the way he's looking at me now, eyes filled with sorrow and sadness, I suddenly don't want him to elaborate. As my stomach churns, I decide I don't want to know.

But it's too late to stop him.

"Rory has multiple circular burns on his arms and chest. From what I understand, they're from a cigarette. He's also severely malnourished and has bruises covering his chest, stomach, and back."

I choke back a sob—barely. How can someone be so cruel to a child? A sick little boy who's never known kindness in this world? Why wouldn't you want to be the one person who lifts him up and gives him something to fight for? I don't understand it.

Elias's hand comes to rest on my shoulder, squeezing gently. "He's going to be okay. The best thing you can do for him is be here. Feed him, let him rest, and give him a stable environment to heal."

I nod, unable to speak. If I open my mouth, I might scream, and I don't want to wake everyone up. Watching the McNeelys get carted off to jail for child abuse tonight wasn't nearly enough punishment for what they've done. I hope they suffer every day they spend behind bars for what they did.

I wish I had the stomach to do it myself. To make sure they can never hurt another child for the rest of their pathetic lives. To see it with my own eyes so I could be sure the message was really sinking in.

Elias lifts his hand from my shoulder, and I glance over at him. "Get some rest," he says, standing up and walking down the stairs. "Doctor's orders."

I watch him go, lost in my own thoughts and knowing there's no way I'll be able to sleep no matter how exhausted I am. I think I've aged a hundred years in a single night. How can things have turned out so spectacularly wrong tonight? It seems like a lifetime ago I was happily watching the McNeelys dragged out of that casino, and I can't help but wonder if what happened to Rory is somehow my fault.

All I want to do is crawl into bed with Indy and let him shelter me from all the bad happening in my world right now.

Rory needs him more, so when I finally do pass out, I know I'll be on my own. Everything's so heavy, though. The weight on my bones is as heavy as an entire mountain and it threatens to buckle my knees and render me completely useless. I can't let it overwhelm me, not when there's so much to do. Giving in to the temptation to turn my back on my problems and get lost in the fantasy of my found family won't actually make anything better.

My situation won't suddenly transform from dangerous and hunted to relaxed and content. I'll still be here, stuck dodging threats from some faceless person. What I need is to ground myself, to sink my toes into the grass, breathe in some fresh air, and toss my head back while I stare at the stars.

I need a reminder that I'm one small person, insignificant really, who's destined to make a difference. A reminder that no matter the cost, I'll pay it to make sure kids like Rory never have to suffer like he has again. One small person can make a hell of a difference when properly motivated, and the potential for my life to be cut short only spurs me on.

It only encourages me to work harder. Smarter. Faster.

With aching muscles and sore bones, I stumble down the stairs and towards the backyard. It's dark, the middle of the night, silent but for some insects and whatever else lives in the trees around my house. The world's asleep and this moment has no expectations. I'm staying close to the house, and Indy and Sebastian have both reassured me that between the perimeter fence, motion detectors, and cameras, I'm safe here.

Well, as safe as I can be while someone is trying to kill me.

I wouldn't take the risk except I feel like I can't breathe. I need the fresh air because otherwise I'm going to suffocate against the weight of everything that's happened tonight, and I have too much to do to let my fear claim me.

I tip my head back, ready to lose myself in the stars and regain some perspective, but there are no stars tonight. Instead, there's a thick layer of clouds obscuring my view, and a slightly hysterical bubble of laughter pushes up my throat. It's just my luck that the one night I'm desperate to lose myself in the cosmos, it's lost to me. I mean, seriously. What is going on with this day?

Is Mercury in retrograde or something?

Not that I believe in that sort of thing, but the terrible energy of this night can't be denied. The earlier parts of this day had been so promising, too. I guess murder attempts could ruin anyone's date, so it's not just me. The thought makes me feel slightly better about the whole thing.

But I'm still disappointed about having to cut my time with my bodyguard short. Is it inappropriate to be sleeping with the man sworn to protect me? Yeah, I'm sure some lines are being crossed. That doesn't mean I care. For once, Penelope Driscoll's thwarting the rules. Playing the bad girl.

What can I say? Indy brings it out in me.

Thunder rumbles in the distance as lightning cracks across the sky, illuminating the whole yard. Rain sprinkles down sporadically, still light enough I hardly feel it misting across my skin. There's an electric charge in the air, the scent of rain and ozone fills my nose as I breathe in and then out, letting go of some of my tension.

It's bleeding out of me like I've been cut, dripping all the day's worries onto the grass at my feet. My toes curl into the soft, cushy blades and I close my eyes. Lightning slashes across my eyelids for a half a second and then again and again. The storm is rolling in fast, the rain picking up in intensity. My hair is soaked as droplets fall from my eyelashes, my nose, my lips.

Another boom of thunder shakes the ground and it's then that I open my eyes. A burst of light from the tree line catches my attention seconds before the sky lights up again, and a hot rush of wind hurtles by the side of my face, blowing my hair wildly in front of my eyes. It sticks to my cheeks and makes it hard to see.

I lift my hand to shield my eyes and stare out into the trees as the rain hammers down. It's impossible to hear anything but the crash of thunder and the sound of rain pounding against the earth. The only time my vision clears enough to see anything through the downpour is when lightning electrifies the sky, and even then, all I can make out is the dark tree line. Shapes of trees like sentries lining the perimeter of my property, but a chill settles into my bones when I look at them now.

The shadows are so thick, they could be hiding anything. Fear explodes in my chest as something hard collides into my side, tackling me to the muddy grass. We roll, and as we do I kick and scream and punch and claw. Whatever it is holds me down, their weight pressing my body into the ground. It's not until a hand clamps over my mouth and Sebastian's icy blue eyes collide with mine, I stop fighting. His glasses are askew and covered in water droplets, and his nose is touching mine. "Stop fighting," he barks out over the crashes of thunder straight over our heads. The expression on his face is fierce, harder than I thought possible from the resident computer nerd.

He's pinning me down as he pulls a gun out from behind his back. He's sitting up on his elbows but keeping his head low while he stares into the trees. "We need to get you inside," he yells over the thunder as more booms go off in the distance.

This time, I can make them out over the crashing of the storm and my blood goes cold. If it weren't for the shitty visibility, I'd probably be dead right now. That hot gust of wind that blew past the side of my face earlier suddenly feels a whole lot like I barely escaped with my life. That had to have been a bullet and the realization splashes over me like a bucket of ice water.

I'm shaking and I don't know if it's from fear or anger. Someone came onto *my* property and is shooting at me. The people I love most in this world are inside, and the clarity of that slams into me with the force of a thousand wrecking balls. I love Indy and Rory, and whoever's here right now trying to take me away from them needs to pay.

If only I was strong enough to make them.

But I'm not. I don't have the training to take someone like that on by myself. All I can do is hide and try to escape, regroup and figure out how to go on the attack.

Sebastian has other ideas. He lifts his gun and fires into the trees. I jump as my heart beats so fast I think it might explode. I throw my hands over my ears too late. There's a buzzing now from the gunshots so I can't hear when Sebastian stares down at me and yells something.

All I can do is grab his wrist as he moves and grips my shirt, yanking me up with him. He moves to cover my back with his body as he pushes me forward, and we run for the doors. I don't know if whoever is in the trees is firing at us or not because between my sudden deafness and the thunder shaking the ground under my feet, I can't hear anything else.

We're almost there, steps away from the door when Indy and Asher both step over the threshold and out into the storm. Indy has a gun in his hand and another strapped to his side and Asher has one in each hand. Indy's eyes briefly flick to mine as they scan down my body but for once they're not full of his usual heat. This is purely a fact-finding mission.

I can tell by the look on his face he's in bodyguard mode, all business as he faces the direction the shots came from. Before I'm ready, he shifts his eyes back out into the dark and without speaking a word to each other, he and Asher start shooting.

I want to stop, to turn around and demand they come inside with me. We don't know how many people are out there in the trees or what weapons they might have. There's a painful ache in my chest knowing there's nothing I can do to stop him from going out there. Hell, he's already beyond the point of me talking sense into him or grabbing him and pulling him back with me.

Even if I wanted to stop, Sebastian's steady hand on my back shoving me forward wouldn't let me. My lungs seize up and the room starts to spin as we walk inside. I want to drop to my knees, to press myself against the glass and stare out into the night to see for myself Indy is safe.

But Sebastian locks the doors and then half drags me across the house. When we get to the stairs, I manage to get to my feet, allowing him to pull me up. As much as my mind is outside under the lightning-filled sky with Indy, tonight I have Rory to think about, too. I can't forget that Sebastian, Elias, and I are the last defense if my attackers somehow manage to get inside.

Outside of Rory's room, my back hits the wall and I slide to the floor. Sebastian opens the door and murmurs something to Elias I'm too far gone to understand. My mind is focused on one thing and one thing only—whether Indy's going to get hurt because of me.

CHAPTER 20
INDY

Every muscle in my body is coiled and ready to spring into action as Asher and I stalk out into the downpour with our guns raised. I'm itching to rain hell down on whoever's in the trees. The perimeter alarm on my phone blared less than two minutes ago, shocking me out of a dead sleep, and my heart hasn't stopped battering my rib cage since.

The rain pelts down on us making it damn near impossible to see more than two feet in front of my face. Droplets of water gather on my eyelashes and drip into my eyes, but I don't dare blink them away. Not when that could mean the difference between finding the motherfucker I'm going to *obliterate* in the Basement when this neverending shit show of a day is done.

Out of my peripheral, Asher uses a hand signal to say he's going left, so I take the right. I rush off into the trees with my gun drawn and my attention focused ahead. I'm scanning everything, looking for so much as a twitch but there's nothing.

Other than the rain hitting the canopy above and the leaves on the way down, there's nothing. I'm breathing hard, trying to keep my head in check and not let my thoughts drift back to the memory of Penelope on the ground while some bastard fucking *shoots* at her.

While I was sleeping.

When I get to the tree line it's so dark, I can't see my own hand in front of my face. Without the use of my eyes, my other senses are on high alert. Not so much as a branch breaks under a heavy boot as I listen to myself breathe and the rain splash the saturated ground. I strain my ears, trying to pick up anything but there's not even a whisper of anyone else out here. If the attacker is a professional, I'd expect nothing less.

Asher's out here searching with me, and I can't hear anything from his direction, either. Stealth, that's what our training has taught us so it's not surprising, but the knowledge a hired assassin is out for Penelope's blood ramps up my already sky-high adrenaline.

The only relief from the absolute darkness is when lightning flashes overhead, and those moments are too few to be of any use. If anything, they blow out my night vision and for a few seconds after each one I'm vulnerable to attack.

I take out my phone and turn on the flashlight, blinking the sting away as my eyes adjust to the sudden brightness. As much as I don't want to draw attention to myself, I can't see shit out here and I need to do something. Stumbling around in the dark isn't going to cut it.

I aim the light at the ground after doing a quick sweep of the area right around me and seeing nobody. If I had to guess, whoever just shot up Penelope is a professional and will try and haul ass out of here before we catch them. It'll be a miracle if I find any evidence that they were ever here at all.

I walk through the trees keeping my flashlight focused on the ground but my eyes on everything all at once. There could be footprints on the ground, but it's hard to tell because everything is saturated with water and mud. If there were distinct prints, they would be halfway washed out and flooded by now.

When I finally reach the perimeter fence, I haven't found anyone and there's no movement, so I circle back. If I was an assassin, I would set up post just inside the tree line. I'd be far enough in that somebody wouldn't be able to see me if they looked out the back door but close enough to the tree line to have a clear shot of my target.

Sometimes you have to think like the enemy to figure out what your next steps are going to be.

Keeping that in mind, I focus my search on that area. My footsteps splash in the rain and mud as I pace back and forth, searching the ground for anything. I'm about to give up until this storm passes when the light from my phone glints off something halfway buried in mud at the base of one of the bigger trees.

I drop to my knees not caring about how the cold wet dirt soaks into my pants. I've just found some bullet casings and my stomach twists staring down at the evidence of how close I came to losing Penelope tonight.

The thick mud coats my fingers as I dig into the ground, lifting a casing up to examine it closer under the light from my phone. I squint through the rain dripping down my face. Fuck. If I didn't think the shooter was a pro before, the AR-15 he used to shoot at my girl just confirmed it. The shell slides into my pocket as I stand up and click off the light, letting my eyes acclimate to the shitty weather and the dark.

I turn, looking for Ash but it's impossible. The storm's too vicious to see through and I need to get back inside and check on Penelope. Barbed wire wraps around my chest as I try to breathe through the pain of nearly losing her.

A branch breaks high in the canopy of the tree beside me, and my head snaps up. I squint into the darkness, but I can't see shit. There's scraping and movement but it's not until a thick arm wraps around my neck from behind and cuts off my air that I realize I may just get my chance for retribution tonight after all.

This stupid motherfucker didn't flee like I thought. He stayed. He climbed a tree. And he waited for his chance.

Too bad for him he's about to spend his last moments in agony while I take out my anger on his flesh.

Because I am fury brought to life.

My rage is all-consuming like an out-of-control wildfire. I'm ready to destroy anything in my path and this asshole just made a fatal mistake.

Every part of me is focused on one thing—ending this threat. So, while his arm may be wrapped around my neck, I still have the upper hand. My heart beats out a steady rhythm as a deadly calm washes over me. I've prepared for this moment, and panic will not interfere with my plans.

My airway is restricted but with the downpour, his skin is slippery against mine and I'm taller. He can't get the leverage he needs to completely cut off my oxygen, so I use that to my advantage, throwing my weight forward so I'm bending at the waist. The would-be assassin flies over my head and lands in a heap at my feet.

I straighten and suck in a breath before dropping down on top of the man. He's dressed all in black with a face so unremarkable, I can't pick out any features. It's dark as fuck and I don't care who he is. The only thing that matters now is what he did and the price he's about to pay for it.

He lifts his hips, trying desperately to buck me off but I'm bigger. I wrap my fingers around his throat using my grip on his neck to push him further into the mud. I hold him down and let him struggle until he's panting and finally goes still. He's not unconscious, just catching his breath and regrouping for his next attempt at escape.

It will fail, too.

When I lean down to look in the eyes of my Duchess's attacker, all I see is defiance. The wheels are turning in his unremarkable brown eyes, so cold and bland compared to Penelope's. His soon to be lifeless eyes.

There's no remorse, but even if there was, I'd never let him keep breathing. Not after what he's done. He doesn't deserve the air in his lungs or mercy from me. His nails dig into my arms as I press him deeper into the mud. I tower above him as he tries to claw and fight his way out from under me, but it'll never happen.

His movements slow and eventually stop. I barely feel the burn where his nails tore at my skin as my chest rises and falls with harsh breaths. Eventually, I let him go, satisfied with his lifeless gaze staring up at nothing.

I don't get pleasure from taking life—not normally. But this is different. I enjoyed every second of that and I almost wish I could bring him back to life to do it all over again. Removing threats from Penelope's life has jumped to one of my favorite things to do. It's a need, an obsession-fueled desire to own her completely. I won't tolerate anyone hurting what's mine.

"Shit," Asher bites out and then immediately turns his phone flashlight up into the tree canopy. "Why the hell didn't we think about them hiding in the trees?"

I stand and search the trees. In my gut, I'm sure this guy was working alone but you can never be too careful. If this guy had been bigger or more skilled hand-to-hand, he might've gotten one over on me earlier because I assumed he'd left. That's a dangerous mistake I won't make again.

Ash does a sweep and then comes back to me and the bloody heap of a corpse at my feet. I might've stabbed him a few times while Asher was double checking the area. Okay, so I definitely stabbed him, but he had it coming. When I thought about those fucking bullets flying past my Duchess, one death didn't seem like enough. If I had more time and the need to see Penelope to be sure she's safe wasn't riding me hard, I'd dismantle this motherfucker piece by piece and then burn him until he turned to ash.

But she's more important than my twisted need for retribution.

"All clear. He's the only one." Asher kicks the guy's leg and then looks up at me with a smirk. "You couldn't hold off long enough to interrogate him, huh?"

"He came at me first."

"Right, after he shot at Penelope." Asher's grin widens. The asshole knows exactly what he's doing riling me up.

I haul back and kick the dead bastard a couple of times in the ribs, not stopping until something cracks. My lungs burn with the effort of dragging in air as adrenaline shoots through my veins.

"I think he learned his lesson," I say when I can finally catch enough oxygen to speak again.

"Who do you think sent him?" Asher asks, back to business as he shoves his gun back into the holster.

"If I knew, they'd be enjoying their last pathetic minutes of life."

Asher eyes me. He and I? We've been through some shit together. We've tortured and killed and never judged each other for it. We have matching pits of darkness where our hearts should be and it's one of the many reasons we work so well together.

He gets me in a way no one else does, even if we've never shared our life stories with each other. We didn't have to. Dark attracts dark.

"What do you want to do with him?" He asks, gesturing to the dead guy at his feet.

"Search him, but we're not going to find anything."

He does it anyway—protocol, remember?—but comes up empty handed. Those unsettling green eyes of his that seem to glow in the dark like some kind of demon settle on me. "I'm not burying him by myself."

"We could have a bonfire, but it'll have to wait until tomorrow."

"Dude, I'm not dealing with a corpse that's been sitting in the woods rotting for hours. Fuck that. We're handling it now." He folds his arms and takes up the stance he uses when he's trying to intimidate me. Except it never works because I don't give a shit.

"I'm going to find Penelope and I don't care if you deal with him on your own now or wait for me to help you tomorrow." That desperation to see her is clawing at me, trying to break through my skin like a beast that's broken free of his chains. It won't be contained any longer and if he tries to fight me on this, it's not going to go well for him. I think he sees it in my eyes because he scowls at me but gestures for me to go.

As I start to take off, he calls out, "I'll add this favor to your tab. That's two, Foster."

I'm fine with that—once shit here dies down and I know my Duchess, and now Rory, are safe, I'll return the favor tenfold if he asks it of me but not a second sooner.

When I get inside, I'm damn near crazed. My heart slams against my ribs like it's trying to break through the cage. I scan the area, but I don't see her. I'll tear this house apart until I know she's not bleeding out somewhere or stolen away from me.

I'm dripping water and mud all over the floor. My clothes are saturated in rainwater, stained with blood, and coated in dirt but I don't care. I sprint up the stairs, every pound of my boots against the tile matching the pounding in my chest.

Elias stands guard outside Rory's door and takes one look at me, shaking his head. "He's fine."

I don't bother stopping, stomping down the hall in search of my Duchess. I've got tunnel vision as I throw open Penelope's bedroom door. It slams against the wall, ricocheting off and bouncing back to almost closed as I search for her, but she's not inside. The longer it takes me to find her, the more frantic I become.

Knots form in my stomach with every room I search. I step back into the hall and my panicked gaze lands on her office. The one Sebastian's commandeered as his own. With Elias on Rory duty, it makes sense Sebastian would've kept her close by and hanging out in her bedroom with her isn't his style.

Which is good for him because if it was, I'd have had to kick his ass.

Low murmured conversation hits me before I even fling the door open, and when I do two heads snap in my direction. I don't pay attention to Sebastian. My attention is solely focused on my Duchess looking like the most beautiful disaster I've ever laid eyes on.

Her hair is tangled, her clothes are wrinkled and torn in places, and she has dirt on her nose but the second those sweet brown eyes settle on mine the storm raging inside of me calms. It's like she's the eye, the reprieve where I can breathe. My heart slows, the beats taking up their regular rhythm as I blow out a relieved breath.

Now that I've looked her over, and the fear has started to subside, a new need begins to take hold—one that won't be ignored or stopped for anyone or anything.

"Get out," I say, my eyes still locked on Penelope. She knows I'm not talking to her, and I smirk at the way her soft lips fall open and a quiet gasp slips out. Her nipples pebble inside her shirt and my gaze drops to get a better look.

Instead of arguing, Sebastian bails like a good little minion. Maybe he can sense the tension coiling in the room. If Penelope and I are in the eye of the storm, there's a raging tempest swirling around us on the verge of tearing everything apart. He's not going to want to be here when it happens.

As if my body has a mind of its own, I prowl towards her, taking her in my arms and running my hands everywhere I can reach. The fury reignites when I find scrapes marring her perfect skin. I run my thumb across one and she winces but then I'm kissing her, distracting her from the pain.

She's kissing me, too, and trembling as her body collides with mine. There isn't an inch of space between us as she clutches my ruined shirt in her fist. Her nails dig into my skin through the fabric, and I breathe her sweet scent down into my lungs. I'm holding her face, desperately trying to pull her closer as we devour each other.

Her taste, her smell... she's everywhere all at once and my dick is fighting to escape my pants and get inside her. I'm so hard, every beat of my heart pulses in my cock and if she notices, all she does is push harder against me.

The need to be inside her, to feel her wrapped around me is all-consuming. She whimpers when I pull back long enough to rip my shirt off over my head. She looks drunk on me with dilated pupils and pink-stained cheeks. Her lips are swollen from my kiss and fuck if it doesn't turn my cock to steel.

"No one ever gets to see you like this again, Duchess. Only me," I growl, spinning her around and pushing her down flat on her desk.

"Only you," she echoes back as I run my hand over the curve of her perfect ass.

She's got on one of those skirts that drive me insane, the ones that hug every curve that she pairs with the stockings with the seams down the back.

"Do you have any idea what these fucking stockings do to me?" I ask while I reach up and pull the zipper down the back of her skirt. Once the fabric falls away, she's left there in nothing but those goddamn stockings and her panties and I'm about two seconds away from coming without even touching her.

"Why do you think I always wear them?" she asks, a little bit of her mischievousness bleeding in and my heart practically somersaults hearing it.

"To torment me, obviously."

I run my fingers across the back of her thighs, above where the stockings end and she shivers. She cries out when I smack her on the ass and it's music to my fucking ears. That sound shoots straight to my dick, and I'm done playing games. If I don't get inside her in the next five seconds, I'm going to explode.

And the next time I come it's going to be in her tight little pussy.

"This is going to be fast and hard, Duchess," I warn her as I pull the knife out of my pocket and slice the panties right off her body. I throw the scrap of lace and cotton onto the floor along with my knife and push a finger inside her while I fumble with the buckle of my belt.

She's dripping and I groan when my finger slides inside her again.

"Indy," she says, breathing out my name like a benediction. A prayer to her dark god, the one she worships with sacrifices of her body on my altar.

I let my fingers explore, but tonight I don't have the patience to get her ready. This isn't about fucking her into oblivion and making her forget everything but me. It's about claiming her again, reminding me she's mine and alive and here with me. It's about satisfying a need to own every part of her.

My wet fingers slide out of her, away from her clit and up to her hips. I guide myself to her entrance, gripping the base of my cock while I drag it across her slick pussy and rub it against her clit.

"Hold onto something, Duchess," I warn before I slam ruthlessly inside her. She screams and my head falls back as I clench my jaw, reveling in her warm, wet heat all around me. It's perfect, an exquisite torture I wouldn't give up for anything in the universe.

Her wet cunt pulses around me and she arches her back, trying to get me to move. I tighten my hold on her hips, my fingers digging into the skin while I remain still and try to get myself under control. All I want to do is fuck her as hard as I can so she'll have bruises on her hips and a raw throat from screaming my name.

But I give her a second to adjust because I may be a lot of things, but at this moment, I'm her protector as much as her tormentor. I want this to be good for her. So good she never wants me to stop.

So good she never wants to let me go.

When I've waited as long as I possibly can, I let go. I snap my hips against her ass, burying myself balls deep over and over. I can't possibly get any further inside of her, but that doesn't stop me from trying.

I'm lost to the madness of the moment, to the sounds of our bodies connecting again and again, to the whimpers and moans Penelope can't hold back no matter how hard she tries.

Nothing has ever felt as good as her cunt gripping me so tightly it's like she's trying to suck the cum right out of my dick. If I don't slow down, her pussy will be overflowing in ten seconds flat, but I can't.

I can't stop, so I need her to come. To give into the inevitable explosion that's barreling down on both of us.

I push my hand between her legs and my palm settles on her clit while my fingers slip to either side of her slit. The wetness that coats us both sticks to my fingers as I feel how my cock slides in and out of her body. I feel where we're connected, and I never want to stop. This right here is heaven, the perfect moment earned in blood, pain, and nightmares.

Penelope is my reward, my redemption, my salvation.

Her walls clench around me, rhythmically pulsing as she shudders and comes, sucking me into her body so hard I have no choice but to fill her up with my cum. I collapse over her back, shooting so much cum inside of her I don't think I have any left in my body. My balls are officially empty because she took it all.

I come so hard my legs damn near buckle, and through all of it she's still gripping me so goddamn tightly I couldn't slide out of her even if I wanted to.

If I had it my way, I'd *never* leave her perfect pussy. I'd live here forever giving her all the orgasms she could possibly want.

Forever and ever.

The end.

When my stupid fucking phone goes off in my pocket—because, yeah, I didn't even manage to get my pants off before I fucked her—I ignore that shit. Yeah, nothing good's blowing up my phone at three a.m. after the longest day of my life. I want to stay in the after sex high for a few more minutes before real life ruins it.

But when it goes off again, I know I can't hide from it any longer. With a massive sigh, I pull out of Penelope and tuck myself back into my pants, watching as my cum leaks out of her cunt. I'm still staring, transfixed, when I pull my phone out and answer the call.

"What?" I bark, already getting hard again and only half paying attention.

"You need to get down here," Asher says, not giving me a chance to respond before he hangs up. Obviously some shit is going down if he's calling me out.

I help Penelope back into her skirt and zip it up for her, sweeping her hair to the side and kissing the back of her neck. "C'mon, Duchess. We need to get downstairs."

After everything that's gone down today, I don't want her out of my sight for even a second. Things are still too raw. My nerves are a hot mess, frayed and tattered and barely holding together.

She slips her hand into mine and squeezes like she knows I need the reassurance. Or maybe she does. Either way, the heat of her skin against mine settles my frantic pulse into something more manageable that will let me think more clearly.

I meet Elias's hardened stare as we leave the office. He's standing guard outside of Rory's room and I'm relieved that he's here even though he doesn't have to be. He hasn't been assigned this case with Sebastian, Asher, and me so he's doing me a solid by keeping the kid safe.

It's a goddamn miracle that Rory's slept through the last couple of hours because after the situation we pulled him out of earlier tonight, the last thing he needs is his new foster parents being shot up and worrying about what that means for his home life.

As Penelope and I walk down the stairs, I shift so my body's slightly in front of hers. I don't know what we're walking into, and despite the high of fucking her only a few minutes ago, an exhaustion settles into my bones. It's almost too much to bear, the weight of everything that's happened tonight.

But there's no other option.

When I went all in with my Duchess, I made a choice and now I have to stick by that no matter the consequences or bullshit I have to deal with. She's mine, and I'm not letting her go no matter how many assassins come out of the shadows and try to take her from me.

At the bottom of the stairs, Asher is leaning against the front door with his arms folded across his chest glaring at our guest as if he feels the need to physically block her from running out the front door. Sebastian's doing the opposite, standing at the bottom of the stairs to keep her from moving deeper into the house.

"Colette?" Penelope asks. I stop as soon as I step off the stairs and she's forced to stay on the bottom step. She's gripping my bicep and leans around me to see her assistant who's just as put together as I've ever seen her despite the fact it's three a.m. "What are you doing here?"

Colette looks shifty as fuck, and her eyes dart between the four of us. She's carrying a big-ass purse and digs around inside. "The Board needed some signatures and I forgot to get them from you last night. They need them first thing in the morning."

She pulls out a stack of papers and waves them around like she's trying to prove her point, and this is the evidence. Asher walks up and snatches them from her from behind, going back to his place by the door and thumbing through them. I'm glaring at her so fucking hard, I wish she'd burst into flames.

It's obvious she's lying by the way she's nervously running her hands over her hair and shuffling from side to side. Her gaze keeps flicking over to Sebastian and then back to me. I open my mouth to call her out on her shit because it's fucking three a.m. and she could've called Penelope in the morning and asked her to come to the office ten minutes early to sign shit. No, this is something else, and while I've had my fill of torture and killing tonight, when it comes to my girlfriend and her safety, I'm always down for more.

Before I can start in on her, Sebastian beats me to it. "That's a lie." He turns to me and Penelope. "She's the one we've been looking for. If you hadn't kicked me out of the office earlier, you'd already know this."

He lifts his chin and pushes his glasses up his nose with his middle finger before he tilts his head in Colette's direction. "She's the one who's been sending the messages we found."

Colette's eyes widen. "No, I—"

"Save it," I snap. "If Sebastian says it was you, it was you. I don't need to hear more lies from your poisonous mouth."

"It took longer than usual because she's good at covering her tracks, but the key you sent helped me unlock the missing pieces." Sebastian's hand moves in my direction, handing me his tablet. I don't take my eyes off of Colette until he's back in place with his eyes locked on her.

"This is all bullshit," Asher says, tossing the papers aside. They flutter to the floor all around him. "Just a user manual, no signature required. It's almost like you wanted to check and see if your boss was still alive."

"You up for another trip to the Basement?" I ask him and his eyes spark back to life. We're both dirty as fuck from the storm, bloody, and dead on our feet but when someone tries to get one over on us, we can't let it slide.

"This has gotta be some kind of record," he says, pulling a zip tie out of one of his cargo pockets and stepping up behind Colette. He's rough when he pulls her wrists behind her back, and her purse makes a loud bang as it drops to the floor at her feet.

"Wait! What are you doing? I'll tell you whatever you want to know," she says, frantically trying to get free of Asher's iron hold.

"Now what fun would that be?" I say, letting my most vicious grin slip onto my face. She pales as Asher tightens the zip ties around her wrists and drags her towards the front door. I turn back to my Duchess and run the back of my fingers over her soft cheek. She leans into my touch and the last thing I want to do right now is leave, but Colette is the first real break we've had into who's after my girl and I have to get whatever information I can out of her.

"I'm sorry, Duchess, but I have to go. I'll be back as soon as I can," I tell her before shooting Sebastian a look that promises dismemberment if anything so much as makes Penelope unhappy while I'm gone. He nods once because what else can he do?

And then I turn and walk out the door.

CHAPTER 21
INDY

"Wait! Stop, please! Just ask me what you want to know," my girlfriend's traitorous assistant begs, kicking and screaming and dragging her damn feet as we haul her down into Connor's basement. "You don't have to do this."

My boss stands holding the door open while Asher tosses a thrashing Colette over his shoulder. Connor nods once looking like he just woke up and his fiancé Gigi is nowhere in sight. I can't blame her. If it were up to me, I'd be in bed with Penelope instead of here about to pry answers out of this woman who betrayed my Duchess.

The reminder of what she's done reignites the fire in my blood as I follow Asher down the stairs, moving past him to open the door so he can go inside. He drops Colette into the chair bolted into the cement floor. She kicks and screams for someone to help her as he straps her legs to the chair. Her hands are bound behind her so he double checks everything's still as it should be before stepping back.

His gaze flicks to me and I nod, ready to step in. I've got an entire day's worth of shit festering inside of me right now and despite torturing a man and killing another, my blood still buzzes with the need for violence. I doubt anything will ever be enough when it comes to avenging my Duchess. Standing in front of this woman who was supposed to help and support Penelope in the hardest year of her life, but instead betrayed her all I want to do is make her regret it.

According to the text I got from Sebastian on the way over here, it was Colette who hired the hitmen who took out Penelope's parents.

It was also Colette who sent the assassin after Penelope in her office. She may play the innocent act well, but she won't fool me with some tears and fake words from pretty lips.

The tools are still out from earlier when Asher and I were down here dealing with the bastard from the accident. Fuck, was that only just last night?

I skim my fingers along them while I let Colette marinate in her fear for a few long seconds, taking my time while I inflict some psychological torture. She has no idea what I'm capable of, and even the worst-case scenarios her brain can think up won't touch the surface of the lengths I'd go to in order to protect the people I love.

A scalpel catches my attention and I decide to start slow with her. A few well-placed slices that don't cut too deep but hurt like a bitch should have her questioning her life choices in no time. No matter what got her involved in this, she's obviously not a well-trained mercenary or assassin or gangster or any of the other types of people we've had our fun down here with before.

No, she's already offered to tell us everything. That would be too simple. After everything she's done, she has this pain coming. The bloodshed will cleanse away some of my guilt for ever letting shit get this far in the first place. I'm as pissed off at her for doing this as I am at myself for not seeing it sooner.

Besides, I made Penelope a promise. When I discovered who took her parents from her, I'd make them suffer.

Even if I spent hardly any time with Penelope's assistant, weeding out threats is my job. This innocent-looking blonde woman with a tear-stained face and wobbly bottom lip trembling where she sits doesn't look like she'd have it in her to do anything malicious, let alone send people in to kill Penelope.

So, either she's an amazing actress or she has help. I'm betting on both. We know from the decoded emails she was responsible for at least some of the attempts on Penelope's life, and since we don't have proof for every plot, I'm betting Colette here had help. And she's just

Penelope's assistant. There's no way she makes enough money to hire a hitman. So, who's funding her?

"Here's how this is going to go," I tell her, sliding the scalpel between my fingers and walking over to where Colette sits. I take my time, strolling leisurely like I don't have a care in the fucking world. My blood is boiling, threatening to spill over with the need for violence, but I can't let my bloodlust consume me. If I lose control, I won't get answers at all and as much as I want to relax and let my demons out to play, I can't.

Someone's helping Colette and I need to know who. Until they're strapped to a chair beside hers, Penelope's still in danger.

I flip the scalpel in my hand so the dull edge rests against Colette's skin and her eyes widen as she pales. "You're going to tell me who you're working with, and if you do it quickly, I'll only cut you as many times as I've had to witness Penelope be afraid this week."

Colette whimpers, probably because she knows that's a fucking *lot*. So much shit has gone down, I honestly don't even have a full count. I think eight is a nice, even number, though. It's one for every day of the week plus an extra because this day has been a shit show.

"It's my father, okay? He wants the tech she's developing and when her father refused to sell it to us, he decided to get creative. Do you have any idea how much that system will be worth? If you let me go, we can split the profit with you." She rushes the words out like she thinks once I hear them, I'll change my mind, but I won't.

She deserves what's coming to her by my hand. I turn the scalpel over and run it through the zip tie holding her hands together. Triumph flashes in her eyes as she shakes out her hands and rubs her wrists. I almost laugh because it's clear she thinks I'm letting her go.

I'm not, not even close.

I nod to Asher. "Strap her hands to the arms of the chair."

He steps forward and grabs one wrist, tying it down before moving to the other. Colette renews her effort to break free, but it's useless. Even if she did manage to snap one of the ties in her frantic thrashing, she's not a fighter. She won't get past Asher and me.

Asher's eyes flash and I think he *wants* her to get free just so he can unleash some of the pent-up rage inside of him.

We both have it; it's why we get along so well and why we can do this job without remorse or stopping to think about what we're doing. I can read him so well because in some ways, we're the same person.

"Please don't do this. Just let me go!" she pleads, breathing hard as she stops fighting her restraints. Her wrists are red and raw and there's fresh blood smeared on the arms of the chair and the plastic ties holding her in place.

"Who's your father?" I ask, ignoring her pathetic attempt to appeal to my humanity. Right now, that part of me is buried so deep I don't know if I'll ever be able to dig it back out. It doesn't matter. Until I get answers, I'll be the monster I need to be. Until my need for retribution is satisfied, I'll exist in the darkness. I'm happy to if it keeps my Duchess in the light and full of life.

"His name's Ricardo Watts." Her head falls forward so her chin hits her chest. Her hair is covering her face as her shoulders shake with sobs.

"And where can we find him?" I ask, trailing the scalpel down her arm, not pressing hard enough to break the skin. Not yet.

"He's at home," she murmurs, her voice shaky.

"Address," I bark, and she rattles it off through her pathetic sobs.

I don't even have to look to know Asher's already on his way out to go collect Colette's father. He's got no idea of the nightmare that hunts him now.

While he goes, I take the opportunity to get as much information out of Colette as I can while still repaying her for the torture she put Penelope through. My fingers twitch around the scalpel as I hold off cutting as deep as I want to, but I press into her forearm, making a line long and deep enough that it'll scar, should I decide to let her live. She's responsible for at least two attempts on Penelope's life and if even one of them succeeded, there would be no question how this is going to go.

She screams as blood pools around the fresh cut and runs down her arm. "One mark for every time you fucked Penelope over," I tell her, slicing a second line into her arm next to the first.

"Please," she begs. "I didn't have a choice."

I click my tongue as I focus on what I'm doing, starting on the third cut. "There's always a choice."

"You don't know my father. He's going to get that technology no matter what, and if I didn't help him, he threatened to cut me off."

I stop mid-slice and look at her. "So, what you're saying is you did all this to Penelope over money? You'd have had her killed so you could buy another handbag?" I frown at her, giving her a look so menacing she shivers. "You would've done it because you're a shallow, vapid bitch. Here's where you had a choice, Colette. Penelope has a huge heart. She's better than all of us, and if you'd come to her and explained the situation, I'd be willing to bet she'd give you all the money you could possibly want. Or did you forget she's a billionaire? Is your daddy a billionaire, Colette?"

She looks up at me with guilt swimming in her eyes, but that shit doesn't sway me at all. If anything, it only pisses me off more. *Now* she feels guilt? After she could've very easily killed Penelope and gone on about her life buying ridiculously expensive shoes and brunching at the country club without an ounce of remorse. No, fuck that. She can keep her guilt and choke on it for however long I decide to let her keep living.

Finally, she shakes her head, letting out a long, shuddering breath. "I messed up."

I laugh. "Messed up? You tried to have your boss *murdered*. That's not a mistake you can come back from. But don't worry, I'll make sure you understand just how badly this went for you before the end. Now, tell me everything," I order as I get back to my work, pressing harder on the scalpel than I need to. I slice through skin and muscle, until I think I see bone, but it doesn't matter. She's got fresh and dried tears on her face, mascara tracks down her cheeks and snot everywhere. She fucking disgusts me, but it's no less than she deserves. In fact, I'm going easy on her by letting her live.

For now.

Colette fills me in through her sobs about how her father got wind of the AI being developed at Driscoll, how her dad told her she'd get the job as Pen's assistant as an in. At the time, she didn't know what he wanted her to do, only that her job was to befriend Penelope and gain her trust as well as access to the Driscoll systems. To sit back and watch.

She didn't know her father's plan, but when he gave her an order, she carried it out. She installed the bug that siphoned Penelope's work outside of the company, sending it to a server her father and his associates have access to. When Penelope refused to budge on selling, her father got increasingly more impatient and put more and more pressure on Colette. That's when she decided to just take out her boss and wash her hands of the whole thing so she could get back to her regular life.

In my eyes, that doesn't make this bitch any less guilty for the part she played. Yeah, her father might've put pressure on her, but she's responsible for her actions. I'm not in the habit of killing women, but she's not getting out of this without a punishment as severe as her crime.

I finish up the last cut, looking down at the eight tallies that have mutilated her arm and I grin down at her. "Sorry, guess my hand's not as steady as a surgeon's." I'm not at all apologetic for that shit and she's looking pale as fuck. I wouldn't be surprised if it's only adrenaline keeping her conscious at this point.

No matter. I'll bring her back around if she passes out. There's no fun in it if I don't know she's actively suffering.

I rinse the scalpel at the utility sink in the corner and dry it off before setting it back on the table. I'm taking my time, in no hurry to wrap this up. I'm dying to get back to Penelope. Every cell in my body is screaming at me to end Colette and go home to my girl. But I can't, not without knowing everything. Not without all the answers that'll make sure she's safe.

The door swings open, and Asher drags in a bloody and unconscious man with thinning brown hair in satin PJs. It looks like Ash dragged his ass straight out of bed. The guy probably tried to put up a fight which is why his face is bloody and he's out, but then Asher might've just had a little fun with him first. It's hard to say.

"Daddy?" Colette cries, straining against her binds. "Daddy! Wake up!" Based on the way she's reacting I almost think she hoped her father would get one over on us and save her. He may be powerful in her eyes, but he's not a true monster. Not like Asher and me. I don't think she's really met true darkness until she was hauled down to this Basement, but she's going to learn today.

The chair makes a horrible scraping noise as I drag it across the concrete floor, securing it to the ground so it won't topple over no matter how much Ricardo here struggles. Asher throws him into the seat, and we make quick work of tying him down. Ash strides across the room and grabs the smelling salts, cracking one up under the man's nose.

He startles awake, his unfocused eyes searching the room until they finally land on Ash, who's standing closer to him than I am. Asher smacks him on the face a couple of times to help the process along. We're both so fucking exhausted. I know I'm willing to stay here as long as it takes to get everything we need, and I'm sure Asher feels the same, but I'm not exactly excited to drag this shit out.

My limbs are heavy and so are my eyelids, but I've got a solid adrenaline boost happening so it's keeping me alert for the time being. When this is done, I already know I'm going to stumble into bed and crash hard.

"Well, hi there," I say as I lean over in front of Ricardo Watts. His tan skin goes ashen when he takes in his surroundings, but it's the eyes that get me. When they land on his daughter, they turn thunderous as if he has any power here at all.

"What the hell is this? You come to my house in the middle of the night, kidnap me, and have the audacity to put Colette through the same fate? Release her! Now!"

I stand tall, looming over this motherfucker. He's trying to talk to me about audacity? That shit's funny as fuck, and I let my laughter out. It's cathartic so I let it go, and even Asher cracks a grin which is essentially the equivalent of him laughing his ass off.

"You want to talk about audacity, old man? How about yours? You've been using your daughter to steal Driscoll's tech, and then what? When you weren't getting what you needed fast enough, you hired someone to kill the CEO?"

He shakes his head. "I don't know what you're talking about."

"You don't? Hmm. How about we test whether or not that's the truth." I walk over to the table of torture tools and pick up a hammer, gripping the handle and letting the heavy end fall into my palm a couple of times.

I waste no time swinging it back and slamming it into his knee. He screams and curses and threatens us, but it's all white noise. The only words I want to hear out of his mouth are confessions about the shit he's done, and until that happens, I'm going to inflict as much pain as I possibly can. In fact, I hand the hammer off to Ash and let him have a turn.

He's been a silent sentinel for the most part during all of this, and he deserves to have some fun, too. Asher doesn't miss a beat, spreading out Ricardo's fingers on the arm of the chair and hitting each one on his left hand with the hammer. The man's a crying, bloody mess, and he's at the point now where he's begging for us to stop.

From experience, I know Ash will take it just a little further before he does and I'm right. That hammer goes straight into Ricardo's ribs once, then again before he stops. Asher's breathing hard as he lets the hammer drop back onto the table and turns back to the bloody lump of a man. He grips his hair in his fingers and yanks his head back.

"Who's involved in the theft from Driscoll Tech? I want every single name, or your right side is going to get the same treatment as your left. Then I'll ask you again, and if you don't give me straight answers, I'll start on your face." Asher stands back, his skin speckled with droplets of blood, and waits to see what Ricardo's going to do.

Ricardo tries to glare at Ash and then shifts it to me, but the effect doesn't quite hit the mark with his swollen shut eye from Asher's fun before he got here.

"I suggest if you want to get out of here alive, you stop fucking around and confess. This might be your last chance," I say, pulling my phone out of my pocket and turning on the camera. Will this shit be admissible in court? Nah, but I could extort the shit out of Ricardo if I wanted to.

And I'm thinking I want to.

But he has to spit the words out first.

Finally, he looks at his daughter who's been quietly crying the entire time he's been down here. At least she's stopped fighting the restraints.

"Do you know how much money we make on our cancer treatments?" Ricardo finally asks. Neither Asher nor I feel compelled to answer. This is Ricardo's show and I'm here to record it, and then make him suffer.

"No, you wouldn't, would you? Let's just say it put my daughter through elite private school, Ivy League college, and pays for my summer house in the Hamptons and my yacht with plenty left over."

My fingers curl into a fist as I imagine smashing it into his greedy face, but I hold steady, recording every word. "If a cure got out, it would decimate that revenue stream. We'd go bankrupt, and I can't let that happen. I've worked too damn hard to build this company into what it is today—"

"Something that keeps people sick enough that they have to keep getting treated and draining their bank accounts so they can't enjoy the lives they're trying to save?" Asher asks, picking up the brass knuckles and sliding his inked fingers into the holes.

Ricardo doesn't miss the movement either and swallows hard. "I knew if we could just get a hold of the tech, I could keep it from the market except in the case of those who could afford to pay a substantial price for it."

"In other words, only the wealthy could afford to cure their cancer while you let everyone else die," I say, debating on if I should throw one of the knives on the table beside me at him just because it'll feel good. This asshole brings out the violence in me. He's so goddamn unrepentant that I'm starting to get the itch to stab him. Multiple times.

"I'm not the only one who sees the potential and the downfalls of something like what Driscoll is developing going onto the open market," he snarls, spit flying as he tries to justify the bullshit spewing out of his mouth.

"Well then by all means, tell us who else helped you with your little plan."

Ricardo, realizing he's backed himself into a corner, snaps his mouth closed and then opens it again as Asher takes a step forward, and then decides to close it again.

"I suggest you speak while you still can," Asher says, curling his fingers into a fist around the brass knuckles.

"Some of the DT board wanted to sell the tech to the highest bidder and move on to other opportunities. Unfortunately, I'm in pharmaceuticals not technology and even if I got my hands on the incomplete AI framework, I wouldn't know what to do with that. That's where Drew came in."

"Drew Reynolds? Field's CEO?" I ask to clarify for the video.

Ricardo glares at me then nods once. "We had a deal. If I got him the tech, he'd finish it and then we'd split the profits. At first, we approached Thomas and offered to buy it from him. We offered more than a fair price, but he turned us down. He threw us out, told us to forget we knew him or the technology and to leave him the hell alone."

"But you didn't let it go, did you?" Asher asks, pulling his arm back and throwing it right into Ricardo's gut. We have to wait a couple of minutes for the wheezing to subside and so he can catch his breath enough to speak again.

He shakes his head. "I couldn't. It would ruin me if that godforsaken program got completed and released without my controlling it. I tried one more time to approach him when we crossed paths at a restaurant, but he had me thrown out." His cheeks turn red with embarrassment.

"That was the final straw. I couldn't play politics anymore. I had to get my hands on the tech, so I took drastic measures."

"Like having Thomas and his family killed but keeping your hands clean by having your daughter do your dirty work," I supply, shifting my weight to avoid doing what I really want, which is picking up the chainsaw and hacking him into tiny cubes of blood and tissue.

"Something like that," he mutters. "I thought if his brother was allowed to step into the CEO role, we'd be able to persuade him to sell us the framework. But Thomas had prepared for that scenario by leaving the company to his daughter. The one building the project. She'd never give it up. Still, we had to try. That's when we approached the Board with our new offer. They declined, but it wasn't a unanimous decision." His swollen, bloody lip curls up.

"There was dissent in the ranks."

"Who?" Asher asks, staring down at Ricardo like he's an ant under his magnifying glass.

"Ira and Franklin. They're on our side."

"Did they have anything to do with the hitmen you and Colette sent after Penelope? With the threats you made?" I ask, suddenly needing to know how much longer this shitfest is going to go on for. If I have more people to torture, so be it.

He shakes his head. "Not directly, no."

"They passed along a message to me to do what needed to be done, but they didn't want the details," Colette added.

"Is that everything?"

"Yes, now let us go," Ricardo demands like he has any control over this situation at all. He doesn't.

"That's not how this works," I say, pulling up a document Sebastian just sent over on my phone. "You're going to sign this or I'm going to send that little video confession all about how you don't want people to get better to every media outlet I can find."

"You can't!" Ricardo rages, twisting his shattered hand against his ties. "It would ruin me."

"Well, Ricky, you're ruined either way, but if you sign this your precious reputation stays intact and no one has to know what a money grubbing, murderous piece of shit you really are." He'll never know that that tape won't see the light of day because it would implicate me in his disappearance. He still thinks he's getting out of this alive. Idiot.

I hold out my phone just under his non-broken finger and he eyes it suspiciously. "What is it?"

"Does it matter?"

His face is turning red with his anger but there's literally nothing he can do.

"I'm going to make you pay for this," he threatens before scribbling out his signature on the document that surrenders all ownership in his company and transfers it to Driscoll—Penelope to be exact.

"Here's the thing," I say, tucking my phone into my pocket after making sure everything looks good. Then I pull out my gun and aim it at his forehead, right between the eyes. My finger wraps around the trigger, and I pull, taking immense joy in the hole that appears between his eyes and the brain matter and blood that spray the room behind him like a work of grotesque art. "I don't think you will."

Colette is screaming and fuck does she have some lungs on her. It's a good thing this room is soundproofed. Even still, I crouch down in front of her and her eyes dart all around the room. Ordinarily I'd kill her too, but that's not the worst punishment I can think of for her.

No, I have something more lingering and much more miserable in mind. She thought she could trade my Duchess's life for high thread count sheets and a credit card without a limit and I've just taken all of that away from her. But it's not enough.

I eye Asher and tilt my head to the side. We sidebar while Colette continues screaming and crying, ignoring her.

"What are you thinking?" he asks, raising an eyebrow.

"Reverse human trafficking."

Asher coughs out a laugh. "The fuck is that?"

"We throw her in a cargo container with some water and a bucket and she sets sail for a third world country where she has nothing. We've got the tape of her father's confession with her on it, too. She comes back or breathes a word of this, and we destroy her for real. Besides, she has no proof of any of this, but we have emails showing her involvement in trying to have Penelope killed. At least this way she still has a chance to redeem herself." I look over at Colette and my stomach turns. She'll never be worth anything in my eyes no matter how she spends the rest of her days, but maybe she can do some good in this world.

Or maybe she'll force my hand and I'll have to kill her anyway. Time will tell.

"I know a guy. I'll set it up," Asher says, back to his usual stoic demeanor but I see the spark of amusement in his eyes. He likes this plan.

I leave him to make the arrangements and walk over and kneel down in front of Colette. She immediately spits in my face. I use my shirt to wipe it off, grossed out but it's not even close to the first bodily fluids I've gotten on myself today. I'm in desperate need of a shower so what's a little spit between hated enemies?

"You can act tough all you want but what's waiting for you when we leave this room should knock the entitlement right out of you," I tell her. "So go ahead and fight back all you want now, but it's not going to make one bit of difference in the end. Just remember you chose this path and now you have to walk it."

With those final words, I stand up and start gathering supplies. The sooner Ash and I deal with shipping Colette off, the sooner I can get home to the family I'm building and put all this shit behind us.

CHAPTER 22
PENELOPE

"I NEED you to call your dad," I say, straightening my spine. After Indy came home in the early hours of the morning, we all passed out. Wrapped in his arms, I fell into the deepest sleep of my life.

Now it's early afternoon and we're gathered around the kitchen island eating breakfast and talking over next steps. As much as I value their opinions, I know what I need to do. I've got a lot of loose ends to tie up, but I've never been happier or more satisfied with the life I see laid out before me. I'd like to think my parents are looking down on me proud of how much I've grown this last year.

"Sorry, but fuck, no." Asher shakes his head and takes a bite of his croissant sandwich. "There's no way."

"Even if I can set you free for good?"

He pauses, sandwich halfway to his mouth and stares me down. "Explain."

"Have a little faith," I counter. If the guys knew my plan, they'd try to talk me out of it, and I can't have that. "C'mon, please? I promise it'll be worth your while."

Asher shakes his head and dusts off his hands. "Fine, but I'm warning you now, getting involved in anything with that man is the worst possible idea. Nothing good will come of it."

"We'll see. Just ask him to meet me here this afternoon, okay?"

Indy's eyeing me with curiosity but even he doesn't know what I'm up to. Wisely, he keeps his mouth shut as he pulls me into his side and kisses the top of my head.

"Oh, he'll love that, being summoned to the queen's castle like a pawn." Asher almost looks *happy* at the idea his father won't be the one in control for once. I can't help wondering if he'll shun my invite and not come at all.

"If it doesn't seem like he's going to agree, promise him I'll make it worth his time to meet with me."

Asher rolls his eyes. "You're a billionaire heiress. He'll find the time."

I nod and go off to change. If I'm going to meet the head of the Mason Family, I need my suit of armor firmly in place.

SEBASTIAN'S EQUIPMENT IS STILL SPREAD OUT ALL OVER MY office but for this meeting, I've kicked him out. When dealing with a man like Nicholas Mason, I learned a long time ago it's important to project absolute confidence and authority.

I don't take my eyes off the man walking through the door. He's got the same penetrating green eyes and dirty blond hair as his son, but instead of the rugged edge Asher has, Nicholas is clean cut and decked out in a tailored suit. He radiates power and danger, and I can see why he's in charge of the largest gang on the west coast. The last thing he looks like is a gangster, yet it's there in his eyes, hidden behind the respectable exterior. The predator, the violence, the bloodlust. The depths of his eyes are ice cold, unrelenting in their cruelty and I can't let myself be fooled by the warm smile he wears now like a mask.

The smile that doesn't touch his eyes.

But I'm here to make a deal with the devil, one I'm positive I won't regret.

"Mr. Mason," I say, standing from my chair and gesturing to the seats in front of my desk. "Thank you for coming on such short notice. Can I get you a drink?"

It's early afternoon, but I know offering something out of my father's expensive liquor collection—what's left after Indy made his way through it, at least—is expected of me.

He eyes me with that cold, penetrating stare like he's sizing me up, weighing whether I'm worthy of his time before he undoes the top button of his suit jacket and sits elegantly in the seat, leaning back like he's the one in charge of this meeting, not me.

"No, thank you."

I can't let him get the upper hand, and once he knows why I called him here, I think the mood of uncertainty with a hint of hostility will morph into something completely different.

"I've got to say I'm curious why you requested this meeting, Miss Driscoll. I know my son's been working for you for a while, but I can't imagine that would be cause for us to cross paths."

I round my desk and take my seat as well, perching right on the edge and keeping my back so straight, it's as if my spine is made of steel. "I've got a proposition for you."

"So my son says." He leans forward slightly, resting his elbow on the arm of the chair and eyeing me like he hopes he can drag my secrets out of my head through my eyeballs. Finally, he sighs. "Let's hear it then. I'd imagine we both have places we'd rather be right now."

I tap the screen on my tablet and slide it across the desk in his direction, waiting for him to pick it up and scan the document already loaded on the screen. He looks at me for a few seconds before he grabs it, and the longer he reads the more his eyebrows pinch together.

Finally, he looks up, and I fight off my smile at the look of surprise on his face. "What is this? A joke?"

I shake my head. "No joke. I'm going to be honest with you, Mr. Mason. I want something, and as I'm sure you're not in the habit of denying yourself what you want, neither am I. I want your son's freedom, totally and completely. If he should come back into your fold, it will be *his* choice, not because you'd guilted or coerced him into it. You won't turn him away from your family, but you won't force him to be a part of your business. He's free to make his own choices, full stop."

I let my request sink in as his eyes darken. His expression is exactly what I feared—that he does in fact have plans for Asher within his organization and this reprieve he's granted is only that—a break. Asher will be dragged kicking and screaming back into this man's organization one way or another if someone doesn't do something.

I've got a company I don't want that's worth millions of dollars, and Asher's dad needs legitimate businesses to funnel his criminal spoils into. It's a win-win, and I can only hope the prize is big enough. After everything Asher's done for me, calling in favors from his father even though he knew it was going to risk the tentative freedom he'd earned himself, he did it anyway.

Besides, neither Indy nor I have any interest in running Watts-Labs. Technically, it's mine but I want it out of my portfolio as fast as humanly possible. As far as I'm concerned, that company is only one step away from a criminal organization as it is. Why not hand it over to someone who can either make it flourish under his iron rule or run it into the ground? I really don't care what he does with it, only that it's no longer in the hands of the people who stole my parents from me and tried to take my life.

"And in exchange for my word on that—"

"Sorry, Nicholas... Can I call you Nicholas?" I plow on without waiting for his permission. "Your word's not going to be good enough, I'm afraid. You'll find I prefer to work in contracts that've gone through an army of lawyers first so we're both protected, and no one falls prey to any of those pesky loopholes."

He glares at me for my interruption, and maybe the way I'm talking to him. But behind that is maybe a glimmer of respect in his dark green eyes. I can't sit back and let this man walk all over me. I won't do it, and I channel every ounce of CEO energy I've accumulated over the last year into this one conversation.

"Just so we're clear—you're offering me WattsLabs in exchange for keeping my son out of my business."

He doesn't ask it like a question. "Unless he makes the choice *on his own* to come to you, yes. It's really that simple." Asher doesn't know what I'm doing, and him having a choice in what he wants for his future is the best gift I can think to give him for all of this. I'm not going to draw a hard line that he can't join his father in the contract, because who knows what he actually wants? I don't know Asher that well. But I can give him this—free will.

Nicholas's gaze drops to the tablet again and he scrolls back through the offer more slowly before he sets the tablet down. We stare at each other across the desk, but eventually his lips tip up into a hint of a smile and he stands, holding out his hand for me to shake. "If you send the contracts over, I'll have my lawyers look them over but if everything's in order, you've got a deal."

My heart flips and I'm giddy, but I lock it down instead reaching out and grasping his hand firmly in mine, shaking and securing Asher's future. After a hasty goodbye, his father sweeps out of my office, and I put in a quick call to my lawyer to send him the contracts.

Now that that's done, I've still got more loose ends to tie up today. I fall back into my chair and let my eyes flutter closed while my nerves settle. A few deep breaths pass and when I open my eyes again, I reach for the tablet Asher's father abandoned on the edge of my desk.

Two days ago, I wrote the last lines of code for my AI framework. I've been quietly running tests in the background during the craziness of the last few days, and all signs point to it being ready. This system is configured to focus on one problem and one problem only—the cure for cancer. It can read numbers and process lines of codes faster than a thousand computers at once, and when chemists and researchers get their hands on it, it's only a matter of time before new treatments and cures start to pop up.

At twenty five, my life's work is already complete.

As I hit the button to send the framework out into the world, and subsequently email Harrison Astley to let mainstream media know it's out there for the taking, an odd sense of grief hits me. I've been so focused for so long on finishing this project, it was my only focus. The one thing that kept me going through my teen years, through college, through the loss of my parents. Without it, I don't know what comes next in my life and there's an emptiness that I'm going to need to figure out how to fill in order to move forward.

But it's not the sadness I thought it would be.

Especially not when Indy walks into my office with his cocky smile, that dimple in his cheek that makes me crazy, with Rory on his heels. When he yanks me up out of my chair, taking my spot and pulling me onto his lap while Rory runs around the office until he stops at the window, that empty spot starts to fill with something new. And when Rory's eyes bug out of his head when he spots my treehouse, I get the feeling everything's going to be okay.

It's been two weeks since the night I almost died.

Two weeks since I released my AI into the world.

Two weeks since I bought Asher his freedom.

Two of the best weeks of my life. Sure, they've been chaotic, but when isn't life that way? I'm starting to think this might be my new normal. Indy's by my side as we walk through the front doors at Driscoll Tech. I haven't been here much over the past two weeks, but I've been working from home behind the scenes to get everything in order for what comes next.

I always said once I got my project done, I had no interest in running this company. I meant it.

We ride the elevator to the top floor, and like always the energy between us heats and sparks to life. Our eyes clash in the small space and my breath catches in my throat. Indy reaches up with the hand that's not holding mine and drags his thumb across my bottom lip. It's so easy to fall into him, to let the world slip away while I get lost in the haunting gray depths of his eyes.

Though these days some of the sadness and cracks inside of him seem to have healed. He's lighter, and the way he and Rory have bonded... it's like they were always meant to be together.

Indy leans in but the doors open before his lips connect with mine, and I reach up and run my fingers along his jaw. "Later," I murmur the promise as my lips brush across his cheek right at the corner of his mouth.

He groans but steps back. "You're going to pay for that later," he promises and my core clenches in anticipation.

But I shake off the sexual haze Indy seems to always keep me in because I've got something more important to take care of right now. Once this is done, all of my other plans will click into place. It's the final piece of everything I've been planning for more than a year and I'm ready for it all to come together today.

He doesn't know I'm coming, so when I step into my Uncle Collin's office with Indy at my back, his eyes widen in surprise. "Penny? Is everything okay?"

His eyes slide to the bodyguard at my back, and I can only imagine how intimidating he looks towering over me dressed in all black with muscles on top of muscles. I shiver thinking about how he looked this morning grinning up at me from between my legs, this powerful man who only kneels for me.

"Everything's fine. Better than fine, actually. Do you mind if I sit?" I ask and he waves me towards the couch he has in the corner of his office.

Uncle Collin follows me over and sits beside me while Indy keeps his stoic pose at my back. "I know you're probably wondering what I'm doing here," I start, knowing that with the AI releasing into the wild Driscoll's been fielding the media and inquiries from people who want to buy the tech, even though it'll never be for sale. It's open source, out in the world for anyone who wants to use it to make a difference.

"I can't say I'm not curious," he says with a wry smile. Now that the danger has passed, Uncle Collin looks ten years younger and has a lightness about him I haven't seen since before we lost my parents.

"Effective immediately, I'm stepping down as CEO and I want you to take my place," I tell him, and his eyes widen.

"Are you sure this is what you want?"

I move closer to him and take his hand, giving it a squeeze as my eyes sting. Sometimes, like right now, he looks so much like my dad it makes my heart hurt. "This is what I wanted from the beginning," I assure him. "But you have to understand that the only way I could be absolutely certain nothing got in the way of finishing the framework, of doing what my father and I set out to do so long ago, was to step in and lead this company myself."

"You didn't trust me?" Uncle Collin asks quietly, and there's hurt in his eyes.

"I didn't trust *anyone*. My parent's death wasn't an accident, and while at the time I may have believed the police reports, I think somewhere deep down I knew the truth." Indy's hand falls heavily onto the back of my neck and strokes the sensitive skin there, letting me know he's here for me if I need to lean on him.

"I couldn't involve anyone else. I love you, but I don't know everything about your life. There's every possibility you have some skeletons in your closet that could've been exploited to get you to turn on me or side with the Board. I *know* I don't have any weaknesses to exploit, so I had to be the one."

His gaze darkens and he tightens his grip on my hand, but it's not painful. More like he's holding on tighter, afraid I'll let go. "I've got nothing like that, either, and I would've stood between you and them if you let me. I'll admit, I had some resentment for my brother leaving things to you. What did you know about running this company when I'd been here by his side from the start? But you did a damn good job, Penny. Damn good. I'm proud of you."

Those pesky tears burn my eyes again, and this time one manages to fall. Indy's hold on me hasn't faltered and his thumb sweeps across my skin as goosebumps run down my spine. "Thank you," I whisper because it's all I can manage unless I want to start sobbing.

"I want you to know I don't take this job or running this company lightly." His expression darkens, and anger burns bright in his eyes. "And the first thing I'm going to do is deal with those backstabbing traitors on the board."

He lets go of my hand and pats my knee before standing to his full height and stalking across the room to his desk. He picks up his phone and murmurs into it, quietly enough that I can't hear what he's saying.

Indy tugs me closer, pulling my hand into his free one and tangling our fingers together. "You did good, Duchess." His lips brush my ear as he speaks quietly into it. "So fucking good."

My nipples tighten at his praise, something he heaps on me in the bedroom and now I'm like Pavlov's dog, conditioned to turn into a horny mess the second he worships me with his words.

I don't hate it.

In fact, I love it.

I love *him*.

"I love you," I tell him, knowing I probably should've waited for the perfect moment, but with us every moment seems to be chaos and perfection blended together into a whirlwind there's no hope of escaping.

He sucks in a breath and leans back, his stormy eyes searching mine for a lie, but he won't find one. "Are you sure?"

I snort, this horrible sound that is so embarrassing that I slap my hand over my mouth. But Indy? He just throws his head back and laughs.

"I take it back," I say, lifting my chin and looking away as my cheeks burn.

Indy lets go of the back of my neck and his fingers grip my chin, forcing me to look back at him. All hints of laughter from earlier are wiped off his face. "I love you, too, Penelope. So fucking much. You're my entire world—you and the kid. You saved me when I didn't think I could be saved, and I hope you know I'll never let you go. There's no escape."

"It's a good thing I like being trapped in your snare then, isn't it?"

That tension from earlier is back and Indy bends down, his lips brushing mine but before it can go any further my uncle takes his spot back on the couch beside me and ruins the moment.

"Sorry to interrupt but I thought you might want to stay for the fireworks. Though, if we're going to watch, we need to go right now."

I blink at my uncle. "Fireworks?"

He grins and stands up, holding out his hand for me but Indy gets there first, tugging me up off the couch by our interlocked fingers. Uncle Collin's gaze slides over to my love and then back to me with a thousand questions in his eyes, none of which I care to answer right now.

"I've just set my first act of CEO in motion," he tells me as I follow him out of the office with Indy at my side and we walk to the conference room where the Board has been hastily assembled.

Uncle Collin pushes through the glass doors, and I bristle at the annoyed and angry expressions on the faces of the five members of this Board, the one my father thought would have his back. He'd be so disappointed in the way they turned out if he were alive to see them now.

"Let's cut the bullshit, shall we?" Uncle Collin starts and everyone's attention snaps to him. They'd been glaring at me, still angry over the missed opportunity of my AI hitting the market for free. But they've always respected his authority over mine so it shouldn't come as a surprise when they immediately comply with his command.

"Finally, someone with a clear head who's talking sense," Franklin says, tilting his head in deference to my uncle. My fingers curl into a fist and Indy stiffens beside me. I can feel the rage wafting off him like cologne that smells like violence and blood. Neither of us make a move, though, or open our mouths. This is Uncle Collin's show and I'm all too glad to hand over the reins.

For once, this isn't my problem to clean up and the knowledge that I'll never have to stand in front of this board again and take their abuse weakens my knees.

"It's come to our attention that at least two of you were assisting WattsLabs CEO Ricardo Watts to steal our proprietary technology, and when that wasn't effective, you conspired with Drew Reynolds and Ricardo to take out your obstacles. As he's gone missing, it falls to you to pay for your crimes against this company and my family."

Ira and Franklin both shift in their seats. Ira pales but Franklin does the opposite—he turns red, his fury rising to the surface of his skin. "What—"

He splutters as Uncle Collin shoots him a glare that could burn him alive. "I don't care to hear your excuses."

Noise from the hall catches everyone's attention and uniformed police officers spill into the room. It erupts into chaos then as Ira and Franklin are put in handcuffs and dragged from the room as they struggle and plead and vow this isn't over. For some reason, their threats do nothing. I have no doubt they'd love to come after me, but they're weak men who need others to do their bidding and if they're locked up in jail with their assets frozen, well... that method's not going to be very effective for them.

When they're gone, the three remaining board members look between my uncle and I with matching shellshocked expressions. "What now, Collin? What will you do with the rest of us?"

"I'm so glad you asked, Hannah." He smiles at her but it's not warm. It's malevolent and cruel, and she flinches when she sees it. "You have two choices. You can resign your positions, or I can have you taken out the same way as Ira and Franklin. It's up to you."

I have a feeling he's bluffing about that last bit. If he had the proof to have the rest of the board thrown out, he'd have used it. But they don't know that. The three remaining members exchange glances and then rise and file out of the room without another word.

"I'll expect your official notices of resignation on my desk by the end of the day," my uncle calls after them.

After they're gone, he turns back to me. "You know I've got a board to fill," he says, his smile turning genuine for the first time since we stepped foot in this room.

"You do."

"I'd love it if you took one of the seats. I could use someone I trust who's got the company's best interests at heart to make sure we're on track."

"Let me think about it," I tell him, stepping forward and into his arms. When he hugs me, it's like for a second my father is back. It's that kind of protective hug that only a parent can give you, the kind that shields you from all the bad in the world and for a brief moment in time you think nothing can touch you because it'll have to get through them first.

Indy's hugs are like that, too, only a whole lot hotter. Still, hugging my uncle, letting everything go is nostalgic in a way I didn't expect.

Once we let go, I step back, ready to get out of here and put Driscoll and the last year behind me. But first, I have to know.

"That was your first act as CEO," I say and Uncle Collin nods. "What's going to be the second?"

Uncle Collin's eyes glimmer and he rubs his hands together. "I'm so glad you asked. You know that tool Drew Reynolds? I hear his board is accepting offers."

I laugh and shake my head. "No way."

"What?" Indy asks, snaking his hand around my waist and pulling me back against his chest.

My stomach loops like a roller coaster when I catch the way he's looking at me. "Uncle Collin is going to take over Fields AI —hostilely."

"Oh, shit," Indy says and then his rumbling laugh vibrates through my back and into my body.

"And what about you, Penny? The price of your freedom was high. Now that you have it, what will you do with it?" Uncle Collin asks, looking at the way Indy's holding me possessively against his body.

"I think I've earned a vacation." It's the first thing that pops into my head and I know it's exactly what we need. "Should we take Rory somewhere? Get away for a while?" I ask Indy, looking up at him.

"Wherever you go, Duchess, you know I'm there. *We're* there."

And with everything inside of me, I know he means it. He and Rory are my family now, one I didn't mean to build but wouldn't give up for anything. I might not have been looking to fix my broken pieces, but somehow Indy Foster did it anyway.

He held me together with willpower and obsession, and I'd rather have a thousand attempts on my life than ever let him go.

Life with him will always be an adventure, and I'm finally ready to shed my inhibitions and enjoy the ride.

EPILOGUE
INDY

Six months later...

The tablet slips through my fingers and falls to the ground as Penelope runs into the room and throws herself into my arms. She wraps her legs around my waist, and my hands go under her ass, effortlessly catching her. She's so open with me now, so affectionate that it's crazy to think back to the cold, closed off, uptight woman she used to be when I first met her.

Getting fucked out of her mind a couple of times every day brought her out of her shell. I take all the credit.

Her palms come to either side of my face and she closes me in, her forehead almost touching mine. My Duchess's warm eyes sparkle and her cheeks are flushed. "Did you see it?"

Instead of answering, I kiss her hard, pushing my tongue in her mouth and tasting her like I'll die if I don't. I'll never get tired of this, having her pressed up against me, the way she submits so perfectly at times and at others fights me with everything she's got. Her body is a work of art, her mind even better. She's the total package, my Duchess.

Her arms wrap around my neck as she loses herself in the kiss, and I'm so fucking hard I can't think straight. She asked me a question, but I don't remember what it was. Eventually, when my head's spinning either from lack of oxygen or all my blood relocating to my cock, I pull back. We're both breathing hard, trying to catch our breath and even after more than six months together, I crave her like the very first day.

Maybe more.

"Mason Pharmaceuticals is starting trials soon," she breathes as her forehead rests against mine. Her lips are curled up into a smile so sweet, I could eat her. Maybe I will.

"Sounds like you're just missing one thing, then," I tell her, letting her drop slowly down my body, feeling every soft curve, until her feet hit the floor. As much as I want to fuck her every second of every day—and even more right now when her eyes are bright and cheeks tinted pink because she's so happy—I've got bigger plans.

Her eyebrows press together as an adorable crease forms between them. "Everyone's going to be here in an hour for the party. What am I missing?"

I can see her starting to drift off, that brain of hers working overtime to figure out what tiny detail she might've missed for the party we're throwing today. It's been her biggest focus over the last month and now that everything's come together, she's struggling to relax and enjoy it.

That, I can fix, but later. Right now, I'm about to do something I've been thinking about for months. It's taken all my willpower to hold off, to wait until she was ready. I'm still not sure she is, but I'm all out of patience.

"The party's fine, Duchess. That's not what I'm talking about," I say, digging into my pocket and pulling out the velvet box.

I'm not all about that archaic bullshit, and honestly, I know my girl isn't either. I don't bother dropping to my knees because Penelope already knows I'd do anything for her, including kneeling at her feet if she wanted me to. But she doesn't want a man who's going to surrender to her. No, we both love the fight too much for that.

Her eyes widen when she sees what I'm holding, and I open the box, slipping the ring out. I reach for her hand, pulling it close and slipping the princess cut diamond onto her finger. She stares down at it for a long time before looking up at me with mischief glimmering in her rich brown eyes. The tiny gold flecks reflect the warm sunlight spilling through the window, and for a second, she looks like a goddess brought to life.

"Aren't you supposed to ask me?"

"What's the point? We both know what your answer's going to be."

Her eyes narrow into a fierce glare—well, it's about as fierce as a kitten's, but she thinks she's intimidating so I won't ruin it for her by laughing my ass off at how cute she is. Then she loses her battle to act like she doesn't want this and launches herself at me for the second time since walking into this room.

She's kissing me hard, and for once I'm not the one devouring her. She's pouring everything into the kiss, all the desire and love she has for me, and I take it all, reveling in the taste of her on my tongue, the way she fits perfectly in my arms like she exists only for me.

"See?" I let a smirk play across my face, using my dimple to draw her in. It never fails, and I know the second that thing pops out in my cheek, it's only a matter of time before she tries to hop on my dick and go for a ride.

"You're such an ass."

"An ass you're going to spend the rest of your life with."

Her palms fall to either side of my face while she stares into my eyes. "You really mean it?" She's whispering like she thinks if she speaks in her regular voice I'll change my mind, but there's no quitting her. I couldn't walk away from her any more than I could rip my own heart out and keep living. It's not possible.

"No. April Fool's," I deadpan.

She scowls. "It's October."

"Guess you have your answer then, don't you Duchess?"

Footsteps in the hallway outside of our room get closer as Penelope reluctantly detaches herself from me. The look she gives me is scorching and promises a long and *hard* celebration when the party's over. I groan and move my dick so it's not so obvious when the kid walks in a second later.

"Mom? Dad? Why are you hiding out in here? Uncle Asher's finally here, and it's been *forever* since I've seen him. Can we go say hi? He brought the *biggest* present!" Rory's practically vibrating with excitement as he hops from foot to foot. When he asked Penelope and I about a month ago if he could call us mom and dad, I wasn't even ashamed of breaking down and sobbing like a baby.

He thinks this party's to celebrate that he's officially in remission... and it is. But it's also so much more than that.

Penelope and I exchange a glance and she nods. For some reason, delivering this news to Rory makes me more nervous than telling her we're getting married. My palms are clammy as I wipe them on my jeans and sit on the edge of our bed.

"Come over here, bud," I say, patting the mattress beside me. Penelope moves to stand beside me with her hand resting on my shoulder. She squeezes gently to let me know she's here with me.

Rory shoots me a curious look and then flies across the room, coming to a skidding stop before flopping down on the bed. Since he's been here with us, he's filled out. He's got a shit ton of energy and never sits still. It's like all the life he missed out on before with that cancer bullshit and his family situations he's making up for now. He's going to school, has tons of friends, and his therapist is impressed with how resilient he is. All in all, we got so lucky with him and not a day goes by I don't wonder if Chase had a hand in bringing Rory into my life.

"Come on, Dad. Jonah's here and we were just about to play a round of Fortnite," Rory whines while he gets more comfortable on the bed, even as one leg hangs off like he's just waiting for the okay to take off.

"Jonah knows his way around, he can hang out by himself for a little while," I say while my heart's like a damn hummingbird in my chest. Rory's best friend practically lives here on the weekends so he can deal with a couple of minutes on his own.

"Do you remember the day you asked us if you could call us mom and dad?" Penelope asks, and Rory lifts his sweet, soulful gaze up to hers while he nods. The vulnerability in his eyes slays me. It's like he thinks we're going to send him packing right when things have gotten to the good part, like he's afraid to hope that he might just get to experience what it's like to have things work out for a change.

I hate that at nine years old, he has a look like that at all. If I could, I'd erase it, banish it from existence and never let anything bad happen to him again.

"That was the day we realized you wanted to stay with us as much as we wanted you here. That was also the day we filed the paperwork to adopt you," I tell him, reaching up to grab Penelope's hand because I need her to anchor me. When I look up at her, she has a tear running down her cheek, but her attention is one hundred percent focused on our boy.

And his eyes are in his lap, his head down as he processes. We give him the space to do it, and when he looks up, that expression I hate so much is wiped away and replaced with hope.

"What does that mean?" he asks as his gaze darts between Penelope and me.

"It means... you're officially a Foster. If you want to be." Though, truthfully, there's no taking it back now. Penelope and I had to pay a fuck ton of money to get a judge to rush the process and sign off without Rory present. We wanted it to be a surprise and based on the look on his face, I'm going to go ahead and say we succeeded.

Rory jumps off the bed. He's breathing hard and his eyes are wide. "Are you serious? Is this real?"

"Yeah, bud. It's real."

A tear rolls down his cheek as he throws himself at me, throwing his little arms around me while he cries, and Penelope moves so she's hugging us both.

"We love you, Rory, and we're never giving you up," Penelope says, and I swear every time I see her with our son the world stops spinning. Time freezes and I'm struck almost by lightning, shocked that I've managed to get this lucky twice in my life. As much as losing Chase killed something inside of me that'll never be whole again, I've realized watching my soon-to-be wife and our son together that I don't need to go back. I don't need to repair what was broken because I'm building something new here.

Something worth every risk of heartbreak.

"Thank you," he mumbles into my shirt after he's wiped all his tears and snot on it. Fuck it, I don't even care. He stands up and dries his eyes before flashing us his wide smile and dimples. "Can I go play with Mason now?"

My Duchess laughs and ruffles his messy hair. "Go, but only one round. Your party's going to start in a few minutes."

He takes off out of the room as I strip off my shirt and toss it on the ground. Penelope's gaze heats as it slowly runs down my chest and abs.

"Keep looking at me like that and I'll have no choice but to bend you over this bed and fuck you until I put a baby in you," I say, and my voice is so low it's practically a growl.

Her attention lifts to my face as her eyes widen and her mouth falls open. "But I thought—"

"I'm full of surprises today, Duchess."

"What did you do?"

"Remember last month when I had that week-long job with Ronin?"

She nods, moving closer so she can wrap her arms around my neck and press her body against mine. It doesn't matter what we're doing, the two of us are like gravity. We can't help orbiting each other, moving closer, always having to touch like we're afraid the other is going to disappear. That's what loss does to you. It makes you appreciate every single moment you have with the people you love most in the world. In this Penelope and I are the same.

"There was no job. I had my vasectomy reversed and spent the week in Ronin and Red's guest room healing up."

She smacks me in the chest with the back of her hand. "I can't believe you lied to me."

I smile at her, knowing she can't stay mad at me. "Is it lying if I did it so I could surprise you? And by the way, one out of ten *do not recommend*. My balls hurt for a fucking week. Nothing is going near them ever again, Duchess. You better prepare yourself for all the babies we're about to make, because the doctor said I'm good to go and I'm not having that shit done again."

Concern is etched into her face, even as her eyes are sparkling. She's so fucking pretty. "But... we haven't been careful."

"No, no we haven't." I smirk.

"Are you sure you're ready for this?"

"We have this huge palace you call a house to fill, Duchess. Besides, I happen to think we kick ass as parents." We may not have gotten here the conventional way; I'm not opposed to doing shit backwards if it gets me the results I want. And a house full of kids with Penelope's genius and my dimples? They'll rule the motherfucking world.

She lets me go and pulls back, and I reach for her, but she bats my hands away with a laugh. "Now is not the time, Indy. We're about to have a house full of people and I don't want to look like I've just had your dick inside of me."

I lift my eyebrow. "You think they don't already know we fuck constantly?"

She blushes hard and mutters, "It's not constant."

I move into her space and press my body along the length of hers, breathing her in while I run my fingers down her spine and watch her shiver. "Keep lying to yourself, Duchess, but we both know the truth. You can't resist me."

She seems to shake off the lusty trance I managed to put her in and glares up at me. "And how do our friends know anything about our sex life?"

"You're not quiet, babe. I'm pretty sure everyone heard you at the twins' first birthday party."

She huffs and folds her arms across her tits, pushing them up so my attention drops straight down to watch. "It's not my fault you dragged me into the guest bathroom. Next time find someplace further away from everybody."

"Like here? In our bedroom? Before everyone shows up?" I close the distance between us, but she catches on and moves back toward the door.

"Don't even think about it," she says, but she's losing the battle and her lips curve up in a smile before she shrieks and takes off running.

I give chase, knowing she'll let me catch her, but giving her a head start because the game is no fun if it ends too fast.

My heart pumps harder as desire for my Duchess tears through my veins. I'll never get tired of this life with her. If our future together lasts a day or a hundred years, I'll savor every second, every smile, every moan of my name that pours from her soft lips knowing each one is a miracle I walked through hell to earn. Penelope? She's my happily ever after.

And sometime tonight, I'm going to have to tell her that I'm taking on a new job with Asher... one that's more dangerous than any I've ever done before.

A favor was promised, and I don't go back on my word. When he called me last night and cashed it in, I had no choice but to agree. So, for tonight I'll savor the time with Penelope and Rory and all our friends, and tomorrow, I'll deal with the fallout of the mess Asher's found himself tangled up in.

With the Masons involved, I have a feeling things are about to get a whole lot bloodier...

Thank you for reading *Hostile*! Find out what Asher's mixed up in, what his stepsister Devon has to do with it, and how Indy's going to help in *Deceit*, book 4 in the Hollywood Guardians series!

ALSO BY HEATHER ASHLEY

For a full updated list of my books, please click HERE.

ABOUT THE AUTHOR

Hi, I'm Heather!

I'm a socially-awkward introvert who loves happy endings, but not the creepy massage parlor type. I'm not awesome at singing or cleaning the house, but I'm obsessed with brining characters to life. My background is in business, but writing's way more fun.

Give me a Wi-Fi signal, a mug of tea (preferably with a cuss word or two on it), and a laptop and life's pretty damn near perfect.